BLOOD IS THE POWER

"You cannot mean to attempt another Opening," gasped Etrascu, still on his knees. "That darkness has a thirst you cannot imagine. You could pour the blood of a dozen worlds into it and not assuage it. Zaru, we are not meant to step beyond the great Cycle."

Vorenzar grunted. "A Csendook must give his life when the occasion demands. We do not question the Marozul."

Vorenzar looked back at the wall, the forest beyond it. "If I have to spill Csendook blood to open this Path, then I will do so. What lies beyond us is too valuable to lose."

Ipsellin nodded.

Together they remounted their beasts, and in both their minds a single word repeated itself, like the calling of a distant bell: *Innasmorn*.

STAR REQUIEM

BOOK 2

THIEF OF DREAMS

ADRIAN COLE

AVON BOOKS • NEW YORK

AVON BOOKS
A division of
The Hearst Corporation
1350 Avenue of the Americas
New York, New York 10019

First AvoNova Printing: January 1993

AVONOVA TRADEMARK REG. U.S. PAT. OFF. AND IN OTHER COUNTRIES, MARCA REGISTRADA, HECHO EN U.S.A.

Printed in the U.S.A.

RA   10   9   8   7   6   5   4   3   2   1

CONTENTS

BOOK FOUR – THE AVIATRIX

BOOK FIVE – THE WORLD SPLINTER

PREFACE

THE LAST DAYS OF MAN

Man once ruled over an Empire that stretched throughout countless worlds, worlds that formed a complex cycle, a self-contained chain.

In his hunger for knowledge, Man unlocked the door to another realm, that of the alien race, the Csendook, and thus began a thousand year war in which these ferocious aliens, faster and stronger than Man, began the inexorable conquest of his Empire.

In desperation, facing extinction, Man's Imperator Elect and his Consulate sought to escape the Csendook tide. On the world of Eannor, the Imperator's Prime Consul and principal scientist, Zellorian, used dark and forbidden powers to create a gate into a separate cycle of worlds, a feat thought to be impossible. Zellorian brought the Imperator Elect, his remaining Consulate and the last of Man's army through to the world of Innasmorn, the Mother of Storms.

Innasmorn is a world of elemental forces, where the storms are worshipped as gods by its inhabitants. They, who are themselves partly elemental, have no use for technology and have almost completely outlawed the use of metals. When they learn of the arrival of the intruders, the Men of the Imperator, they begin preparations for a war.

However, a small group of Innasmornians under Ussemitus, a woodsman, question the decision of the shamen, the Windmasters, to carry war to the intruders, about whom little is known. Ussemitus meets Aru Casruel, a girl who flees the Sculpted City, where the Imperator has built a base in the mountains. Aru warns Ussemitus that Zellorian is prompting the Imperator to subdue the people of Innasmorn. Those in the Sculpted City who would prefer an alliance and peace with the races of Innasmorn are being eliminated by the ruthless Zellorian.

Ussemitus and Aru begin a search for a forbidden land far in the west of Innasmorn, which is said to contain ancient powers. They fear that Zellorian will seek out these powers and attempt to harness them in his new thirst for control. With the help of a renegade Windmaster, Quareem, Zellorian attempts to release the storm-of-the-dark, terrible destructive forces chained by the gods of Innasmorn, but Ussemitus and his companions enlist the help of the Windmasters and thwart Zellorian's ambitions.

They now begin their search for the western lands anew, knowing that it will be a matter of time before Zellorian finds what he seeks and taps in to these dreadful forces.

As the shadow of a new war threatens to embroil Man on Innasmorn, the victorious Csendook declare their own Crusade against Mankind ended. A Supreme Sanguinary is appointed, Auganzar, and he is given the task of subduing the last surviving men in the original world cycle. Auganzar creates gladiatorial schools, where Men are trained as *moillum*, human gladiators who have exchanged their freedom for services to the Csendook. They perform in the games and are used in hunting down their own fellow Men who will not capitulate, for which the *moillum* are well rewarded.

But Auganzar is obsessed with the belief that the Imperator Elect is still alive and that somehow he has evaded the Csendook and achieved the unthinkable, breaking through the very fabric of the world cycle to whatever lies beyond. When the Csendook military rulers, the Garazenda, learn that Auganzar may be seeking the Imperator Elect, some of them, led by Zuldamar, embark on a secret plot to assassinate him, as they have no desire to renew the costly Crusade.

Auganzar sends one of his loyal commanders, Vorenzar, to the world of Eannor, where it is believed by most Csendook that the Imperator Elect perished along with Zellorian and his principal supporters. But Vorenzar has been charged by Auganzar with searching for any trail that might lead to the Imperator: he has been told to find him at any cost.

THE CSENDOOK MILITARY REGIME

The Csendook are governed by the GARAZENDA, a body comprised of all the principal generals, the foremost of which form an inner council, the MAROZUL.

Subordinate to the generals are the military commanders, the ZARU, their captains, the ZOLUTARS, and their armies, or Swarms, which are comprised of warriors, the ZEMOKS.

Csendook names are generally family names, with rank or title built into the name, usually as a suffix. Thus a member of the Marozul would have a name ending in -MAR, such as Zuldamar; a member of the Garazenda, who was not one of the Marozul, would have a name ending in -GAR, such as Xeltagar; a Zaru would have a name ending in -ZAR, such as Auganzar, and so on.

Certain Csendook, who have not earned enough battle honours to give them the right to their full title, do not have part of the title suffixed to their name, such as Cmizen, the Keeper of Eannor.

Apart from the Zemoks, Csendook are usually addressed by subordinates by their rank or title, thus Vorenzar is addressed by his warriors as 'Zaru' and not by his name. Auganzar, the Supreme Sanguinary (a title unique to him) is also a Zaru, and is addressed as such by his contemporaries.

The principal Csendook characters encountered in MOTHER OF STORMS and THIEF OF DREAMS are:

ZULDAMAR,   a member of the Marozul
HORZUMAR,   a member of the Marozul and friend of Zuldamar
XELTAGAR,   one of the Garazenda, a renowned Csendook fighter and veteran of the wars, fiercely supportive of Auganzar

AUGANZAR,	the Supreme Sanguinary, appointed to develop the process of Man's enslavement
VORENZAR,	a Zaru loyal to Auganzar, one of his personal bodyguard, Auganzar's Thousand
GANNORZOL,	a Zolutar under the secret orders of Zuldamar, with certain responsibilities for the world of Eannor
CMIZEN,	the Keeper of Eannor
ETRASCU,	an Opener, a hybrid being used specifically for the creating of gates between worlds of the world cycle, assigned to Cmizen and Eannor
IPSELLIN,	another Opener, assigned to Auganzar, and through him to Vorenzar

STAR REQUIEM

BOOK 2

THIEF OF DREAMS

BOOK ONE

VORENZAR

1

EANNOR

The tunnel stretched ahead into the distance, its walls seeming to contract and expand in the wavering lights held by the frontrunners of the company, an illusion of instability and change. Vorenzar, the new Keeper of Eannor, rode at the head of the company, two hundred strong, and not once on the long march did he look back or to the side, his eyes filled with visions of the future and the world he was about to take control of. Eannor, a world of mystery, shunned by the Csendook, abandoned because of the catastrophic events that were said to have taken place there, events that had resulted in the near annihilation of the world, the death of the renegades, the servants of the Imperator Elect, last of Mankind.

Beside Vorenzar, on a smaller beast, rode Ipsellin, his Opener, a being who was half the size of the huge Csendook, partly of the warrior race, and partly something else, a hybrid whose origins were lost in the far past of the Warhive's creation. The Openers were strangely rotund, neckless and with wattles of fat hanging under their chins, their eyes milky, their hair like a wiry down across their skull and upper backs. Ipsellin was no exception, his broad face creased in an almost permanent frown. He wore a voluminous tunic, emblazoned across its chest the twin scarlet rings that were the emblem of Auganzar, Supreme Sanguinary of the Csendook, whom Vorenzar served.

Vorenzar was dressed in dark war-mail; at his side he carried the twin swords of a commander going forward to battle, though he was on a peaceful mission. Strapped to his back was a long rectangular shield, embossed with the scarlet twin rings, the 'eyes of Auganzar' as they had been dubbed by his troops, his selected Thousand. Beyond Vorenzar were a score of his own picked Csendook, the

3

finest fighting beings he could find, and behind them were two hundred of the new warriors, the *moillum*, the gladiators: these were Men, trained by Csendook, Men who began as slaves, captured in the last of the wars, who had elected to become what they were rather than die in some pit, slaughtered by beasts for the amusement of their conquerors. They had accepted a new role, knowing that if they fulfilled it well, they could expect more from life than any defeated army should ever hope for.

Ipsellin held aloft a light, nudging his charger closer to the beast ridden by his master. It was a xillatraal, a quadruped that resembled a huge horse, but which also had reptilian features, a scaly hide, an elongated head and a forked tongue; it was carnivorous, prone to temper, and took firm handling, though the Csendook had formed as unique a relationship with the fierce creatures as Man had with the horse. Vorenzar's beast, though large and terrifying, accepted its burden without complaint, as though it shared the power of his position.

Vorenzar glanced down at the bulbous figure riding uneasily beside him. 'This Pathway seems to me to be unduly long. I seem to recall a shorter one.' He was referring to the fact that the Opener had brought him to Eannor before, on a spying mission for Auganzar. It had been a different trip then, with only the two of them, garbed in secrecy and stealth.

Ispellin's eyes rolled. 'The journey always changes,' he said in a hoarse whisper, as though his voice would offend the walls. His mouth was a scarlet orifice: the Openers had no teeth, they ate no solids. 'It is to do with conjunctions, Zaru. But the Path I have opened for you is nearing its end. Eannor is not far.'

Vorenzar grunted. He understood a little about timing. Only an Opener could bridge the worlds of the great Cycle with a gate, a Path, and without proper timing the Path could snap like a stretched thread, a ruptured artery. It was an uncomfortable thought, for if it happened, travellers would be flicked into instant oblivion. Vorenzar had visited numerous worlds of the new Csendook empire, but he never

4

relished the journeys between them. And this one seemed to be taking far too long: there was a smell of blood in the air.

However, the tunnel began to open out, light streaming into it from a source ahead. A short while later the company came to the end of the Path. Like a cave into a hillside, it widened, revealing the terrain and vegetation of a world. Eannor. The almost forgotten world, the place where Man had made his last stand, and where his Imperator Elect and all the leaders had perished.

Vorenzar grinned as he surveyed the peaceful scene below in the deep valley. Trees grew thickly, a river gleamed beyond them, and hills rose up, verdant and fertile, beyond them high mountains dressed in a lace of snow. The sky was a blue vault, smudges of clouds in the distance. There was no hint of desolation, no trace of destruction, no gaping world-wound, no ruins. Eannor looked almost a virgin world. Did the Garazenda who controlled the Csendook really think this place was Man's tomb? Auganzar had never believed it. Which was why he had first sent Vorenzar here. To search. To find the means by which Man's Imperator Elect had eluded the Csendook, and to track him down to whatever world he now hid upon.

Movement on the slopes caught Vorenzar's eye, and he dropped his visor. In a moment a small figure rode towards him from the low trees, behind it two others, though they were more cautious than the first figure. Vorenzar grunted: they were Csendook warriors, Zemoks, and therefore born cautious.

The first rider, mounted on a young, temperamental xillatraal, came upon him swiftly. The being was not unlike Ipsellin, though not as rotund. An Opener, its face coated in sweat from the unprecedented exertion, its eyes filled with agitation. Its beast bucked and turned, reflecting the anxiety of its rider.

'I was expecting you,' said the Opener. 'I am Etrascu. But, Zaru, I was to fetch you – to meet you beyond the Path at –'

'I have an Opener of my own,' said Vorenzar

impatiently, dismissing Etrascu's protestations with a brief wave.

Etrascu glared open-mouthed at Ipsellin, his eyes coming to rest on the renowned twin circles of the latter's tunic. 'It was not necessary, Zaru – '

'You seem offended,' said Ipsellin, his voice thickening with scorn.

Etrascu's xillatraal turned and he struggled to bring it under control. It had sensed the beast that Vorenzar rode, the mass of creatures arrayed behind it, emerging from the Path. 'Not at all,' stammered Etrascu. 'Merely surprised. As you know, Eannor is a restricted world – '

'Indeed,' cut in Vorenzar. 'I intend to keep it so. Everything I do here will be in absolute secrecy. The Garazenda are most specific.'

'I should have been told,' muttered Etrascu. 'No one should open a Way to Eannor without – '

'Where is your master?' snapped Vorenzar, ignoring the complaints.

Etrascu was looking in horror at the *moillum* who had formed ranks on the hill slope. They were *Men*! How many of them were there? And they were all armed! Was there to be a battle here? But why? Surely the Supreme Sanguinary had not sent them here to do battle with the Csendook guardians, the watchdogs of Eannor, his own people? But Etrascu knew it would be dangerous to ask more questions. Instead he began to ride back. As he did so, the two Csendook that had followed him came up, their faces set.

'You are the Zaru, Vorenzar?' said one of them stiffly.

Vorenzar nodded, acknowledging the commandership.

'You are welcome, Zaru.' The Csendook looked back at the company, the large number of *moillum*. Behind them the hillside was as closed as it had been before Ipsellin's working. 'I am Ulbok, serving under the Zolutar, Cmizen. I am to take you to him.'

'Have arrangements been made to accommodate my Zemoks?' said Vorenzar, gesturing to his Csendook.

'They have, Zaru,' nodded Ulbok. 'And there is an area

set aside for the others, as was ordered.' He made no attempt to hide his distaste for the Men.

'Then lead on,' said Vorenzar, ignoring it.

Etrascu heard this exchange with mounting dread. What did it mean? Why had he not been told? Why should Vorenzar have been allowed to open his own Way here? Etrascu looked at Ipsellin, but the Opener ignored him, his gaze deliberately fixed elsewhere as the entire company began to move down the mountain, led by the two Csendook of Eannor.

The ride took two hours and brought them down into the cool trees of the valley and to a place where it widened out. On a precipitous hill overlooking the river, a castle had been carved out of the native rock, its black windows gaping down with interest on the newcomers. Ulbok and his companion picked their way up the single, winding path that led to the base of the castle, and one by one the company followed, entering the shadows of another tunnel that took them out to the sunlight of the inner castle court. Walls towered over them ominously, dwarfing them.

Vorenzar, however, did not feel in the least humbled. He was too elated to be on Eannor again. His previous trip here had been furtive, dangerous. This time it would be very different. The taste of power had given him an appetite. He looked about the sombre court, wondering if its captain, Cmizen, would show himself. He evidently preferred to try to hold on to his dignity; he would be waiting in the castle, in his hall of office. Vorenzar grinned inside his helm. He dismounted slowly.

'See that the *moillum* are properly housed,' he told one of his Csendook. He turned to Ulbok. 'You will attend to my Zemoks.'

'Of course, Zaru. Ovarz will show them to their quarters. If you will come with me.'

Vorenzar gestured to Ipsellin to join him. Etrascu shuffled out of view, but Vorenzar guessed that he would be scuttling up some inner stair to have a last word with his master before Vorenzar confronted him. Vorenzar smiled to himself. He felt completely at ease here, though he

7

wondered how many eyes looked down upon him from the huge fortress walls. But those eyes would have seen the twin circles, the eyes of Auganzar. And they would know how far-seeing those eyes were.

Vorenzar took a leather satchel from his saddlebags and nodded to Ulbok. Together with Ipsellin they mounted the outer stair and passed within the fortress.

It was a gloomy, cold place, not built for pleasure, but as a house of war, a testament to the battles that had once been fought on Eannor. Man had first built this bastion, but Csendook had added to it, expanding it. Vorenzar nodded to himself. It would be a fitting setting for what he had planned.

High up in the castle, he approached a chamber where several guards waited stiffly. Their eyes gazed ahead of them, but Vorenzar knew they would be longing to gaze at him, to see what kind of a Csendook the legendary Supreme Sanguinary had sent here to their forgotten realm.

Ulbok spoke to them and they opened the thick doors to the chamber beyond. A voice spoke in low, guttural tones. Vorenzar and Ipsellin walked past Ulbok and into the chamber. Like the castle, it was austere, its walls bare except for a number of stacked weapons, spears and shields.

There was an elaborate desk between Vorenzar and the Csendook he had come to see, Zolutar Cmizen, who had risen, keeping himself behind his desk. He was unusually short, his stature not as broad as one would expect for a Csendook Zolutar, but Vorenzar knew that he had been picked to come to Eannor because he was weak and unambitious, a warrior who could be trusted to keep to himself and to do the minimum required of him. His skin was pale, as though, unlike his Zemoks, he did not spend much time in the sunlight of this pleasant world, and his eyes were sunken, his large teeth uneven in his mouth.

Cmizen saluted, too stiffly, holding himself rigid. His fear of the intruder he could not quite disguise. His eyes shifted nervously from Vorenzar to Ipsellin, who himself felt no awe at being before the Zolutar. There were other captains

8

in the ranks of the Csendook who filled him with coldness with a mere glance.

'It is a pleasure to have you here, Zaru,' said Cmizen, though his expression suggested that pleasure was the last thing he felt.

Vorenzar took off his war helm and dropped it noisily on the desk. Papers fluttered to the floor. He ignored them, enjoying Cmizen's expression as the latter's eyes followed the drift of the sheets, and did not meet his own cold eyes. 'Good. I am sure I shall enjoy Eannor.'

'Yes, of course. As you know, Zaru, it is not the devastated world it was believed to be –'

'I understand all that,' said Vorenzar, cutting him off. He dragged one of the wooden chairs over and sat comfortably in it, gesturing for Cmizen to sit. The Zolutar did so, though slowly and as if he might be in pain.

'Quite so, Zaru,' he said, clearly unsure of himself and how to react to the commander. Vorenzar's face was the face of a true warrior, the hunger for battle, for the hunt, carved there in every fierce line. Such a warrior had not stood on Eannor for many years.

'You have received orders from the Supreme Sanguinary, I believe?' said Vorenzar.

'I have.' Cmizen reached across the desk and fumbled among the papers until he brought out written instructions, though he knew by heart what they contained.

'And do they refer to further instructions?'

Cmizen nodded. 'To be brought by you, Zaru.'

Vorenzar grunted and thrust the leather pouch across the desk. 'You'll see that they are signed by the Supreme Sanguinary himself, approved by the Garazenda.'

Cmizen broke the seal and pulled out the papers, reading them quickly, a sheen of perspiration gathering above his brows. He nodded, sitting back.

Vorenzar could see the mixed reaction on Cmizen's face. 'They are clear?'

Cmizen looked up at him. 'Why, yes. Yes, Zaru, quite clear. Though I am a little puzzled –'

'Oh? What is it that puzzles you?'

9

'I had assumed that you were coming here to relieve me of my command and that my Zemoks and I were to return to the Warhive, or to be sent to another region to act as Keeper, or something appropriate to my rank.' He was beginning to babble. 'But I see from these orders that I am to remain here, under your command – '

'It concerns you?'

'No, no,' said Cmizen quickly. 'I just thought it perhaps wasteful. I know I am not the most valuable of the Gara-zenda's servants – '

Vorenzar scowled. Such a Csendook was hardly worthy to be a warrior. But the Zaru masked his thoughts. Cmizen had been picked for his weakness. In the past the Gara-zenda had wanted Eannor sealed off. In that sense, Cmizen had been useful.

'But you know Eannor better than anyone,' said Vorenzar.

Cmizen glanced uncomfortably at Ipsellin. Why had the Zaru found it necessary to bring his own Opener? Surely Etrascu was ideally discreet? No one could have attempted to study Eannor without alerting him. 'I have not made a study of the world,' said Cmizen. 'That was not my brief – '

'You know its history.'

'Well – '

'Its true history. You have kept its secrets well. To the Csendook nations it is a desolate world, a world destroyed by Man in his abortive attempt to break free of the cycle of worlds. The Supreme Sanguinary is most pleased with the way you have strengthened these myths.'

Cmizen waited. He knew there was more to this, far more.

'The Garazenda have decreed that Eannor should be forbidden to all Csendook. In a sense they have cursed it. You understand why?'

Cmizen straightened, speaking now as if reciting lines he had learned by heart. 'Man is worthy of contempt. In attempting to escape us, he destroyed Eannor. It is a testament to his folly, and a witness to the futility of all Man's works, the evil of his ways, his lust for sorcerous powers – '

Vorenzar nodded impatiently. 'Yes, yes. It is the picture that the Csendook nations have, and rightly so. But you know better.'

Cmizen's pallor became paler. 'I know that Eannor is not a wasteland – '

'And?'

'It would be a fine world for Csendook to live upon.'

Vorenzar leaned forward. 'And what of Man?'

Cmizen frowned, his fingers interweaving, his tension evident. 'Man, Zaru? There are no Men here. Only those you have brought.'

'You've searched the entire world?'

Cmizen nodded. 'There are no Men here, Zaru. No intelligent life forms.'

Vorenzar sat back with something approaching satisfaction on his face. 'I'm sure you are right.'

'Man may not have destroyed Eannor, Zaru, but clearly he destroyed himself in his efforts to create a Path into another realm – '

'Beyond the world circle?'

'So it is believed.'

'By whom?'

'I have had Etrascu, my Opener, study the ruins – '

'So there are ruins?'

'Yes. It is a place I have sealed off. I think it unsafe. The reek of death clings to it still.'

Vorenzar nodded thoughtfully. 'I will have to visit this place. Where is your Opener?' He had guessed that Etrascu must be lurking somewhere near at hand.

Cmizen reached for a tiny bell and shook it. It tinkled musically and within minutes the Opener appeared from behind some thick drapes. He came forward and bowed.

'The Zolutar tells me you have studied ruins here on Eannor,' said Vorenzar.

Etrascu looked up at Cmizen, but the latter nodded.

'The place where the last of the Men attempted their making of a Way,' said Etrascu. He shifted uneasily, as if speaking of things that disturbed him.

'I understand,' said Vorenzar, 'that they failed, and in

11

so doing destroyed themselves. Have you any proof, any evidence, to suggest the contrary?'

Etrascu looked stunned by the question. His eyes rolled and his wet mouth opened and closed. But he recovered himself. 'Zaru, I have not. Forgive me, but probing the ruins is very dangerous – '

Ipsellin's voice hissed from the shadows. 'Have you attempted an Opening?'

Etrascu gasped. Was *that* why he was here? To attempt such lunacy? 'Of course not! As an Opener, you know the fundamental laws that govern our chain of worlds. To break out of the circle would lead to a void, a vacuum. Utter annihilation. Had you seen the ruins – '

'Oh, we shall,' said Vorenzar with a smile.

'Zaru, you cannot mean to attempt an Opening,' Etrascu suddenly blurted, falling on his knees before Vorenzar. 'You cannot!'

'Why should you think I would do such a thing?'

'You have brought this Opener. You have no need of one here! I am the Opener. Assigned to the Keeper – '

'Your master has been relieved of that post. I am the Keeper of Eannor. Ipsellin is my assigned Opener, by Auganzar's hand.'

'But you must not attempt an Opening!'

Vorenzar was not angered by the sudden outburst, but it intrigued him. 'I ask you again, have you already done so?'

Etrascu looked up imploringly at Cmizen, who nodded once more.

'We have,' said the Zolutar, as Etrascu seemed incapable of answering.

Vorenzar leaned back. 'I see. What happened?'

'Etrascu almost died. He made a number of attempts to probe beyond the ruins, beyond the very walls of Eannor. He is not without skill,' added Cmizen, looking accusingly at Ipsellin. 'But he encountered a darkness, an atmosphere of pain, of death. It is as if the area around the ruins and beyond them is drowned in suffering, in the disaster that befell the Men who died there.' He fell silent, eyes down-cast, though it was not out of pity for Man.

'You talk of ghosts?' said Vorenzar coldly. 'Of Man's mythologies? Have they drawn you in, Zolutar? Have Man's dark gods claimed you?'

Cmizen shuddered, but did not look up. 'I am Csendook. I abjure such things, Zaru. But there are dark places we do not understand. Nor should we try to.' He lowered his voice. 'Have you come to attempt an Opening?'

Vorenzar gestured for Etrascu to get up off his knees. 'It seems to me,' he said after a moment, 'that such a course would be foolish.'

Both Etrascu and Cmizen looked relieved. Etrascu turned to see Ipsellin looking smugly at him, as if he enjoyed the discomfort of the Opener.

'I have other instructions,' said Vorenzar. 'And you will learn them soon enough.' He waved Etrascu away, and with a brief bow the Opener left the chamber. Ipsellin looked behind the drapes after he had gone, but there was a door beyond, and Etrascu had indeed left the company.

'You are to remain here on Eannor, with your full comp-lement,' Vorenzar told Cmizen. 'For you, nothing has changed, except that you will answer direct to me and it will no longer be necessary for you to forward any reports to the Warhive. All reports will be through me, and through me alone. I must make that clear at the outset.'

Cmizen indicated his written orders. 'It is in here, Zaru.'

'Excellent. And any reports that I send back to the War-hive will go with my Opener, Ipsellin. For the time being, Etrascu is not to be used for any duties connected with Opening. If he is, I will have him executed. Is that clearly understood?'

Cmizen frowned, but nodded. 'Of course, Zaru. But I must assure you that he has my implicit trust –'

'I'm not doubting his loyalty. But my orders are precise and they are from the Supreme Sanguinary, who appointed Ipsellin.'

Cmizen looked at the twin rings, the eyes of Auganzar

on Ipsellin's robe. Did any other Opener wear them? 'Then have no reservations, Zaru, Etrascu will not be used.'

Vorenzar cleared his throat as if he had said all that he intended to on the matter. He rose and walked around the chamber, studying the weapons, some of which were very old, possibly once belonging to the armies of Man. 'Tell me, Zolutar, are you familiar with the policies of the Garazenda regarding Man?'

Cmizen had also risen, but he felt dwarfed by the bulk of the warrior. 'Why, yes. I hear that the Crusade against Man is virtually at an end. Auganzar has initiated a new way forward. An enslavement policy.'

Vorenzar turned to him. 'Not all of the Garazenda approve of this policy. They would rather we pursued Man to the ends of the world cycle and wiped him out. What do you say to that?'

'Laudable, Zaru, but possibly not very practical.'

'That is how the weight of opinion went,' agreed Vorenzar. 'And it's why I'm here. You are no doubt aware that I've brought two hundred *moillum* with me.'

'Yes, Zaru. It is also in these papers.'

And you'll have seen them from your high tower, unless I miss my guess, thought Vorenzar. 'Quite. They are the first phase. I will have many more such gladiators brought here. Eannor will remain a restricted world. A world where the very best *moillum* can be bred and trained.'

'I see,' said Cmizen, not understanding at all.

'Think of it,' said Vorenzar, with unfeigned enthusiasm. 'Armies of them! Trained to serve us. Can you imagine what it will mean to the Csendook worlds, having entire battalions of enslaved gladiators, fighting each other for our pleasure! The Crusade may be over, but the wars go on, Zolutar. But in a new way. And where there are pockets of resistance in our worlds, where Man still struggles against us, we shall send in the *moillum*. They will do our work for us.'

'Forgive me, Zaru, but can we be sure of their loyalty?'

Vorenzar grinned. 'Ah, a question repeatedly asked. But the *moillum* will have everything they could wish for. And

14

Eannor is a splendid world, is it not? A world that any Man would enjoy. There will be every pleasure here for him. We shall bring his women to him, and breed selectively. Eannor will become a farm.' He laughed as he thought of it. 'Yes, a farm, with the *moillum* our beasts of burden.'

Cmizen's eyes widened. There was much in what Vorenzar said. Eannor was far from being devastated. It seemed to be an excellent world, and one which the Csendook nations would have revelled in. Doubtless they would have wondered at the fairness of using it to breed human warriors, but the Garazenda had obviously given much thought to their grand design.

'It will take time, naturally,' ended Vorenzar. 'Lifetimes, perhaps, but you will be here at the inception, Zolutar Cmizen. Something to be proud of, I think.'

'Indeed, Zaru.'

Vorenzar grunted with satisfaction. 'Very well. We will discuss this in greater detail later. For now, I'll see to the housing of my Zemoks, and the *moillum*.' He waved Ipsellin to him, and together they left the slightly bewildered captain behind them.

Alone on the stairs, descending to the lower courts, Vorenzar and Ipsellin spoke quietly. 'You are certain that his Opener cannot work without your knowing it?' said Vorenzar.

Ipsellin's face screwed up with contempt. 'Quite sure, Zaru. He is little better than a first cell Opener. He would not dare an Opening, not matter how small, for fear of my knowing.'

'When we have used him, we will dispose of him.'

Ipsellin did not hide his smile. 'Do you think that fool Cmizen was taken in?'

'About the colonising of Eannor?' Vorenzar grinned. 'Oh yes, he'll believe it. He has to, because he needs to feel secure. Terror rules him. He will have to know why we are here eventually, but by then it will not matter. How many Zemoks does he have?'

15

'I sensed only a few in this fortress,' said Ipsellin. 'Perhaps a hundred.'

Vorenzar shook his head. 'Auganzar is sure there must be more. As many as a thousand. And unlike Cmizen, I suspect they will be hardened warriors. They were sent here to make sure no one interfered.'

Ipsellin's fleshy smile widened. 'Ah, but you command them now, Zaru.'

Vorenzar nodded. 'Yes, they will be in no doubt of that. When they see the eyes of Auganzar upon them, they'll be swift to obey me.'

'In everything, Zaru?'

Vorenzar looked down questioningly at his Opener.

'Even to death?' said the bloated figure, his voice like that of a serpent in the shadows.

'That is the duty of any Csendook warrior. To make whatever sacrifice is required of him. Even to death.'

Ipsellin watched the Zaru stride off to attend to his Zemoks, knowing that for Vorenzar there was no remorse, no pity. His course was set, no matter how deeply the blood ran. It was ever the Csendook way, a thirst they would carry with them until they, too, were overrun. If such a thing would ever happen.

2

A HUNTING ACCIDENT

Zuldamar stared at the reports before him, though he had read them all a number of times. They were well written, their details clear, concise, so that nothing had been left open, at least in the eyes of anyone who did not guess the truth, that the reports were a fabrication. In exasperation, Zuldamar got up and paced slowly about his huge chamber. He was one of the principals of the Marozul, the High Command of the Csendook nations, and yet even here, in the comfort of his own offices, he felt threatened. Murder stalked among his colleagues, he knew it.

A voice whispered politely in the air, transmitted from beyond the great double doors of the chamber. It was a guard announcing the arrival of his colleague and fellow Marozul, Horzumar. Zuldamar admitted him, knowing at once by his friend's face that he was equally as disturbed by recent events.

'You've seen the reports?' said Horzumar. In his belt he wore a short stabbing sword, something he had not always carried in the halls of office.

Zuldamar gestured to the papers on his desk.

Horzumar grunted. 'Yes, I have a copy. They have been very thorough.'

Zuldamar crossed to another table where a tall pitcher and glasses rested. 'Drink?'

Horzumar nodded tiredly, sitting down as if this was as much his own chamber as Zuldamar's. No other Csendook would have taken such a liberty, but Horzumar and Zuldamar worked these days in almost constant companionship, a fact which would, ironically, work in their enemies' favour in some respects.

Zuldamar handed him a glass of wine and he himself sat. For a while they did not speak, as though gathering their troubled thoughts. Zuldamar was the elder of them by a number of years, a huge being, in his prime, seven feet tall and with the formidable build of a Csendook warrior, battle-trained and experienced, though he had not fought for a long time. Horzumar was younger, slightly less heavily built, though to a Man he would have still seemed huge. His head seemed always to be moving, his eyes restless, looking about him as if he were on the field of battle, suspecting every shadow, though he, too, had not fought for a long while, though he had lately taken to energetic training, as if he expected to be sent to some remote battle front.

'Another assassination,' said Zuldamar at last.

'Is it time we expressed our thoughts to the Marozul?'

Zuldamar shook his head. 'How can we? What would an investigation reveal? Xindezar got himself into a compromising position. It was too easy in the end for the death to be arranged.'

'Auganzar is overreaching himself,' replied Horzumar, banging down his empty glass so that he had to steady it.

Zuldamar could see that the death had badly shaken him, which was unusual. Horzumar was usually able to remain exceptionally calm in any crisis.

'We know that he murdered Gannorzol, then other Zolutars. That was bad enough, Zuldamar. But now a Zaru! How long before he begins eliminating members of the Garazenda?'

'You think we are the targets?'

Horzumar snorted. 'At first I presumed that all Auganzar wanted was to dispose of all those who stood in his way over this business about Eannor. We made the mistake of thinking he would be quite content to control the training of the gladiatorial armies, the new enslavement of Mankind. But this obsession he has with searching for the Imperator Elect – '

'He seems to want him very badly. I never could understand why. Man has fallen. Even if the Imperator Elect were to come back, what powers would he have? Or Zellorian? Even if he is alive – '

18

'I cannot believe it.'

'Auganzar believes it.'

'He has no proof.'

'But he'll scour Eannor for it.'

'Yes,' nodded Horzumar. 'I had assumed we could forget about Auganzar once we allowed him to use Eannor as a base for the gladiatorial armies. Let him play his hunting games. But his ambitions grow.'

'Just as his power grows,' observed Zuldamar. 'It is incredible, is it not? Since that incident in the arena, Auganzar has become almost a creature of myth.'

'Our race does not enjoy peace,' said Horzumar irritably. 'The Supreme Sanguinary has become the new warlord. In the eyes of the warriors, he is the hope for the future, the wielder of the sword, the one who will feed them.'

'Their adoration feeds him,' agreed Zuldamar. 'I think he wants to take his place among the Marozul. He already has as much say in military matters as any one of us.'

'I think he wants more than that. I think he wants to replace the Marozul.'

Zuldamar would have sneered at such a statement once, but not now. The traditions of centuries were undoubtedly in danger. 'Become supreme ruler?'

'That is what he seeks,' said Horzumar coldly. 'Xindezar's death has convinced me of that. Consider: he was loyal to us and to the Marozul who are strongly with us in the belief that the Crusade should have ended, a stop put to the colossal wastage of the wars. More than once Xindezar had been given an opportunity to join the ranks of Auganzar's Thousand, his elite corps – '

'Had he?' said Zuldamar.

'Oh yes. He had been approached.'

'It does not surprise me. He was a superb warrior, very quick on his feet. He served under Xeltagar before transferring to our internal guard.'

'Some of the veterans wanted Xindezar with them. But he refused. He was training up his own small school of *moillum*, and had a family – '

Zuldamar gasped. 'They are not mentioned in the report. Have they – ?'

'They are safe. I have seen to that. Auganzar is careful about the extent of his murders. He wiped out the entire household of Gannorzol, but since then has been careful not to arouse suspicions by such wholesale murder.'

Zuldamar nodded, picturing in his mind's eye the flying accident that had brought the death of Gannorzol and every living member of his household, his entire line felled in one stroke. It had seemed curious that they should all be together at the time, but nothing could be done to show that it was anything other than a crash, a mysterious fault in their craft that could never be identified. Gannorzol, too, had been loyal. He had known all there was to know about Eannor and its secrets, and he had carefully monitored all reports from there, ensuring that Zuldamar and no one else saw them. Without Gannorzol's complete dependability, the secret of Eannor could never have been kept. But Auganzar had taken that secret from him. And from that moment the sword in his hand, given to him by the Marozul, had begun to swing round to face them.

'Where will he strike next?' said Horzumar.

'He seems to know which of the Zolutars and Zaru are closest to us, even though some are secretive about it. He has a network among us, and yet we have none among his followers.'

Horzumar glowered at the polished stone floor as though something in its design infuriated him. 'Three times I have tried to infiltrate his system. Each time my spies have failed.'

'Murdered?'

'No. Released from duty. Transferred back. Auganzar has been careful, even in that. He reported back to my Zolutars that he was grateful for the suggested promotions, but felt that the quality of the Zemoks sent to him did not quite match that quality looked for in a member of the Thousand, or indeed in the forces they command. Somehow, if we send in spies, Auganzar knows they are from

20

us, no matter how indirect and discreet we are when we plant them.'

'So he is able to toss our agents back in our faces. "Grateful for the suggested promotions" indeed!'

'He feels very secure in his strength,' nodded Horzumar. 'But even so, he takes no risks and shows no hint of complacency.'

Zuldamar got up and poured more wine for them. 'Then what are we to do? If we take no action at all, we are like stones upon a beach, awaiting the incoming tide.'

'I agree,' said Horzumar, taking the wine and sipping at it thoughtfully.

'Can assassination be considered?'

'I've thought of it a hundred times,' replied Horzumar. 'But Auganzar will have thought of it above all. He must know that he has enemies who would gladly strike off his head, or thrust a knife in his heart. But aside from an open kill, how could we get near him?'

'It would have to be indirect.'

'So indirect that it would be complicated, and so complicated that it could fail on any number of accounts.'

'Open opposition to Auganzar would not work,' said Zuldamar, again pacing about. 'There are too many of the Garazenda who either support him in his new role, or who are blind to the assassination committed in his name. I am afraid, my friend, that you and I are seen by too many of our colleagues as alarmists. They simply don't believe in the dangers we point to. And some of them may think we are deliberately attempting to fabricate deceits aimed at bringing Auganzar down.'

'I'm sure you are right,' nodded Horzumar bleakly.

'There may be another way,' went on Zuldamar thoughtfully. He put down his glass. Horzumar waited for him to say more, knowing that if there were useful ideas to be found anywhere, they would come from Zuldamar. 'These schools, farms, whatever we call them – '

'For the *moillum*?'

'Men. Our hated enemies. Who once hated us as

passionately as our warriors hated them. Now that they have been subjugated, do they forget their old hatreds?'

'They are settled very carefully. I hear that those who serve in Auganzar's *moillum* are very content.'

'Can they all be? Content? As slaves?'

'The alternative is death.'

'So they feign contentment to remain alive?'

Horzumar sighed. 'In theory, one would expect it. But from what I have learned, Auganzar's Zemoks are able to select Men who are genuinely content. Their lives as gladiators are, in some ways, to be envied. They are well treated, and in many cases have more pleasure in life than they would have had hiding from our Swarms on some remote world, where many of them are culled from. Again, the Supreme Sanguinary has excelled. No other schools are as eagerly sought by Men as his.'

If Horzumar had expected his friend to scowl resignedly at this, he was surprised. Zuldamar nodded as though the words brought some comfort to his troubled mind. Abruptly he thumped the table, rocking the glass pitcher. 'There! An opening in his armour. His vanity.'

'What do you mean?'

Zuldamar turned to Horzumar with a faint grin. 'We cannot get a Csendook in to his system. He has everyone vetted. But could we get a Man into it?'

'A gladiator?'

'Yes.'

'But what good would it do? The *moillum* never get near Auganzar. He may see them in training, or in battles, but always from a distance. None of the *moillum* could kill him.'

Zuldamar shrugged. 'No. But it will be a beginning. One Man. One who hates us –'

'He would serve us no better than Auganzar, surely –'

'Then he must be schooled by his fellows. Men who do serve us. There must be *moillum* who are as content with their lots serving our schools as those of Auganzar.'

Horzumar suddenly gasped. 'Why, of course! Xindezar's *moillum*. They would be appalled by his death, fearing the worst for their own futures.'

'Secure them,' said Zuldamar. 'See that they are promised the protection of one of our own schools, the best we have. And find from among them a Man who we can use against Auganzar. A Man we can teach to hate. And if there is none among them, then we will find one from outside the Warhive, fresh from one of the worlds, a Man still burning with hatred. Let his own fellows teach him that there is a way for him to strike back at the Csendook.'

'By joining Auganzar's *moillum*.'

'A beginning,' nodded Zuldamar, sitting again, looking more content.

'This Man will have to be exceptional. A warrior of the highest order. Auganzar's agents are not easily satisfied.'

'The Man will have to be exceptional if he is to survive as a spy.'

'Then we must begin searching at once.'

They fell silent, considering their plan, until one of the guards spoke, his voice gentle in the air. 'There is a request from the lower chambers, sir. A visitor requests permission to be admitted.'

'Who is it?' said Zuldamar, annoyed at being disturbed at such a time.

'The Supreme Sanguinary, sir.'

Zuldamar and Horzumar looked at each other for a moment, neither able to cover his surprise.

'You are expecting him?' said Horzumar, though it was perfectly clear that Zuldamar was not.

'An uncomfortable coincidence. Shall I admit him, or would you rather leave first?'

Horzumar gave the matter a moment's thought. 'On reflection, I'd like to remain, if I may. Auganzar will learn nothing by seeing us together that he does not already know. And I would like to see his reaction to the death of Xindezar.'

'Very well.' Zuldamar called out to the door, 'You may admit the Supreme Sanguinary.' He rose and put away the wine, tidying his desk, though he left the report of Xindezar's death upon it.

They waited in silence, thinking over the brief plan they

23

had made, wondering how they could extend it towards their committed goal, the downfall of the Csendook about to visit them.

The guard signalled Auganzar's arrival and he was admitted. He bowed to them both as he came in, showing no emotion whatsoever at meeting both of them, as if he had known they were together. Had Horzumar left clandestinely, Zuldamar realised, the Supreme Sanguinary would have suspected his actions.

Auganzar's face was handsome, though its lines were hard, as if they spoke of the wars he had known, the terrible battles in which he had fought as a young Zemok, when the conflict with Man was still raging on a dozen worlds. He was dressed in sombre, military colours, and in the present company these leant more than a hint of aggression to his bearing. At his side he wore the twin swords of a warrior, and both his hosts glanced at them disapprovingly, though there was no reaction from the huge warrior. His entire mien was well studied, a presence that put terror into the hearts of his enemies with a mere glance. Even the Marozul flinched before this embodiment of power.

'And what brings you to us?' said Zuldamar as affably as he could, after they had all seated themselves. They might have been discussing a military banquet.

'Two matters, Marozul,' said Auganzar, getting straight to the point. These Csendook were his enemies, he knew that. They would have his head today if they could find a legitimate way to remove it. Probably they had been conspiring against him only a few moments ago. But it did not greatly concern him. He knew their strengths. Ironic that it was these two who spoke so strongly in favour of having a Supreme Sanguinary in the first place! How they regretted that decision now.

'Presumably,' said Zuldamar, 'the first is the untimely death of our colleague, Zaru Xindezar.'

'Exactly that,' said Auganzar, a faint smile on his lips. He tapped a report he had been carrying. 'I have studied this in depth. I take it you have also done so?'

'We both have,' said Horzumar, staring directly at the

Supreme Sanguinary. He had faced him before, and knew the absolute coolness with which this warrior went about his business. He could generate deep fear with a single glance, but Horzumar was not prepared to back down an inch.

'An unfortunate business,' said Auganzar.

'Indeed,' nodded Zuldamar, waiting.

'I wanted to speak about the death to you informally, which is why I did not ask for an audience with the full Marozul.'

Still Zuldamar said nothing, face bland.

'In a way, I feel partly responsible for the young warrior's death.'

Horzumar felt himself tensing. *He's taunting us! Throwing this killing in our faces! Damn him* –

'How can that be so?' said Zuldamar mildly.

'Xindezar was an excellent warrior. He fought under the veteran Xeltagar, as you probably know – '

'Xindezar's record is well known to both of us,' said Horzumar, unable to remain silent, though he could sense that Zuldamar wanted him to be so.

'I was considering approaching Xindezar, formally requesting that he be released to my own corps.'

'Really?' said Zuldamar, as though this was a surprise to him. 'Though I have to say again, Xindezar was excellent. I am sure he would have been greatly honoured.'

'Regrettably,' Auganzar went on, moulding his deceit effortlessly, 'he must have heard of my intentions prematurely. Sometimes word does leak out, though I am very hard on those responsible. Very hard.'

'Ah, then Xindezar knew that you would ask for his transferral?' said Zuldamar.

'I think so. Otherwise, why would he have made such a rash attempt to impress me with his competence as a warrior? This expedition that he was on,' and again Auganzar tapped the report. 'Baiting killdreen. He was understaffed and underequipped. And then he attempted to bring one of the beasts down on his own.'

'That's your interpretation?' said Zuldamar.

'I can hazard a guess, Marozul – '

'You haven't considered the possibility,' cut in Horzumar, 'that he had no intention of hunting killdreen at all, that he was merely taking a party of Zemoks and *moillum* into the hills for other training.'

Auganzar smiled gently, as though consoling a relative. 'I am afraid I am party to certain things not contained in the report, Marozul.'

'Such as?' said Zuldamar.

'Some of the Zemoks talk among themselves. My own Zemoks hear things. Apparently they are saying that Xindezar deliberately went out in search of killdreen in order to fulfil an old custom. That of a hand-to-hand killing of a black lion. Of course, I cannot substantiate this, which is why I would not wish to bring it before the full Marozul. But it suggests to me that Xindezar did this foolish thing in an attempt to secure a place among the Thousand.'

Clever, thought Zuldamar. Very neat, and typical of him. Should he be challenged on it, he'll produce witnesses, naturally. A dozen Zemoks who will swear that Xindezar would have done anything to join the Thousand. Like so many other Csendook.

'I am sure we are grateful for this news,' said Zuldamar with a deliberate look at Horzumar that told him, be silent! It's no time to argue. Already Auganzar would have ensured that other Marozul had heard of this, indirectly.

'I also think,' said Auganzar, 'that should this be made public, it would reflect badly on Xindezar, and his family. It would be better, I think, that such a promising warrior be remembered for his past. The report says that the attack of the killdreen pack was unforeseen, and that there were more of them than usual, and that they were in an area where it was thought they no longer hunted.'

'None of the beasts were killed or captured?' said Horzumar.

'They had fled back over the mountains,' confirmed Auganzar.

If they had been caught, Horzumar knew, they would

have been found full of drugs, their tempers enflamed. No investigation would ever uncover such facts now.

'Your advice, as always, is sound,' said Zuldamar, and Horzumar marvelled at his friend's duplicity. 'Let us honour Xindezar, and do our best to cover over his impetuosity. I don't think we need to display it, do you?'

'Of course not, Marozul. And again, I am troubled by my own, indirect, part in this tragedy.'

'You set the highest of standards,' said Zuldamar. 'It is what we asked of you.'

Auganzar nodded, displaying just enough hint of remorse to have been convincing to anyone who did not know the truth. After a brief silence he went on. 'The other matter, Marozul, concerns Eannor.'

Again Horzumar felt his blood heating. Auganzar could hardly have touched on a more sensitive nerve.

'The new Keeper has taken up his post?' said Zuldamar, as if they were once more discussing trivial matters that he had no real interest in, but as a Marozul must recognise as an act of protocol.

'Vorenzar is there, Marozul. But I am asking that the former Keeper, Zolutar Cmizen, be asked to remain there. In fact, I have taken the liberty of issuing orders to him that he does so, under the command of the new Keeper, Zaru Vorenzar.'

Zuldamar thought over this quickly. Cmizen was weak, but like Gannorzol, he was loyal, his fear of the Supreme Sanguinary goading him to remain loyal to Zuldamar, who received his reports. If Cmizen remained on Eannor, he would fall prey to Vorenzar quickly, having no stomach for conflict.

'Is there a particular reason?' said Zuldamar mildly, as though he had no concern one way or the other. 'Cmizen is not very gifted, and no warrior. I'm not sure what use he would be if we recalled him, but what is there for him to do on Eannor now that he is to be, as far as I can tell, redundant?'

'As I understand it,' said Auganzar, 'Cmizen has had

very little to do on Eannor, the world being as it is, badly ravaged by events there.'

'Come, come,' said Horzumar. 'You are well aware that Eannor is not the devastated world that it was given to be. The Marozul have their own reasons for wanting to perpetuate the myth of its dangers –'

Auganzar raised his hands gently. 'Of course, I realise I have not had the support of all the Marozul in pressing for the use of Eannor. I know that it is not a graveyard, but I do agree it should be a forbidden place. It will be, to all but the chosen few who are sent to it, under Vorenzar. I have to say, at risk of incurring your further anger, that I believe Eannor to be the perfect breeding ground for the *moillum*. With the imposition of secrecy, we could make a formidable force of them.

'The subjugation programme goes better than we could have hoped.' He held up more reports. 'On six worlds that were a constant problem to us, Man has capitulated. Many have been brought to the Warhive and have already been put into *moillum* schools. My intention, with approval, is to use Eannor to create a force that can go out to the last of the renegades and bring Man to heel, fully to heel.'

'Admirable,' said Zuldamar, knowing that this was yet further deceit. The Supreme Sanguinary had his Zemoks on Eannor for one reason, and one reason only: to hunt for the Imperator Elect, whom he believed to be alive. Auganzar was, Zuldamar was sure, obsessed. Perhaps there would be a way to turn that obsession on him, use it as the weapon that would ultimately bring him down?

Horzumar had no alternative but to follow Zuldamar's lead. He nodded. 'We may yet differ over how Eannor should be used,' he said. 'But that's as may be. Tell me, what possible use could you have for Cmizen? If you intend to make Eannor a training ground, and a hard one, probably the most exacting in the cycle of worlds, I would have thought that Cmizen would be the last Csendook you would want there.'

Auganzar smiled as though taking the point well. 'Of course, Cmizen will have no place in Vorenzar's force. He would indeed be the last one chosen for it! But he has other abilities. Since he has been there, he has kept the secrets of Eannor well. Let him continue to do so. Vorenzar will be busy. I will be sending to him some of the most difficult *moillum*, those who refuse to do as we wish. I know that we have promised death to those who cannot accept our lordship of them – '

'You would use Eannor as a prison, too?' said Zuldamar.

'Dissidents should be killed. But some of them could be potentially fine *moillum*. On Eannor their rebellions would be wasted, for they would have no one to turn to. I would have them segregated. There would be two schools. One for the converted Men, the finest *moillum* we could train. The other for the rebels.'

Horzumar smiled. 'And you could pit them against each other, use their rivalry to tighten up their strengths.'

Something struck Zuldamar, an idea as bright as a shaft of sunlight, but he showed none of his inner emotion. 'Supreme Sanguinary, you and I have not always agreed on matters. But in this matter I find your arguments most persuasive. Your ideas impress me.'

'Thank you, Marozul. I confess I brought them to you rather than the full Marozul, knowing that if I could convince you of the worth of my ideas – '

'Not quite the correct protocol,' smiled Zuldamar. 'But it does you credit, as your tactics so often have. Yes, I think we can support such an idea. Do you not agree, Marozul Horzumar?'

Horzumar read the promptings of his friend and smiled. 'Well, if you want the truth, I was wondering what we could possibly do with Zolutar Cmizen anyway.' And they laughed gently as though the matter was sealed.

After a few brief pleasantries, Auganzar departed. As soon as he had gone, Horzumar's face clouded.

'I have missed something,' he said. 'But I went with you, Zuldamar. What is it?'

Zuldamar patted him on the arm, an oddly intimate gesture. 'Don't you see? We have our lever. Eannor as an off-loading place for Man's dissidents! How perfectly this fits into our thoughts of earlier.'

Horzumar's eyes widened. 'Of course! And if Cmizen is to remain there, we may yet depend on him to help us.'

'If his nerve holds. But Eannor is where we will breed our assassin, my friend. When Auganzar puts his proposals to the Marozul, we'll agree, but on condition that we send a percentage of the *moillum* from our own schools. So that the Marozul are properly represented.'

'And we'll have a team of assassins, an elite corps. The sword that bends back on its wielder.'

They laughed gently together - and Zuldamar again brought out the wine. But in his mind one unspoken thought remained. Why did Auganzar want so many *moillum* on Eannor?

3

WORLD GATE

Ipsellin sat in the centre of the gloomy chamber, his eyes closed, his mind focused on his deep thoughts, all else closed to him. The search time was almost over, the listening, the attuning as the Openers called it. He did not know that he had a visitor, who sat silently opposite him in the shadows, watching his face patiently, not making a sound, expression blank. Vorenzar had his own thoughts to consider.

When Ipsellin opened his eyes, he was immediately alert, as though he had been pretending sleep, but Vorenzar knew better. The Csendook waited.

'As I thought,' said Ipsellin. 'There have been no attempts to send information back to the Warhive.'

'How can you be certain?'

'Only the Opener could do it. And since we have come, he has made no attempt.'

Vorenzar relaxed. 'He knows you would sense such an attempt.'

'Of course. He is very concerned for his future.'

'Now that you have confirmed Cmizen's fear of communicating with the Warhive, it is time to proceed with our work. And we shall need Etrascu for that.' Vorenzar stood up and left the chamber, his Opener walking softly behind him.

Cmizen was also in his chamber, brooding over papers that he did not really see. Whatever it was that Vorenzar wanted here on Eannor, the real truth of it had yet to emerge. But Cmizen's nights had been sleepless since his coming. And Etrascu had smelled fresh blood in the air, a breeze from the future perhaps. Cmizen was a Csendook: he should not believe such things. But this was Eannor,

31

and the hidden horrors of its past were very tangible ghosts to him.

There was a knock on the door, which opened at once to admit Vorenzar. Cmizen stood up, noting with distaste that his Opener was with him. The eyes of Ipsellin strengthened Cmizen's fear, as though the bulbous figure had its own purpose, a purpose of pain, murder perhaps. Ipsellin's contempt for Cmizen was very clear, though Cmizen dared say nothing of it to Vorenzar, who would have been offended.

'Are things to your satisfaction, Zaru?' asked Cmizen.

Vorenzar grunted. 'Excellent. We have begun the training programme for the *moillum*. As I anticipated, they feel at home in this place. My Zemoks report that they behave well, not like slaves at all.'

'That is good,' said Cmizen, relieved. But why should Csendook make life comfortable for our slaves?

'In view of this, I feel I can afford the time to look around. Travel further afield.'

Cmizen felt the coldness gathering in his gut. He knew well enough what was coming. He had been expecting it since Vorenzar's arrival several weeks before.

'If your duties are not too pressing,' Vorenzar went on, 'perhaps you could show me something of Eannor.'

'Of course, Zaru.'

'And we'll need your Opener.'

'Zaru?'

'Fetch him.'

Behind him, Ipsellin's face wore the smug grin that Cmizen assumed must always be fixed there. It had become part of his own restless dreams.

They had not travelled far from the fortress. A range of low hills rose up before them, wooded and innocuous to the eye, though an odd silence hung over them, and even a long look at them revealed no sign of life, no distant flap of wings.

Vorenzar gently stroked the long neck of his xillatraal.

He had felt it tense beneath him, a reaction to the hills. Cmizen's own beast was decidedly uneasy, rising up on its hind legs, having to be brought sharply to order; it unsettled the smaller beasts of Ipsellin and Etrascu. Vorenzar had elected to bring none of his Zemoks or *moillum* with them, and again Cmizen wondered at the secrecy of his purpose.

'Beyond these hills,' he said. 'Sealed.'

Vorenzar said nothing, nodding for his guide to lead them upwards.

The path they found was overgrown, bushes tangled on either side of it, spilling over, almost blocking the way, but the xillatraal forged through the obstructions, Cmizen leading. The journey upward into the hills was conducted in silence, though Cmizen felt as though he would cry out in protest, his nerves wearing thinner by the seeming indifference of the Zaru and his Opener. Could they not feel the air of this place? Hear its murmurs of outrage like tiny waterfalls?

Vorenzar understood the peculiar powers of the Openers, which in some ways cut across the beliefs of the Csendook, the rejection of the supernatural, of sorcery. But he was himself rigid in his own rejection of such things. There would be no demons here, and if there were guardians, his warriors would deal with them, without recourse to the trickery of so-called magic. Even so, Cmizen's dread had become more deep-rooted than it had been at the fortress. Whatever they would find beyond the hills, it was a focus for that fear, and Etrascu seemed likewise disturbed by it.

Ipsellin glanced up at his master, his own brows clouded. 'There is an evil here,' he said softly so that neither Cmizen nor Etrascu heard him.

'A trap?' mouthed Vorenzar. 'Should I return with a force?'

Ipsellin shook his head. 'I can deal with it. But it may be dangerous. There is a smell of old blood. Overpowering.'

Vorenzar frowned. He could sense nothing, only the silence. But he had known it was a place of death they were coming to.

They entered the low trees which huddled over them, blotting out most of the light. There was no undergrowth, as if the earth here could support the life of the trees and nothing more: their trunks were thin and pale and reminded Vorenzar of corroded spars.

Over the brow of the hills they went, the land dropping away steeply, almost as if in to a gorge, chiselled by streams that whispered through it like spirits, loosening the dark loam, making it unsafe. The company had to pick their way carefully downward. Etrascu led now, knowing the path by instinct, for none was visible. Cmizen had pulled his cloak tightly about him as if caught in a sudden winter's breeze, though Vorenzar ignored the cold embrace of the air among these trees. Their trunks were pale, like leeched corpses, but he shook himself free of the images of death.

The journey downwards seemed interminable, the slope far deeper than the one they had climbed to reach the hill crest. But at length Etrascu pulled up his snorting beast and indicated a darkness below. It seemed to be a wall cut from huge blocks of black rock, stretching across the forest, its top obscured among a wild tangle of branches and vegetation.

'Who built this?' said Vorenzar, his voice almost smothered by the air. It had become even colder, almost as though the coldness seeped out of the wall like a miasma.

'Man,' answered Cmizen.

'The valley of sacrifice is beyond,' said Etrascu.

'You've seen it?' said Vorenzar.

'Once,' said Etrascu, with an anxious look at Cmizen, who was visibly shivering, his face white in the shadows.

'And is this where Zellorian brought the remnants of the Imperator Elect's people? His last desperate stand against us?' said Vorenzar, raising his voice, throwing it at the wall in contempt. But the black stone absorbed the sounds as if he had whispered.

'Yes,' nodded Etrascu. 'It is where they attempted the Opening.'

Vorenzar nodded slowly, guiding his beast up and down the wall, looking at it, trying to fathom it, weigh its strength. It did not seem high, but there was a strange solidness about it, as if it could resist the might of an ocean. But somehow he had the distinct impression that it had not been set here to keep back an army, but to contain something. The mythical power of Zellorian?

'Where is the gate?' Vorenzar challenged Etrascu, ignoring Cmizen, who seemed incapable of speech anyway.

Etrascu looked to his master, but got no response.

'One will have to be made,' said Ipsellin, coming forward. 'The wall is continuous, self-sealing. I have seen the constructions of Men on other worlds.'

Vorenzar did not criticise him, valuing his judgements. 'Then let Etrascu make an Opening through it.'

Etrascu shuddered. 'It will take blood?'

Vorenzar frowned. 'The place beyond is part of Eannor. Why should it need blood.'

'It is Eannor, Zaru,' nodded Etrascu. 'But the Men who came here were powerful. Just as the Openings between worlds are made in blood, so is the gate to this wall.'

Ipsellin trotted his xillatraal down the slope, closer to the wall. He could hear the fears trapped within the wall, almost see the faces of the dead as they watched him. They were in the blood, he told himself. A Csendook would not understand that, but as an Opener, blood spoke to him, a river of life, with its own recording of what was once the flesh that housed it. And blood was the flesh of the world cycle.

He turned and trotted his beast slowly back. He looked meaningfully at Etrascu. 'I agree. A little blood will open this wall.'

Vorenzar ignored Etrascu's look of horror. 'Do it,' he hissed.

Cmizen stared down at the ground, his body shaking. He said nothing.

Vorenzar pulled out one of the swords. It grated against the metal of its scabbard, but it did not shine in this place. He lowered his visor.

Etrascu nudged his reluctant beast forward to the wall, dismounting. His robes concealed what he did, but

Vorenzar caught a glimpse of metal, a tiny cloud of steam. The Csendook looked away. Beside him, Ipsellin was grinning, enjoying the ordeal of the other Opener.

On the wall above Etrascu there seemed to be a stain, growing like a pool of shadow. Etrascu slumped to one side, his face pale. There was blood on his hands, but he quickly rubbed them, using his cloak to wipe them. Without looking at the wall he climbed on to his xillatraal, which bucked under him, almost throwing him, disturbed by the blood. Etrascu steadied it, gazing at Vorenzar, nodding like a man in pain.

'He has made the Opening,' said Ipsellin.

'I cannot see it,' said Vorenzar, though there was a deep shadow across the wall.

'It is there,' said his Opener. 'Shall I take us through?'

Vorenzar nodded, and Ipsellin again led his beast down to the wall, entering the cleft of darkness. Cmizen and Etrascu followed him, with Vorenzar behind them. He held his sword before him like a torch, his own nerves stretched taut as the cold darkness engulfed him like a pool.

Through the gate they went, like shadows on a moonless night. Vorenzar closed out the images that tried to form in his mind, waking dreams that spoke of pain, of terror, of bloody death.

Then they were through.

Sunlight streamed down into the valley into which they had emerged. It was a treeless place, rock walls rising up on all sides like polished glass. There were ruins, toppled columns, statues, large dwellings that might once have been temples or storehouses, Vorenzar could not tell which. But the awful cold of the passage was behind them. Here it was warm, though not welcoming. A wide area opened up before them, its flagstones huge, cracked, some thrust up by the roots that quested beneath them. And there were bones.

At first Vorenzar thought he was looking at collapsed buildings, walls, but as he came closer he realised that there were innumerable skeletons here, stacked in heaps, or scattered like leaves before a storm. The entire valley was choked with them. He dismounted and picked up the broken rib cage of one of these grim relics. It was the rib cage of a Man.

'You have found the Imperator Elect,' said a voice behind him, so that for a moment he jerked.

It was Cmizen, moving like a ghost through the open graves. 'Man's last grave,' he whispered.

Vorenzar thrust up his visor, cold eyes gazing about him, amazed by the destruction that must have taken place here. Countless thousands. Row upon row of the dead.

'This was the result of their sorcery,' Cmizen went on, taking a deep breath.

Vorenzar still said nothing. He had seen the heaped slain many times in the field of battle, heard their screams. But the silence here was more harrowing. He walked across the plaza, feet kicking through bones and skulls. Near the centre of the natural arena there was a large mound of these skulls, most of them badly broken, some mere fragments. Almost hidden beneath them there was a huge dais, and Vorenzar used his sword to clear away some of the piled remnants. Ipsellin came to his side.

'You were right,' Vorenzar said to him softly. 'There is a smell of blood here. Even now.'

Ipsellin looked about him in disgust. 'So many,' he said, shaking his head. 'Enough to open a hundred gates, a thousand.'

Vorenzar, like most of his race, knew little about the Opener's craft, its grim details. He knew that certain sacrifices had to be made in order that Paths could be made between worlds. Blood was shed, through the Openers, as far as Vorenzar understood, and they were bred for this purpose, to give a little of their blood to perform this function. It did them no harm, so it seemed, and they quickly replenished their blood. Difficult gates, it was said, took greater sacrifices.

'Is that what they attempted?' said Vorenzar, still surprised at the enormity of the implications. 'To open a Path *out* of the cycle of worlds?'

37

Ipsellin scowled. 'So it would seem. They were not killed in battle.'

Etrascu's face was white. 'You see the stupidity of Man before you. The results of his madness.'

'The price of failure,' murmured Cmizen, pulling his cloak about him, though the sun beat down here, as abnormally hot as the forest had been cold.

'What Openers did they use?' said Vorenzar. He knew that Men had had their own methods of moving from world to world in his empire, methods which were not unlike those employed by the Openers. But Man had cloaked the rituals in mystery and sacred lore. Even the Openers had not been able to learn as much of it as they would have desired.

'Man opened gates with his own blood,' said Ipsellin. 'His sorcerers – your pardon, Zaru – his men of knowledge did this, as we Openers do it. But the key remains the same, Blood. Blood of Man, blood of Csendook, of Opener, it all has power.'

Vorenzar studied the chaos of bones about him. 'You are certain Man failed here?' he said to Etrascu.

Etrascu stiffened. 'Zaru, I once attempted an Opening in this place.' His eyes opened wide on some inner experience, some deep torment as he said this. 'To learn if Man had succeeded in his madness.'

'And?' said Vorenzar. Ipsellin studied Etrascu, as though trying to probe the mind of his fellow Opener.

Etrascu indicated the heaped bones. 'These people thought they had been brought here to go through. But they were used. *Used.* The Path was to be made for a *select* company. The Imperator Elect and a few thousand of his people. That is my guess. And these, these countless thousands, were used. The blood in their veins. Like a river. Pouring out into – ' But he stopped.

'Into what?' hissed Vorenzar. 'The gate?'

Etrascu shook his head. 'I cannot read the stones. Nor can I hear the voices of the dead, though it is as if they shout at me. It is all pain.'

Vorenzar looked angrily at Ipsellin.

'Something of them clings to this place,' nodded the latter. 'But I read no message for us. Only their suffering.'

Vorenzar grunted. Superstition, typical of the Openers and beneath a Csendook.

'I tried to look beyond,' said Etrascu, shrivelling from the vision of memory. 'But there is only a void there, a terrible void, worse than any vault between worlds of the great Cycle.'

'Is that where they went?' said Vorenzar. 'Into oblivion?'

Etrascu nodded. 'I am sure of it.'

'What did you use?' said Vorenzar ruthlessly.

Etrascu gazed at him blankly.

Vorenzar gripped his arm and shook him as he would have shaken a child. 'Well? You attempted an Opening. What did you use?'

Etrascu looked imploringly at Cmizen, who closed his eyes but nodded. 'Answer the Zaru.'

'Life,' gasped Etrascu.

'What life? Men? Men were hiding here? Men who escaped this carnage?'

But it was Ipsellin who provided the answer. 'Zaru, there are Csendook bones among the skeletons.'

Vorenzar released Etrascu and hovered over his own Opener like a storm about to break. '*Csendook* bones?'

'A score of Zemoks,' said Etrascu behind him.

Vorenzar whirled on him. 'You used Zemoks to make a gate?'

Etrascu fell to his knees, his hands on the stone before Vorenzar. 'Zaru, it was the only way to search. To be sure that Man had failed.'

Cmizen stood behind him, his face wearing the wretched look of one condemned. 'I gave the instruction. And it was given to me from the Warhive.'

Vorenzar turned slowly to face Cmizen. 'The Warhive? By whom? The Garazenda?'

Cmizen nodded. 'Yes. From Marozul Zuldamar himself.'

Vorenzar's eyes narrowed. '*He* gave the order to use Zemoks for this attempt on an Opening to – '

'A search, Zaru. The Garazenda had to know the truth.

39

And when we learned that Zellorian's attempt to flee had ended in disaster, I was ordered to seal this place, to sow the myths of Eannor –'

'By Zuldamar?'

'Yes, Zaru. The Marozul. And now that you have seen this place –'

'You cannot mean to attempt another Opening,' gasped Etrascu, still on his knees. 'That darkness has a thirst you cannot imagine. You could pour the blood of a dozen worlds into it and not assuage it. Zaru, we are not meant to step beyond the great Cycle.'

Vorenzar grunted as if agreeing with him. He looked about him, his anger, if such it was, cooling, his thoughts hidden. So Zuldamar had given orders for Csendook to be sacrificed in an attempt to try and find Zellorian and the Imperator Elect! And having failed, had covered up the atrocity. Is this where the seeds of the new peace had been sewn? Auganzar would treasure this news. If the entire Garazenda did not know of this, would there not be outrage if they were told?

'Very well,' said Vorenzar at last. 'You have done what was asked of you, Zolutar. A Csendook must give his life when the occasion demands. We do not question the Marozul.'

'No, Zaru.'

'Go back to the fortress. Say nothing of our visit to this place.'

Etrascu struggled to his feet. He had left a pool of blood where his hands had touched the flagstones. He looked down at it in horror, as though by putting it there he had committed a blasphemy. He turned quickly away.

'Ipsellin and I will spend some time here,' said Vorenzar. 'There is no need for you to distress yourself any longer, Zolutar. The past must hold many unpleasantnesses for you. But the Garazenda rule us, and justly.'

Cmizen's relief was visible.

'Take Etrascu with you. And leave the gate. Ipsellin will seal it behind us. When we have finished, matters will be ended in this valley.'

Cmizen nodded, mounting his xillatraal, Etrascu beside him. They said nothing more, going across the plaza and into the shadow of the wall. Vorenzar waited until they had gone before he turned, laughing, to his Opener.

'Fools!' he growled. 'They swallowed my fury at the death of a few Zemoks.'

'Etrascu is a coward. It embarrasses me, as an Opener, to say so. He does not speak well for my breed. But it was that cowardice that hid from him the fact that you cared nothing for the Zemoks who were sacrificed. He and Cmizen will assume, quite wrongly, that you would fiercely protect the life of every one of your Zemoks. They may even assume you would be as protective with the *moillum*.'

Vorenzar nodded, though his smile had faded. He did not like using Zemoks, good warriors, as fodder, whatever the cause. 'The Supreme Sanguinary is correct in his belief that there is no more powerful a weapon than fear.'

Ipsellin bowed gently.

'It is good,' Vorenzar went on, 'that you, Ipsellin, have a stiffer spine. And that you do not shrink from the things that I intend to do in this place.'

Ipsellin controlled his fear, for when he contemplated attempting to make an Opening here, in this realm of nightmare, his flesh crawled with it. But before he could frame a suitable reply, he found himself gazing down at the blood on the stones, the blood of Etrascu. To his amazement he saw that it was fanning out as if the wind was playing upon it, creating a pattern.

'What is wrong?' said Vorenzar, for he could see that something had disturbed the Opener.

Ipsellin gasped, taken aback. The blood had shaped itself into more than a pattern. 'It is a form of, of writing.'

Vorenzar snorted, looking down at the blood. 'Your imagination has the better of you. In this place – ' But his words trailed off in shock. The blood was unquestionably shaping itself into script, though it was alien to the Csendook.

'I cannot read it,' said Ipsellin. 'But it is *Man's* language – '

41

'A trick!' snarled Vorenzar, wielding his blade as though antagonists would appear at any moment. Etrascu and Cmizen had gone: there was no sign of them. The plaza was utterly silent.

Ipsellin jerked back as something else happened to the blood. It had pooled again, and from its centre there now issued a thread of steam, as if it had again become hot. Ipsellin pulled Vorenzar back and they stood among the bones, watching the steam turning to a thick mist, forming into a tall, white column. It spun like a vortex and for a moment Vorenzar contemplated striking at it with his blade, but checked himself. The mist began to spread, but its core coalesced into a dark form. Gradually the mist seeped away into the stone, like skin shed by a serpent, leaving behind it a figure, though it was insubstantial and incomplete. It was neither Man nor Csendook, slightly taller than the Opener, but nothing like as obese, being instead angular and thin, almost emaciated. From the blur of face, eyes watched as though from beneath a pool.

Vorenzar felt, to his surprise, no fear at being confronted by this being, although Ipsellin drew back, frightened by it and the powers that its presence suggested.

The figure spoke, its voice thick and distorted, though nothing it said was intelligible to Vorenzar. Ipsellin frowned, hearing an echo of the words in his mind, where they gathered an intelligence to them.

'Do you understand it?' Vorenzar asked him.

'It claims to be a *guide*,' said Ipsellin, his face drawn.

'To where?'

Ipsellin shook his head. 'To beyond. Etrascu's blood called it. The blood is the key and the price.'

'But what manner of being is it?'

'It seems to be formed from the very elements, as though the air has been given form,' said Ipsellin, amazed by the creature. Vorenzar would have ridiculed him for such remarks, but his own fascination gripped his interest.

'I am the servant of Innasmorn,' the creature told Ipsellin in its contorted voice. 'Should you desire to go there, I will guide you.'

42

'What is the toll?' said Ipsellin.

The creature understood him. 'What price will you pay?'

Ipsellin let his thoughts answer for him, a pact in blood that Vorenzar did not hear but would sanction.

The figure's dull, empty eyes seemed to swing towards the Csendook, free of judgements, of emotions. It nodded.

'It speaks to you?' said Vorenzar, frustrated by his own inability to understand it.

'It claims to be from a place called Innasmorn. If it is a world, Zaru, it is one I have never heard of before.'

'Nor I,' said Vorenzar. 'Ask this messenger if others have gone before us.'

In answer, the figure's arms spread out, thin as a sapling's boughs, and indicated the mass of bones littering the plaza. 'All these were given that others might pass to Innasmorn.'

Vorenzar felt a stab of pleasure as Ipsellin interpreted this for him. 'But *where*, Ipsellin? Where is this place it speaks of?'

Ipsellin shrugged, his fears beginning to lessen. 'This thing is yet prepared to guide us.'

'Could it be a trap? Set by Zellorian?'

Ipsellin spoke again to the figure, but it would divulge no more than it already had. 'It is merely waiting,' the Opener told Vorenzar.

'For how long?'

Ipsellin spoke to the creature again, listening to its faint whispers. 'It will not wait long. But if we come again, with the sacrifices it demands, I can summon it. It has taught me how to do this. A little blood.'

Vorenzar nodded. 'Then dismiss it.'

Ipsellin did so, and within moments the figure had dissolved, again as if formed of the air, slipping away to the secret realm from which it had come.

Vorenzar studied the place where it had been for a long time. There was no longer a trace of blood there. He turned to Ipsellin. 'If Etrascu's blood summoned this thing, why did he not speak of it before?'

'It never came to him.'

43

'It told you this?'

'In its way.'

'Then why did it not answer his own attempts to open a Path? This was his blood today.'

Ipsellin shrugged. 'That puzzles me, Zaru. But it has clearly chosen to offer us guidance. The price will be high. The *moillum* – '

'I don't care about the toll. You must get word swiftly to the Warhive, to the Supreme Sanguinary. I need as many as he can spare.'

'And . . . the Zemoks?'

Vorenzar looked back at the wall, the forest beyond it. 'If I have to spill Csendook blood to open this Path, then I will do so. What lies beyond us is too valuable to lose.'

Ipsellin nodded.

Together they remounted their beasts, and in both their minds a single word repeated itself, like the calling of a distant bell. *Innasmorn*.

4

GUIDE

Cmizen struggled with another bad dream, twisting and turning in his bed, his head rolling. It was no use trying to sleep: his eyes opened. There was torchlight about him, for he no longer trusted darkness and could not sleep without lights. Eannor did that, populated as it was by phantoms from another age.

Something moved at the edge of Cmizen's bed. A length of steel gleamed, a sword resting on his abdomen. A face loomed above it, lips drawn back over white teeth. Vorenzar.

'Zaru!' gasped Cmizen, trying to move, but he found his muscles would not respond. Again fear controlled him.

'One simple question,' said the new Keeper.

It was deep into the night. When Cmizen had gone to bed, neither Vorenzar nor the loathsome Ipsellin had returned from the valley of sacrifice. Cmizen had half hoped that they had succumbed to that dreadful place.

'Of course, Zaru. If you'll allow me to sit up.'

But the sword point moved upwards, resting on his chest. 'What is Innasmorn?'

Cmizen frowned. The question made no sense to him. 'But I have never heard of it, Zaru.'

'Don't lie to me,' said Vorenzar gently.

'No, Zaru. I have no reason to lie. But I have never heard of Innasmorn.'

Vorenzar scowled. He and Ipsellin had already questioned Etrascu, but Ipsellin had been forced to conclude that Cmizen's Opener had never heard of Innasmorn.

'Where did you hear the name, Zaru?' asked Cmizen, limbs trembling.

'No matter,' said Vorenzar, withdrawing the sword. He stood up abruptly, partly concealed by shadows. 'I am sending for more *moillum*, and there will be additional Zemoks with them. They will be here very soon. Ipsellin will go to prepare a Path for them.'

'Very well, Zaru,' nodded Cmizen, finally wriggling to a sitting position. He was utterly baffled by this intrusion. Had Vorenzar found something in the valley? Innasmorn. But the word was in no way familiar to him. 'I will prepare the fortress for their accommodation.'

Vorenzar grunted, turned on his heel, and left as though he had already dismissed Cmizen from his mind.

Cmizen slipped from his bed and dressed himself. He also left his chamber, but did so through another door, going down a spiral stairway that led to a private part of the fortress, one that he had not shown to Vorenzar, though he felt that his Opener could look through walls. Ipsellin possessed a far higher degree of skill than Etrascu.

As Cmizen came down into another chamber, Etrascu was waiting for him, sitting on a narrow stone bench, staring into the blankness of the wall before him. He seemed drained of power, his face haggard, his body slumped.

'They came to you?' said Cmizen, his voice very low, as if every whisper would be transmitted to other ears.

Etrascu nodded. 'They found something in the valley. I don't know what.'

'What is this Innasmorn?'

Etrascu shook his head. 'I cannot fathom it. It has the sound of a place. Perhaps,' he said hoarsely, 'it is where the Men went.'

'But all our attempts to find them failed!' gasped Cmizen. 'Surely they did not survive?'

Again Etrascu shook his head. 'Ipsellin would say nothing. He just gloated in that insufferable way he has. To him I am an infant.'

'Do they believe us?'

'That we know nothing? I think so. Ipsellin knows my mind. I cannot close it all from him. He would have known that Innasmorn meant nothing to me.'

'Then surely we have no reason to fear them.'

Etrascu pulled his robe about him tightly. 'We have every reason to fear them.'

'But we acted on the orders of the Marozul – '

'Yes. And does it not puzzle you, Cmizen, that they used me, a modest second cell Opener, to probe Eannor's secrets? Instead of an Ultimate, one of the most powerful of my kind?'

Cmizen stared at him. 'Well, I suppose – '

'I have given it much thought this night. I draw one conclusion. The Marozul did not want the Way beyond the cycle of worlds found. They did not want to extend the Crusade. Zuldamar wanted us to fail.'

Cmizen's jaw sagged. 'Is Ipsellin an Ultimate?'

'Probably. There is much secrecy among the Openers. But you see the twin circles on his robes. The eyes.'

'Of Auganzar!'

'Who serves the Marozul. Or does he? I wonder.'

Cmizen turned away, and in the dark he imagined he saw the glow of those twin circles, eating into him.

Ipsellin was waiting. He had dressed himself for the journey back to the Warhive. Vorenzar's instructions were still clear in his mind.

Vorenzar closed the door and nodded. 'I've spoken to him. He would have no reason to conceal the truth. Innasmorn means nothing to him.'

'Then the guide spoke to us and not to them,' said Ipsellin, seeing in his mind the spectral guide in the plaza.

'But why?' snapped Vorenzar. 'Why us?'

'Zaru, I have far more skill than Etrascu. He is as weak among my breed as Cmizen is among yours. Perhaps he was sent here with Cmizen in the hope that he would not find the Path created by Zellorian. If it had been Zuldamar who chose Etrascu, would that not explain much? Those loyal to him wanted Man out of the great Cycle, thus ending the Crusade.'

Vorenzar was nodding as he thought. 'I'm sure you are

right, Ipsellin. But one thing still worries me. It was Etrascu's blood that summoned the guide.'

'There is power in all blood. Etrascu opened a Way. But only to the void. My presence focused the voice of the guide.'

'You are certain that Etrascu has no control over that being? That this is no trap?'

'Quite certain, Zaru. I am an Ultimate. There is no higher order among my breed.'

Vorenzar smiled coldly. 'I imagined you must be. My master selects his servants with extreme care.'

'Nothing Etrascu could have done here would escape me, Zaru. He has no power that I cannot break.'

'Very well. Do as I bid you earlier. Fetch the next wave. And see that our master is informed.' He tapped the twin rings on Ipsellin's chest.

It was only a matter of days before the second wave from the Warhive arrived on Eannor. Two thousand *moillum*, marshalled by a hundred Csendook. Vorenzar marvelled that he did not have a rebellion on his hands, for his own Zemoks were well outnumbered by the Men. Yet already these gladiators had been won over to the new Csendook ideals. Besides, they knew that if they killed their masters on Eannor and fled to the sanctuary of the world, it would only be a matter of time before a Csendook force came for them and destroyed them to a Man. Their compliance to Csendook rule was not won easily, and they complained, sometimes revealing an inner bitterness, but for the most part they got on with their tasks, their training. The rewards promised them were rich, and for all of them a future beckoned that would be infinitely more enjoyable than the future they would have had, holed up on some remote world, harassed by Csendook Swarms, their numbers dwindling, death a breath away.

Vorenzar summoned his Zolutars to him and informed them that they must prepare for yet another journey, one that would be far more hazardous than the simple crossing to Eannor. He did not tell them where they were going, only that it would be to another realm, a possible war zone, which like Eannor, was on the outer rim of the world cycle. The Zolutars grinned at the thought of real conflict. Auganzar had vetted them personally, and all wore the twin circles of the Supreme Sanguinary with pride. There was no higher honour than to be a member of Auganzar's Thousand.

On the eve of the intended search for Innasmorn, Vorenzar called his Zolutars to his war chamber. There were ten of them, each in command of twenty Zemoks, and over two hundred *moillum*. Already they had begun calling themselves Vorenzar's Swarm, though in numbers they were nowhere near as vast as a Csendook Swarm. They boasted that their particular skills and strengths would make up for any differences. Vorenzar allowed them their boasts, delighted that morale was so high.

'Remember that you are here on Eannor at the express command of the Supreme Sanguinary,' he told them. 'Make no mistake about that. I have his seal.' They knew this, as they knew that very few Zaru had their master's seal. In many ways, Vorenzar was Auganzar's deputy, or so it was said. 'And you are not here merely to train *moillum*. At dawn, you'll find that out. But as far as your *moillum* are concerned, this is just another training exercise. Neither my Opener nor I know what lies beyond Eannor, and there may be strong opposition to us. Above all, we have to be careful that the *moillum* do not rebel. Yes, I know they have shown great willingness to conform, but if we run into a rebel army of any strength, they may yet defect and leave us in difficulty.' It was enough to persuade the Zolutars that Vorenzar had every intention of taking the entire battalion through to this other place.

Ipsellin, sitting as ever at the edge of the meeting, watched and listened with his strange powers for any suggestions of doubt or suspicion. Should any of the warriors have thought that sacrifices would be made, their mood might change, but Ipsellin read no such suspicions in this gathering, although he sensed that far below them,

49

in the fortress, the *moillum* were uneasy. He also sensed that Cmizen and Etrascu, who had not been admitted to the meeting, were quiescent, hiding their own terrors, which would be gathering like clouds about them.

Vorenzar went over a number of battle plans with his Zolutars, most of which he had concocted for the sake of veracity, and the enthusiasm with which his warriors greeted them and discussed them for a moment filled him with regret. He cared little for Zemoks who had to die for the cause of war, but he had no way of knowing how many of these Zolutars would die in the crossing, no way of knowing how thirsty this creature that would guide them would be.

Cmizen had no god. Like any other Csendook, his only deities were war, the perfection of self as warrior, the glory of the nation. But as he rode through the forest, he found himself praying to some great outer darkness, where maybe his voice would be heard by unknown powers, powers that knew pity. Beside him, riding in total silence, closed in on himself as if he, too, were praying to whatever dark powers governed his own inner universe, sat Etrascu, his fat body diminished, his blood running cold, sluggish. He knew what Vorenzar intended. The Zaru had found something in the valley of sacrifice that he had not. And he intended Ipsellin to effect an Opening. He knew, too, that his own blood would be used, possibly his life. But he could do nothing to prevent it. He must prepare himself mentally. He must perform as an Opener should, and put aside base fear, wear an impassive face. The dark closed around him.

Ipsellin rode directly behind Cmizen, their party following the leading group of Vorenzar and his principal Zolutars. Ipsellin could feel Cmizen's terror: he had been instructed to keep it in check, to kill the former Keeper if he lost his nerve and tried to flee from the coming rituals. Ipsellin looked at Cmizen coldly. The Csendook was unworthy of the name. Only his sacrifice would absolve him from his cowardice. Etrascu was little better, though

50

circumstances had made his promotion difficult. Elsewhere he might have advanced his power, but Eannor had made a weakling of him. He had settled for a life of ease and self-indulgence. No, I shall feel no remorse when these two give blood to the making of a Way.

In the lower depths of the forest, the company came to the black wall and as before, Etrascu was summoned by Vorenzar to make a way through it. He did so in silence, head bowed, careful to cover his hands, to seal any wounds he inflicted on himself.

Beyond the wall the entire company gathered in the plaza among the bones, the heaped skulls. The atmosphere was no better, but the presence of so many living beings dampened it down, and Vorenzar felt nothing of the apprehension he had felt on his previous visit. He had the huge stone dais cleared of debris, skulls rattling and scattering like broken balls as his Zemoks removed them. The irreverence of the act added to the confidence of the company. The terror of Cmizen was not infectious. There were even a few laughs and shouts of amusement from the gathered *moillum*.

Vorenzar nodded to Ipsellin. 'Summon the guide.'

Behind him his Zolutars stiffened, and the ranks of the Zemoks and the *moillum* quietened. This was, to them, a routine crossing, but at such times they always fell quiet until the first few steps along the opened Path were taken.

Ipsellin beckoned to Etrascu. 'Step forward.'

Etrascu had known it would be him, his blood that would be used. It was unfair, unreasonable! Why should Ipsellin, by far the more potent of them, not be the one to give blood? But Etrascu had known. Woodenly he stepped up to the foot of the dais, unable to resist, knowing that if he did he would quickly be butchered, like an ox used to open a minor Way. This way he could at least cling to his dignity, his hope for life.

Ipsellin's face was close to his as he took from his robe a slender tool, sharp and fine-pointed. 'I am not about to take your life, Etrascu,' said the Ultimate in a language

51

that only the Openers understood, conscious that every eye in the plaza was upon them.

There were tears in Etrascu's eyes, his hands were shaking. He could not speak for fear.

'There is work for you here after we have gone.'

It was like a douche of cold water. Etrascu's eyes widened, his heart thudding. He was to live?

'When we are through the gate, you must get word to the Warhive. To the Garazenda. I will give you the message, but be most careful. The words are of absolute importance and must be learned by heart. Not one of them must be changed, or said out of place.'

'I understand,' said Etrascu, nodding so that the fresh tears ran. Allowed to live! Safe?

Ipsellin gave him the message then, repeating it and having Etrascu say it several times so that he was satisfied he had learned it. For an Opener it would be easy to recall it verbatim.

Satisfied, Ipsellin rolled back Etrascu's sleeves and began to work on his bare arms with his tool. No one in the company saw what happened, but they knew there would be a letting of blood. Sometimes, with common Paths, the blood of animals was enough, but usually the Openers, bred for such work, used their own blood. No one understood why it should be necessary for blood to open a Way, but it was a fundamental law of the world cycle, the common link of life between worlds.

Ipsellin allowed some of Estrascu's blood to fall on the stone of the dais. Neither of them spoke, and Etrascu rolled his sleeves back, standing down, eyes fixed on the dark stain. This would never be enough to open a gate from here, not if Ipsellin sought the elusive place to which Man had aspired. Did he seek some other realm, some world that would be a simple link in the world cycle? If so, then Etrascu's blood would be ample for such a purpose.

Ipsellin watched the coagulating blood, wondering if there were words he should speak, but as he watched, the strange writing formed as it had before. He glanced down from the steps at Vorenzar, who could tell by his expression that something was happening. Before long the mist began to curl upward and Etrascu gasped, understanding. Something had been summoned by his blood, a force within the mist. Fascinated, he watched as the mist figure took shape, a short, thin being, with eyes like milk. The company strained for a view of it, Vorenzar's Zolutars nodding to each other in understanding of the potency of Ipsellin's summoning.

Cmizen, who had himself expected to be taken to the block, dropped to his knees, but he was ignored. The mist figure spoke to Ipsellin, though no one else understood it.

Ipsellin suddenly called out to the gathering. 'A Way is prepared for us! Ready yourselves! The passage beyond will not be an easy one.'

One of Vorenzar's Zolutars, Durrazol, touched him lightly on the arm. 'Your pardon, Zaru, but what is this place we seek?'

'A war zone. Where glory waits,' was all Vorenzar would say.

The figure in the mist raised it skeletal arms and beyond it, over the dais, a rushing of air filled the plaza, as though a storm had been abruptly snatched from across the world and focused here. Winds howled from nothing, swirling in a vortex that enclosed the entire plaza. The warriors felt themselves cuffed by it. Clouds had scudded in like vast battleships, darkening the sky; behind the roar of the wind there came the rolling conflict of thunder.

Ipsellin gazed back beyond the dais. A huge column of darkness rose there, like a cleft in a cliff wall. It was impossible to see through it to the plaza beyond, as though an opening had been made in the very fabric of Eannor, an opening that allowed only the void to show through. Ipsellin heard the voice of the guide, urging him to begin the march into the gateway. It would only be held open for a short time.

The figure swayed forward, drifting like silk towards the high portal. It hovered at the entrance, waiting. Ipsellin turned to Vorenzar, who looked at him avidly. He nodded, for he could not make himself heard above the roar of the wind, which threatened to gather itself into a hurricane. Vorenzar waved his Zolutars forward, and as one, the entire company surged toward the Path, eager to move along it to whatever realm was beyond.

Cmizen felt himself jostled and nudged, pushed aside. He was ignored in the flow. Vorenzar had not seen him, or had no more need of him. He slid away until he saw Etrascu ducking down. Together they watched as the storm burst overhead.

The mist guide had disappeared, swallowed by the gaping dark, and Ipsellin waited at the portal until Vorenzar reached him. He could read a plea for assurance in the Zaru's eyes, and for a moment the Opener thought he detected fear there. But he nodded.

The exodus from Eannor began. Vorenzar and Ipsellin led it, walking into a swirling dark that roared like the storm, as though they had stepped from one storm into another, vaster one, one that threatened to swamp a world. Their steps were groggy, for the ground seemed to waver beneath them, and a dreadful dizziness assailed them. They were forced to lean on each other in order to stumble on, but they did so, trying without success to peer into the darkness ahead of them. There was no light, no hint of a star. Was this, after all, the void they had been warned of? But they could see the ghost guide, drifting on, not looking back at them, never far from view, the only object in all the chaos of night they could fix on.

Behind them their warriors were stepping over the threshold into the Way. They clung to each other, but their fears were lessened by the weight of their numbers. Sight was denied them all, and they moved on by feel, by touch, by blind instinct, shouting encouragement above the din.

Etrascu and Cmizen had stumbled further away from the portal, agog at the extent of that huge rip, that gash of night. They backed from the steps, across the plaza, almost tripping over the bones. They had been spared. But from what? The glory of Vorenzar's crusade beyond Eannor, in whatever realm he would find? Innasmorn. Was Man really there, beyond the world cycle? Impossible.

Cmizen watched as the last of the *moillum* went into the dark, disappearing, a final trio of Zemoks going with them, looking back only once to see that no one else needed help. They ignored Etrascu and Cmizen as they had ignored the bones of the fallen. And they steadied each other, Zemok and *moillum*.

The Way closed, its sides knitting so quickly that it was done in the blink of an eye. And as the darkness winked out, the storm shut off at once. Etrascu's ears rang to the echoes. He slumped down. But he looked at Cmizen, smiling thinly. Alive! The silence of the plaza rushed in on them, but if it brought its ghosts with it, they were unaware of them. They got to their feet together and laughed, fighting back hysteria. They were safe.

'Are they through?' said Cmizen.

'Who knows?' said Etrascu. 'That is not the message I must take to the Warhive. Ipsellin told me to report that they were lost.' Turning, he looked for his xillatraal, which was chewing indifferently at a crop of weed.

Cmizen stared at the place where the Way had been, puzzled by the Opener's words. Lost? Well, let them be. He would go with Etrascu to the Warhive. After that he would be free. Free of Eannor, free to go somewhere that did not echo to the slaughter of years gone by, of the beckoning ghost of the Imperator Elect.

Zuldamar and his fellow Marozul waited in silence at the great table in their hall. Light streamed down on them from above, but there was an air of unease in the huge hall. There were no Zolutars here, no other warriors, and even the guards had been dismissed. Only one other Csendook had been asked to attend the special meeting, and he sat, alone, beyond the great table where so many decisions had been made in the history of the Warhive. Auganzar's face was, as always on these occasions, inscrutable. He looked directly ahead of him, no hint of what was going through his mind on his broad features.

Finally the Opener was admitted. He waddled forward to the great table and bowed.

Zuldamar leaned forward, his face creased in annoyance. 'We understand that you have an important message for us.' It was already known that this Opener, Etrascu, had rushed to the Warhive from Eannor, where some great disaster had overtaken the new Keeper.

'Great lords, I have,' said Etrascu breathlessly. He prayed that the act he had been asked to put on would fool the Marozul as it was intended to. There were mercifully no other Openers present, but Ipsellin had promised that none would be. The Garazenda had no reason to expect lies from an Opener, particularly Zuldamar, to whom Etrascu had always been loyal.

'The new Keeper,' said Etrascu, glancing once at the Supreme Sanguinary, though Auganzar did not so much as blink. He might have been a statue.

'Vorenzar,' said Xeltagar, the old veteran. 'Fine Csendook. What has happened?'

'He began the training of the *moillum* on Eannor – '

'We know that,' said Horzumar impatiently. 'We recently granted permission to the Supreme Sanguinary to deploy a further two thousand of them to Eannor. Did they not arrive safely?'

'They did, sire.' Etrascu went on to speak of how training for them had begun at once, how Vorenzar was tireless in his efforts to ensure that they worked to perfect their skills. The Opener used the words Ipsellin had given him, guessing that they were the keys to a code that someone in this hall would understand. That could only be the Supreme Sanguinary. Vorenzar was undisputably his servant.

'This hardly seems good reason to call a meeting of the Marozul,' said Juntagar, another of the more senior members. 'We have sanctioned the use of Eannor for such work. It fits in admirably with our intention to subjugate the remnants of Mankind. Is there a problem on Eannor?'

Etrascu nodded. 'Forgive me, sirs. A disaster.'

Zuldamar again leaned forward. 'What disaster?'

'Vorenzar himself led an exercise that brought him

dangerously close to the area that we call the zone of sacrifice, the place where the Imperator Elect and his legions sought to escape our closing forces.'

'Where their experiments blew up in their faces?' said Juntagar.

'Yes, sire. It is a strange land. I myself warned the noble Vorenzar about its dangers, its strange discharges of power. But the Zaru was curious to know more about the region. He took a large force there, to investigate it.'

Zuldamar looked across at the Supreme Sanguinary. 'That was not a part of his brief.'

Etrascu answered. 'Sire, he scorned any suggestion that the region was haunted, a place of evil and sorcery.'

'As any Csendook would,' growled Xeltagar.

'Vorenzar and his host were caught up in a storm,' Etrascu went on. 'It was no ordinary storm. It annihilated them.'

The Marozul all murmured at this, exchanging glances of shock and surprise. At last there was a reaction from Auganzar. He stood up, his eyes narrowing, his massive fists clenched. He stepped forward, looming over the Opener like the threat of execution.

'They are dead?' he said bitterly. '*All* of them?'

'Yes, sire,' said Etrascu, cowering. 'Even Ipsellin, most worthy of my breed.'

'You are telling us,' said Auganzar, as though not believing the testimony of the Opener, 'that Vorenzar, his Opener, all his prime Zemoks and *moillum* are no more? Destroyed?'

'Annihilated,' said Etrascu. It was the word he had been told he must use.

'What do you mean by this?' called Xeltagar, evidently furious.

'Sire, there was chaos. Indescribable chaos,' babbled Etrascu, and he did begin to describe the storm he had in truth witnessed. But he embellished his tale with descriptions of Csendook being stripped by the winds, of blood, of bones tossed before the storm. Of fresh skulls. Annihilation.

A long silence followed his report, broken only by the

57

low whisper of Auganzar, who seemed to speak the word 'annihilation'. He swung on his heel and faced the Marozul.

'My lords, I am concerned that it was myself who suggested we use Eannor as a training ground, a breeding pen for our *moillum*. Just as I chose Vorenzar to take over the wardenship. His foolish interference with this forbidden zone dishonours me.'

'Perhaps we should reconsider the use of Eannor,' said Juntagar.

'Firstly, lords,' Auganzar went on, 'I crave your permission to go to Eannor myself to see the extent of the damage.'

'It may not be necessary to remove the new schools we have set up,' said Zuldamar, his eyes locking with those of the Supreme Sanguinary. 'If this was mere carelessness on behalf of Vorenzar, perhaps it will teach our people to be more cautious in their studies of Eannor.'

'Yes,' said Horzumar. 'I think Auganzar should investigate this matter. And perhaps we should make Cmizen, the former Keeper, a temporary warden, until a suitable replacement can be found.'

'I agree,' said Juntagar, and many others called their own agreement.

'I will select some of my own warriors to accompany me,' said Auganzar. 'As a mark of respect for Vorenzar.'

To his surprise, Zuldamar gave immediate support to this. 'But as Marozul,' Zuldamar added, 'I think we should impose certain rules. You, Supreme Sanguinary, must ensure that this place of evil, as it has been described, is properly sealed off. I suggest the death penalty for anyone found near it.'

The Marozul agreed at once.

'And I think we owe it to ourselves as the Garazenda,' Zuldamar went further, 'to send Zemoks of our own to swell the ranks of the Supreme Sanguinary's forces – '

'But lords, I need only a small force – '

'You are too modest, Supreme Sanguinary,' said Horzumar. 'And you have lost some of your worthiest troops in this disaster. No, I think we should all shoulder our responsibilities where Eannor is concerned. Zemoks from us all. And to quell any fears those left on Eannor might have, *moillum* for the schools.'

'An excellent idea,' said Xeltagar.

Auganzar hid his fury, bowing. 'But of course, Marozul.'

Zuldamar pointed to Etrascu. 'You, Opener. While the future of Eannor is resolved, you remain as Opener to it. You are assigned to the temporary Keeper, as before. Meanwhile you will take your commands from the Supreme Sanguinary.'

Auganzar winced, again bowing.

'And,' Horzumar added with a brief smile, 'you will bring full reports directly to the Marozul.'

Once more, his colleagues nodded agreement.

Etrascu bowed in thanks, but his heart felt cold. Free? No, this was hardly over. It was never over. And he was tied to Eannor as surely as if by blood. Only one of the company felt more cheated than he. But the Supreme Sanguinary had again become as stone.

In his chamber, Auganzar sat back and enjoyed the rarity of a good wine. It was always available to him, but he rarely permitted himself its luxury. Today, however, he felt he had at last made real progress in the true quest. Never mind the minor setbacks of Zuldamar's statesmanship. A small price to pay.

Annihilation.

Not death, destruction, slaughter, or any one of a hundred words that Etrascu could have used. Annihilation. The code. Vorenzar had found the Path! And Ipsellin had opened it. They had gone through.

And the Supreme Sanguinary had a name. One word, given to him by Etrascu before he had quitted the attention of his superiors, a word that no one else had heard.

Innasmorn.

Auganzar said it to himself softly. Like a mistress, it lured him, and that night, when he slept, it filled his dreams with a fresh and delicious temptation.

5

THE NARROW WAY

Vorenzar saw the darkness beyond him beginning to glow, as though a sun had risen above an unseen horizon. At first it was as if his company travelled along an endless, flat plain, but as the light spread, so the edges of the plain appeared to curl upwards, forming themselves into an illusion of curves, a tunnel of immense proportions. Between worlds, Vorenzar thought. Ahead of him the ghost guide drifted on without looking back. The tunnel shrank quickly, painted in by the light, narrowing until it had become no more than a hundred feet across. Its walls were of no substance Vorenzar could recognise, being neither stone, metal, nor flesh, though they had a translucent quality that somehow suggested life. Beyond them was the darkness of a void that threatened those who studied it with a dreadful kind of fear. Vorenzar found himself concentrating hard on the being ahead of him.

Ipsellin's face was a study of anxiety, his eyes roving from side to side as though he almost expected the sides of the tunnel to bulge inward and split under the weight of an ocean. The Csendook and *moillum* who followed them talked softly: although they had all crossed between worlds many times they felt the strangeness of this Path, its uniqueness. It studied them like a live thing, and seemingly with a mounting interest. The xillatraal were restless, and all of them had to be led and not ridden, their noses high in the air as they tried to scent the heavy air.

The ghost guide abruptly stopped. It appeared to have reached a breach in the walls of the Path, and on closer inspection, Vorenzar saw that it was a branch, another Path that led down into an infinite distance. There were more such Paths, so that the way ahead became something like a complex system of roots, branches within branches.

'You have chosen Innasmorn,' the ghost guide told Ipsellin with seeming indifference.

The Opener nodded, though a coldness grew in him.

'There will be a toll. Be ready.'

The ghost guide said nothing more, drifting downward and entering the mouth of one of the many branches. Ipsellin followed, waiting. From the depths of the Way, he heard the wind rising, coming up to meet them like the first wave of an unleashed tide. The coldness within him turned icy. He pulled back the sleeves of his robes, his arms white and bloated in the light.

Vorenzar motioned for him to do what was needed, and moments later there was a gleam of blood. It dripped gently on to the soft floor of the Way.

The wind came racing up the tunnel, a living thing, and before Ipsellin could brace himself, it tore into him, bowling him over, slamming him into the side of the tunnel. It felt like pulpy flesh and he could hear a roar of sound, like blood gushing through the arteries of a giant. Vorenzar was knocked off his balance and behind him a united howl went up as the full force of the gale reached the Zemoks and the xillatraal. As the wind whirled about them, the peace of the tunnel was shattered by the din, a wailing that tore at the ears, gathering in pitch.

Vorenzar tried to stand, but it was as though he had been tossed into a hurricane. The very sides of the tunnel stretched, pulled awry by the sheer force of the wind.

'Innasmorn comes for you,' said the ghost guide, and for once its voice reached the ears of every one of the company, cutting into the yell of the wind.

Ipsellin tried to balance himself, but was pinned by the force of the gale. He watched in horror as his arms bled, and he felt the sudden clutch at his chest, as though an invisible giant had closed a hand about him. It squeezed, and he felt his organs throb with protest.

Vorenzar, on his knees, looked back. His company had entered chaos incarnate. But he had known there would be a price.

The air seemed to be full of writhing shapes, not properly

61

visible, an illusion, but they moved at incredible speeds, so fast they defied the eye. The tunnel itself was rotating, as though they were in the heart of a vortex, a whirlpool of air. The sides of the tunnel lost perspective, the tunnel churning, the sound adding to the confusion. Warriors were flung upwards, sideways, picked up like rags and scattered. Some smashed into the walls, sank into them, were absorbed, digested. Others bounced into each other with sickening force, breaking limbs, crushing ribs. Not one warrior stood; all were mercilessly punched to their backs by the weight of the storm. The xillatraal were likewise powerless to resist such force, flung over, their shrill squeals adding to the din.

Vorenzar tried to see the ghost guide, but the power in the air forced him to squint, wind bringing water to his eyes. But he saw Ipsellin lift up, rotating like a doll. The Opener was screaming, his eyes bulging from the moon-like face. Blood gushed from his arms, his entire robe saturated. As he spun faster, he blurred, then burst. Vorenzar was flung backwards by the force, almost knocked senseless as he again hit the wall. He felt the stickiness of blood on him, wiping at it as he tried to understand what had happened. Surely he had imagined this! And yet there was nothing left of the Opener. The tunnel was pure crimson, the walls dripping, closing in like a mouth.

Behind Vorenzar, the horror began. Whatever the toll for this transition, it was now being extracted. The wind drowned out the shrieks of the Zemoks and *moillum* as the power of the tunnel struck into them, the flashing shapes reaping a terrible harvest of flesh and blood.

Vorenzar curled himself into a ball, unable to watch this massacre, unable to defend himself. A trap! He had no power against this. All his strength, his magnificent Csendook training, could do nothing for him now, not in the face of this impossible storm. He closed his eyes, as though in a dream. But he could not close out the screams, the horrible blasts of the wind.

The tunnel opened and closed like the gills of a fish. The wind lifted its chosen corpses, flinging them this way and that as a river in flood plays with dead wood. Blood ran deeply, glossing the livid walls of the Way until they were pure crimson. The ghost guide waited, motionless, the only point of calm, its features blank. It might have been in another place, remote from this, unaffected by it.

Vorenzar forced terror away from him. He got to his knees, appalled by what he now saw, by what he had brought his warriors into. Had any of them survived? Around them the tunnel pulsed, its walls the ruby lips of a mouth. But the wind began to drop, the spinning slowing. Vorenzar saw the ghost guide and dragged himself to his feet. The wind did not attempt to prevent him this time. He staggered over to the ghost guide, pulling out his sword.

'You led us into this slaughter!' he roared, the blade whistling as it came down. But it passed through the ghost guide as if it were made of air. There was no response. Again Vorenzar struck, but his efforts were wasted.

The ghost guide began to drift down the Way, and as it went, the winds pulled themselves into one last swirling blast and followed, racing on before the figure as quickly as they had come.

'The Path to Innasmorn is open for you.'

Vorenzar choked back a howl of rage, turning. The tunnel was still, but it was a tangle of corpses. Their mutilation was vile to look upon, and to Vorenzar's further horror, he saw movement. Zemoks were crawling from that dripping fusion. A few of them dropped down before him, and with them were *moillum*, though none of the latter looked as though they would live much longer. In disgust, Vorenzar saw the trail of blood that ran like a cord away down into the sloping Path, as if drawn to the ghost guide. The toll. He had agreed it, but could never have expected this.

Gripping his sword in both hands, he began the march downward, into the smaller tunnel. The only sound now was the groan of those behind him, the squeal of a xillatraal. A handful of his Zemoks, smeared in the blood of their dead fellows, lurched after him, together with the beasts which had survived. By the time they had gone any distance down the way, the last of the *moillum* were dead.

The light dimmed, the walls shrank, and ahead of them there was only a blur of movement, a hint of life. But Vorenzar focused all his attention on it, using it to goad him on, to keep moving. He had no strength left to encourage his Zemoks. If they were to survive, they must rely on their own efforts.

The dark closed in. There was no way back.

He did not remember anything of the rest of the crossing. He had walked into a kind of dream, a daze, almost an unconsciousness. If his Zemoks and a few xillatraal were following, he did not know it. Everything closed inward, and his senses became utterly numbed, the pain and horror of what had been were shut out.

The voice woke him.

Looking up, he saw the war helm of a Zemok. Beyond it was a deep blue sky where curved clouds moved sluggishly by. Vorenzar lifted his head, blinking in the light. Sensation returned quickly. He was stretched out on a bed of short, stubby grass. Beyond his immediate surroundings he saw the hills, low and clustered with trees. This could not be Eannor?

The Zemok bent down. 'You are well, Zaru?'

Vorenzar nodded slowly. 'How many came through?'

'With you, Zaru, eight of us. And a dozen xillatraal.' The Zemok pointed. Beyond him, sitting on the slopes of the hill, were six other Zemoks. They had found a stream, stripped themselves and washed the filth from them. Water was brought to Vorenzar in a small container. He drank thirstily, wiping at the blood on his face. None of it was his own.

'Where is this place?'

The Zemok laid aside his helm. 'We thought it must be Eannor again. But you have brought us through to another realm, Zaru.' He spoke gruffly, impassively, no trace of resentment in his tone.

64

A shout from below made the Zemok turn. Vorenzar got to his feet, using his sword. One of the other Zemoks had seen movement in trees beyond them. Something drifted out of them, soft as a breeze and almost as insubstantial. Vorenzar growled in his chest like a hound. It was the ghost guide.

'Innasmorn greets you,' whispered the voice. They all heard it. 'The toll is paid.'

Vorenzar's anger gave him the strength to stride forward, a curse on his lips, but the ghost guide abruptly dissipated like river mist. Vorenzar turned to study the skies, the rolling landscape, but could see no further sign of the creature or possible allies. Instead he went to his Zemoks.

'So we are through,' he said at last.

They stood up, saluting him. Their faces gave away nothing of their reaction to the horrors they had survived. They had a mission here, a duty. Nothing else was important to them.

'Eight of us,' said Vorenzar, drawing himself up. 'When you are rested, we'll search these hills. There must be some kind of circle, or ruins. Something to indicate where Zellorian must have arrived.'

'*Zellorian*, Zaru?' said the Zemok who had woken him.

Vorenzar's grim features warped into a smile. 'He's here. Which is why we have come. Auganzar knew it, and charged me with finding him. As I charge you now. If it takes the life of every one of us, we must find him!'

The Zemoks nodded, and Vorenzar saw at once their pleasure.

'We have already searched this hill and those immediate to it, Zaru,' said their leader.

'How long have I been unconscious?' Vorenzar snapped, angry that he had been the last to come to.

'It was early morning when the first of us woke, Zaru. It is now little after midday.'

Vorenzar grunted. 'And what have you found?'

'I regret, nothing, Zaru. No ruins such as we left on Eannor. No sign of a temple, nor of anything that would suggest Man has been here. But such evidence could have been removed.'

Vorenzar nodded, glad that his Zemoks were thinking and acting as warriors should. The crossing had been a nightmare, but there would be no time to dwell on it. This was a war zone, and if they were to survive, they must treat it as such.

'What about food?'

The Zemok grinned, calling down to one of the others. 'Gazem! Our Zaru is hungry. Bring some of that beast you slew.' He turned back to Vorenzar. 'Provisions survived with the xillatraal, which we have tethered in a hollow below us. But there is food on the hoof here.'

Vorenzar smiled for the first time since arriving when he saw the meat. It had been cut from the carcass of a small deer-like creature, and when he sank his teeth into the almost raw flesh, he grunted his pleasure.

After he had scrubbed himself in the stream, he called all the Zemoks to him. 'There are people here somewhere,' he told them. 'In country like this, I would expect to find small communities. Villages, perhaps.'

The leader of the Zemoks, Ondrazem, spoke for them all. 'Other than Men, Zaru?'

Vorenzar shrugged. 'This was not Man's world before Zellorian came here. Nor is it part of the great Cycle.'

'It's true then, Zaru?' said Ondrazem. 'We have entered some other chain of worlds?'

'I am sure of that. Before our Opener died, he spoke to that creature that guided us. It told him that it had already brought the Men of Eannor to this world, which it calls Innasmorn. Those bones you saw on Eannor were the bones of sacrifice.'

'A great sacrifice,' said one of the Zemoks.

Ondrazem turned to him, his face made ugly by his anger. 'Those of us who have survived are honoured. We have been chosen to find our enemies. And are we not proud to bear the eyes before us?' He tapped the twin circles of his tunic, though their pattern had almost been erased by bloodstains.

66

The Zemok stiffened, bowing quickly. 'No Zemok could win greater honour. No price is too great to pay.'

At that, the others agreed at once. What had happened had been necessary. They must close it from their minds. The dead were dead.

Vorenzar straightened, sheathing his sword and pointing southwards. 'Wherever Zellorian went, he will have left a trail. There will be those who saw him, or heard him. There's a river. We'll follow it.'

There was no further discussion and they began the trek at once, going down through the trees beyond the slope, making for the stream that fed into the river. They were all trained woodsmen, specialists in terrain, having been in far more hostile environments than the one in which they now found themselves. Its similarity to Eannor was uncanny, but they accepted that this was another world entirely, and possibly hostile, no matter how tranquil it seemed.

After an hour's ride, one of the advance scouts came back to them. 'A trail, Zaru,' he announced. 'A single being. Injured, for there is blood.'

'Which way?' said Vorenzar.

'Westwards. Leaving the river.'

'We'll follow.'

They fanned out in the forest and moved swiftly to the trail that the Zemok had found. Vorenzar gave the command and the hunt began. Silent as ghosts, the Csendook closed in on their quarry. Within an hour they had found it. But they were cautious. The lone being had been met by others.

From the dense undergrowth of the forest, Vorenzar watched a small clearing where the solitary figure had slumped down. Other figures stood round it, creatures that did not resemble Csendook, who were far smaller, their arms and legs spindly as though they could hardly support them, their faces narrow and pinched. They carried bows, and several of them had arrows trained on the fallen figure.

Vorenzar's eyes narrowed. The wounded being was a

Zemok. Somehow it had also survived the dreadful crossing from Eannor.

'How many are there?' he whispered to Ondrazem.

'The Zemoks report six here, another six in the forest.'

'Those arrows look frail.'

'Shall we slay them, Zaru?'

Vorenzar considered. 'They must be from a village. But I don't want the village alerted to us. If we attack these, some of them may escape.' He was watching the wounded Zemok as he spoke. He was being questioned by his amazed captors, but it was clear they understood none of the Zemok's growls. The Zemok was badly hurt. There was a wide stain across his tunic, his armour hanging off him, and when he tried to rise, his right leg failed him. It did not appear to be broken, but his leggings were sodden with blood.

The archers were alert to his every move, their arrow-heads never wavering from his neck, but the Zemok showed no trace of fear.

'Zaru, if they attempt to kill him – '·

Vorenzar waved Ondrazem to silence. 'Then let them. We'll follow them. No attack.'

Ondrazem did not question this. For all Vorenzar knew, the wounded Zemok could have been Ondrazem's brother, but there were more important things to consider.

'I want to see their village. We may be able to enter it without a skirmish, though it will not be easy to speak to them.'

Ondrazem was watching the wounded Zemok. The forest people seemed to have dismissed the idea of killing him. Instead they had brought ponies, and with difficulty they helped the Zemok mount one, though he was far too large to sit comfortably. He looked about him, and Vorenzar knew he was looking to see if help would come, but without alerting the forest people to the fact that other Csendook might be near.

The small party began to leave the clearing. Vorenzar passed the orders for his Zemok to track.

The Csendook were superb huntsmen, and they revelled

in the easy terrain of Innasmorn's forest lands. All through the afternoon they tracked the party of foresters and the wounded Zemok, who had slumped over the tiny pony, unconscious for most of the journey. By evening the party had reached a huge mound, on top of which was a stockade, its posts close-packed and sharpened against intrusion. The village contained within was small, and Ondrazem's scouts calculated that the village held at most about fifty of the forest people, including their women.

Vorenzar waited until the Zemok had been taken inside and guards had been set on the single gate of the stockade.

'You favour a night attack, Zaru?' said Ondrazem.

Vorenzar shook his head. 'I wish to communicate with these people somehow. There are ways. We will wait until the first light of dawn.'

Ondrazem grinned as he went to give the orders to the Zemoks. Dawn. The hour when an enemy was least prepared for a surprise attack, still sluggish with sleep, his muscles not quite as ready to respond as they would be later in the morning.

'Is it to be a kill?' several of the Zemoks asked, but Ondrazem shook his head. 'We wait. Do nothing until Vorenzar commands it. Spill no blood.' He knew he would not have to repeat this.

Shortly before dawn, after the Zemoks had rested, the company mounted their xillatraal, strapping on their armour, preparing themselves in case they came under fire from the arrows of the foresters. Their armour, their shields, would be enough to protect them, and as they filed out of the forest, it was with typical Csendook confidence. In this place they felt like warriors facing naked children. If Vorenzar called for blood, they would take out every living being in the village effortlessly.

Vorenzar donned his war helm and rode to the gates. Above him the sleepy guards gasped in horror, suddenly leaping up as if they had been scalded. They struck the hanging bells that were placed on either side of the gate, so that the chimes rang back through the village. Moments later a score of heads poked up over the palisade wall. They saw the Csendook apparitions: huge, black-clad shapes on equally huge beasts, like monsters from a bad dream, demons from the far reaches of the night. The warriors were silent, though their very presence was a threat. At once the villagers knew that these were the allies of the being who had been brought in to the village last night, the promise of vengeance for any slight to him.

Vorenzar could sense the terror of the little people up on the palisade, which was as he had intended. He pointed deliberately to the gate and called out for it to be opened. His words were alien to the villagers, but their meaning was clear.

Some minutes elapsed, but the gate did open. Vorenzar rode forward slowly, his Zemoks behind him. He was surprised that there was no resistance at all, but the villagers had decided to take no chances. Did they know of Csendook? But no, how could they? Vorenzar told himself. Unless Man had been here and warned them. Would the villagers warn Man, if they had contact? But he had placed one guard outside, to ensure that no one made off while the Csendook were in the village.

The huts of the village clustered together among the trees, and villagers stood at every door, wide-eyed children, tiny hands grasped in their mothers' hands, their parents hardly less afraid than they were. The warriors all had bows, but none of them were primed. Caution ruled here.

Vorenzar did not dismount. He took his beast to the centre of the little village, where it gulped at the water of a small pool. The wounded Zemok had already been brought out; he sat on a felled log that served as a bench. He looked up at the armoured giant, still exhausted, it seemed, but with relief in his eyes. The villagers were absolutely silent, every one of them watching the armoured Zemoks, stunned by them, their size, their impression of terrible power.

'You survived the crossing,' Vorenzar said to the wounded Zemok.

The latter nodded. 'I am glad to see you alive, Zaru. But are you all that is left?'

'It would seem so,' said Vorenzar.

The warrior shuddered, looking around him at the faces of the villagers. They were like Men, but so much smaller. So frail. 'They don't understand us.'

'No, but they will have to,' Vorenzar told him. 'Who is their spokesman?'

The warrior indicated one of the villagers behind him, motioning him forward. The forester stiffened proudly, bow at his side. In his belt he wore a knife, but it was made, Vorenzar noted with surprise, from wood. Did they have no steel? Their bows were tipped with stone.

'His name is Assantis,' said the wounded Zemok, pausing for breath. 'He seems to be the chief here, Zaru.'

'Have you asked him about Men?' said Vorenzar, leaning forward across the thick neck of his charger.

The Zemok shook his head, mildly surprised. 'Men, Zaru?'

Vorenzar said nothing. He got down slowly from his xillatraal and went to Assantis, removing his war helm as he did so. There was a gasp from the villagers, for Vorenzar's face was even more of a shock to them than the wounded Zemok's. They saw the power in the eyes, the coldness, the glare of a being afraid of nothing. Vorenzar bent down and smoothed a patch of bare earth, patting it flat. He then pointed to Assantis and sketched something in the earth.

Intrigued, Assantis dropped on to his haunches and studied the sketch closely. His eyes, Vorenzar noted, were intelligent, the brain keen. They were not ignorant, these foresters, despite their silence.

Assantis could see that the huge warrior had drawn, crudely, a picture of a forester. Assantis nodded, tapping his chest.

Vorenzar grinned, though to the foresters it was a grimace, a flash of feral teeth. The Csendook then sketched himself next to the forester. He waited for Assantis to respond.

The chief did so, indicating Vorenzar.

Then Vorenzar drew, as accurately as he could, a Man.

71

He drew him with minimal clothing, trying to emphasise the body structure, the size of the chest and head, the variations between Man and Csendook, and Man and forester.

Assantis scowled at this third drawing, looking at it from a number of angles. Eventually he shook his head, baffled.

Vorenzar mentally cursed. Assantis had never seen a Man. 'Is he lying, do you think?' he asked the wounded Zemok, though he did not think so.

The Zemok shrugged. 'Protecting them?'

Vorenzar stood up, towering over Assantis. 'It's possible.'

Assantis turned and spoke to one of his archers and at once the villager slipped away on some private mission. Vorenzar watched with mild interest.

'Someone will know,' he said. 'Zellorian must have arrived near here. And not so long ago. That guide brought him, just as it brought us. Someone here must know something.' He looked down at his wounded warrior. 'Perhaps it will be necessary to threaten these little beings. Break one like a stick.' He walked slowly away from Assantis. The villagers drew back as he approached them, but he stood at the door of a hut where a mother and two tiny boys were rooted to the ground. Vorenzar grinned at them, turning to face Assantis.

Assantis could not hide his alarm, his hand slipping down to his bow.

'Perhaps,' went on Vorenzar, 'we will have to prod their memories.'

Before his warrior could speak, the forester who had slipped away came back, and with him was an older villager, a wizened being with a bald pate and a sparse beard that he scratched thoughtfully. He eyed the Zemoks more in surprise than fear, swaying like a gnarled tree, his thin arms as dry and scratched.

Assantis pointed to the sketches in the earth. The old forester had to peer at them closely. He recognised the representations of his people and of the larger warrior-creatures. But, as with Assantis, he did not seem to recognise the Man-sketch.

Vorenzar went back to his drawings. He pointed at them, then gestured at the lands around the village. 'Where are they?' he said. No one could have any doubts about what he meant.

The old villager scratched himself as if in aid to memory, but he shook his head. He shuffled over to a small pool and dipped his hands in it, as though no longer interested.

'We may have to look elsewhere, Zaru,' said the Zemok, wondering if Vorenzar would decide to eliminate these creatures.

'Is that your advice?'

But the old villager returned, clutching something. It was a slippery rock, little bigger than his fist, that he had pulled from the side of the pool. He got down on his knees and smoothed out a patch of earth next to Vorenzar's sketches. Then he used what little strength he had to drive the rock at an angle into the ground. Satisfied that he had the oblique angle correct, he stood up, pointing down to the rock. Then he used his hands to indicate that the rock represented another one that was far larger, almost as though he were trying to describe a world. Finally he pointed, with positive surety, to the west.

'This rock is significant,' murmured the wounded Zemok.

Vorenzar snorted. 'Obviously. But what is it? Part of a ruin?'

'Could it be an arena like the one we left on Eannor, Zaru?'

Vorenzar studied the old villager. The latter was squinting at him, waiting. Vorenzar pointed again to his sketch of a Man and then at the rock. The question was again obvious.

The old villager neither agreed nor disagreed, but the faces he pulled and the gestures he made spoke volumes for him, so much so that Vorenzar was mildly amused.

'You understand him, Zaru?' said the Zemok.

'I think so. He's trying to say that he knows nothing of

73

Men, but if we are going to find them anywhere, it'll be in the land of this rock.'

'Then we go west, Zaru.'

'Yes. But we'll need a guide.' Vorenzar turned to the old villager, using signs to show him that the Csendook, including the wounded Zemok, must journey to the rock. But he was able to make it understood that he wanted someone from the village to be their guide.

The old villager spoke briefly to Assantis, who was at first appalled by the idea. He looked down at the rock as though it was a source of deep terror to him. It confirmed Vorenzar's belief that the rock had something to do with the temple of Zellorian.

Further soft words from the old villager quietened Assantis. Then there was an argument. Assantis shook his head, but the old villager was persistent, pleading, and in the end seemed to have won his point.

Vorenzar waited for them to finish. If they could not agree on a guide, he would take one, or possibly several. He could not afford to waste time here, and his patience was not inexhaustible.

In the end it was the old one who stepped forward, proclaiming by his manner that he himself would be the guide.

Vorenzar considered protesting, but decided that this old fool was probably the only one who knew the way to the land of the rock anyway. He nodded, and a pony was found at once.

BOOK TWO

SEARCH

6

BEING

The gliderboat cruised silently over the lower hills of the Thunderreach, taking its passengers further and further from the city of Amerandabad. They had spent the previous night in a small inn on the road to the pass, a place where few travellers were questioned about their business and where they had been able to obtain the supplies they needed for a crossing. As they moved on, further from the lands of the Vaza, each of them gazed at the mountains that rose majestically to their left, soaring peaks of orange and brown, tipped with snow, gleaming like frozen fire in the late afternoon.

Aru was almost asleep, her hands on the craft in front of her, her mind linked to it, pre-occupied with its need, its fears that Innasmorn would yet attempt to drive it from the skies. But she calmed it, steering it gently on, searching for the pass that Jubaia had promised her would be their way through the range to the west.

Jubaia himself was quiet for once. He hung over the side of the craft like a child, exulting in the aerial journey, his eyes wide as he drank in the experience of flight, his single lock of hair streaming out behind him like a pennant. Every now and then he would exclaim something, usually in a language the others did not understand, but it was evident that he was in a state of great excitement. Unlike the rest, he had taken to flight at once, so that even Aru, whose concentration was fixed on her task, was aware of his pleasure. She sensed that the gliderboat could feel Jubaia's joy at flight, and it gave strength to the craft, just as the foresters' fears had once unnerved it.

Armestor, unlike Jubaia, would never come to terms with the aerial journey, always crouched down as far as he could get in the rear of the craft, though he had learned to relax a little now that he was becoming accustomed to the swooping motion as the gliderboat rode the winds and their changes. Aru guessed that he did not enjoy being this close to the gods of his world. Fomond masked his own anxieties better, finding that he could do this best if he studied the terrain. He could see that the Thunderreach was like nothing he had seen in his own lands, for the cliffs were oddly sculpted, weathered and cracked into bizarre formations that looked as though one rough push would send them crashing into the jagged canyons far below. And their colours baffled the eye, as if the sunlight had been trapped within pillars of glass, concentrated in scarlet and orange layers.

Ussemitus was the least relaxed of them all. His experiences in the Dhumvald had opened a host of passages in his mind, showed him doorways that he only had to touch to open. And yet he was afraid to open them. Innasmorn had taught him the taste of strange powers, and he knew he would have to use them and not shie from them.

'Is the pass far?' called Aru, breaking into his thoughts, though she was talking to Jubaia. 'Better to rest for tonight and attempt the crossing in the morning.'

Jubaia nodded, his face serious but slightly comical as he stood up and appeared to sniff the wind like a hound. Ussemitus was certain he would topple out of the gliderboat, but the little being was perfectly safe.

'Early evening at best,' said Jubaia.

'I'll take us into the lower mountains,' said Aru, pointing above them. 'There must be flat ground somewhere.'

Jubaia was scowling, and the others thought he would argue, but then he nodded in agreement.

'Something wrong?' said Ussemitus, quick to catch Jubaia's sudden change of mood.

Jubaia stared ahead as if trying to peer into the remote distances of the north, where the pass would be. 'Storm, perhaps,' he murmured, then sat down.

With a shock, Ussemitus realised that he could have probed into the thoughts of the little being, but he withdrew at once, appalled by this gift. Jubaia glanced at him as if he understood, but Ussemitus looked away.

Aru took the craft through several columns of twisted rock, the air swirling gently about them like a gentle tide. For the moment at least there seemed no danger of a storm, and the air was still, with enough afternoon warmth in it to keep them comfortable. The craft settled on a flat expanse of rock, and an overhang protected the company from any likely abrupt change in the weather, although Ussemitus said he did not think there would be any. He had not used his power to reach out into Innasmorn and search weather patterns, but he did not say so. How much responsibility did the others expect him to shoulder? Did they think he would assume the mantle of a Windmaster without deeper thought?

They were tired, although they had done little on the flight, and they ate quietly. Fomond and Armestor, after a brief exchange, were curled up like children, deep in sleep. Jubaia finished his own brief meal and excused himself, saying he would study the rocks above before settling down for the night.

Aru checked the gliderboat, soothing it, knowing that it, too, needed rest. She felt it shut out the world, herself included, and submerge itself into the oblivion of a private sleep.

Ussemitus sat with his back to the rocks, watching her as she came towards him. She could sense his tiredness.

'You have powers,' he told her softly. With the dying light behind her, she looked particularly beautiful, he thought. A girl from beyond Innasmorn, a creature almost of legend. If she had been anything else, he might have put out his hand to touch her, pull her to him and speak softly to her. But there were too many conflicting thoughts in his mind.

'My link with the gliderboat?' she answered him, sitting. 'Few of my people master the link. But here on Innasmorn, your own kind – ' She stopped, as if she had said something foolish.

'We are different,' he said. 'And yet alike in many ways.'

She turned to him, only to see a sudden fear in his eyes. Behind her she heard the soft footfall of Jubaia.

He squatted down before them, lowering his voice. 'The way through the pass may be dangerous. I climbed upward. From my vantage point I could hear the winds of the north.'

'What did they tell you?' said Ussemitus.

'The pass has a guardian.'

Aru frowned at him. 'You waited until now to tell us this?'

Jubaia shook his head. 'The pass has been used for many years. Now and then there are seasonal storms. But this is something new.'

'What guardian?' said Ussemitus.

Jubaia shuddered, his frame seeming even more diminutive. 'An elemental, a storm being of the mountains.'

'Why is it there?' said Aru.

'It has been put there,' replied Jubaia simply.

Ussemitus nodded slowly and got up. He looked out at the thickening darkness. 'I'd better learn what I can.'

'Where are you going?' said Aru, scrambling up, realising that he meant to leave the overhang.

'I'll be quite safe. But I'll climb, as Jubaia did.'

'I'll show you – ' began Jubaia.

'No. Stay here. Look after the gliderboat. I don't intend to disturb anything. But I must look.'

Aru would have argued, but Jubaia lightly touched her arm as Ussemitus slipped out into the shadows. 'He is still unused to his abilities. They embarrass him a little. Let him use his mind to search the land ahead. Who better than him to do this?'

Aru slowly subsided, knowing that Ussemitus would be able to look after himself. But it was not that that troubled her. She sat, and Jubaia squatted with her.

'Interesting,' said Aru. 'This power of the mind. You seem to have talents of your own in that direction.' She smiled at him.

He raised his brows in protest. 'You mock me, my lady – '

'No, I don't think so, Jubaia.'

He grinned, resisting the urge to continue the deceit. 'Well, I am Innasmornian. We all have certain powers. In some they are wholly dormant. And you, too, have powers. Is it so with other Men?'

She shook her head. 'A few of us. But apart from linking with the gliderboats, it is all.'

He spread his hands almost dismissively. 'Well, my gifts are no greater. Only the Windmasters have true power. It sets them apart from others.'

As it sets Ussemitus apart? she asked herself. But she did not pursue it with Jubaia. She felt the onset of tiredness, drawn by sleep. Yawning, she leaned back, trying to keep her eyes open. By the time Ussemitus returned, her eyes had closed. But she jerked awake as he came to them.

'You should have slept,' he told her gently.

'Later. What did you learn?'

Ussemitus knelt down and they huddled together as if they were afraid of being overheard. 'It is as you said, Jubaia. Something waits in the pass, a darkness that cannot be probed, a raw power. What we faced in the Dhumvald was different, but the power of this elemental is as black.'

'Did it sense you?' asked Jubaia.

'No. I shielded myself – '

Aru was wide awake now, her eyes fixed on Ussemitus. He felt the need to share with them the understanding he had of the powers that had awakened in him. For a long time he had wanted to close himself off from them, afraid of them, but he knew he had to face them. He glanced at Armestor and Fomond, and both were snoring lightly. For some reason he did not want the two foresters to hear this. I am afraid to distance them from myself, he thought. If they knew the depth of power I have, we could never be as we have been.

Conscious that Aru and Jubaia were leaning very close, he began to speak. 'When I was in the Dhumvald, linking my mind with that of the Windmasters, it was as though I had opened a gate through which many things entered. Some of them I understood and used, others rushed into

81

some dark part of my mind. They hide there yet, like a nest of snakes, but I seem to hear them, their voices. Some of them I have been able to reach. Others I may reach at another time.'

Jubaia was nodding at this.

'I learned things about the Windmasters, and touched on certain of their own fears. Azrand, for example. He has many doubts about the inner circle that he rules. There are a few of the Windmasters who do not agree with the policies of the Blue Hairs. Renegades, who, like Quareem, seek power for different reasons. Some of them welcome war with Aru's people and seek the utter destruction of the Sculpted City and all Men on Innasmorn. Azrand felt this way once. But recently he has come to understand that there may be a better way of achieving peace on Innasmorn. The events in the Dhumvald swayed him to this new way. I read his uncertainty, his fear of Man, but already he ponders the future. He is no warmonger, and neither are most of the Blue Hairs.

'But those who press for war have used Vittargattus. They have toyed with his very mind.'

'He resented freeing us,' said Aru. 'It seemed an effort for him to accept us as allies.'

'They fuelled his bloodlust with evil sendings.'

'Sendings?' said Jubaia. 'Dreams?'

Ussemitus nodded. 'Yes. Certain Blue Hairs have used dreams to control Vittargattus. But after the battle of the Dhumvald, his mind was cleansed. It may have something to do with my part in the battle, my linking with Azrand and the others. I did not consciously attempt to free Vittargattus from his visions, but such things have been removed from him.

'And now the Blue Hairs who manipulated him are angered. They believe it is my power that has thwarted them and they fear now that Vittargattus will modify his plans to destroy the Sculpted City, especially with Azrand to support him. They also believe that in order to win back control of Vittargattus, to pour more evil into him, they must destroy the power that protects him.'

Aru frowned. 'Are you protecting him? Even now?'

'Not consciously. I don't know enough about what has happened to me to say. But the mountain elemental that waits for us intends to destroy us all. It has been set to guard the pass by the renegades. And if we do not get past it, we will be set upon by other forces that are gathering on this side of the Thunderreach.'

'Forces?' echoed Jubaia. 'Storms?'

Ussemitus shrugged. 'I cannot tell. But the Blue Hairs have many such powers at their disposal.'

They contemplated this for several moments, Jubaia screwing his face up so that he looked like a wizened old man. Aru chuckled at his expression, explaining herself, and for a brief moment they all enjoyed the humour. But again the darkness closed in.

'We dare not attempt to get through the pass by night,' said Jubaia. 'The elemental is oblivious to daylight. It will be raw energy, pure power. Time means nothing. Whereas we would struggle at night.'

'How do we pass it?' said Ussemitus. 'What do we use against it? Should I attempt to unlock more of the powers that seem to be within me?'

Jubaia shook his head. 'It will not be as it was on the Spiderway. There we all added fuel to your fire. But the evil powers there were puny compared to this thing. It has been focused by many Blue Hairs – '

'You know that?' said Aru.

'Ah, well, yes,' stammered Jubaia. 'Ussemitus just said so – '

'We have no choice as I see it,' said Ussemitus. 'We must use what powers we have.'

'The Blue Hairs may well have shielded the pass,' said Jubaia. 'Which would make it hard for you to summon help from the Mother. She may not hear us, once we are in the pass.'

'What about the gliderboat?' Ussemitus asked Aru.

She looked apprehensively towards the dark craft. It blended into the rock like a part of it. She shook her head.

'It will need all its own power to stay in the air. And I won't be able to do anything except pilot it.'

Ussemitus looked at Jubaia. 'Are you certain we cannot climb over the mountains any other way?'

But Jubaia confirmed what he had already told him. The mountains were too high and airless. And likely filled with other hostile elements. Only the pass would do.

Ussemitus looked hard at him for some time, as though there was something else he expected the little being to tell him, but Jubaia remained silent as stone. Eventually he nodded, as if all had been said, and found himself a place in the rocks where he settled down for sleep.

Aru watched Ussemitus's face. He was still studying Jubaia.

'What is it?' she asked him softly.

'I can't say. But Jubaia is hiding something, I'm sure. He's closed his mind like a fist.'

'Can you – read minds?' she said, her eyes dropping.

'I didn't mean that. But I can sense when a mind is as tightly shut as that of Jubaia. I don't think he's afraid of me, but there are things he knows that he doesn't want to share.'

'About the elemental?'

'Perhaps. He's afraid of it, very afraid. That much he cannot hide.' But he sighed and rubbed tiredly at his face. 'I think we should sleep.'

Moments later he had stretched back, eyes closed, and was silent.

Aru tried to sleep, but now found that she could not. She looked away from Ussemitus, afraid that if he could reach into her mind he would find – what? She did not know herself. Her own emotions were confused, but they troubled her. It was a long time before exhaustion claimed her.

She woke with the dawn. Ussemitus was already gone, but Fomond and Armestor were struggling up stiffly, stretching themselves and grumbling about being thirsty. Armestor lifted his beloved bow.

'You don't mean to *hunt*?' snorted Fomond. 'We've food enough with us to last the crossing.'

'Those of us who have certain skills use them,' Armestor said with mock scorn. He was up and away in a moment.

Fomond chuckled as he saw Aru shaking her head. 'You think he'll come back empty-handed? Even on this rock he'll find something. You should know that by now.'

Aru smiled. She knew that Armestor needed to combat his personal fears in his own way. 'I won't wager against it.' She began preparing a fire.

Ussemitus and Jubaia joined her shortly afterwards, having both been up on the higher rocks. 'It seems a peaceful day,' Ussemitus commented. But no one replied.

Armestor returned later, having killed a single creature; it seemed neither lizard nor mammal, but he insisted on cooking it and trying it, proclaiming that it was excellent. The others chewed on their provisions, expressing their doubts but laughing at Armestor's enthusiasm.

The moment came to leave, with the sun still low, the sky still partly hung with shadows. The company got into the gliderboat, and Aru spoke softly to it as though coaxing a horse from its stable and out into a chilling day. But it rose and they left the little plateau, threading their way through the strangely eroded peaks, the leaning stacks. They had decided not to go out to the edge of the range, but to weave through the minor passes and peaks until they came to the main pass to the west at an angle, disguising their coming as best they could.

Out over the lands below the mountains, mist rose, fusing with the low clouds that now drifted in, obscuring the sky. The company knew that rain would come, and high up in the mountains they saw the ominous gathering of grey, the huge, billowing clouds that would soon discharge a heavy deluge.

The opening to the pass was not many miles distant, and they came to it in silence, the wind having still expectantly, the swollen-bellied clouds lowering themselves on to the upper crags, rain falling as they did.

'We should find the most sheltered path through,' Jubaia told Aru. 'Go as low down as you can. The storm being will find it more difficult to assail us if we are near the ground. And we can take shelter if we have to.'

'Would it be safer to go through the pass on foot?' said Armestor. 'Do we have to fly?'

'And carry the gliderboat?' said Ussemitus.

'Couldn't we secure it somewhere?' Armestor persisted.

'Leave it?' said Aru, horrified.

'We have a long journey ahead of us,' said Jubaia, calming them both. 'Without the gliderboat it would be hopeless.'

'Well, we can't carry the craft,' said Fomond.

'We're wasting time,' said Ussemitus. 'Take us down, Aru.'

She did so, dropping down into the steep-sided pass, the mountains closing around them like bleak gods, the clouds opening, rain tumbling from the sky. The gliderboat dipped from side to side, rain beating upon it, but Aru knew that it was unmoved by rain. Only the unpredictable winds caused it alarm, and here in this deep pass they would be difficult to navigate. But for now they were not hostile, the turbulence minimal.

Far below, a river ran downwards to the east, carving a broad channel for itself as it foamed and danced, while further up in the pass it flashed and sparkled, dropping over hard bands of rock in white cataracts, tumbling into deep pools, filling the air around it with clouds of spray like steam. The gliderboat followed the twisting river up into the pass, and its crew saw the narrow road that also ran up into the pass, though no caravans moved along it today.

The rain beat down harder, obscuring the view ahead, and clouds began to dip lower, filling the pass, billowing outwards and down, bringing with them the first rush of air, the wind gathering itself, swirling and eddying like the waters of the river below. The sides of the pass became more sheer, rising upwards and outward as though their own weight would topple them over, so that the company felt threatened by them, tempted to cover their heads in case of rockfall. But the gliderboat moved on easily, navigating the shouting wind smoothly. Innasmorn had not decided on an attack, Aru thought. She wondered if this had anything to do with Ussemitus, but she could not read his expression. He merely gazed ahead, his eyes fixed on some point beyond the thick cloud mists.

Then he jerked, his mouth opening. 'Jubaia!' he called, and the little being was beside him at once. Ussemitus pointed.

Aru could see only the thick cloud, but Jubaia was nodding, his face creased with fear. 'It is there,' he breathed.

Behind him Fomond and Armestor had fitted arrows to their bows, but Jubaia waved them away.

'Get down, flat to the floor,' he told them.

'You'll help me?' Ussemitus asked him.

Jubaia nodded, but the fear was growing in him visibly. Aru kept as low as she dared, feeling the sudden tension in the gliderboat. It veered towards the side of the pass and she struggled to keep it from glancing off the rock.

'It's struggling against me,' she cried. 'What is ahead of us?'

Ussemitus was trying to see into the thick mist. A sudden blast of air hit the craft like a fist and it swung upwards so that they were all almost flung out. But they held on as the craft righted, then dived. It swung around in a tight curve, but Aru forced it back to face up the pass.

'The entire pass is blocked!' shouted Ussemitus over the scream of the wind.

'By what?' said Aru.

Ussemitus shook his head. 'Darkness. Thick clouds. And there's something in them, binding them. A fury. Madness. If we try to break through, we'll be pulled to pieces. Jubaia –'

The little man drew back. 'We cannot face that! Ussemitus, the Mother will not hear us. You don't have that kind of power – '

Ussemitus shielded his eyes from the sting of the rain. The wind grew stronger, buffeting the craft as though an immense hand reached out from the clouds beyond. A sudden peal of thunder sounded above them and light flickered, whipping chunks of rock from the cliff face that sped by only feet away.

Again Aru had to fight for control of the gliderboat. Its terror rose up like bile, threatening to engulf and overpower her. She was forced to turn the craft back down the pass. More thunder sounded, and above it a deafening roar.

'The voice of the gods!' cried Armestor, closing his eyes.

Ussemitus gasped as the rain lashed at them with renewed fury. Jubaia had also flung himself down, covering his head. It was impossible to go up against this monstrous force. The entire pass was thick with it and it rolled forward like a tidal wave, pulsing with hatred, its intent focusing on the pathetic leaf that was the gliderboat.

Aru maintained her grip with an effort, guiding the craft as straight as she could back down the pass. It skimmed over the crest of a waterfall, almost ripping its belly on the rocks that groped upward for it. The lower end of the pass was alive with another storm, the clouds boiling upwards. They reached them and plunged into them, Aru almost blacking out from the effort.

Ussemitus was stunned by the intensity of the elemental powers that pursued them. They were not as powerful as the deathstorm, but when he had opposed that nightmare, Azrand and the Windmasters had poured their own power into breaking it up, and it had never been allowed a true birth. But the storm being of the mountains was far too terrible to match. Ussemitus was afraid that if he unleashed everything within him, disaster would follow, his own reason for falling back under the stress. Reason told him to flee this horror.

The gliderboat swung out over the plain, turning to run parallel to the range until Aru could bring herself to control it once more. She swerved to dip into a narrow canyon, and as the craft entered it, they all felt the sudden hush as though the storm had rushed on past them, losing them in its pell-mell flight.

They hovered a few feet from the ground. All of them were spent. The rain pitied them: it had become a gentle drizzle.

Aru slumped back.

Fomond and Armestor struggled to sit up, both looking wretched in the back of the craft, and Jubaia looked little better.

Ussemitus grinned weakly. 'The pass is closed to us.'

'So now what?' said Aru. 'I could sleep for a week.'

Jubaia shook his head. 'You had to see it. To know how impassable it was. You had to believe me.'

'I would have taken your word for it,' muttered Armestor.

Fomond nodded. 'Did you know it would be that bad, Jubaia?' he asked, but Ussemitus sensed that the question was also directed at him.

'There's another way through,' said Jubaia after he had recovered his breath. 'I didn't mention it before, in case you shouted me down. But now you know what lies in the pass – '

'If you're going to tell us there's another way through, like the Spiderway – ' began Fomond.

Jubaia shrugged. 'Not overland, or by river, or by sea.'

'Jubaia,' said Aru, her look admonishing him. 'Is this another of your secrets? A mystery from the past?'

'Well, we could go under the range,' nodded Jubaia.

'*Under* the range?' said Aru, her eyes looking up to the skies.

Jubaia nodded even more vigorously as the others groaned. 'It is very dangerous – '

'Naturally,' said Aru.

'The caverns of Windsong.'

Ussemitus and the foresters exchanged frowns, shaking their heads. They had not heard of these caverns.

'So what is the particular problem this time?' said Aru.

Jubaia looked at her in mock innocence. 'No tricks, my lady. But danger. Possibly far more than on the Spiderway.'

Armestor grunted. 'Well, nothing could be as bad as the pass.'

'Could it, Jubaia?' said Fomond.

'There are worse things in Innasmorn,' said the little being. 'But as far as I know, they are not under the Thunderreach.'

'It is a great comfort to hear it,' said Fomond, and for a while the humour offered a little relief from the horrors of the pass.

7

MAZE

Aru guided the gliderboat through a number of canyons, following Jubaia's instructions; they were getting further into the range, though to the west the peaks rose even higher, looking every bit as impassable as Jubaia had said they would be. As the rain lashed down at them, almost as though servants of the elemental had found them and were preparing for another assault, they saw an opening in the side of the gorge below them, an almost perfect circle of darkness. Ussemitus glanced at his companions, reading their faces: to all of them it looked as if a giant worm had buried itself into the cliff face. They dropped towards the ring of dark, and as they did so they heard the first strains of sound, an eerie, musical wind. Whether it issued from the cave or whether it was made by the sound of the air rushing inwards, they could not tell, but it grew steadily in pitch, fluctuating rhythmically.

'The song of the wind,' said Jubaia.

'Before we enter this place,' Ussemitus told him, 'you had better explain something of its history. Who made it?'

Jubaia shrugged. 'It's as old as the mountains themselves. Legend says that the wind opened the stone on a whim. But Thunderreach was angered by its insolence and so closed up the wall, trapping the wind within. For centuries the wind sought ways out of the mountains, moving this way and that inside, creating a maze, opening channels, tormenting the mountain, until at last it relented and permitted the wind to return to the outside. The caverns of Windsong each have their own music, for the shape of the cavern walls, the sculpture of the rocks, varies and reacts in many ways to the rush of air, for the air is no longer at odds with the mountains. Whatever feud there once was is long ended. But the harmony of wind and stone are not always good for the likes of us. These are not our songs you will hear. It may be necessary for us to stop up our ears. And the air sometimes grows cold, at others it can be as rough as any mountain torrent.'

'And these tunnels go right through Thunderreach?' said Fomond.

Jubaia nodded. 'Yes, to the west, high up over the lands there.'

Armestor leaned forward cautiously, though the growing dark of the cave had become very quiet. 'It seems far less dangerous than the pass of the elemental.'

'You've never been through?' Ussemitus asked Jubaia. 'Has anyone?'

'Not as far as I know. But then, the mountain pass is never usually protected by such hostile forces.'

The gliderboat hovered close to the dark opening, which the company now saw to be over two hundred feet high, and not quite as symmetrical as they had first thought. But it still looked disturbingly like a mouth. They could hear a distant roaring within it, like the sound of a cataract plunging over a gorge, but it was a steady, fixed sound, seemingly innocent.

Aru frowned at the wall of darkness, and Ussemitus could sense her uncertainty.

'You seem troubled by it,' he said softly to her.

She nodded. 'It's not me. It's the gliderboat.' She had felt the mounting of its unease. Now that they were poised to go under the rock overhang, the craft trembled, then gave a shudder that the entire company felt.

'What's wrong!' gasped Armestor.

Jubaia had joined Aru in the prow of the craft. 'We have to go on this way,' he whispered. 'There's no other way through the range.'

'The gliderboat is terrified!' said Aru suddenly, and the craft swerved aside from the cave so that she had to bank it steeply and level it out slowly. She turned it and tried to come forward again, but this time it dipped downwards, narrowly avoiding a jutting crag.

'Aru!' called Ussemitus, who had almost been flung from the craft. 'Can't you steer?'

'Something in the cavern is preventing the gliderboat from entering.'

'There's nothing there,' insisted Jubaia. 'The air is troubled, that's all. You must keep trying.'

Twice more Aru sought to take the gliderboat into the cave, but she could not keep its nose pointed forward and was forced to swerve aside. It was becoming dangerous and she knew if she tried to force her way in, the gliderboat would overturn and send them all plummeting to their deaths on the rocks below.

She hovered some distance from the cave mouth, her face glistening, her chest heaving with effort, as if she had been physically wrestling with the craft. She could feel its fear deeply, knowing that the craft was like a horse, ready to bolt wildly at the first opportunity.

'The gliderboat has never been underground,' she told them. 'The darkness and the uncertainty of the maze would disorientate it. I dare not bend its will too much to mine. If I try, I won't be able to control it properly. It has to be a shared working. The gliderboat is not a slave.'

'What exactly is the craft?' said Ussemitus. 'Sometimes I wonder if it's as sentient as we are. As if you can talk to it. Is it some kind of creature?'

Armestor and Fomond stiffened, looking about them at the sleek lines of the craft as if it had suddenly become a winged beast.

Aru nodded slowly. 'It is alive, yes. I don't know all its secrets. I can't penetrate its mind, but it has one. And I often feel it is far deeper than we know. But I have no real power to explore such a thing. Besides, I am afraid to. And I cannot try to fathom it now. Not this dread it has. It's put there as a protection, for self-preservation. So don't ask me to probe it.'

They were still circling gently, watching the cave, which had again fallen very silent.

'Jubaia,' said Ussemitus. 'Can we go through the cavern on foot?'

Jubaia screwed up his face, for a moment looking like a wizened old man. 'Possibly,' he murmured. 'But it would take so long. And what would we eat once our provisions ended. I doubt we'd find prey within.'

'You want me to abandon the craft?' said Aru.

Ussemitus could not meet her gaze, as if she were asking him if he wanted her to abandon a friend. He thought of the death of the gliderboat she had been flying the first time they had met, and the pain it had caused her to think of it.

'It would die,' she said flatly.

Ussemitus shook his head. 'No, no. We cannot permit that.'

Fomond broke their glum silence. 'Then we have to find another way over the mountains. Or go round them.'

This time Jubaia demurred. 'If we try to go round them, we'll be set upon by the agents of the Blue Hairs. The rebels. Some of them, like Quareem, have gone a long way down the dark paths.'

'So what do we do?' blurted Armestor. 'We can't stay here. Sooner or later that elemental will find us – '

'We have to go into the caverns,' said Jubaia, his voice cutting into them with a fresh edge.

Ussemitus stared at him. 'How?'

'The gliderboat can go below,' said the little man. 'If it is calmed. If it is made to understand that the danger is not as severe as it seems to think. Its fear is irrational.'

'How do you know?' said Aru, trying to keep a trace of alarm from her voice.

Jubaia looked very serious, but for once the company did not laugh at his expression.

'Well?' prompted Ussemitus, sensing that Jubaia was about to reveal something of his own nature that he had been keeping back. He knew there must be far more to the half being than they had ever learned.

Jubaia seemed to be tormented by some inner argument, but at last he spoke. 'I could steer the gliderboat.'

'*You*?' gasped Aru, the word almost punched from her.

Jubaia nodded. 'Yes. I know its mind.'

'How?'

He lifted a hand as if asking for peace. 'I have certain gifts. Modesty has forced me to keep them from you –'

'Jubaia,' growled Ussemitus.

'I know. I should be open and honest. But I am cautious, that is all.'

'Minds are open to you?' said Aru.

'Not exactly.'

'Then be more precise,' said Ussemitus. He was conscious that Fomond and Armestor were scowling at the little man with more than a little resentment, hands straying to their bows.

'To be more precise,' said Jubaia hesitantly, 'I am able to sift dreams. It is more easily done when people are asleep. But even when we are awake, there are dreams in our minds.'

'You *sift* them?' echoed Aru.

Jubaia nodded. 'It is a talent of my people.'

'Then you can read the mind of the gliderboat?' said Aru.

Again he nodded. 'More clearly that I can your minds, for she is in a kind of constant sleep.'

'Can you speak to it?'

'I can. As you do, lady. Though more clearly and openly.'

Aru did not know whether to be pleased or angry. She just went on staring at him as if she would be able to see inside the workings of his mind, the machinery that would confirm his outrageous claims.

'Why have you not told us before?' said Fomond, and for once there was no humour in his tone.

'It is a gift that alarms people, though unnecessarily. I do not pry into dreams for amusement. I use my skills only when I must.'

'As you did when we first met?' said Ussemitus.

Jubaia flinched, looking sheepish. 'Well, I was in a dilemma –'

'You put thoughts, commands, into our minds,'

Ussemitus went on. 'We unleashed our arrows on the soldiers who pursued you, killing them. That was your doing.'

Jubaia fidgeted. 'Ah, yes, well, you see, I was desperate. They would have killed me – '

'You manipulated us!' said Fomond, suddenly grinning. 'You entered our minds and gave us the command to kill? I don't believe it – '

'Oh, it's true,' nodded Ussemitus. 'I have suspected as much for a long time. But there are more positive ways to interfere with minds, are there not, Jubaia?'

Jubaia grinned. 'Of course! I would not use my art as a weapon unless I was threatened.'

'Tell us about Vittargattus,' said Ussemitus. 'His dreams.'

'Ah,' breathed Jubaia, as though he had decided he had been caught out at a prank and could no longer avoid admitting to it. 'Yes. Vittargattus. You have only a part of the tale. His mind was indeed cluttered up with evil visions. Dreams sent to him by the renegades.'

'But *I* didn't remove them,' said Ussemitus.

'Well, no,' said Jubaia, looking away. 'What the Blue Hairs put there, I took away. I cleansed Vittargattus's mind of evil dreams.'

Fomond and Armestor gaped at him.

Ussemitus chuckled. 'I seem to have certain powers, but I could not understand how I could have helped Vittargattus. Then it was you.'

Jubaia nodded. 'But you can surely see why I wanted no one to know of this.'

'Naturally,' said Aru. 'Now the renegade Windmasters are after Ussemitus and not you!'

'No, no, that's not what I meant – '

'Of course not,' smiled Aru.

Ussemitus held up his hand before Jubaia could say anything else. 'This is something we must discuss in greater detail. But not now. We must decide on our immediate course. Which path do we take?'

Jubaia looked at Aru. 'Lady, you must trust me. Let

me guide the craft. I can persuade it to go under the mountains.'

'You will control it?'

'You must let me do this. I know the craft's mind. Already I have spoken to her.'

'You refer to the craft as "her", ' said Ussemitus, puzzled by the tenderness in Jubaia's tone.

Jubaia inclined his head. 'Yes, she is a lady.'

'How can you know that?' said Aru, amazed. 'To me the craft has always been a machine, even though it has a mind – '

'I think once, long ago,' said Jubaia, 'she was more than just a gliderboat. Much of that former life is within her yet, though her mind has been amended.'

Aru felt herself shudder. 'What do you mean?'

'She is now a gliderboat. As such she only needs to respond to simple commands. She does not need to think, to dream. All that part of her mind has been closed down, covered, if you like, by a blanket. But I have felt the things beneath. I have touched them. What you have sensed, lady, is the deeper part of her mind. And it is not unlike your own.'

'Sleeping,' said Ussemitus.

'Exactly,' said Jubaia. 'Dreaming. But it would be dangerous to waken her. Not too abruptly. That part of her mind does not know what she has become.'

Aru studied him with a renewed intensity, as if she could burn her way into his thoughts, layer by layer. 'What was she, Jubaia?'

But he shook his head, turning away. 'Perhaps we will know one day.' He seemed to want to close any more discussion of the matter.

Aru clenched her fists, anger flushing her cheeks, but Ussemitus realised that her anger was not aimed at the little man.

'Who made the gliderboats?' he asked her.

'I am not sure. But they are new things. I can guess at their origin. Only too well. Who else would be cruel enough to – '

Ussemitus put an arm about her, sensing that she was close to tears. She held him for a moment, but her expression hardened.

'Jubaia,' she said. 'If you can speak to the craft, then do so. Guide it – her – gently.'

'Very well,' he nodded. At once he sat beside her, and Ussemitus dropped back with his companions. None of them spoke, watching the churning skies, the cold walls of stone.

Jubaia let his mind slip away into the dark places where he knew he would locate the gliderboat's fear. He worked at it, his eyes closing, his hands pressed to the bow of the craft as though they, too, were establishing contact of a kind. Aru could feel the craft's fears yet, the way in which it still baulked any attempt to move it towards the cavern.

Then the nose of the craft dipped and Jubaia began murmuring to himself, soft words that Aru did not catch. The gliderboat steadied, dropping closer to the darkness. Somewhere in the mountains high overhead there was a deep boom of thunder. The rain lashed down with renewed spite, and clouds shouldered their way over the crest of the canyon. But the gliderboat had entered another world, and the maze opened up before it, a world of shadows and far sounds, where the wind danced, rising and falling.

Inside the cavern all was not total darkness as the company had expected. There were huge twists of rock curling up from the floor, bent this way and that as they rose to the ceiling, and other great incisors of rock hung down like the fangs of giants. The gliderboat threaded in and out of these like an expertly wielded needle. Aru could feel the sudden calmness of the craft, like a horse that has been stroked into gentle submission, complete trust. She felt, too, a stab of jealousy, for Jubaia had exercised this control effortlessly in a way that she could never hope to duplicate. There were a hundred questions she wanted to ask him, but he studied the surroundings, his concentration locked, and she dared not break it.

Ussemitus and the foresters gaped at the bizarre scenery of the caverns. Tunnels curled and twisted in all directions, the massive ceilings held up, it seemed, by thin columns of rock, and they all wondered how such weak supports could prop up such a weight. Light from outside reached in for a great distance, but they knew there would come a point where it no longer shone. How would Jubaia steer then?

But their unspoken questions were answered when darkness closed around them. The gliderboat had no need of eyes. It was sensitive to the air, to its currents, as a bird was, and to the smells of the caverns. Jubaia shared them, locked into this subterranean world, its curling columns of rock, the bends in its great maze.

Armestor could not bear the silence. 'There seems to be no wind any more,' he said. His voice carried more loudly than he would have expected, but Jubaia never flinched.

'Feels to me as if the entire mountain is alive,' said Fomond. 'And we're slipping through its gut.'

'The storms will never find us here,' added Armestor, though his tone implied uncertainty.

They ate a little food as they went, though Jubaia demurred, and as their nerves eased and they began to relax, they heard the first sounds of any significance. A distant rush of air came to them, as though a vast door had been opened and a blast admitted. The air trembled, and somewhere ahead of them, they heard a high-pitched moaning, a fugue of sounds that gathered strength instead of diminishing.

There came an abrupt flash of light, a zigzag of brightness that imposed itself on the eye, leaving its traces behind it after it had gone. The craft veered to the left, but Jubaia called something out and it corrected itself in time to miss one of the many tall columns. More light flickered and there were roars, as though several winds had come tearing down tunnels and met in a cross-current like the turbulence of a number of torrents. The gliderboat began to buck and toss as if being bounced along between rapids, and the company hung on grimly. Around them the swirl of noise rose in pitch, the mad laughter of invisible beings.

Aru fell backwards, gripping the craft to steady herself, unable to help Jubaia control it. But he seemed to have

99

become one with the craft, his form etched in dazzling light as the underground storm grew in intensity, as if he were no more than a component of the gliderboat. His eyes were closed, but he smiled, and Aru could sense in him an elation, an ecstasy almost, as if this wild flight through the maze had suffused his blood with a new level of power. She could feel his mind, a wild thing, racing with the wind, but there was no madness in it, only a great strength, a surge of power from within the little man that seemed impossible for one so small.

The forked lightning was so frequent now that the entire cave system was lit by it in a flashing effect that gave a bizarre dimension to their movements, making them seem jerky as dolls, trapped in a kind of half time. The gliderboat rose up and dipped down, swinging from side to side at great speed, but Aru knew that its fear had been turned into an exultation, as if it drew on the unbridled energy about it and fed upon it.

Armestor peered through his fingers at the walls around him. They seemed to stretch and pull out of shape, contorting into faces that mocked and leered, the wind roaring from their open mouths. Fomond, too, shut out this grotesque parade of images, and Ussemitus used his own powers to pour what calm he could upon his terrors.

Gradually the light eased, but in the remaining glow there seemed to be an army of shapes marching along the tunnels, huge, twisted forms, gargantuan beings crossing from one dimension to another, like homeless colossi searching for new realms to plunder.

Aru wanted to call out to Jubaia for some kind of explanation, but he was locked into his task, fused with the gliderboat, ignoring everything but the need to avoid disaster. Aru gaped at his skill, for she had never been able to control the gliderboat as he did. She had always considered herself skilled at control, but Jubaia moved the craft in a new way, and with a speed and grace that she could never hope to emulate. She found herself shrinking away from his ecstasy, his sudden surges of wonder at the flight.

'What is happening?' gasped Ussemitus at her shoulder.

'Has he lost his reason? I can feel it, as though he has become possessed.'

'He shares the mind of the gliderboat, and through it feels every fibre of its flight,' she answered, her face drained. 'No Controller ever achieved this, Ussemitus. It is something that goes beyond the capabilities of my people. And Jubaia tastes every ripple of air, every crosswind. They give strength to him! Power. He is as one with the air as a fish would be with the seas.'

Ussemitus nodded. Not madness then. While Jubaia piloted the gliderboat, he could feel no menace in the things around them, dangerous though they must have been. 'I think we have much to learn about him yet.'

The light dimmed away, and soon afterwards the winds died down, as though they had tired of the game, for it seemed no more than that to them.

In the darkness, Jubaia turned, and though his companions could hardly see him, they felt his eyes on them.

'You have heard the Windsongs,' he called, his voice tremulous, as if the excitement of the flight still had hold of him. 'There's a strange beauty in them.'

'Beauty!' shouted Fomond. 'Much more of that and I'd have gone over the side!'

'Did you not taste the freedom of the wind?' Jubaia called back. 'The lure of the air, the spirit of Innasmorn, even in this place.'

'I was too busy hanging on to my sanity!' shouted Fomond.

'Yet there was a sadness in it,' Jubaia went on. 'The winds of Innasmorn should blow across the world, not down here in the darkness of another age. They are not completely free, you see.' He seemed to understand this, as though he had a sympathy with the plight of the winds that were trapped down in this underworld realm, and Aru sensed his melancholy.

But the company, exhausted by the flight, lapsed into silence; the gliderboat moved on more gently, until Jubaia brought it to rest on a shelf high above the floor of the caverns. Within moments he was asleep. Aru sought signs of awareness in the gliderboat, but it, too, had sunk down into a private darkness that was, to her, impenetrable.

Fomond and Armestor chewed thoughtfully on some dried meat, and Ussemitus stretched back, yawning. 'Have we been travelling all day?'

They realised they must have, and though there were many things they wanted to discuss, the darkness seeped into them so that they were soon all asleep, their minds empty. No dreams troubled them.

Movement brought them all out of sleep, many hours later. It was not the cool caress of the wind, no gentle breeze, but the faint stirring beneath them of the gliderboat, for none of them had ventured over its side on to the rock. There was no light to see by, but Ussemitus knew that Jubaia was alert, preparing to begin the next part of the journey.

'How far to the exit?' he asked him.

'A few more hours. I can feel the wind from the west already,' came his voice. It held a new warmth, a new confidence.

'Will there be dangers beyond the caves?' said Fomond.

Jubaia chuckled. 'Of course! Innasmorn crawls with dangers for the unwary. Especially in the lands we will visit. But we have thwarted the guardian of the pass. He will not be waiting for us.'

'How can you be sure?' said Aru, trying not to sound petulant.

'Did you not hear the voice of the winds?'

Aru snorted.

'And you, Ussemitus?'

'I heard many voices in the storm. They confused me. Like children shouting all at once.'

'Yes, a good image,' said Jubaia. 'Lost children. But they spoke of the elemental of the snows high above us. He stamps about in his fury and shakes the roots of the mountains. But he has lost us. His storms failed to find us. When we go beyond the Thunderreach, he will not be there.'

Armestor was muttering something, but only Fomond heard him say, 'So he can talk to the wind as well.'

Aru made no comment, but she knew that the little thief they had known in the east was no longer with them. The Jubaia who guided them now was an altogether different being, and she felt more estranged from the company, more alien, than she had done before. Even the gliderboat seemed to be more in tune with Innasmorn than she was.

8

DEATHLESS CITY

From their vantage high in the mountains, they could look down and see the western slopes of the Thunderreach spreading out below them to where the sea glistened in the distance. Rich green forests spread up towards them from the lowlands and beyond them were open areas that became yellowed, stretches of dune and beach, barely visible from this distance. Behind them the company had left the last of the incredible maze, the gliderboat resting on the ledge where they had emerged. Jubaia told them she was tired, but the emergence into sunlight would quickly restore her energy.

Armestor was more relieved than anyone, it seemed, skipping off like a child, in search of food. Fomond went with him. Ussemitus warned them not to venture far, though Jubaia said it was probably safe hereabouts. Above them the high peaks soared, white and clouded, but of the snow being and its storms there was no sign. Even Aru felt the relief of coming out of the near-dark into daylight, as if Innasmorn welcomed her as much as the others. She tried to forget the sombre thoughts that had beset her on the way through the mountains.

They found a small stream and used its icy water to wash away the last of the fears of the caverns, sitting together on a rock outcrop, content for a time to drink in the spectacular view.

'There's a small town beyond the dunes, almost directly west of us,' said Jubaia. 'It's a rough place, filled with traders, pirates and vagabonds from the north and south roads that run up and down these coastal plains. So no one will question us too closely. I doubt that the Blue Hairs will have extended their influence here.'

'If they think we're beyond the Thunderreach,' said Ussemitus, 'they'll treat us as less of a threat.'

Jubaia nodded, 'Probably.'

In a while Fomond and Armestor arrived, both having killed large hare-like creatures with their bows. They were arguing good-naturedly over who had killed the largest, and for once it was Fomond who was given the benefit of the doubt. But Armestor took this with good grace, only too glad to be out in the open. Jubaia pronounced it safe to cook the meat, which they did, and they ate heartily. It was the most relaxed they had been for many days, and they stretched back among the rocks, able to put the difficulties of their quest from their minds for a while.

Aru examined the gliderboat, but as Jubaia had said, it was recovering quickly from its exhausting race through the caverns. Aru tried briefly to reach deeper into its mind, but found the same evasiveness she always found. If Jubaia had unlocked areas, it was his own particular secret.

When Aru joined the others, Ussemitus seemed thoughtful. She sat with him, and he knew from her eyes that she wanted to know if something troubled him. He shied from any hint of touching her mind with his own, afraid to offend her, and also unsure of what he would find.

He smiled. 'When I saw what was in the pass, I confess I despaired. Yet Jubaia surprised us as he has done before. And no doubt will again, eh?'

'There were reasons why I kept my abilities to myself. Had you known them, Ussemitus, the knowledge in your mind might have been discovered by others,' said Jubaia.

'I think you ought to tell us more about who you are,' replied Ussemitus.

Fomond grunted. 'More, I think, than an itinerant thief. What really brought you to the forests of the east?'

'It really was pure chance,' insisted the little man. 'Though to be truthful, I wonder now if Innasmorn had something to do with it. I was searching for items of interest, for as you know, I make my living from what I can barter – '

'Thievery,' said Armestor.

Jubaia laughed. 'Why, yes. You look through your nose at such things, but I should tell you that there are certain races on Innasmorn that have made an art of theft. It is considered an honourable profession.'

The others all laughed at this.

'Come, Jubaia,' said Aru. 'Even among Men it is difficult to justify thievery. It is good to share things, but without approval – '

Jubaia nodded. 'Let me tell you about the city of Shung Nang. Has any of you heard of it?'

There were shrugs among the Innasmornians, to whom the name was unknown.

'No,' said Jubaia. 'I expected not. Well, let me go back in history. You may know that once the people of Innasmorn, those who were here *first*, were as you are, physical beings, flesh and blood and bone. As time went by, they grew closer to their gods, to Innasmorn's many elemental forces, and took new forms, until they became one with them.

'Other, newer races evolved, races from which you foresters possibly began. But the old races, the first people, were almost gone. Only a few were left. One of the last of these was a race of winged beings, creatures of the skies. Perhaps they did not entirely give up their physical form and become one with the winds because they were already so close to them, racing with them, at one in many other ways.

'The winged ones dwell, even now, in the sacred city of Shung Nang, or the Deathless City as it is called. It is a forbidden place, where no other Innasmornians may set foot, and it is hidden away in the remote western lands, beyond the Ocean of Hurricanes. To many people on Innasmorn, those that have heard of Shung Nang, it is no more than a legend, a name from history, long dead.'

The others listened avidly, each picturing for himself this distant place, with its winged citizens. Aru felt the glider-boat stir, as though it, too, was listening to Jubaia's history.

'The winged ones of Shung Nang, the windriders,' he went on, 'are master thieves. It is their great joy to steal from all other races on Innasmorn, whom they consider to be intruders, vermin. They have, so the windriders insist, usurped the lands of Innasmorn and have no right to them.'

'You call my ancestors intruders,' said Ussemitus with interest. 'What do you mean by that?'

Jubaia merely shrugged. 'It is how they are thought of by the men of Shung Nang. They brought artefacts to Innasmorn and did great damage with them. The stories of the Curse are part of Shung Nang's history as much as they are a part of the rest of the legends of Innasmorn.'

'But if my ancestors are intruders,' said Ussemitus, not prepared to let this pass, 'where did they come from?'

Jubaia frowned, looking far out as if searching the distant sea for an answer. 'Ah, that is a source of mystery.'

Aru gasped. 'Through a Path? Is that what you mean, Jubaia? From another realm, just as my race has come here?'

Jubaia seemed to be uncomfortable. 'The myths are full of strange conjectures.'

Armestor snorted. 'So according to the winged beings of this city, the rest of us have no right to be here!'

Jubaia grinned at last. 'Oh yes. That is precisely how they see us. So you see how they justify stealing from us! Anything and everything. Shung Nang has become a city of staggering wealth and beauty, so it is said. The windriders thrive on contests that involve them in daring, in ever more fantastic thefts. They issue each other great challenges and seek to belittle each other with their own prowess.'

'Who rules these people?' said Ussemitus.

'The Aviatrix. The queen who few ever see. Her word is absolute law and it is believed she spends her life in communion with the wind gods of Innasmorn, from whom all power in Shung Nang is derived. She breathes the power of the wind gods into her people.'

Aru knew that the gliderboat was indeed aware of Jubaia's words; she felt sure that he was deliberately directing part of his mind to this end. It annoyed her, she began to realise, trying to rationalise her anger.

'So obsessed were the windriders,' Jubaia went on, 'that one day they issued a challenge to see who could become the master of thieves. They are a very jealous race, full of self-esteem and bombast. You can imagine how such a challenge would appeal to them. What would the ultimate theft be? They spent many weeks thinking over this, until at last they came forward with a suggestion that caught the imaginations of them all.

'The windriders, like me, like the Blue Hairs, can enter the dreams of others and steal them, or put fresh ones there. The ultimate theft would, therefore, be the theft of a dream of the Aviatrix.

'There was much debate, most of it hovering around fear. But it was agreed. And one of the windriders was daring enough to be first to make the attempt.'

'It has the ring of lunacy to me,' ventured Armestor, though he was fascinated by the tale.

'Perhaps,' smiled Jubaia. 'But you are a master of the bow, Armestor. You are modest enough to deny it, but in your heart you know it's true. Would you not respond to a challenge, a test to see just how fine a bowman you are? If you could become the finest in all Innasmorn, perhaps the finest ever known, how would that be?'

'I don't know about that,' said Armestor, looking away, but Fomond laughed aloud and clapped him on the shoulder.

'Yes, he'd like that!'

'There's pride in us all,' said Jubaia. 'And the windriders are a race who thrive on pride. It is true they are beautiful: tall, elegant, with superb balance, and when they take to the skies!'

'So you've seen them?' said Aru.

Jubaia nodded. 'I have. Majestic they are. No bird ever soared as they soar, nor mastered the winds as they do. It is no wonder they have never changed. They are perfect, or so their pride tells them.'

Ussemitus grunted. 'And what of this mad scheme to steal from their ruler?'

Jubaia snorted. 'It went wrong, of course! Though the

windrider almost won through. He entered her mind while she was oblivious, deep in communion with the gods of the air. But he was greedy and overreached himself. He was found out and taken before he could escape with his prize. It was as much to do with bad luck as bad judgement, I gather.'

'And what was the fate of this thief?' said Ussemitus.

Jubaia shook his head. 'Ah, it is a sad tale. Obviously he was discredited, for although he was much respected and honoured by his fellows for even attempting such a reckless venture, the Aviatrix decreed his punishment. She was without mercy, saying that he had endangered her life and the stability of all Shung Nang. Which he had.'

'So he was killed?' said Aru.

Jubaia shook his head. 'No, that would have been too kind. Or so the Aviatrix thought. No, he was taken before his people and his wings were cut away so that he would never again be able to fly.' Jubaia stiffened as he said this, again looking far out over the sea. 'And he was banished. Sent from the Deathless City, carried from it by six of his brethren, for there is no way to reach Shung Nang except by air, and cast on a distant shore. The last words they said to him were that if he returned to Shung Nang, he would die.'

For a long time, no one spoke. Aru felt the surge of pain from the gliderboat, as if it lamented for the things that Jubaia had told them. She turned to Ussemitus, but he was staring at Jubaia, his eyes moist with tears. And then she realised.

She sat back with a little gasp and for a moment could not speak. 'Jubaia,' she said softly.

Ussemitus nodded. 'This is your own story, little thief. Shung Nang is your city.'

Jubaia stood up, raising his tiny arms to the sky. 'Yes! Shung Nang is my city. They said I could never fly again. I had disgraced the wind gods. But I *have* flown, have I not!' He laughed and turned to them. 'Perhaps you understand now why I took such joy from the gliderboat. How I could control her as I did.'

'You had wings,' gasped Armestor.

Jubaia shrugged, managing a grin. 'Yes. But it was a long time ago, my friend. I am used to my new shape. But you see, the old habit of thievery is with me yet.' And he laughed.

Again no one knew what to say, saddened by Jubaia's tale. But he sensed their pity and quickly sought to cheer them. 'Anyway, I have told you all this for good reason. It will affect our quest.

'When I entered the dreams of the Aviatrix, and I can tell you it was as complex a system as the caverns of the Windsongs, I found myself caught in many currents. There were many secret things to be found there. I had entered a treasure trove of myths and fables, some of which are true and offer the keys to fabulous powers. It was there that I paused to learn of the great mystery of the western lands. The very lands we seek now. The lands of the World Splinter.'

'The World Splinter,' murmured Ussemitus. 'What is that?'

'It is tied to the legends we spoke of earlier, those that tell of a race of intruders. Somewhere in the far west lies a land that is protected by ancient powers and sorceries, a land where the Curse is said to have made the terrain impassable, a nightmare region. And the Curse, the black powers, all spread like waves from the World Splinter.

'This is a huge mountain,' Jubaia went on, but then shook his head. 'No, I cannot describe the thing I saw in the dreams of the Aviatrix. Let me show you.' He jumped from the rock and looked about him, suddenly finding what he sought. It was an elongated sliver of rock, its edges jagged. He made a circle in some soil, patted it down and then dug the sliver of rock into the earth at an angle so that it thrust out, leaning as if it might topple. 'There,' he said. 'A crude model. But the World Splinter is huge, thousands of feet high. And it lies in the heart of the west.'

'How did it get its name?' said Aru.

Jubaia nodded. 'As you might guess, it was part of another realm, another world, that broke off, either by accident or in some grim catastrophe, and tore through the fabric of Innasmorn to lodge here. A splinter of unimaginable proportions.'

Fomond and Armestor gazed at it, almost hypnotised. 'That's what we are searching for?' said Fomond.

Jubaia nodded. 'It houses vast powers, though what they are, I have no idea.'

'And this must be what Zellorian is searching for,' said Aru.

'Should he find it and learn to use its powers,' said Jubaia, 'he would have far more power than he would have won for himself had he controlled the deathstorm. And he could use that power to reach down into the darkness of Innasmorn. It is that which we must fear the most.'

Ussemitus rose and looked out over the land, his mind dwelling on Jubaia's disclosures. He knew of that dark, of the terrible forces that the gods of Innasmorn had recognised within their own cycle, forces that could surge up and wreak havoc if they were tapped.

'My people speak of a war of long ago,' Jubaia said. 'A terrible war of the elements, when Innasmorn rocked to storms beyond our imagining. But the darkness that threatened chaos was overcome and suppressed. Whatever powers are in the west, embodied in the World Splinter, they, too, have been suppressed. But the old darkness would use those powers if it could tap them.'

'Through Zellorian,' said Aru.

'He can have no idea what it is he will unleash.'

Ussemitus abruptly turned, his expression tired, almost defeated. 'How do we stop him? How do we even find him? We know he'll search for the World Splinter, but if it's as large as Jubaia says, we may never meet him, our paths never crossing.'

'He has allies,' said Jubaia. 'Allies that he does not even know about. They will be gathering, waiting for Zellorian's agents. And the wind gods will be watching them all.'

'Can you – talk to them?' said Armestor, and this time there was no derision in his voice.

'I can find them.'

'You spoke of allies,' said Aru. 'For Zellorian.'

Jubaia took a deep breath. 'When my people were young, when all life on Innasmorn was young, and when all races were of the flesh, as it were, the gods were divided. Some sought complete freedom, freedom to create, to control and not be controlled, to experiment, fearing nothing of the consequences. Evolution, they declared, was random, choosing its own path, its own dark genesis, finding its successes through change, often painful change. Others said this was wasteful, lacking in compassion. It was the beginning of the war, the war that shaped the evolution of Innasmorn. The power warping.

'Perhaps it would have been better had there been a compromise, with some of the gods calling to them some of the races and allowing others to go on as they had. But the wind gods pulled all races to them, insisting that if they were one with the elements they would be one with each other, unified, divine.

'A dark fury possessed the other gods. They turned the many tribes away from the wind gods and gave them powers over the earth, resisting the changes. But given such freedom, so the legends say, the people evolved into an army of the night, selfish, arrogant, disparate, always at war. Many died in their conflicts, and much harm was done to the world.

'The gods of Innasmorn argued and then clashed, and in the end the gods of the flesh were defeated, their slave peoples given a choice: relent or be smitten. Many would not give up their black pacts and were ploughed back into the earth by the fury of the storms. But most races, as I have said, evolved into the elemental powers they are today. My own race, the windriders, are another compromise. They serve the wind gods, but are of the flesh. Yet they are proud of their loyalties.'

'And the dark?' said Fomond.

'Being repressed, its slaves destroyed or converted, it sought ways to escape its shackles, for it could not be utterly destroyed. It lives yet, and is ever devious. It has had to seek even darker places for itself. But it has festered

112

like a wound, never healing, and the poison within it has worsened.'

'Then,' said Ussemitus, glancing warily at the skies, 'Innasmorn has created this evil from herself. By chaining these powers.'

'The Mother acknowledges that,' said Jubaia. 'But the powers have become corrupted beyond any reasoning now. And they are even more determined to rebel, now that you are here.'

'Man?' said Aru.

But Jubaia was looking at Ussemitus. 'Wherever your ancestors came from, it was long after my own evolved into elementals. Your people, Ussemitus, were the second wave.'

Ussemitus felt a coldness creeping over him, and could sense the fears in Fomond and Armestor gathering like a pall. 'What do you mean?'

'Your own genesis began elsewhere, beyond Innasmorn.'

'That's a lie!' snapped Armestor.

Ussemitus put a hand on him to still him. 'Is this so, Jubaia?'

'It is in the legends of Shung Nang.'

'Legends!' snorted Armestor.

'Whatever they say,' Jubaia went on, unmoved by Armestor's anger, 'we can be sure that the dark powers will use the flesh to their ends. They will seek to bend it to their will. As with Quareem, as with the renegade Blue Hairs. And as with all of our races, and of Aru's.'

'To do what?' said Ussemitus, though in his heart he already knew.

'To control Innasmorn. To harness and enslave those who rule it now. To bring down the wind gods.'

Around them the air moaned softly and they looked up as though shapes would drift down from it, guardians of the great powers of old. But the skies were clear, the wind soft.

'Zellorian has no idea what he taps,' said Jubaia. 'He is in danger of being used. Just as Vittargattus was.'

Aru was frowning. 'But Vittargattus was being used to

113

attack the Sculpted City. My people. Zellorian. Why should these powers work against each other?'

'A pretty paradox,' grinned Jubaia. 'For a war between Man and the Vaza nations would destroy many of them. But it would be a selective slaughter. The faithful to the elements would die, as would those of your own people, Aru, who would not bow to the dark powers of Innasmorn. Victory would go to those who sold themselves to the dark. A union forged between the survivors, a union forged in blood and earth. And a new army to begin a bloodier crusade here on Innasmorn.'

Ussemitus was again sitting, his chin resting in his hands as he listened to Jubaia's grave words. The others turned to him, sensing his unease.

'It seems hopeless,' murmured Aru.

To her surprise, Ussemitus reached out and took her hand. 'No, not hopeless,' he said softly. 'We each of us have a gift. From whom? Gods? Who knows? I certainly possess powers of which I once knew nothing. As does Jubaia. And you, Aru. Your mind is not closed.'

'Armestor has his skill with the bow,' grinned Fomond. 'But what do I have?'

Ussemitus smiled at him. 'Your spirit, I suspect. Whatever it is, Fomond, it is part of us, and vital to us.'

'You sense something else in us?' said Jubaia.

Ussemitus shrugged. 'A greater purpose? Perhaps. You have said that the dark powers seek to move through the flesh. I doubt if they move through us, but perhaps other powers do –'

Jubaia screwed up his face. 'We dare not be complacent. The darkness will tempt us, test us, believe me.'

'But the Mother will protect us.'

'Let us pray so,' nodded Jubaia.

'It is strange,' Ussemitus went on. 'If what you have told us is true, the wind gods turned aside from the flesh and transformed the people of Innasmorn into elemental beings. If we are the second wave, as you have called us, why should the same wind gods seek to help us? Are we so different?'

'Yes, why?' said Aru. 'How are the Vaza different from your ancestors, Jubaia?'

'If you are not truly native to Innasmorn, children of some other world, there must be something.'

'But what?' persisted Aru.

Jubaia merely shook his head. 'Perhaps we will discover this on our journey.'

As they prepared for a new flight in the gliderboat, they thought over this and the other mysteries Jubaia had set before them.

'So what is it to be?' called Ussemitus as Jubaia studied the land from another high vantage point. 'How do we get to the west?'

When Jubaia came down to the others, he wore an even graver expression and had become the troubled creature he had been before. 'Ah, yes. The west. Getting there will be very difficult. Crossing the ocean will be bad enough. But after that – '

'The lands are dangerous, we know that,' agreed Ussemitus.

'Yes, but in order to reach the World Splinter, we have to win the key that will unlock the way through its guardians. We cannot merely fly there, nor walk.'

'And where is this key?' said Aru.

'In Shung Nang, the Deathless City.'

The others gazed at Jubaia in uniform amazement.

He nodded. 'The Aviatrix. Many of the secrets of the Mother are hers. She guards the key to the door of the World Splinter jealously, knowing that there are great powers there that could be harmful to Innasmorn. And only she has the key.'

Fomond groaned. 'You mean you will go back and attempt what you once attempted before?'

Jubaia flinched. 'Attempted. Oh yes. Yes, that is what I must do.'

'That's madness,' said Armestor.

Jubaia shook his head. 'If we do not secure the key, we will never find the World Splinter. We have to thwart the powers that have been set to guard it.'

'And Zellorian?' said Aru. 'How does he expect to reach this place if he, too, does not have a key?'

Jubaia shuddered as though a cold wind had passed through him. 'The powers that guard this place are moulded from darkness, slave to the wind gods. But who knows what alliances they might form, given an opportunity?'

'Jubaia,' said Ussemitus calmly. 'Is there a reasonable chance of your stealing this key?'

The little being laughed softly. 'Ah, but this time they will be completely off their guard. They would never expect me to return to Shung Nang. They do not know that I can ride through the air, as well as any of them.' He looked across at the gliderboat.

'And we have powers,' said Aru, nudging Ussemitus.

In spite of himself, he laughed. 'Such confidence!'

'For the time being,' said Jubaia, 'we ought to be going. I'd sooner have a roof over my head tonight than spend a night in the lands below.'

'They look no more hostile than our forests at home,' said Fomond.

'That's what concerns me,' grunted Jubaia, the first to board the gliderboat.

Aru felt its suffusion of warmth as the little being settled himself in its prow. She sat beside him, aware of his hunger to take control of it again, though she was only too glad to let him have his way. She felt a degree of inner warmth herself, in spite of the strange things she had learned about Innasmorn. She put her hand to her neck, realising as she did so that she had imagined the eyes of Ussemitus on her. She yet felt the warmth of his hand where he had gripped hers in reassurance. Or had it been more than that? But she pushed the thought away, telling herself that if he discovered it by reading her mind – but the thought dissolved as she realised that it disturbed her more than it did him.

TRANSFORMATION

Zellorian looked through the soldier who stood before him, not seeing him. The man kept perfectly still and had been standing rigidly to attention throughout his report. It was remarkable, Zellorian thought, how he had managed to control his nerves, his fear. The best of the soldiers had not, after all, been destroyed in the Csendook wars. There was good material here yet.

Eventually Zellorian nodded, having digested the report, which had not pleased him, and the soldier dismissed himself, closing the door as he went. Only after he had gone did Zellorian's face alter. He swore, striding to his desk and sitting at it in fresh concentration.

There was one other person in the room, a short man dressed in the white robes of a Consul: he sniffed and continued to gaze out of the window at the mist that gathered over the Sculpted City.

'That's the fifth report I've had since my return from the west,' said Zellorian. 'And every one of them reports defections. Men leaving the Sculpted City to go east into the unknown mountain regions.'

'To Gannatyne. Yes, Prime Consul, but Gannatyne is a prisoner. He has been banished. And he does not have the heart for rebellion.'

'Maybe not, but Consul Pyramors has. He's behind this. You know that well enough, Onando.'

The Consul bowed, light striking his peculiarly pale face. It seemed bloodless, deficient, though his eyes were alive, almost mesmeric, his body fat, his hands fleshy, as white as his remarkable face. 'There is an undercurrent of ill-will towards the Imperator, it is true,' he said cautiously. 'Since the fall of Gannatyne, there has been a degree of unrest.'

'Trained men have left this city,' said Zellorian. 'A few

hundred of them. Where are they? Hiding in the eastern mass, beyond Gannatyne's retreat?'

Onando shrugged. He had waited a long time to get this close to the Prime Consul, the man who wielded more power than any other and who, Onando knew, was the master of other dark powers that most men would not even have dreamed of. His own hunger for such things had driven fear out of him in his attempt to move closer to the Prime Consul. And since the apparently disastrous events in the west, where it was rumoured Zellorian had suffered some sort of defeat at the hands of the Innasmornians, Zellorian had been gathering as many supporters to his side as he could. His unease at internal strife had sharpened.

'I am sure, Prime Consul, that any deserters are wasting their energies in leaving us. Gannatyne is quite secure in the stronghold in the mountains. He is well guarded, and those who do guard him – '

'Don't lecture me,' snapped Zellorian. 'I know the situation. I want to know what is being done about Consul Pyramors.'

The rebuke slipped off Onando like water across oil. 'He has his own supporters, but few of my fellow Consuls are foolish enough to pay more than lip service to him.'

'You are quite sure of that?'

Onando bowed. 'Indeed, sire. I have spoken to many of them, and have tried to inveigle my way into their confidence. Some have been quite open about their fears. They do not want to see the City riven by dispute. And they have no desire to communicate with the Innasmornians. Others do, but will not have a rebellion at any price. Very few would openly oppose you and the Imperator.'

'You understand how careful I must be, Onando, in how I deal with the insurgents. Knives in the dark, disappearances, are no longer possible in the main. Besides, Pyramors protects himself thoroughly. He has an excellent network.'

'I have failed to breach it, sire, and I am not without skill in such matters.'

Zellorian frowned at him, but then nodded. It was true.

Onando did have ability when it came to finding out what went on in the Sculpted City, down to its lowest gutters. The fat Consul was unscrupulous and quite cold-blooded about such matters. But he was known too well: any direct approach to some of the Consulate would have met with silence.

'What is Pyramors planning? Would he dare attempt assassination?'

Onando dabbed at his white face with a silk kerchief. 'Oh, I think not. Not yet, at least. He would not find anyone to employ in such a role.'

'Not from within the city, no. But from outside it? What about the Innasmornians?'

Onando raised his brows. 'I know little of them, sire. I am sure your own knowledge – '

Zellorian silenced him with a cold stare. But after a moment he relaxed. 'Yes, I've had dealings with them. I made the mistake of underestimating them. And the Casruel bitch.'

'Could Pyramors be in contact with her?'

'It is possible. But even so, I cannot imagine how Pyramors could turn it to his advantage in the city.'

'I am certain, Prime Consul, that there can be very few Innasmornians here, in secret. As your reports have pointed out, people are leaving the city, not coming into it. I can arrange for spies to be secreted amongst any other soldiers who might be leaving. I'm sure I can find a few traitors.'

Zellorian grunted. 'See to it at once. And have reports sent to me as soon as you can get them back from wherever these scum are hiding.'

'And you, sire? Will you be going westward again?' Onando's voice dripped with curiosity.

Zellorian could smell it on him, the lust for power, the desire for the unknown things that Innasmorn might be able to give him. He shook his head. 'Not yet. Pyramors was very active during my last absence. If I should leave the Sculpted City again now, he might consider it an opportunity to strike at me, or the Imperator. I want this canker cut out!'

Onando waited patiently. He was here to serve, for in that he would grow stronger. If he could uncover a way of destroying Pyramors, ah, then he would be truly rewarded. But for the moment he would be content to take whatever responsibilities were meted out to him.

'The Casruel girl must be found,' said Zellorian suddenly. 'She has made contact with the Innasmornians and there are certain skills they have that could be dangerous to us.'

'Do you wish me to organise an expedition to the west?'

Zellorian shook his head. 'No. I want you to use your networks in the city to make contact with any remaining Casruel knights, or anyone connected to the family. There must be some. Gain their confidences. Find out everything you can about what they do, what they say, what they feel. If a Casruel breathes, I want to know about it.'

'And you, Prime Consul?'

'I will be here. I'll make that clear to the entire city.'

Onando bowed and was about to shuffle away, but Zellorian called him back.

'Tell me,' he asked, 'are you aware of any weaknesses Pyramors might have? Anything at all. Speak your mind.'

It was something Onando had already considered. 'He is a most careful man, Prime Consul. He may not be without sin, but I am sure there is nothing we could use against him. Unless you wish to trap him as you trapped Gannatyne.'

But Zellorian shook his head thoughtfully. 'It would be dangerous to try such a ploy again. And it might undo what we achieved the first time.'

'He has no significant weaknesses,' said Onando. 'Unless you include his sadness.' Onando had come back to the centre of the room.

'He is troubled? By what? Gannatyne's fall?'

'That is a small matter, I think, compared to his sorrow at the loss of his woman.'

Zellorian's eyes narrowed. 'Explain this.'

'Pyramors once had a woman. She was named Jannovar.

It was before the exodus from our own worlds. I have heard that their love was particularly strong. A great passion – '

Zellorian snorted impatiently as if Onando was wasting his time.

But the Consul went on. 'It is said that Pyramors was besotted with her and that there was nothing he would not do for her. She was his obsession. And some say that she remains so.'

'Where is she?'

'Lost, or dead. Left behind.'

'Where?'

'She was the wife of a commander whose force was left to protect our crossing from Eannor. Thus she was parted from Pyramors and, like many others, never came here.'

'And he broods over this?'

'Not openly, Prime Consul. But he has not taken a woman to his bed since coming here. The loss of Jannovar is his great burden.'

'So for all he knows, the woman may yet be alive?'

Onando nodded. 'Somewhere beyond Innasmorn. Lost to him forever.'

Zellorian got up and paced slowly about as he thought. 'I imagine that Pyramors would give much to win this woman back, if it were possible.'

Onando grinned, though there was little humour in his eyes. 'His soul, sire, if he possessed one.'

Zellorian stopped pacing. 'His honour, his position?'

Onando shrugged. 'That, too. But surely the woman is lost – '

'But if he could have her back,' Zellorian went on, 'he would give everything for her. His political freedom.'

'As I said, Prime Consul, Jannovar was his obsession.'

Zellorian nodded a final time. 'Very well. I will give the matter some thought. You may leave.'

Onando bowed and left the chamber, delighted that he had been able to present his master with information that the Prime Consul evidently valued greatly. And there was work to do now, a great deal of it. Onando smiled to himself, enjoying his trade, the intrigue, the scent of blood, for there would be blood spilled in this issue. And for every drop of it he would advance another step.

Zellorian relaxed when the fat Consul had gone. His side ached where he had been wounded by the Innasmornian arrow; the best surgery had not made it entirely whole. But he had made no show of his discomfort to Onando. He thought for a short time only about the Consul's last words, searching his own memory for the name Jannovar, which seemed to mean something, but which eluded him. If she were alive – but she was beyond reach.

He was still thinking about the name as he left his chambers and went down into the lower parts of the citadel, to the corridors where he had set his own guards to watch carefully. It was a dismal place, cut deep into the bedrock of the mountain. No one else came there, except occasionally by accident, but they were calmly and politely moved on by Zellorian's watchful soldiers.

He admitted himself to a particular chamber. It was cut from the stone, a little cold, its lighting poor. There was almost no furniture and unlike other rooms, no plants. Stretched on a cot was a single figure, beside it a tray of food which had gone cold, untouched.

Zellorian sat in the only chair and studied the figure. It was a man, and he seemed to be asleep, but Zellorian knew he was not. Presently the eyes opened. They were ringed with pain, the lines of the face drawn in suffering. With a great effort, the man heaved himself to his elbows. He was unshaven, his neck and upper chest exposed, the skin blotched, drawn and puckered like that of a very old man, though this man was not old at all.

He peered across at Zellorian, opening his lips as if to speak, but a sound like pain came out.

'How are your wounds?' said Zellorian, though there was no need to ask. The man was severely crippled. He tried to rise but sank back.

'*They are killing me,*' rasped the voice.

'Your mind refuses to accept that you could be healed.'

'I was a warrior!' snarled the wretch suddenly, flinging up an arm. Beneath it the trunk of his body was emaciated,

122

a series of wounds that had been sewn up carefully, showing like white lines across him.

'You could be again – '

'*No!* Never. I might walk, even run. But I could never be what I was. I don't want anything less, Zellorian. If I cannot be what I was, then finish me. Do it now. *Here!*' Again he tried to rise, but fell back, exhausted by his efforts.

'It would be such a cruel end,' said Zellorian, his face utterly impassive, no trace of his feelings showing.

'The only thing that would give me any pleasure now would be to see the heads of the creatures who did this to me,' said the wounded man, his eyes widening as if he could see the very thing he had asked for.

'You think I am not pursuing them?'

The man glared at him, no fear in him any more. 'You'll go back? To that chaos?'

Zellorian shook his head. 'I dare not leave the Sculpted City at this time. My enemies are active here. If I were to leave again, they would work harder for my downfall.'

'Then the Innasmornians will be free. And their powers will grow against you and the Imperator.'

'No,' said Zellorian. 'I'll hunt them. Wouldn't you like to hunt them, too, Vymark? For what they have done to you?'

Vymark tried to speak, but he suddenly shook, the tears rolling down his cheeks, his body heaving with great sobs. Zellorian waited patiently. He had seen this many times in the former warrior. But it was necessary. Vymark had to be prepared, conditioned, for what was to follow.

'You cannot expect to live many years,' he told him when he had at last brought himself under control.

'I am as one already dead,' said Vymark, the words barely audible. 'You should have left me there to die when the arrow took me. The arrow that was meant for you – '

'I know that. But I have kept you alive for good reason, Vymark. Your work is far from over.'

'You mock me.'

'No. I am offering you the one thing you crave most.

Your revenge. A chance to destroy the Casruel bitch and her allies.'

Vymark eyed him desperately, but he shook his head. It was not possible.

'You were my most loyal warrior,' Zellorian told him. 'And you took the arrow meant for me, as you said. For that I will give you power. Power that few are fortunate enough to attain.'

Vymark's feverish mind worked with the possibilities. Zellorian was as much a sorcerer as a scientist. What powers did he have? Vymark knew that he could only guess at the things Zellorian might achieve. Was there any way out of this living nightmare?

'You must trust me,' said Zellorian softly.

Slowly Vymark reached out with his bony hand, his fingers reaching for Zellorian's sleeve. The touch through the fabric was as cold as that of a corpse. 'Yes. I served you well. Serve me well now, Prime Consul.'

Zellorian rose and left. It was time to prepare Vymark. His mind was as conditioned as it was ever likely to be. If it was to work for him, it would have to be soon.

Vymark gazed into the shadows beyond his cot, seeing in them the twisted faces of the elemental beings who had attacked him and his master in the Dhumvald, the western mountains where they had tried to raise and control the deathstorm. Those whirling, maniacal creatures of Innasmorn had invaded Vymark's dreams night after night since the disaster, and he wondered if at last he was to have surcease from them.

Zellorian did not return to the room quickly, but when he did come, he had two others with him. They were strange warriors, their thin bodies sheathed in mesh, their heads masked in steel, their hands also gloved in steel.

'What are these?' said Vymark, fear suddenly clawing at him.

The two warriors lifted him as easily as they would have lifted a new-born child.

Zellorian smiled. 'Good servants, Vymark. Clear your mind of fear. Gather its strength. You will need it. I will put power into it, but it will be stronger than the strongest wine you have ever tasted. There will be confusion, but at the end, absolute clarity. And a new kind of strength.'

Vymark glanced fearfully at the automatons as they took him from the room in absolute silence. Were they made from metal or from flesh?

'Thank you,' sighed Vymark, and for a moment he felt a surge of emotion, of deep gratitude.

Zellorian watched him as they carried him down the winding tunnel, deeper into the secret bowels of the mountain, though he was as silent and expressionless as the two servants.

The cavern was brightly lit from above, its convex ceiling curving symmetrically away into the distance, its contours never failing to please the eye of Zellorian as he studied it. So much of the art of the scientist had survived the crossing, and here, at least, some of his best servants thrived. He looked down from the balcony into the nearest of the glider-boat beds. A dozen constructors were working busily, though they made little sound. Lights blazed and fizzed occasionally, and there were equally sudden bursts of noise, of metal scraped on metal, but otherwise the beds were peaceful. Wires ran down into them like arteries, curling up singly or in thickly-banded clusters, and huge domes pulsed with inner light like transparent organs taken from some unimaginable leviathan.

At Zellorian's elbow, Artificer Wyarne watched the beds with equal interest, almost parental in its intensity.

'Five new craft within the next few days,' he said proudly. 'I have already commissioned Controllers for them.'

'Good. Let me know as soon as they are ready,' said Zellorian.

Wyarne cleared his throat, looking away. He was a tall, hunched man, his face long, lined with years of strain that could never be erased, even though he was devoted to his work on the gliderboats, his children as he called them.

Zellorian knew that what they had suffered here on Innasmorn was eating away at Wyarne like an illness.

'Sire,' said the Artificer hesitantly, 'have you given thought to the idea we spoke about – ?'

'Protection for the craft?' said Zellorian. 'Yes. I am ready to try an experiment. As you are aware, I've been far across Innasmorn and I've tasted first hand the elements of this world. What destroys our gliderboats can also be used to enhance them. I'm certain of that.' Quareem had taught him much, though he had not yet passed any of this dark knowledge on to the Artificer. He was not afraid of doing so, for Wyarne was only too pleased to serve Zellorian, with a fanatic's zeal. Zellorian had done everything in his power to advance the use of the gliderboats.

'This world has already killed a number of gliderboats,' said Wyarne bitterly, his hands wringing themselves in illsuppressed frustration. 'The fleet, such as it is, is almost grounded. Restricted by the boundaries of the city, unable to travel far beyond them – '

'Necessary precautions,' said Zellorian. 'For the while, at least. Your craft are essential to the future of our race.'

'Yes, of course, Prime Consul,' said Wyarne, again glowing with pride.

'I wish to attempt an experiment. If I am able to utilise the power of Innasmorn properly, then our gliderboats will work *with* the winds here and not against them.'

Wyarne looked delighted. 'Excellent, sire. If I might suggest the craft there, in bed five – '

Zellorian shook his head. 'No. I am more interested in the one that you are working on for me personally.'

Wyarne's smile evaporated. 'But sire, there is so much to be done – '

'There are difficulties?'

The Artificer swallowed hard. 'In a manner of speaking, sire. As you know, it is not always possible to create what we desire. Some craft are never completed in view of the immense pressures put on the minds, the trauma – '

Zellorian grasped the Artificer's thin arm. 'What are you telling me, that my craft is to be terminated?'

'No, no. But if you wish to experiment – '

'Without protection, it will be useless. As will all our craft. So either we experiment, or we terminate the entire programme now.'

Wyarne's eyes widened. He knew it would be utterly pointless to argue with the Prime Consul. 'Of course, sire.'

'Take me to it.'

They walked in silence through the beds to a chamber that had been sectioned off from the others. The lighting had been dimmed, scores of coiled wires looping into it, from overhead and from the walls, as though they were entering the entrails of a great beast. A number of mesh-clad constructors moved about, stepping aside as their visitors approached. In the centre of the chamber was the gliderboat bed, a sunken pen, where the wires converged. Many of them were translucent and the passage of fluid could be seen through them, flowing in and out of the tank in the sunken bed.

Zellorian leaned over the tank. A partially constructed gliderboat was below, the top half of it not yet fitted, or grafted, for the craft was more of a living organism than a metal object. As Zellorian watched, one of the robotic constructors appeared from within the hull, and in its hands it carried a pulpy mass, dripping blood, that could have been a fusion of human organs. The constructor bent down, working with his grisly offering within the body of the craft.

'It is almost complete,' said Wyarne, again pleased. 'As you requested, sire, I have not commissioned a Controller for it.'

'You will not require one.'

'I fail to understand, sire – '

Zellorian did not take his eyes from the sleek lines of the gliderboat. It looked superb, a perfect job. Wyarne had surpassed himself with it, just as Zellorian had hoped. 'I will control this craft myself. To the exclusion of all others.'

'You intend to go out over Innasmorn?'

'No. Perhaps in the future. But I want to be able to control this craft from *here*, in the Sculpted City. I want to be able to send it far to the west. I want it to be my eyes and ears.'

Wyarne listened, his own eyes searching a distant horizon, as if crystallising Zellorian's vision.

'Do this for me,' said the Prime Consul.

Wyarne nodded slowly. 'It was in my mind so to develop the gliderboats, sire.'

'This one only. No other. Not yet.'

'As you wish, sire. With you as its Controller –'

'It will have the protection it needs. I have that power.'

Wyarne straightened, a head taller than Zellorian. 'It will be a triumph, sire –'

Zellorian nodded. 'When the craft is ready, we shall see.'

They spent the next hour inspecting other craft, and Wyarne talked animatedly about modifications he was making, and about progress he had made in the communications of the craft. Zellorian let him speak, listening to the dissertation patiently, noting each new development in silence but with growing satisfaction. With the new powers fused into them, the gliderboats would be a powerful force on Innasmorn, more than a match for its people.

At length Wyarne announced that Zellorian's gliderboat was ready, and they returned to its private bed. The shell had been fitted to it and the craft looked even more sleek than it had before.

'Wake it,' said Zellorian.

Wyarne bowed and went down in to the bed. Zellorian did not see what he did, but the gliderboat trembled, and in his mind he felt a sudden flare of pain, anger almost. Just as at the moment of birth of human kind, the awakening of a gliderboat was a traumatic moment. Zellorian could already feel the mental thrashing of the thing below him, the surge upward from darkness to light and pain, utter confusion. He was drawn into it for a moment, and as he felt himself caught in the churning sensation, he felt Wyarne also struggling, like a man flung overboard during a storm. But Zellorian's mind took control of the situation firmly, directing the wild release of energy, channelling it, forging it into a coherent pattern.

The chaos began to die down, as if the gliderboat was being pulled towards sleep, relaxation.

'Do you hear me?' Zellorian asked it.

Wyarne had climbed from the bed, shaking himself, his mind clearing of the emotional maelstrom. He sank down, watching Zellorian with awe. The fury of the birth had been unique, like a storm, a mirror of the elements reputed to be beyond the Sculpted City.

Somewhere deep in the darkness of the gliderboat's mind there was a response. A cry for help, one almost of despair.

'Do you hear me?' Zellorian asked again.

Then, like a man reaching under water and finding a hand, he gripped and tugged with his mind. And there was an answer. He pulled the response upward, through layers of agony, uncertainty and fear.

I hear you.

'Then you are reborn.'

What have you done to me?

They all asked this, but Zellorian almost recoiled at the ferocity of the anger. But that was good, he told himself. He would use that, point it, aim it where it would do the most hurt to his enemies.

'There is more to be done yet,' he told the gliderboat. 'I feel your power. But when you take to the air, you will have far more. Prepare yourself for it. Once the testing is over, you'll drink deep of this power. You will be like a god, lord of the heavens.'

Zellorian moved away, ignoring the sounds of anger that still welled up. He walked past the exhausted Artificer. As he left the chamber, readying himself for the final act of preparing the gliderboat, he saw the remains of the corpse, the thing that had once been Vymark, the mortal flesh, now no more than a shell of discarded bone and tissue.

10

STORMWEAVE

It seemed that they would never find their way out of the mountainous dunes which rose up on all sides, steep and crumbling, an infinity of little hills that had created a maze where the unwary could wander until exhaustion or possibly madness claimed them. There seemed to be no track or path, and merely skirting the wide, sliding bases of the dunes was so circuitous that it served only to confuse further the sense of direction.

Even so, Jubaia insisted they were close to the outlet, beyond which there was, he persisted in telling the others, a long stretch of beach that swept on to the small town of Kelpoora. Fomond grunted something about this terrain being the most unsuitable imaginable in which to build a town, but Jubaia merely smiled, secure in his knowledge.

They had deliberately left the gliderboat at the edge of the forest area, which stretched between the foothills and the reeds before the vast dunelands. Jubaia did not want to arouse the suspicions of the inhabitants of Kelpoora, nor their greed, for he said they were, like his own people, particularly acquisitive. Kelpoora, was, in fact, a pirate port, home of smugglers, slavers, thieves, all the characters that Jubaia respected most. That he knew so much about them and their ways had finally convinced the company that he would find a way through the dune maze. The gliderboat had been secured in the forest, with Armestor left to guard it. He had been quite content to remain in the stunted trees, waiting for the outcome of his companions' visit to the pirate town.

The company emerged from the maze and stood at the edge of the beach that swept away in a great curve before them, the sand a shimmering gold, the sea whispering across its edge as gently as the ripples of a lake.

'Surely this is not the Ocean of Hurricanes?' said Fomond.

Jubaia screwed up his face. 'Oh yes. She is a wily one. This is how she woos the unwary to her breast. A calm sky, gulls wheeling lazily. Waves that hardly seem to stir. When they do, they breathe seductively. Tranquillity. But, should you venture out without proper care, ah, then you see the other side of her face! She is a cruel one. But the people of Kelpoora love her for all her vices. They see in her a reflection of their own restlessness, their contempt for others.'

Aru winced. 'You keep mentioning the nature of these people, Jubaia. Are you sure we will be welcome?'

Jubaia tapped his nose and winked. 'I have friends here.'

'Sometimes,' said Ussemitus, 'I think you must be several lifetimes old. There can be few places on Innasmorn you do not have friends.'

Jubaia shook his head. 'I'm not made welcome everywhere.'

They laughed at that, glad to be out of the huge dunes, their stifling heat, and soon were moving along the upper reach of the beach, the sand dry and less shifting. In the dunes it had dragged at their feet, but here they were able to walk in comfort.

'We would have been made extremely welcome here if we had arrived in the gliderboat,' Jubaia went on. 'But we would have lost her within the hour. Such a prize!'

He had argued this a number of times on the way over the forest, saying that to have brought the craft too close to Kelpoora would have invited disaster. And he would not hear of the craft being flown over the Ocean of Hurricanes. The hunger in that particularly lady, he promised, was far more voracious than that of the Kelpoori.

Aru had argued against leaving the craft, but again allowed Jubaia to convince her that his plan was better. 'We must show ourselves to those we wish to use,' he had said. 'If we charter a ship, we will have to let its captain know who we are. We can arrange for a rendezvous with the craft, though the captain may suspect a trap.'

'Then I'll remain with the craft and meet you later – '

'No, we'll need you in the town,' he had insisted.

'Why?'

He had looked mildly embarrassed and at once Fomond and Ussemitus had scowled at him, thinking that here was yet more deviousness showing itself.

'Well,' he had said hesitantly, 'the Kelpoori are slavers. If we had you with us, lady, we could pass you off as a prize we had won – '

'What! I'm not going to be humiliated – '

He had shaken his head violently. 'No, no! A pretense. You do not have to be roped. Merely act a part. We are a group of freebooters making our way to the west, where we will sell you for a fine price. Your rare beauty would – '

'I don't like this,' Ussemitus had said. 'If Aru is so valuable, what is to stop these people trying to abduct her?'

'They won't,' Jubaia had insisted. 'Kelpoora would never have survived if they acted that way. They have their codes.'

'But you fear for the safety of the gliderboat!' Fomond had pointed out.

Jubaia had looked acutely embarrassed. 'Ah, well, there are some prizes that would tempt the morals of a god – '

His discomfort had, ironically, made them all laugh, and to the surprise of the Innasmornians, Aru had capitulated. Strangely, she had felt something within her, a response to Jubaia's suggestions, and it had seemed as though the gliderboat itself had put it there. Thus is had been agreed that Armestor would watch over the craft, which would be fetched once a bargain had been struck in Kelpoora.

Now they could see the misty outline of the town. It had been built on a dark green outcrop of rock that pushed up through the sand as if it had no business to be there, glistening in the sunlight, thick with seaweed. The town itself was built from other materials, a combination of shell, wood and other plant life, a bizarre hybrid that matched perfectly the qualities of the residents, so Jubaia avowed.

As they approached the town, walking across a wide stretch of beach where there was not an inch of cover, they saw a gate in the town open and riders emerging. These galloped furiously towards them as though intent on charging them down, but the three riders swerved at the last moment, circling the company on their tiny ponies. These beasts were slender, but with huge feet, spread to make travel over the soft sand easier, and they snorted like forest predators, their eyes livid. The riders were no bigger than Ussemitus and Fomond, though their skins were far darker, bronzed by exposure to the open spaces of the beaches and seas. They carried short swords, though these were not cast in metal but seemed to be made from some other hard substance. They eyed the metal swords of the travellers with ill-concealed interest.

'What is your business?' called one of them, his voice indifferent.

'I have friends in the dockways,' said Jubaia. He took something from one of his many concealed pouches and tossed it towards the rider. It flashed in the air and the rider snatched at it and caught it with stunning precision.

He examined it, eyes widening, then quickly slipped it away inside his ragged shirt. 'Traders?' he said simply.

'Going west.'

The rider twisted and looked up at the calm heavens, but he shook his head. 'Not for a few days, friend. She's getting ready for a tantrum. No one is putting out.'

Jubaia nodded. 'Then we'll take lodgings until we can charter.'

The rider examined the company, his eyes fixed on Aru for a long time, but she kept her head down, mastering her fury and acting the part she had been given. Ussemitus stood close beside her; she had told him if there was any trouble, she would use her concealed sword. He had laughed softly, but had promised that he would never be more than a step away. Fomond, too, kept very near at hand.

Satisfied, the three riders wheeled, spurring away back to the town.

When Jubaia and his companions reached the gates, they

stood open, though as soon as they had passed within, they closed again, great bolts being slipped noisily into place.

There was little activity in this part of the town, and what people were here busily moved about, suggesting that they were preparing to shelter from the promised storm. Aru was surprised, for the weather had been particularly pleasant, but she knew better than to question the Innasmornians about its temperament. Ussemitus whispered to her that he also felt something gathering out across the Ocean of Hurricanes.

Jubaia led them down through the narrowest of streets, the extraordinary jumble of buildings that seemed to have been thrown together in a hurry, almost as if the sea itself had cast up a mountain of flotsam and jetsam that the people had assembled in a parody of a town. There were, indeed, broken ships and spars among the housing, some upended, their keels now roofs, others broken in half, while in still other places there were what appeared to be giant sponges, hard as stone, with numerous windows, and in other streets walls that were studded with shells. The sandy floor of the town was littered with such shells, some of which were as tiny as the sand particles, others which were like great plates. The largest were the size of small rooms, incorporated into the houses, along with glittering banks of coral.

Jubaia led his companions to the dockways, as he called them, a system of canal-like openings into the seaward side of the town, where the water was deep, constantly sloshing up against the base rock. Various ships bobbed up and down on the waves, none of them very large, and Aru gaped at the shape of some of them, which seemed even more unusual than the houses. There were beautifully sleek craft, low in the water and built, it seemed, for speed, while others looked as though they should never have floated at all, bulky and overweight, with immense spars hanging low in the water. She said nothing. The craft, obviously, had been constructed to suit the whims of the strange seas beyond. Their waters heaved, the horizon narrowed by banks of mist, the clouds curdling overhead out of nothing. Over everything hung the pungent reek of weed.

Aru turned from the mesmeric pull of the waters, sure now that some sort of storm would erupt.

Along the quays of the dockways there were innumerable taverns, and Jubaia chose a particular one, ducking low under its beamed doorway, gesturing for his colleagues to join him. They stooped and entered, and it was with an effort that Aru kept her head down in the manner she had been practising. There were not many people in the narrow room, but all were staring at her, their gazes blatant, their fascination open and intense. All were Innasmornians of slight build, all with the weatherbeaten skin that the riders beyond the gate had had. They swigged at their jars of beer, several of them coming across to the company.

'What's the Mother tossed up on the shore today?' said one of them, a pot-bellied being with teeth that were too big for his mouth. His beard was full, stained with beer, his wide eyes slightly out of focus, suggesting he had been in the tavern for some considerable time.

'My name is Jubaia,' said the little thief and went on to introduce his companions. 'And this woman is our prize.'

Aru steeled herself to look at the floor.

'Where'd ya get her?' snorted the fat Kelpoori. 'Never seen a woman so *tall*. And fat with it.'

It took all Aru's self-control to keep from kicking the fat slob's feet out from under him. *Fat?* No man had ever called her fat.

'Got her way over Thunderreach,' said Jubaia. 'In the lands beyond the Vaza forests. These lads are Vaza themselves. Fetch them drinks! They're difficult when insulted.'

Ussemitus's brows raised, but the men in the tavern laughed good-naturedly.

'We're none of us happy when our jars are empty!' laughed the fat one, wiping his mouth on his sleeve. 'Let's see to it for you.' He sent one of his companions to the bar and drinks were soon provided. 'Bound for where?'

'Umtar,' said Jubaia, following the line he had already planned with his companions. 'Up the river and beyond

135

to the tribes who enjoy such unusual gifts,' he added, indicating Aru with the skilled practice of a merchant who had sold scores of women into slavery.

'She'll fetch an excellent price,' the fat man belched. 'You haven't considered selling her here in Kelpoora? Why trouble yourself with a difficult voyage across the Ocean of Hurricanes? I know someone who'll pay you handsomely. Not as much as you'd get in remote Umtar, it's true, but then, he has his own profits to consider.' The fat man guided them expertly to a corner of the room and they sat.

Ussemitus and Fomond sipped at the beer, a thick brew that seemed to have been concocted from the all-pervasive weed. They found it disgusting but did not say so. Jubaia swigged at his as though it was nectar, listening with apparent avidity to his rough companion.

'I'm Corvash,' said the latter, and a number of his own companions draped themselves over the benches around him there, Ussemitus could see, to keep other interested parties at bay while these discussions took place. And they were Corvash's henchmen, that was clear.

'And I serve Stormweave,' said the fat seaman. 'You've heard of him?'

Jubaia eyes lit up and he clapped his hands. 'Of course! Who has not heard of the illustrious captain?'

'More guts than a dockfull of pirates,' snorted Corvash. 'And none fairer. You'll not get a better price from any trader if you've a prize worth selling. Which you have.' He made to pat Aru's arm, but Fomond moved gently, his own arm blocking the way. He looked straight into the bloodshot eyes of Corvash, who for a moment looked angered, but then he laughed loudly, calling for more beer.

'I'll not part with the girl here,' said Jubaia pleasantly.

'You haven't heard Stormweave's offer.'

'You haven't heard the price.'

Ussemitus and Fomond listened in fascination as the argument began, the haggling, the threats, the curses, until at last, exasperated, Corvash sat back with a belch that shook the beer jars.

'Storm and waves! You're a stubborn little bastard, Jubaia! There's no reasoning with you.'

Jubaia bowed, not in the least intimidated. 'I have enjoyed our discourse. You argue your master's case well. Stormweave should be proud of you. But take consolation from the fact that I am not in Kelpoora to sell. Not to anyone. The girl is for the Lord of Umtar. I will accept bids from him personally, and no other.'

Corvash rose. 'Well enough.' He seemed no longer interested. 'And I've other business. Securing the craft for the storm. You've lodgings?'

Jubaia nodded. 'There is a place I always use. I am quite well known in the ratways.'

Corvash's bushy brows rose. 'Is that so? Well, you're a dark one, little trader. If you have friends there, you're in good hands.' He leaned across the table, meaning to whisper, though his voice was loud enough for Ussemitus and Fomond to hear him. 'But a man could spend a dozen lifetimes finding his way across the Ocean of Hurricanes.' He stood up, bowed awkwardly, then swept away, his men following, and the door to the tavern banged behind him.

Jubaia grinned, but his companions were glaring at him. 'I almost put my boot in his fat gut,' snorted Aru.

Fomond tried not to laugh. 'Ironic that *he* should have thought you fat.' But his smile died as he saw the look of fury on her face.

Ussemitus touched Jubaia's arm. 'You provoked him. We have an enemy there. Why did you get involved?' Ussemitus kept his voice low, his own irritation under tight control.

Jubaia looked around him calmly. Several of the men watched his group, but no one else made a move to join it. 'We need Stormweave. He's the best there is. If we're to get across the Ocean of Hurricanes, we'll need his skill. And his respect.'

Ussemitus frowned. 'So you annoyed his men?'

'There'll be a fight,' said Jubaia calmly.

Aru looked down at him. 'What are you playing at?' she hissed.

'This is Kelpoora, lady. We have to play the game by the rules here. And we will embarrass Stormweave, mighty though his reputation is.'

'How?' said Ussemitus.

'Trust me. And keep your hands on your swords.'

They left the tavern and Jubaia took them by the most devious route imaginable to a part of the town that reeked even more of seaweed, almost overpowering in its intensity. The streets were slick and treacherous, Jubaia explaining that for much of the time they were under water, especially when the sea winds blew. These were the ratways, and it was not difficult to understand why they were so called, for numerous rats scuttled hither and thither, contemptuous of the company.

Aru grimaced, horrified by the size of them. She kept close to Ussemitus, who himself had no love of these sleek-skinned creatures and their pointed, inquisitive faces. Jubaia ignored them, reaching a door that looked as though one hard knock would reduce it to splinters. But it held, opening to reveal a peering face that had much in common with those of the scurrying rodents of the gutters.

'Nitoc!' said Jubaia, offering his hand. 'It is your old companion, Jubaia. Quickly, admit us. We are hunted by the dock vermin.'

Nitoc's tiny eyes swivelled to and fro, taking in the company, his nose sniffing as if it could penetrate the stench of the ratways and learn something about his visitors. He did not smile, but nodded slowly. 'Jubaia, the little thief of Shung Nang. Come in.' There was little warmth in his voice, and his expression was fixed. But he shuffled aside and admitted the company, watching the street.

They climbed some steps that had been cut into the slippery rock and found themselves in a chamber that could have been a cave, its walls curved and blotched with algae. It was lit by a number of thick candles, and the seats were hewn from what appeared to be bone, as if at some time they had been part of some monstrous creature from the deep that had been beached and plundered.

'Nitoc,' said Jubaia to his companions, 'is an old friend of mine. We have done much business together.'

Nitoc nodded, hands tucked out of sight in his ragged coat. 'No one else brings me the spoils you bring, Jubaia. You are a thief among thieves. A loss to Shung Nang.' Still his expression was fixed, as if an illness had condemned him to wear it until his death. 'You are hungry?' he asked. 'You must be.' He snapped his fingers suddenly, a dry crack that startled them all.

'I have nothing for you this time Nitoc,' said Jubaia, but he pulled a tiny pouch from his shirt. 'There are these, but their worth is minor – '

Nitoc took the pouch eagerly and examined the contents close up to one of the candles. What he had been given seemed to be rings of metal, plundered on one of Jubaia's countless escapades. Nitoc nodded, pocketing them. 'I'll take them, though they only add to the services I owe you, Jubaia. What is it you wish of me?'

'Passage to the west. Across the Ocean of Hurricanes. And I will need Stormweave.'

'He is the best of them. But expensive. And busy. I am not his agent. Choose another.'

Jubaia shook his head. 'No, I must have Stormweave. His craft is the only one capable of transporting my prize. But he will agree. First, however, I will need some of your gutter rats.'

Ussemitus and Fomond glanced at one another, guessing that they were already deep in the meshes of another of Jubaia's complicated schemes. They turned to Aru, but she shrugged, shaking her head in bewilderment. She envied Armestor in the distant forest.

'How many?' said Nitoc.

'A score.'

'How soon?'

'By dusk. Stormweave isn't likely to move until then. When does the storm begin?'

'In the night, I think,' said Nitoc without hesitation.

Jubaia turned to his companions. 'He is never wrong.'

'What is Stormweave likely to do?' asked Ussemitus.

'Corvash will have told him about Aru,' said Jubaia. 'He'll want to bargain for her himself.'

'And when we tell him I'm *not* for sale?' said Aru.

'He will attempt a more basic kind of persuasion.'

Aru stood up, hands on her hips. 'What! You told us there were certain codes here in Kelpoora. Now you're saying that this pirate is going to use force – '

'Which is quite contrary to the codes,' said Jubaia, still calm. 'But help will be on hand to protect us.'

Aru looked up at the ceiling, groaning.

Ussemitus snorted. 'Jubaia, you should tell us these things before you undertake them! We must discuss them!'

Jubaia looked away sheepishly. 'There was little time. And I thought perhaps you might not agree, or suggest some other, less plausible plan – '

'Indeed!' snapped Aru. 'It would be nice to have some say in my fate! Perhaps you'd like to fetch a good price for me in the west? Perhaps you'd sell us all? How do we know what you're planning, you, you – '

But she felt a faint voice calming her inwardly. 'And you can stop that!' she added, pointing at Jubaia. 'Don't try and placate me by invading – '

Jubaia mouth hung open comically. 'No, my lady. I would never! No, it is she – '

Aru stiffened. 'The gliderboat?' she said, suddenly realising.

'She speaks to you.'

But the voice had gone, though it had served its purpose. Aru sat down, bewildered. She was lost in her own thoughts for a moment. Food was brought in by a silent figure, a smaller version of Nitoc, and the company ate in silence.

'Are we resolved?' ventured Jubaia when they had finished.

Ussemitus grunted. 'Very well.'

Later, Jubaia led them back out into the alleys. It was near dark, the only sound was that of the gurgling waves. The company left Nitoc's house, and he closed the door as if they had never been to him, shutting himself back into his darkness.

'Draw your weapons,' said Jubaia.

They did so, Aru keeping her sword hidden under her cloak.

'So where are the ones Nitoc promised us?' said Ussemitus.

'Close. It is not easy to hear the gutter rats.'

They would have pressed him for more information, but they concentrated instead on watching their surroundings. As they came towards the end of the area that Jubaia had called the ratways, a figure spoke to them from a low doorway.

'Well, well, it's the little merchant,' came its familiar voice, and Corvash stepped into the dim light, bowing ostentatiously. Two of his silent companions also came into the light, their faces hidden in shadow.

Fomond swung round: behind the company were another three pirates. All had their swords drawn. None of them spoke.

'I was under the impression we had concluded our discussions,' said Jubaia.

Corvash shrugged, his fat belly quivering. 'I speak for my captain, but not always. Sometimes he prefers to speak for himself. In matters of weight.'

Another figure moved in the shadows. It was taller than Corvash, far thinner, dressed in dark clothes, though the light shifted around them like a veil of mist. The face was in shadow, occasionally dipping into the light, shining briefly like glass.

'Ah, this must be the good captain,' said Jubaia, bowing. 'This is an expected pleasure.'

The voice of the pirate was surprisingly deep-toned. 'When Corvash told me you were in Kelpoora, I had to seek you out.' The figure moved forward, but the darkness clung to it as if somehow woven into a cloak for it. 'And this must be your prize. Do bring her into the light.'

Another of his men stepped from an alley, lifting a torch, the smoke curling overhead like a serpent banner.

Jubaia raised his sword gently as Stormweave took another step, his face glistening by the light of the flames.

They seemed to shine through it as they would have the face of a spectre.

Fomond and Ussemitus eyed the pirates, their own weapons lifting in warning. Aru felt herself shudder, a coldness creeping over her at the appearance of the strange captain.

'Come, come,' said Stormweave smoothly. 'I am not here to fight you. You're a man who likes to barter, little thief. If your prize is as worthy as Corvash tells me, I'll meet your price. I am a wealthy trader.'

Jubaia shook his head. 'No, but I'll pay you well enough for a passage to Umtar.'

'It is not a good time to make a voyage across the Ocean of Hurricanes. Why expend energy unnecessarily? Sell me the girl here. You'll be rich, I promise you.' He chuckled as he spoke, but there was a note of deep menace underlying the sound. Still he did not reveal himself clearly. Aru's fingers tightened on her hidden blade, but Jubaia had warned her not to show it unless death threatened her. Her disguise was essential to her success.

Again Jubaia shook his head. 'I cannot be persuaded.'

Stormweave sighed, the air frosting about him like a halo. 'But you have not reckoned with my powers of persuasion.'

'I think you are not as rich as the Lord of Umtar.'

'You are rich in wit,' said Stormweave. 'But alas, not so rich in companions.'

'Is that relevant to our discussion?'

'I rather think it is,' breathed Stormweave. 'After all, we are not merely discussing coins or jewels. We are discussing this creature. Flesh and blood. Blood is a commodity, of course. And we all have a certain amount of it.'

Jubaia yet kept his voice remarkably cool. 'Forgive me, are you saying you would pay for this girl in blood?'

Ussemitus felt his own blood chilling, sensing the gathering storm here in this alley, feeling the eyes of the pirates weighing him up.

'In a manner of speaking,' said Stormweave. 'She is the sort of prize for whom much blood could be spilled. Perhaps beginning here.'

'Is this not contrary to the codes of Kelpoora?'

142

Stormweave laughed softly, but it was like a wave pushed ahead of an ice floe. 'I am an honourable trader. But even honour is marketable. Will you sell your prize to me?'

Jubaia shook his head. 'I regret that I will not. But I wish to purchase a passage on your ship.'

There was a protracted silence. Finally Stormweave, who seemed to have accepted Jubaia's stubborn defiance, spoke quietly to Corvash.

Aru felt the air about her like frost. Swords turned in the light from the torch. The pirates closed in. The attack had started.

BOOK THREE

THE ELEMENTALS

11

THE URMUREL

Vorenzar waited patiently for the reports, using the thick forest as a screen while he viewed the land beyond the valleys. It was a spectacular vista, the land lush with vegetation, cataracts bubbling over cliff walls; the Csendook felt something stir within him, a response to such beauty. His small party had crossed through a range of low hills on its journey west, now preparing to turn slightly south. The old Innasmornian, Korborus, had become their guide, eager to learn their speech and to teach Vorenzar the Innasmornian tongue. Vorenzar had picked up the brogue well enough, though many of the things the old man had tried to teach him were meaningless. Korborus seemed to be obsessed with a kind of sorcery, a belief that the very air was alive with spirits and beings that followed everything and knew all that occurred. Vorenzar grew irritable when Korborus rambled on about his gods, but the old man seemed not to care about causing offence. He knew his worth.

He had warned Vorenzar that it would be a long journey to the lands that surrounded the place of the rock, or the World Splinter as he called it. There would be powerful forces guarding the place.

Vorenzar studied the green landscape, the placid skies. He might have been back on Eannor. In the south west he could see a configuration of clouds that for a moment put him in mind of a face, with arms that reached up and over the land, but the image quickly dissolved.

Ondrazem watched his leader with interest. The disaster of the crossing must haunt him, with so many lost, and yet the Zaru seemed to consider it a great triumph in spite of the enormous sacrifice. How could they get back? If it had taken so much life to cross, what would it take to go back?

147

But Ondrazem also looked out at the land around him. Better not to go back. This world would be an excellent base, once the enemy had been rooted out.

He took reports to the Zaru. 'There is animal life in plenty, Zaru, but we are unable to trace human life. Our xillatraal have picked up the scent of simple life forms only. We'll not go hungry, Zaru, but we'll not find our enemies in these lands.'

Vorenzar nodded, preparing to mount up for another day's ride. He called Korborus to him. 'Are there any of your tribes in the lands below us?'

Korborus shrugged. 'Unlikely, master. Far to the south there may be villages, along the edge of the great sea. I've not been there, but I've met those who have seen the ports and their ships. If there are Innasmornians here, there will not be many.'

'If we are seen,' Vorenzar went on, 'how will your people react? Will they bring others, attack us?'

Korborus hunched up his shoulders, his face wrinkling like bark. 'That would take a powerful force, master. Such a force would take many weeks to gather. I doubt that it will come, though we will be watched.' He looked up at the skies.

'By your gods,' nodded Vorenzar with a snort.

'You do not fear them,' said Korborus, a note of awe in his voice that was always there when he referred to the Csendook lack of respect for the Mother. Surely she would punish them for their scorn. But at least, Korborus told himself, my own villagers will be safe from these monsters, and will have moved far to the north east where they will not again be found by them.

Vorenzar signalled for the party to leave the hills, and in a while they moved on, their scouts tracking ahead on their flanks, careful to study the terrain in spite of what Korborus had told them. Vorenzar was cautious, though he was amazed by the peacefulness of the land. Yes, this would be the perfect sanctuary for Zellorian and his rabble. But it would be extremely difficult to find them. How many of them were there? A few thousand? How quickly could they breed? In ten years, twenty, they would begin to spread. But there would be time enough to find them, to return to Eannor and get word to Auganzar. And then the true hunt would begin.

For a number of days they moved on across the lowlands, their journey dull, unbroken. There was food enough, for they took what game they needed, and the streams were pure. The Csendook exercised strictly, and Korborus watched them, perched on a rock like a bird, saying nothing. If he marvelled at the speed and strange grace of these fighting machines, he did not show it.

Towards the end of the lowlands, where the land began to rise in a fresh line of hills, they felt the gathering of the clouds, which drifted over the higher hills and spread out like the outriders of an aerial army. Vorenzar watched them, face drawn in a scowl, but Korborus was very quiet, pretending that he saw nothing out of the ordinary in the silent formations. The wind rose, coming down off the hills in gusts, driving dust before it, and the strong sunlight weakened. Vorenzar could sense the unease of the xilla-traal. They could taste the air, sense the change in temperature, the smell of an enemy. But nothing could be seen.

'Is there to be a storm?' Vorenzar asked Korborus.

The old man pulled his rags more tightly about him. 'Innasmorn is not pleased. The elements here are offended by your presence, as I knew they would be.'

'Where are the warriors?' said Ondrazem, his blade held before him, eager for a contest.

Korborus shook his head. 'You must find shelter!' he hissed suddenly.

Vorenzar gripped him, almost lifting him from the ground. 'You have served us well, old crow. But if this is a trap, I'll feed you to the worms, piece by piece. *Who comes?*'

'The elementals seek you. The Mother has sent them. Find shelter.'

Vorenzar snorted, thrusting the old man away and he tumbled like leaves across the grass, picking himself up and scuttling away for the cover of the nearby rocks.

149

A rumble of thunder beyond the hills disturbed the xilla-traal, and the Csendook controlled them with difficulty. Vorenzar gave the command to ready for an attack and the party formed itself into a defensive wedge, choosing ground that was reasonably covered and which would not be easy for an enemy to attack without exposing itself on the open ground beyond it.

The sky darkened with a peculiar suddenness and the rumbles of thunder rolled on overhead, the forks of lightning dazzling. Vorenzar's warriors were prepared for the worst. There was no panic among them, though the xilla-traal were restless, not eager as they usually were when battle drew close. The Zemoks waited, themselves hungry: it would be a relief to fight. Only Korborus was afraid, his eyes darting this way and that as he watched the trees, the rocks, every cloud. Vorenzar could see him and would find him when he wanted him. Escape was out of the question.

As the wind swirled about the company, buffeting the Csendook, almost lashing at them, Vorenzar caught sight of figures emerging from the shadows beyond the rim of the ground he defended. The darkness had become unnatural, both in the speed of its coming and in its density. Like a false twilight, it wrapped the land. But there were only three figures approaching. Each of them stood on an elevation, now no more than twenty yards from the Csendook.

They were not tall, dressed in flowing, dark robes, and they had hair that spread about them like white clouds, their beards equally as long. Each of them held a short wooden implement, neither a weapon nor a staff. Vorenzar thought at first it must be something they used to work the soil.

'You are not of Innasmorn,' the central figure called. As this being spoke, the winds dropped, drifting away as if these creatures had arranged for their orchestration. The clouds and darkness remained, but the air had become extraordinarily still. Even so, Vorenzar could sense that something waited beyond the edge of vision, eager to respond to commands that these beings would give out.

'Who are you?' challenged Vorenzar in the alien tongue.

One hand steadied his xillatraal, which hissed at these beings, while the other gripped his blade menacingly.

He thought the central figure replied that they were lords of the wind. 'We share the powers of the Mother. You speak our tongue?'

'A little,' said Vorenzar.

'Why are you here?'

'We seek a common enemy.'

'Common to whom? To your kind and mine?' said another of the figures.

Vorenzar nodded. 'There are intruders in your world. We are here to find them.'

The three figures began to converse, evidently intrigued by Vorenzar's words. He strained to see their faces clearly, but in this light it was not easy. There was an impression of age, but with it wisdom and unquestionable power. But the thought of these beings controlling the weather was ludicrous, Vorenzar told himself. No matter how alien this world was, such powers existed in the mind only. He focused his own thoughts, driving out all hint of the supernatural.

'We know of intruders,' said the central figure. 'But you are moving across Innasmorn away from them. They are in the east, beyond the sea. Somewhere far from here in the mountains beyond the lands of the Vaza tribes.'

Vorenzar felt himself judder at this news. But he calmed himself. 'You have seen them?'

'No. But word has come to our enclave. We share knowledge with the brotherhood. Though these intruders are far away, we know of them.'

Vorenzar nodded. 'Have your people fought with them?'

'The Vaza, the tribes of the east, are riding against them in war. They will send storms upon them. In their wake, they will crush them.'

'Storms?' said Vorenzar.

'The Windmasters of the east are strong. They have greater gifts than any other. They are the Blue Hairs, most ancient of our order. They serve the Mother well, and she imparts great gifts to them. She gives power in their hands

151

and such storms as flow from them will raze the city of the intruders.'

'A *city*?' said Vorenzar. So soon? How much of a grip did Man have?

'What is your purpose?'

Vorenzar brandished his blade. 'These intruders fled my people. We have been at war for many lifetimes. Man sought to escape his destiny. We are here to seek justice. We are not here to interfere with your own kind. If you are at war with Man, then we are your allies.'

The Windmasters considered this for a long time, and Vorenzar could sense the unease of the Zemoks. They had not learned the tongue of the Innasmornians as well as he had, but Korborus was whispering to them, imparting as much as he could.

At length the spokesman for the Windmasters lifted his rod and pointed to the east, behind the Csendook. 'Your path lies that way. There are no intruders in this continent. You must not go on to the west. Your enemies are behind you.'

Vorenzar grinned, his visor up. 'In good time, we shall do so. If you wish to aid us, or if you have allies, these Vaza, in the east, we shall be glad to meet them and combine our strengths. But first I would see the lands in the west.'

'They are forbidden lands, even to the Windmasters,' was the cold reply.

'Why is that?'

'They are filled with dangerous powers. Things better left as they are. The Mother locks them within the confines of those lands for good reason. If you go there, you will be in peril of your lives. Your mission would fail before it began. Turn about, and travel to the east. We will see that you are protected. We will advise the Vaza of your coming.'

'Do not trust them, Zaru,' breathed Ondrazem, who had been trying to follow the words.

Vorenzar made no show of having heard, but he was not about to discard caution. He needed time to think and plan. It would have been very easy to turn back and find the place where his enemies had hidden. But if there was a city, Zellorian would be powerful. Even with the help of the inhabitants of this backward world, it would be difficult to overcome him. This power in the west was intriguing. Korborus knew the way to it. Surely it would be better to find it, use it, turn it upon Zellorian.

'I will consider your advice,' he called to the figures.

'Very well,' was the reply. 'But if you seek the west, Innasmorn will be angered, and will turn against you. You are intruders here, too. You would be no loss to the Mother.'

Vorenzar watched the three figures; they remained immobile for a long time, until, eventually, they turned away and disappeared into the shadows that had spawned them. The wind again whipped up, like a cloak drawn about the three beings, and tore away across the hills. Above, the skies began to surge, clouds parting to permit fresh sunlight through, and the day that had become premature evening changed its guise once more.

The Csendook were stunned by the abruptness of the transition. But they were on an alien world, and as veterans they did not allow themselves to be too deeply moved. There was no fear in them.

'A clever deception,' said Vorenzar, sensing the quiet.

'You see their sorcery,' said Korborus reverently.

'Sorcery! To the weak-minded, the gullible,' said Vorenzar contemptuously.

Korborus turned away, saying nothing. The Csendook laughed.

'Which way, Zaru?' asked Ondrazem. 'We are eager to ride.'

'We'll turn south, but when we have the opportunity, we'll turn up into these hills. Fetch the old one and put him in front. He'll take us.'

Korborus was prodded ahead of the company, trembling. When he knew what was intended, he seemed to shrivel up even more, his face pale, his hands clenched together in fear. 'Must go back,' he breathed. 'If they unleash their powers on us here – '

153

'What is it they protect?' said Vorenzar. 'What is this power?'

'I have not seen it,' said Korborus. 'But I know what the Windmasters can do. We should go back.'

'We'll allow them to think we are,' said Vorenzar. 'But I wish to find your World Splinter. If I have to shed blood to do so, so be it.'

In the brightening light, they swung southwards, down into a winding river valley, until Vorenzar felt it might be safe to turn again to the west and ride up into the hills. These were the first range of many and beyond them there were mountains, stringing out towards the north west. It would not be difficult to pass through the hills to the south west, and Korborus confirmed it could be done, though he had lost all his enthusiasm for the journey. More than once he tried to persuade Vorenzar to release him, saying that all the Csendook had to do was keep riding and they would inevitably come to the promised lands of the World Splinter without his help. But Vorenzar would not let him go and warned him he would have him spitted if he tried to escape him.

As evening began to fall, the wind again rose, singing through the hills, bending the trees. The Csendook were preparing camp, and a fire to cook the game they had brought down. Vorenzar had not been conscious of being watched and his scouts had reported nothing significant, though the land here was very quiet, unusually so.

Thunder constantly rolled in the distance, though Korborus said it was a common feature of the west, where unnatural lights flickered. He curled himself into a ball and slept beneath a fallen tree, meek as a rabbit.

Ondrazem joined Vorenzar, who still studied the gnarled trees, the escarpment beyond them.

'This land frightens the old one,' said Vorenzar.

Ondrazem shrugged. 'Superstition weakens.'

'The Zemoks are not concerned?'

'They are good Csendook, Zaru. They wonder at not going eastward, in search of the Men, but they will not question you.'

'Perhaps Zellorian is not in the east.'

Ondrazem's eyes narrowed, scarlet with reflected camp-fire light. 'You think the Innasmornians lied?'

'Perhaps they are allies of Zellorian. Perhaps the way back to the east is a trap for us.'

'But the west is – '

'Full of evils and danger? These people are protecting something. Supernatural power? I have no time for sorcery. But what else is hidden in this World Splinter? What is it? A fragment of what?'

Ondrazem looked out at the gathering night, certain that he could see whirling forms in the low clouds.

Vorenzar grinned, his teeth like the fangs of his xillatraal. 'I think, Ondrazem, that our enemies are not in the east at all. I think,' he added, stabbing with a thick finger at the western horizon, 'they are there. Protected by the vermin of this world. Powers! We shall see these powers.' He turned, quietly dismissing his companion and checking over the camp, speaking to each of his Zemoks in turn, praising them gently, sharing a joke with them.

Ondrazem stiffened. This was indeed an unnatural world. But Vorenzar was quite correct. Such things were to be scorned. Even so, this was not the Warhive, nor any Csendook outpost. It would offer new experiences, and they must be guarded against.

As if in answer to his unspoken caution, he heard a new note in the wind, a howling that suggested hunting animals. He felt movement beside him and jumped back, hand on his sword. But it was Korborus, eyes wide, nose up like a hound, sniffing the air.

'If they have loosed the windwraiths – ' murmured the old man.

Ondrazem gripped his shoulders, not really understanding him. 'What are you babbling about?'

'They'll tear us to pieces!' gasped Korborus. 'Windwraiths.'

'Are these things coming?'

'Did you not hear them?'

They listened again, though Ondrazem thought only of

the wind, which could twist itself into many sounds. But the suggestion of a hunt was strong.

Korborus turned and ran back to the cover of the rocks. 'Hide! Find cover under the earth!' he piped, but few of the Csendook understood his garbled words. They looked about them, searching for the source of his panic, but could see nothing, only the tossing of the trees high on the escarpment.

'Another cursed storm,' said Ondrazem. 'Take shelter as best you can,' he told the Zemoks.

'What has the old fool seen?' said Vorenzar beside him.

'He talks of an attack.'

'He's jabbering. Get under cover. The overhang. I don't want the xillatraal stirred up. They're reacting badly to this damn wind.' Vorenzar forced his own beast to cover and the entire company moved under the shadow of a projecting rock overhang, the xillatraal bucking and snarling until they were cuffed into obeying. Their eyes blazed as the sounds of the wind grew, as if they dreaded that wind more than any beasts that might come hurling out of it.

'Zaru!' cried Ondrazem, pointing to the opposite ridge. Suddenly something had swirled down from above, like thick clouds, coiled in a serpent-like movement, shrieking hideously. Dozens of shapes burst from the cloud, translucent bodies that moved back and forth in the wild air with tremendous speed, their faces grotesque, mouths open, a funnel for the wind. The sounds they made were like the high wail of hounds, yet hounds unlike anything the Csendook had ever heard before. They were unnatural, bizarre, and in them was the tearing of flesh, the drinking of blood, for these creatures were hunting, and they sought the flesh below them, eager for it.

'The air has shape,' said Vorenzar softly. 'A clever illusion!' But he backed into the shadows, his blade before him. 'Hold your ground, Zemoks!'

Around the clearing the elemental beings whirled, like a maelstrom from which a score of talons reached. Closer they span to the sheltering Csendook. But the Zemoks stood their ground, faces impassive under their visors. Only Korborus was riven by dread, pressed to the earth.

As the windwraiths were about to surge forward into the Csendook, the ground about them heaved, as though some vast monster had stirred itself. The earth split in several places across the clearing, and boulders rolled aside, trees splintering and toppling. Something stood in the open, shadows gathering about it like bats, smothering the shape, blurring it, making it a focus for yet more illusions. Around this dark sentinel the windwraiths swirled, like huge moths drawn to a beacon of darkness that tugged at them as fire attracts insects. It lured the aerial horrors away from their intended prey.

Vorenzar gasped, unable to see more than a pillar of darkness, though it seemed to have malformed arms, a head that seemed shaped from black loam. As it collected the darkness to it, other things crawled in the earth, shapeless things, elongated, twisting, fat maggots of soil. Boulders split with loud cracks and from them, like creatures emerging from cocoons, other pulpy forms toppled, trying to rise on the bed of churned earth that the clearing had become.

The Csendook closed ranks, unable to tear their eyes from the madness that was unfolding before them. The windwraiths tore downwards, clawing at the earth, scattering it and the undulating shapes. But these fresh creatures were not intent on attacking the Csendook. They rose up, amalgamating, forced to do so by the hideous central shape, as if it conducted its own mad war against the aerial beings. Earth burst and flew in hot gouts across the clearing. Screams tore the air and the elemental beings were ripped apart, dissipating and reforming, though the shapes below reformed just as quickly.

The battle, for such it was, raged on, wild and tempestuous, with no weapons used, only the blind fury of two elements which seemed locked in mutual hatred, destroying and re-destroying each other. Nothing seemed capable of damaging the central darkness, while about it the earth writhed, vomiting out other shadows that swung upwards, only to fall again.

The Zemoks watched in fascination, shaking their heads as if they could not credit this.

'What are they?' called Vorenzar above the din. Behind his warriors the xillatraal tried to break free, but the Zemoks kept them in check, knowing if they left the cover of the rock, they would be ripped to shreds like rags.

'Slaves of the dark,' said Korborus, which meant nothing to the Csendook. 'We are at the very edge of the dark lands. They abjure the servants of the Mother.'

'Will they attack us?' said Vorenzar. 'Or is there a way we can escape this turmoil?'

But Korborus had no answer.

The struggle in the clearing raged on and on, well into the night, but finally it began to end. The Csendook had not been harmed, though they watched in trepidation as the swirling aerial beings broke up for a last time and began to withdraw, their energies seemingly spent. As they went, so did the things of the earth sink down, their movements less urgent.

A sudden calm fell over the valley. In the centre of the clearing the dark mass that was the orchestrator of the mayhem remained like a monolith.

'Prepare,' breathed Vorenzar as the heavens cleared. Moonlight seeped down over a strange scene. The earth was pounded, rucked up. Tree roots poked up like frozen snakes, some trees snapped off at the trunk. Rocks had been churned up from their beds and tossed aside like pebbles, some of them shattered. It would not be easy to find a path through this devastation.

But no attack came.

Korborus ventured out into the clearing, the moonlight daubing him so that the Csendook watched him as if he were a ghost in a land of the dead.

Vorenzar waited until he was sure there would be no more movement. Then he stepped out, joining the old man. 'What were those things?'

Korborus had stopped shaking, but he seemed aghast, as if he had witnessed something from a nightmare. 'An ancient evil,' he murmured. 'It was no accident that these things attacked the windwraiths. If they had not done so, we would all have been destroyed.'

'What are you saying, that they *defended* us?' said Vorenzar, though the idea was ridiculous.

Korborus nodded, though he seemed amazed by the idea. 'I hope I am wrong. But they understood your plight. They held back the winds.'

'Why?'

'The Windmasters sent the windwraiths. They declared themselves to be your enemies by so doing, and thus also declared you the enemies of Innasmorn. And the darkness of this land rebels. It feeds itself, not the Mother. It has been alienated from her.'

'Who rules it?'

Korborus shook his head. 'No one could rule such evil. It is a power unto itself.'

Vorenzar grunted. He pointed to the earth monolith, its arms by its side, moulded to it. 'That is earth. You are saying it is capable of thought?'

Korborus began to shrivel again, his fears renewed. He looked away from the earth monument. 'It is an urmurel. A shaped one.'

'Shaped by whom? Or by what?' snapped Vorenzar.

'The darkness.'

Vorenzar controlled his annoyance at the old man and his aversion to simple answers.

'The earth has been shaped by the old darkness,' Korborus said, trying to explain. 'It has had power put into it, for the purpose of serving. You saw this.'

'Is this power still in it?'

Korborus shuddered. 'I think not. The windwraiths have been dispersed.'

'And if they come again?'

'You have been protected, marked – '

'Why should anyone in your world protect Csendook?'

'I have said – '

'Because we are enemies of the *winds*? This is sheer nonsense,' snarled Vorenzar. He edged closer to the urmurel. Moonlight fell over its hunched shoulders. The thing stood about eight feet high, but it seemed lifeless, a solid column of earth.

The Zemoks watched as their Zaru confronted the thing. He prodded at it with his weapon, but if it had once been alive, it was now no more than earth. As Vorenzar turned from it, it began to crack, pieces sloughing off it like skin. But no new creature emerged from this grotesque chrysalis.

'We camp under the overhang,' said Vorenzar. 'In the morning we move on. To the west.'

They placed an extra guard. Neither Korborus nor Vorenzar slept, watching instead the gradual decline of the urmurel. By morning it was half its original height, a husk of what it had been, and all sense of power, of dread, had long fled. Except for that which was lodged in Korborus, who moved as if something dark and unseen dogged his every step.

12

BLACK GLIDERBOAT

The gliderboat slipped silently out of the mountains, soaring into the open expanses of sky, its long, skeletal wings pulsing up and down like the fins of a fish propelling it through water. From the ground it would have been invisible, blending as it did with the skies, its hues and colour tones changing as the sky changed, its camouflage complete. No one sat in the craft: it was complete in itself. It conducted its own trials, its own tests to see how the skies of Innasmorn would react to it, the sacrilege of its flight. But this craft had far greater powers built into its components than any of its predecessors. Zellorian had breathed a new kind of life into it, a subtle blend of technology and what? Sorcery? Perhaps that was it, the craft mused to itself. But it could feel the coursing of unknown properties through its construction, its myriad steel veins.

It felt the wind race about it, tasting its shape, varying its currents to encourage a reaction, but the gliderboat merely adjusted its glide, its soar, its swoop. Innasmorn knew that here was an entity that, in some ways, was of itself, a living organism that pulsed with the elements of Innasmorn, a bizarre fusion of the alien and the known.

Zellorian had perfected his science well. Vymark was the greatest stride he had yet taken since his arrival on Innasmorn. No other gliderboat had been able to survive for long in Innasmornian skies. And no other gliderboat could be controlled from a distance. Vymark needed no pilot.

Yet he was controlled.

'A rebirth,' Vymark thought to the void that contained his invisible master.

As clearly as if Zellorian stood at his side, the voice answered. 'I share this with you, Vymark! I see through your eyes, I feel the air of this world about you. It pries, searches, but you are protected. This is a triumph.'

Vymark had been encased in misery for so long that Zellorian had feared for the stability of his mind during the transformation, but his warrior had survived it. There was a coldness about him, perhaps a reaction to the loss of his original identity, his form, but in time that would go. As a gliderboat, Vymark would have powers beyond those of any man.

Although Vymark projected his thoughts as easily as speech to his master, he was able to keep his own feelings to himself, resenting any intrusion into them. But Zellorian was careful how he viewed such things. The Prime Consul knew that gliderboats usually had much of their identity suppressed, their emotions buried: they were little more than machines. Many would have rebelled or suffered mental collapse if they had known what they had become, the humanity they had lost. But in this respect Vymark would differ from them again. He was still Vymark, most of his old identity preserved. And with it, the anger, the bitterness, the hatred lived on. These would fuel him on his quest. And Zellorian would use them to manipulate his angel of destruction.

'How soon can I begin my work?' said Vymark. His voice was cold in Zellorian's mind, harsher than Zellorian remembered, but there was purpose in it.

'It will be a while before we understand fully your relationship with Innasmorn. There may be difficulties – '

'No,' said Vymark. 'The winds have found me and are not sure of me, but they veer from the darker powers you have used. If I am to be attacked, I will focus this other strength. It will come to me gladly. Let me go westward, sire. Let me hunt our enemies.'

Zellorian felt the stab of Vymark's fury: his desire for revenge was potent, and the darkness fed on that, too, revelling in such destructive emotions. Here was a weapon to plunge into the very vitals of Innasmorn's controlling powers!

'As you wish, Vymark. But exercise caution.'

'You are my Controller, sire.'

It was true. Zellorian could still manipulate the craft, drag it back. Yet time was critical to his plans. The source of unknown power in the west had to be found, and it was difficult to assess the strength of the Innasmornians and the damned Casruel girl. They, too, had to be found and eliminated.

Vymark, elated by his new freedom, sped across the miles of forest that stretched out below him in dark green waves. From time to time an eddy of wind took him, trying to shape his course, but he used what was within him to master it. The power of the sun fuelled him, its rays igniting other powers in his many systems, and all human longings for sustenance quickly dispersed. He still thought of his body, the way it had been, but as a gliderboat he was far more aware of himself, of every vein. And there were parts of himself which he had yet to test. The talons that could reach down eagerly. But he pulled his mind from the pleasure of contemplating the first bloody kill.

'Go westward,' Zellorian told him. 'If you have a report to make, do so. I will not be with you always, but I can always be reached.'

Vymark felt the contact broken. He was truly free, for a while at least. The forest sped beneath him and as it did so, new emotions raced through him, faster than the air that he moved through at such graceful speed.

Some time later, still quivering with elation, he sensed the deeps of the forest of Spellavar below. He recalled vividly his meeting there with Quareem, the renegade Blue Hair who had aided Zellorian, and who had taught him so much about the powers of Innasmorn. But Quareem had not survived the battle in the Dhumvald. Vymark had not been able to save his life as he had saved Zellorian's.

He dived down, almost at treetop height, listening to the wind talking to itself. He took pleasure from the fact that it felt him as an intruder, the restless voices falling silent as he passed. But other powers curled up like smoke from below. The dark was with him, the part of Innasmorn that was kept in check like a hound on a lead, eager to tug free of its shackles. Vymark could reach into himself for this. He did so now, savouring the abrupt snarl of hatred, the fury that echoed his own.

They had been here. His enemies. The dark had felt them pass. Close to him when he had flown another craft, as a man. But they had moved on, journeying to Amerandabad, and after that, up into the Dhumvald.

Vymark was about to rise, away from the whisperings, for he knew these facts. They served only to frustrate him, pointing up as they did his anger at the disaster in the north. But he learned other facts. The Innasmornians and the alien girl had appeared again, west of the forest lands, at the edge of the great range of Thunderreach. They had taken to the skies in another gliderboat.

How could such a craft survive? Vymark asked himself.

Voices from the dark answered him. There was one who flew it who had a deep understanding of the elements and who could use them. A creature of the skies. It was he who controlled the gliderboat. He had taken it into the Thunderreach. But there was no other news. The forest things could not penetrate the western range, though there were dark powers there which would aid Vymark in his search.

He was away at once, lifting high on the air currents, using them, forcing them to his will with a growing confidence. There were far storms on the horizons, banks of thick cloud, but none of them seemed to drift his way. If Innasmorn resented his flight, she did not consider it significant enough to curtail. Whatever Zellorian had called upon to protect Vymark had power enough for that.

The miles blurred below him as Vymark sped toward the Thunderreach range. He ignored the night, though it tired him to fly in the darkness. It was a relief to feel the dawn, and as the sun grew in strength, so did his own strength regenerate, his spirits with it.

Peaks began to loom from their banks of cloud, and he felt other powers in this place, elemental forces that drifted in the air peculiar to these mountains, some of which fled from him, others of which enveloped him, curious to know what powered him. Few contacted his mind, but there were allies here, he quickly discovered. Allies fed by the same dark desire he had to find and destroy the other craft. He sensed the frustration of the powers.

So the Casruel girl had been here! With her companions she had sought the pass that would take them through to the sea in the west. Vymark lost no time in finding the great gash in the mountains. He soared into it, followed by streams of air, alive with spirits and creatures that clamoured for recognition, hungry to share in the knowledge with him. They served the mountain powers, they told him, loyal to the brotherhood of renegade Windmasters and not to the inner circle of Azrand.

Vymark found it difficult to follow their lines of garbled dialogue, unfamiliar with the plots against Vittargattus and the movements of the Vaza. Whatever original plans Zellorian had had, shaped as they had been with Quareem, events had superseded them. There was only the need now to find the gliderboat, destroy it, and move on to the far west.

As he moved up the deep pass, Vymark began to feel something beyond him, shrouded in the thick banks of cloud that swathed the sheer rock walls. A surge of power struck him, a wave that made him sail upward, almost tipping him over, but he righted himself and focused his energy. What confronted him was far too powerful to probe, a rich source of elemental power, like the core of a storm, balled tightly into something with a will, a distinct purpose.

Was this a god? One of Innasmorn's elusive masters?

It did not speak to him, neither in the way that Zellorian did, nor in the way that the elementals of the forest and rocks spoke to him, but something of its thoughts permeated his own. He had to fight to control his fears, knowing that the power before him was colossal, a wall of energy that, unleashed, could sweep down and destroy with the intensity of a hurricane.

He felt the coming of the storm and tried to swerve back, but its outer tendrils pulled him in, and within moments the clouds took him, so that he tumbled and rolled, his mind exposed to a merciless inspection. He must have cried out to Zellorian, for somewhere in that confusion, the threatening madness, the Prime Consul spoke.

Words became tumbled images, the thoughts of all interlocking in such a way as to make identities uncertain, as though Vymark had fallen into a sudden dream, with little control over its convolutions. Darkness swirled in, and although Vymark seemed to be falling, there was no up and no down. There was a deep, livid anger, like the heart of a storm, searching for release.

Yet it did not fall upon him, nor tear him piece from piece as he thought it surely must. The clouds broke up, the mountains shrieked by on either side like gods, and he was flying again, on through the pass, the storm being behind him. It was as though he had been ejected, blown out, the air behind him a giant wave, pushing a swimmer before it. Vymark wanted to scream with the joy of that wild flight, his mind leaping.

Zellorian's voice pulled him back from the brink. 'The darkness gathers itself against our enemies! The very mountains closed in on them. But they got through, Vymark. Our will to find them has saved you from destruction. The storm elemental has given you greater powers to use in the hunt. You must go on to the west. Somewhere in the coastal lands there is a town, Kelpoora. The others are there. Find them!'

Vymark laughed within, a howl of silence that went out into his every fibre, and in his veins ran the power of the storm he had come through, his blood roaring with fresh purpose, his hatred honed to a fine cutting edge.

In the Sculpted City, Zellorian slumped back on the couch, his face glistening in the semi-darkness of the chamber. He had felt Vymark's cry like the point of a knife at his brow. But he had survived that storm creature! And would use it. Vymark's baptism was over. In him burned a new fire.

Zellorian closed his eyes. He dared not rest. There would be other gliderboats to build, to perfect. Each new infusion of power from this unexpected quarter gave him a deeper belief in his cause. In the storm being he had sensed a link to something even more staggering, something akin to the immense powers that had attempted to burst through the barriers of their confinement in the deathstorm. In time he would unlock those shackles. In time.

Swords danced like spirits in the drab light; other shadows moved at the edge of vision. Stormweave's henchmen were alert as hawks, swinging round to face whatever the ratways were disgorging.

Aru and Ussemitus gasped. A score of beings, no bigger than Jubaia and dressed in black tatters, faces peering from cowls like those of the rats that infested this part of Kelpoora, crept in on the party. They held short, curved weapons that whispered of murder.

Silently they set about the pirates and the shadow shape of Stormweave drew back out of the light, hissing angrily. His weapon sliced the air with stunning speed, and he moved so swiftly and liquidly that he seemed to be more shadow than man. The rat beings were also fast, three of them weaving about the captain, while Corvash and the others cursed crudely as they, too, were forced to defend themselves instead of attack as had been their intention.

Jubaia motioned his companions to him and they were able to watch the dazzlingly quick interchange. One of the seamen was hurt, dropping his blade and falling to his knees, but the rat-like beings did not kill him, though they could easily have done so.

'You set this up, you filth!' Corvash snarled at Jubaia as a curved weapon nicked his arm and he winced at the pain.

Jubaia bowed. 'Lay down your weapons and we'll discuss the terms again.'

Corvash said something obscene, but Jubaia only laughed.

Someone else was coming down the alleyway. It was Nitoc, but with him was another figure, wearing a long robe and some kind of wooden medallion around his neck, carved in the shape of a crab.

'Ah,' said Jubaia. 'Fancy meeting an Arbitrator in such a place as this and at such an hour.'

Corvash saw the two approaching figures and groaned. The fighting had stopped at once. A number of the rat-like beings melted into the shadows, but the seamen were forced to stand their ground, some of them trying to stem the flow of blood from their wounds. Stormweave himself was invisible, but the air where he hid shimmered like mist.

'What in the name of the Ocean is going on here!' snorted the taller of the two newcomers. His hood had fallen back to reveal a long face, the eyes keen, the expression one of offended dignity. Ussemitus almost chuckled, turning from Fomond, who himself had to glance at the ground to prevent himself from laughing. Jubaia had indeed primed and sprung a trap for the pirates.

'A modest dispute,' said Corvash with as graceful a bow as he could manage, slipping his weapon out of sight.

'Over an item of merchandise?' said the Arbitrator haughtily, his gaze sweeping the entire company. His eyes fell upon Aru and his brows rose up quizzically. 'I gather from this person,' he said, indicating Nïtoc, 'that there was an intention by certain parties to rob his colleagues. Theft is considered anathema to the inhabitants of Kelpoora. I have to say that I find it disturbingly distasteful that I have to state such a fundamental law of the community!

'Who is the injured party?' he ended, ignoring the pirates who were clutching their injuries, their faces clouded with fury at this betrayal.

Jubaia stepped forward. 'I am, your worthiness.'

'You seem familiar to me.'

'I am not a resident, worthiness, though I have been here many times. I have always sought to control my behaviour in the best interests of your society. I am certain that the good gentleman who stands with you will testify to the veracity of this statement,' said the little man with another bow.

'What are you trading?'

'Nothing, worthiness. I am merely seeking a passage to Umtal. I am to deliver a certain item to the monarch there.'

The Arbitrator again studied Aru, who had slipped her weapon away and was doing her best to look downcast and pitiful, though her cheeks were flushed with anger at having to play this role. 'I take it that this woman is the item referred to?'

Jubaia inclined his head. 'Quite so, worthiness.'

The Arbitrator swung round on the shadows where Stormweave waited. 'You there! What is your part in this dispute?'

Stormweave showed only a fraction of his face, his voice like ice in the night. 'I believe I have been duped, sir,' he said. 'The item in question had already been promised to me. I came here at the behest of these people to collect my merchandise and pay over the agreed price. However, as you can clearly see, when I arrived here with my men, so few of them, as you'll note, we were set upon. Not only were we to be robbed, but our craft was to be purloined, our services pressed. Why, they carry steel, sir. Quite obviously this person does not have the means at his disposal to pay for a passage across the Ocean of Hurricanes, so he intended to trap me into taking him. My men and I have been the victims of a terrible deceit.'

Jubaia laughed sharply, though Ussemitus and the others began to wonder if their own trap had been sprung. 'What arrant nonsense!' said Jubaia. 'I had been warned that this pirate had a glib tongue, but this is a lie.'

The Administrator snorted impatiently, unsure which way he should conduct this tasteless affair. 'As you are aware, this matter ought to be aired in the House of Assessment. It is, however, a most inconvenient hour for such a meeting. I am therefore prepared to consider an arrangement here and now. I am so empowered. Well?'

Jubaia shrugged, the smile still on his face. Nitoc had done well to rouse this official. The smell of bribery was quite pungent.

Stormweave's emotions were unreadable.

'I am sure,' said Jubaia, 'that we can settle this matter very easily. There has been a misunderstanding, that is all. I am quite capable of paying my way.'

169

'And what price had you agreed upon?' cut in the Administrator.

Stormweave answered quickly. 'I suggest we bow to your own judgement, sir.'

'If you cannot agree – '

'We did, of course,' said Stormweave. 'But as you are here, I would be quite prepared to accept your weighing of the matter.' His men were silent, eyes ahead of them, not eager to speak unless prompted by their leader.

The Arbitrator turned to Jubaia. 'You claim to be the injured party. How is that?'

Jubaia spread his hands. 'Why, worthiness, you arrived in time to avert an abduction. I was about to be robbed. Fortunately the inhabitants of the ratways came to my aid, otherwise my friends and I would have been outnumbered.'

The Arbitrator looked askance at the heavens. 'Evidently one party is lying. Has any payment been made?'

'None,' said Stormweave.

'I was on my way to make arrangements for passage,' said Jubaia.

The Arbitrator eyed Stormweave dubiously. 'Captain, you are known to be an able seaman, with a craft that has a singularly high reputation among those which ply the Ocean of Hurricanes. Though many of the tales told in the docks about your prowess are questionable, I am sure that you are more than able to defend yourself against abduction. And you expect me to believe that such an odd company as this would have *purloined* your craft?' He indicated Jubaia and the others.

'There were a score or more of the rat people,' said Stormweave calmly. 'Quite appalling how they flocked.'

'You are known to be a cautious man, Stormweave. Your stepping ashore is rare, is it not? Yet you came here tonight. You must have been assured of a successful venture. You do not seem to have been expecting a trap, else why such a small bodyguard?'

'How could I know that treachery had been planned?'

'You assumed not? Careless. The renowned Stormweave.' The Arbitrator shook his head. 'No, I am beginning to form an opinion in this matter. I would not like to think you have broken the codes of our humble town. Theft is not tolerated here. You, above all, know that. Elsewhere, of course, it is an established thing, and rightly so.'

'I have no desire to press charges officially,' said Jubaia quickly.

'You surprise me,' said the Arbitrator. 'Should they be upheld, this captain would not be admitted to Kelpoora again.'

'I understand that,' nodded Jubaia, still smiling. 'But I have no wish to discredit him. In fact, I came here for the express purpose of securing his services, having heard that there are none better.'

The Arbitrator snorted. 'I believe there has been some talk on this matter. It is not my business to favour anyone.'

'Quite so,' Jubaia bowed yet again. 'But I seek justice. In view of what has happened here, I am sure that the good captain would consider giving me passage to Umtal, for an agreed fee, with the understanding that my prize is not to be interfered with in any way.'

'You surprise me further,' said the Arbitrator, eyes widening. 'You would still seek passage with the one who has tried to cheat you?'

'I am sure Captain Stormweave values his reputation,' said Jubaia. 'It would be reckless of him, would it not, to toss it away with one rash act of piracy now?'

The Arbitrator tried to see Stormweave's expression, but could not.

'My honour is at stake,' came the captain's smooth voice, the irony evident in it.

'Then you'll place this issue in my hands?' said the Arbitrator.

'Absolutely, worthiness,' said Jubaia. 'Though I must say I am in great haste. An early decision would be appreciated.'

'When do you wish to sail?'

'On the first tide after dawn.'

Corvash cursed under his breath, but the Arbitrator held

up his hand for silence. 'All such matters are taken into consideration when a fee is waged. How many go with you?'

Jubaia indicated Ussemitus and Fomond, and lastly Aru.

'That is all?' said the Arbitrator.

'Two more will join us once we are at sea,' Jubaia told him. 'One man and . . . one woman.'

The Arbitrator considered, stroking his chin thoughtfully. Finally he turned to the shadow of Stormweave. 'First tide tomorrow. Five of them. Umtal. What is your opinion of this?'

'Expensive,' said Stormweave. 'There will be a storm soon. A bad one.'

'You are equipped with your magnificent reputation,' commented the Arbitrator. 'Surely compensation enough.'

'I will have to abandon all my other dealings for a while. It is not a short journey. That will cost me.'

'Noted,' said the Arbitrator.

'What supplies do they carry?' said Stormweave.

Jubaia explained.

'Then I have to provide food and water. For many days.'

Between them they argued and discussed the matter for many minutes longer, until at length they seemed to have compromised on a coherent plan, and one to which a price could be fixed.

'Am I to take it,' said Stormweave to the Arbitrator, 'that this is to be an Assessed charter?'

'I can have it made official and affix the seal. But if we have to go through official channels this very hour, you'll both spend the rest of the night going from one chamber to another having the charter endorsed. I do, of course, have the power to make a verbal referral. Tomorrow I can have the papers signed confirming the matter. But yet, it will be an Assessed charter, bound by the laws of the League.'

'Then I have no choice,' Stormweave conceded.

'If you refuse – ' began the Arbitrator, but Jubaia politely interrupted him.

'Then I would consider pressing charges,' he smiled.

A low chuckle came from Stormweave's direction. Even now he had still not shown himself clearly. 'Very well. Let us agree on a price.'

The Arbitrator turned to Jubaia. 'As offended party, you may make the first suggestion.'

Jubaia nodded. He stepped close to the Arbitrator and spoke into his ear, much to the annoyance of Ussemitus and his companions. Aru could barely keep herself from shouting at him, but she remained very still.

The Arbitrator drew himself up and sniffed, as if with a degree of disapproval. 'It is not for me to guess where you came across such a prize,' he said to Jubaia.

'Corvash,' said Stormweave.

Corvash went to the Arbitrator, who spoke softly to him. The pirate listened, grunted, then went to the shadows that concealed his master.

The moments ticked away silently until the soft voice of Stormweave gave its reply. 'I accept.'

'Then I confirm this as an Assessed charter,' said the Arbitrator. 'Captain Stormweave, you are to report back to myself or at least two of my colleagues as soon as you have made delivery of your five charges to Umtal and returned, direct to Kelpoora. Any goods you currently hold will be placed with the League until you return. Including, of course, the fee, one tenth of which will be kept by the League for our service in this matter.'

Corvash glared at Jubaia, but nodded.

'An hour before the tide,' said the Arbitrator, 'be on the Key of Crabs. Unless you wish to sail from another?'

'That will be admirable,' smiled Jubaia.

Stormweave had dissipated like mist, and with him went the others, looking back like hounds disappointed at not making a kill. The Arbitrator ignored them and turned once more to Jubaia. 'Of course, had this gone before the full House, it would have cost you a good deal more.'

For answer Jubaia held out a small pouch. 'I'm certain it would have, worthiness. You have been extremely tolerant, a monument to patience. Please take this.'

'I shouldn't,' said the Arbitrator, hastily pocketing the

173

pouch without examining it. 'You must excuse me. We'll meet before the tide.' At that, he, too, was gone.

Jubaia clapped his hands and turned, only to meet the angry stares of Ussemitus, Fomond and Aru.

Aru gripped him by the scruff of the neck.

'Wait, wait!' he gasped. 'Nitoc is still here.'

It was true, for the strange fellow and some of his even stranger companions were circling the party, unsure of what Aru intended.

'All is well,' Jubaia called to them. 'Our plan worked immaculately. Please disperse.'

Nitoc nodded, his teeth flashing, though it did not seem to be a smile. Then he and his fellows from the ratways were gone.

'Jubaia,' said Ussemitus. 'What has all this charade been for? Why did you not commission Stormweave at the outset?'

The little thief wriggled free, straightening his tunic. 'I know his heart. If we had, he would have agreed to take us, quite possibly. And then he would have killed us all and taken you, good lady, for himself. He has limitless taste, a strange appetite. If we had applied in the first instance to the House of Assessment, they might have called upon Stormweave, but only as a recommendation. He would have been in a position to refuse us, and in view of the fact that it will be a hazardous voyage, he likely would have. So we have instead compromised him! Now he is forced, by charter, to take us. And he is sworn to our protection!'

'Yes, and he'll undo us at the first opportunity!' said Fomond. 'He'll not accept this with good grace.'

Jubaia laughed. 'I think he will, once we get to sea. This is the sort of deceit in which he revels. But he values his membership of the League. It is a brotherhood that keeps the pirates strong. None of them would jeopardise their membership of it, or anger the Arbitrators. No, I vow we'll be drunk together more often than not before we reach the far shore. Mark my words.'

Aru snorted in exasperation. 'Jubaia, you are quite incorrigible.'

'My lady! I think only of our safety.'

'Tell me something,' said Ussemitus. 'I hate to be impertinent, but what in the winds did you offer as payment for our crossing?'

Jubaia sniffed. 'Well, I've been here before, you know. And I've more than one cache. Nitoc looks after some of them for me. Let us just say that I offered Stormweave something that will take his mind off all of us, and any thoughts of revenge.'

13

OCEAN OF HURRICANES

As they waited on the Key of Crabs, they could smell the gathering of the storm, which smothered the sharp reek of weed. Even Aru, who had no Innasmornian blood, could sense the powerful forces shaping beyond the armada of waves. She wondered if the company was wise to attempt this voyage, though the seamen of Kelpoora were going about their business as though this were another day for them. And Jubaia had insisted they had to cross this Ocean: that going around it would be far too perilous.

Earlier, before dawn, he had slipped away and visited Corvash before the pirate and his mates had come to the Key of Crabs, and had presented them with whatever fee had been agreed for the passage, though he would not tell his companions what this was, in spite of their attempts to find out. It irritated Ussemitus intensely, but he was forced to give up asking for the time being.

'We may be under the protection of the charter,' he told Fomond and Aru, 'but we'd better sleep with our swords in our hands.'

Corvash arrived on the key with a number of his rugged mates. He grinned hugely when he saw Aru, bowing in an exaggerated way. If there was any fury left in him after the incident in the ratways, he hid it extremely well. He clapped his hands together and rubbed them as though in eager anticipation of the voyage. 'So! We are prepared. It's to be a rough crossing. Still time to reconsider. If you're not used to the sea – '

Jubaia, who had been studying the waters as they heaved up against the wall of the quay, shook his head. 'We'll take our chances. Where's your ship?'

'This way,' grinned Corvash, leading them along the

quay. The Administrator had still not shown himself, though Jubaia said that he would probably not come.

Corvash took them to where the quay pinched in to its narrowest, leaning at an angle towards the swelling waters, and beyond a curve that seemed to be taking them away from the buildings they came to a vessel. It was elongated and low in the water, like some half-surfaced predator of the deep, its stern tapered, its rudder a pale fin, trailing like a line into the water. As they walked alongside it, they could see below the water line another trailing fin, almost like the great wing of a bird, folded to its side, while the prow rose up in a gentle curve, waves braking over it in a constant spray. Two mast-like projections swung back at steep angles and what passed for sail seemed to Aru more like membranes. She immediately thought of the gliderboat, for here was a craft that seemed even more alive. The keel was a deep green, matching that of the waters, glistening like the body of a great fish, and the entire craft had a smell that was like the ocean itself.

'We call her the *Restless Venture*,' said Corvash, his face lit with pride. 'Though she has other names. A rare and priceless beauty. Have you ever seen anything more desirable?'

Aru noticed Jubaia's eyes turn for a moment to the east of the city, where the dunes lay, but he met Corvash's challenging gaze calmly.

'She is quite superb,' said the little man.

Corvash grunted, pleased at the acknowledgement. He hopped from the quay to the craft easily, timing his leap expertly, for the craft bobbed up and down in the moving waves. Fomond also crossed, and although Aru would have preferred to see to herself, Ussemitus reminded her softly that she still had a part to play. He guided her over and she did as well as she could to seem downcast and less able, though the annoyance welled in her.

'Are there no cabins?' she whispered to Jubaia. 'Surely we're to have some protection against the storm.'

Jubaia shook his head. 'There may be a way down into

the belly of the craft, though I shudder to go into it. These pirates live with the elements. Close to the Mother.'

Aru groaned. The sea looked suddenly darker, the sky more threatening. Beneath her the deck was slippery, smoothed almost like glass, and she thought of the patterned scales of a great fish, though pushed the image from her mind.

Jubaia excused himself and went forward in search of the captain, who had not been seen. Something stirred near the prow, a shadow draped in a fine halo of spray, spectre-like. It was Stormweave, studying the waves, his concentration very deep.

It was a while before he acknowledged the little man, doing so with a nod, though he never turned his face from the water, as if to do so would damage his calculations. His head was partially hidden by a membranous hood which trailed down his back, itself wrapped in dark material that could have been the skin of a sea creature.

'We're almost ready,' came his voice above the hiss of the spray. 'Is the cargo secure?'

'It is.'

'I intend a direct crossing. The tide is about ready to bear us. Your companions understand what this storm will do?'

Jubaia nodded. 'Yes. But before you plot a course for Umtal, we must travel east along the dunes for a short way.'

Stormweave almost turned to him, making an effort to keep his invisible face fixed to the sea. 'The agreement was that we met your other passengers *at sea*. My ship travels the water as a fish does. Every current, every ripple, is important, as is timing. You, a creature of the skies, should understand this, Jubaia of Shung Nang.' His voice hardened as he spoke.

Jubaia felt the ship move under him. 'The appropriate adjustment in the fee can be made – '

'Good, but the adjustments to the voyage will not be so easy. I have my ship to think of.'

'If you are unable to make this adjustment to collect my

companions, we will have to renegotiate,' said Jubaia levelly. He was aware that Corvash had come to stand behind him, listening to the exchange.

'The Arbitrator has the fee,' said the seaman.

'And you,' said Stormweave, 'will forfeit it. There'll be no voyage.'

'The Arbitrator may not agree with you,' he said confidently.

Stormweave guessed that the Arbitrator had been bribed. He kept his gaze fixed on the sea with an effort of will. 'You gave your terms. Your companions were to be picked up at sea.'

'So they shall be. You have no need to put ashore. The Arbitrator is a reasonable man. Are you certain he will find for you if there is an official dispute? He considered me the injured party, after all.'

Corvash growled something, but Jubaia ignored him. The laws of the contract bound their hands as surely as leather.

Stormweave said nothing for a long time, his body tensing in preparation for taking the ship out into the bay. 'How far?' he said at last, the words like frost.

'Not far,' said Jubaia. 'No closer to shore than a mile.'

'If the storm breaks, there will be complications.'

'I understand.'

'The fee is doubled.'

'I'll give you half as much again of what I've paid you.'

'Two thirds.'

Jubaia watched Stormweave's hunched body. It had grown very tense, as if, like a diver, it was preparing to launch itself. The precise moment to leave the quay was almost upon them.

'Half is all I have,' said Jubaia.

Stormweave lurched forward, then back, and the ship moved at once, picking up a wave that had slapped against the quayside and rebounded with some force. The voyage was under way.

'I agree,' whispered Stormweave, the words like surf, almost lost.

Jubaia gripped the sleek side of the craft as it moved forward, dancing over the procession of waves. Beyond it the sky had blackened like a gigantic pot, spilling its contents over its side and downward so that the sea seemed as if it had come gushing out of it, one vast, churning mass. The wind had funnelled into an army of sounds, and as the ship slipped from the sanctuary of Kelpoora, the sounds increased, whipping at the craft, buffeting it as if in an effort to roll it over. But smoothly it adjusted itself and its lines, using the wind without fighting it, just as it used the tide, a perfect fusion of the elements.

Stormweave silently guided his craft round to the east, though Jubaia sensed the anger in him. The captain seemed to be in constant conversation with his ship, as if speaking softly to a steed, something which the little thief understood perfectly. He thought of the gliderboat, his own communication with it. He had not dared to contact it since he had been in Kelpoora, concerned for its well-being, as he was for Armestor. But he dare not risk contact until they were close, not knowing the extent of Stormweave's powers. He had his suspicions about this captain, this master of the seas.

Corvash rejoined the crew, of which there were no more than a dozen. They had already sensed the slight swing to the east, their eyes betraying concern. They plied Corvash with muted questions and he explained to them, scowling across at Ussemitus and the others as he did so.

Aru sat at the base of one of the spine-like masts, Ussemitus and Fomond squatting beside her. They had no fear of the racing of the winds, but the ocean was something new to them. They could feel its wild power, as if they moved across the hide of some unimaginably huge beast, though it was far too large to give them a second's consideration. Aru thought of the gliderboat, but apart from that one moment when it had spoken to her, she had lost all contact with it.

Jubaia could feel the pull of the sea as it sought to prevent the ship from moving eastward. It was as if some unspoken bond with the storm had been broken by this variation, and he regretted it, but there were sacrifices to be made if they were to get the gliderboat aboard safely. Stormweave seemed to suffer discomfort, and Jubaia would have offered to help, but the contact between a captain and a ship like this was a sacred thing, not to be disturbed. Jubaia knew his duplicity was unfortunate, but it had been necessary.

'How far?' came the stabbing voice of Stormweave above the din of the waves, which rose up dangerously, the more so because his ship was sideways-on to them, far less easy to control.

Jubaia went to the landward side of the ship and tried to see into the false darkness. The line of dunes was barely visible. He leaned outwards, gripping the craft hard as it rose and fell. Carefully he sent out a probe. It was answered faintly. The gliderboat stirred.

'You'll need to turn north west to pull away, I take it?' Jubaia shouted against a sudden burst of spray, his feet slipping.

'Aye. I'll swing around, landward, with the stern facing south. We'll ride the surf in to the land, then turn again, through south west, west, then north and away. But I must begin it now. I'll honour the bargain, but it must be now.'

'Very well,' nodded Jubaia, returning to the captain's side. Stormweave had almost merged with his craft, a projection of it, blurred by the thick spray. Any animosity or bitterness he might have felt for Jubaia was lost for the moment as he worked his craft, urging her to do his bidding, dropping down into a trough where there was an area of calm water, then rising up across another line of waves in perfect timing with them. Jubaia could feel the elation in the seaman, the knowledge that he was still in control, feeding on the elemental forces, a living part of them.

Jubaia looked straight ahead to where the low dunes could be seen as the craft rose up to crest each tossing wave. He called again to the gliderboat, knowing that it was coming, with Armestor aboard. The craft transmitted Armestor's fear to him, and he could visualise the woodsman flat to the deck of the gliderboat, the wind howling about him without pity. But he was safe.

As Stormweave began the manoeuvre that would swing the ship back along the coast, Jubaia sensed an emotional change in the captain. Stormweave had sensed the presence of something else within the storm. Jubaia would have spoken to him, but he focused his own attention on guiding the gliderboat, helping it as he had helped it under the Thunderreach, protecting it from the grasping hands of the elements.

'Where is the ship that will bring your companions?' shouted Stormweave.

Jubaia could not speak, his eyes searching the darkness overhead. The gliderboat came onward, but its flight was difficult, the storm jealous of its flight. Then he saw it circling, low over the waves. 'She comes,' he said. 'She will land upon our deck.'

'*Board* us?' gasped Stormweave, voice cutting the air like a blade.

'She comes from the air.' Jubaia pointed as he spoke, and the dark shape of the gliderboat drifted alongside, somehow frail and small beside the racing ship. Jubaia could not see Armestor, but he could feel the thoughts of the gliderboat.

Corvash had seen the gliderboat, alarmed by it, but Ussemitus was beside him, calming him.

'*This* is your craft?' came Stormweave's rasp as he swung the prow of his ship into the storm, forcing it to take the line of his original course. The gliderboat was now flying parallel to the ship.

'It is,' called Jubaia. 'I must bring her aboard. She does not ride the storm as your ship does. It will bring her down.'

Stormweave slowed his ship a fraction; Jubaia guided the gliderboat across and down on to the deck. Slowly it settled. He could feel its exhaustion.

Ussemitus leapt aboard it at once, dropping down to tend to Armestor. The latter was cold and forlorn, but by the time Fomond had shaken him and called him a few ribald names, he sat up, coming out of his self-induced trance.

Aru had also entered the gliderboat, running her hands over it, checking to see that it was not damaged. She and her companions were so intent on their reunion that they paid little attention to the crew of Stormweave's ship, who watched them with renewed interest.

When Jubaia climbed out of the gliderboat, satisfied that it was no more than exhausted by its brief flight into the wind, he found himself facing the enigmatic figure of the captain, which had slipped down from the prow like a ghost. Its lower body was obscured by the long robe that it wore, trailing like silky fronds to the deck, and it swayed as if it clung there, a part of it. Stormweave's face was a white blur, one eye in shadow, the other a bright oval, deep green, like the eye of a sea dweller.

Stormweave nodded, arms folded across his narrow chest. He gazed with open fascination at the lines of the gliderboat. 'An intriguing craft,' he said. 'Is this also a gift for the king of Umtal?'

'No more so than your own ship,' said Jubaia.

'You would compare this craft to mine?' said Stormweave, the soft flesh of his mouth curling. 'But surely, this is an artefact.'

Aru was stunned by the look that crossed Jubaia's face, and she could almost feel the fury in him, like a blast of heat.

'No more so, captain, than your own craft is a fish.'

Stormweave was not stung by the retort. His expression said clearly that he had found a weakness in Jubaia's coolness. He turned his attention from the little man to Aru. It was only then that she realised just how much of her own mask she had let slip.

'Your prize, Jubaia, appears to have a special relationship with this craft,' Stormweave said, his eye unblinking. He drifted towards Aru, and she could not take her face from his. He had become as forbidding to her as a Csendook, the storm poised at his shoulder like his servant.

'That is nothing to you,' said Jubaia.

'Oh, but it is. The safety of my craft, my crew, depends upon my judgement. I am confused by this development. Who brought the craft here? Certainly not that creature.' He lifted an arm to indicate Armestor.

Jubaia straightened. 'I am responsible,' he said, seeing no reason to deny what Stormweave must already know.

'You communicate with this craft?' said the captain.

Jubaia inclined his head.

'And does the girl?'

Jubaia's eyes warned Aru not to speak. 'Of course not! But she serves it. As your crew serve this ship.'

Stormweave studied Aru again, but he smiled. 'I am not sure the terms of the charter cover these developments. Two companions were to be picked up. A man and a woman. I wonder if we should put back into Kelpoora. It is not far away. We should, possibly, seek clarification about the exact status of this craft. We will, in all fairness, have to re-negotiate the fee for this voyage. I feel I have been somewhat misled.'

Jubaia snorted. 'It was not specified that one of the companions to be collected would be of a different form.'

Stormweave nodded gently. 'That is true, of course. But I find myself confused by the arguments. In a voyage under a charter, with fixed fees and penalties, and with the House requiring a percentage, forfeits, and so on, one has to be very sure of one's terms. Would you not agree?'

Jubaia said nothing.

'Whereas, under a private enterprise, the rules can be far more flexible. As you insisted on a formal procedure, I have to insist on my own rights.'

'You want to go back to Kelpoora?' said Ussemitus.

Jubaia put a hand on his arm. 'There's too little time.'

'Well, if you wish to continue with the voyage,' said Stormweave, glancing once more at the gliderboat, 'we had better come to a fresh agreement at once.'

'You have one in mind?' Jubaia asked him.

'I think so. You see, I have never enjoyed sailing under charter. You may be aware of that fact, as I do have a reputation among my brothers of the League. To be under charter now irks me. Oh, I'm not suggesting we should abandon our voyage. I'll sail to Umtal. And I'll carry your companions, whatever form they take.'

'But you wish to rescind the charter.'

'I think that would satisfy me.'

'How should this be done?'

'I would require a fresh document, signed by yourself and your companions. I will return to Kelpoora after I have landed you and claim my fee, although the House will keep a tenth of it. You will have to meet this figure.'

'That could be arranged,' said Jubaia, ignoring the anxious glances of his companions.

'Even though you have already agreed to part with the last of your wealth to bring me this far off course?' said Stormweave, again smiling.

Jubaia looked away. 'Well, naturally I kept something back as a contingency against disaster –'

'My revised fee,' said Stormweave coldly, 'will be the original price, including the tenth for the House, and a further two thirds.'

Aru glared at Jubaia, who could not meet her gaze. 'Your greed exceeds your honour in this matter,' muttered the little thief, but he nodded glumly.

'Excellent. And as we would then be sailing independently, you would have to accept any decisions I made as pilot of this craft,' Stormweave went on.

'Meaning what?' snapped Aru, no longer concerned with keeping up the guise of a slave.

Stormweave's eyes flashed in response to her anger, which appeared to delight rather than annoy him. 'Meaning that, should circumstances dictate, I may be forced to deviate from your best possible interests. This is, after all, the Ocean of Hurricanes.'

'And you are supposed to be the finest sailor ever to take a ship across it!' snorted Jubaia.

Stormweave laughed softly. 'That has been said, but I am at the whim of the Mother. She may not always listen to my demands. Which is why I am unhappy to be under charter. I need to exercise my own discretion.'

Aru was about to say something quietly to Jubaia, but she saw him stiffen, though it was not at anything the captain had said. He was looking hard at the gliderboat, almost as though it had spoken aloud to him, and there was concern in his face. Abruptly he turned from the deck and went to the stern, gazing across the turbulent water as if he could see something bearing down upon the ship.

Stormweave's strange shape bobbed near him, moving with easy agility, as light as air. He, too, seemed mesmerised by the waves.

'What do you see?' he asked Jubaia, their debate forgotten for the moment.

'There is no time for delay,' said the little man. 'You must hasten on across the sea.'

'What is it?' said Aru beside him.

Jubaia shook his head, face clouded. 'We are pursued. She senses it. Some dark shadow in the eastern skies.'

'Who sends this?' said Stormweave. 'Is it a servant of the Mother?'

'I cannot tell. I dare not attempt to reach it,' said Jubaia. 'But it is looking for us.'

Aru glanced at Jubaia. Now Stormweave would almost certainly want to put back into Kelpoora! Was Jubaia wise to speak openly?

'It seems you have enemies,' commented Stormweave, though he smiled. 'You must furnish me with a complete history of your cause. I am intrigued.'

Jubaia moved away from the stern. 'Give me a little time to discuss the position with my companions.'

'Of course,' nodded Stormweave. He moved away to the prow of his ship, once more facing the waves beyond, the storm that was already breaking directly ahead of them.

'What have you sensed?' Aru asked Jubaia, while the others huddled around them.

'Another gliderboat, though it is quite unlike our own. There is a grimness about it, as there was over the Dhumvald when you grappled with the deathstorm,' Jubaia told Ussemitus. 'Neither I nor our gliderboat dare attempt contact with it for fear of alerting it to our exact position.

186

There is some terrible power in it, a brooding anger, a destructiveness drawn from many sources. But the dark shadow of Innasmorn's past is linked to it.'

'Zellorian's work?' said Aru.

'It must be. But it may be that this thing cannot cross the Ocean of Hurricanes as we can. It could not charter a ship as we have. Listen, I cannot risk our gliderboat being seen in Kelpoora. I think we will have to accede to Stormweave's demands.'

'Rescind our charter?' said Ussemitus. 'But if we do so, will we not be at his mercy? His discretion, as he puts it, would give him the power to attempt an abduction. The League would no longer protect us.'

'We dare not go back to Kelpoora,' Jubaia insisted. 'Delay will be disastrous. The League would impound the gliderboat, possibly imprison us.'

'Why?' gasped Aru.

'The League are as opposed to artefacts as the Vaza. They trade in whatever suits them, however, and it would suit them to trade the gliderboat. They would simply manipulate the law to take it from us, then trade it.'

Ussemitus grunted. 'Surely you knew how Stormweave would react when he saw the gliderboat!'

'I underestimated him greatly. He is not as I imagined him. How could I know he would *hear* my thoughts, read my very mind? I did not think he would realise how alive the gliderboat is. I just assumed he would protest, but agree to continue the voyage. But he has elemental powers beyond what I expected. I suggest we accept his proposals. Without a ship like *Restless Venture* under us, we'll never cross the Ocean of Hurricanes.'

'Without the charter,' said Ussemitus, 'will he not simply choose his moment to kill us?'

'No, he'll not kill us. But he may, in the end, sell us.'

'*Sell us!*' said Armestor. 'To whom?'

'There are lands beyond the northern coasts where slaves are considered valuable assets – '

Aru threw up her hands in horror. 'I should have expected this!'

'Wait,' said Ussemitus. 'What about the fee that you've promised him? The one the House is holding. You said it was something he wanted badly. Will he sacrifice it for us and the gliderboat?'

'No. Unfortunately by rescinding the charter, we forfeit it to him. He would return and reclaim it.'

Aru groaned. 'Jubaia, this is madness. You knew we might be faced with such a dilemma. Have you made no alternative plans? You thought Stormweave would mildly allow the gliderboat aboard and sail on? You are usually far more devious.'

'Oh, I expected to have to haggle a little, admitting that I misled him over the nature of the second lady passenger. But the gliderboat and I were to shield her powers from him. He saw through the deceit! Even so, the voyage fascinates him. I think he would make it, even if he had to continue under charter.'

'Then he'll simply attack us if we rescind it?' repeated Ussemitus.

'I think not. You see, he is an elemental, more a creature of the storm than he is of flesh and blood, though his true nature is beyond my understanding. It is the same with this craft, for the *Restless Venture* is pure water elemental. Certain things are of real value to such creatures. They have needs, appetites.'

'And the gliderboat?' said Fomond.

'To Stormweave it would be a toy. But he would sell it for something which, to him, would be far more valuable.'

'So what is it he really wants?' said Armestor.

'And what did you use as a fee for this voyage?' said Fomond.

Jubaia drew them all in closer. 'There are certain substances that the elementals crave. Things which give them mastery over their form. My own people used them, centuries gone by, to accelerate their evolution. But they eschew them now, having no wish to become one with the elements, the things that we have seen in the atmosphere of Innasmorn. Stormweave and his crew use these substances, and the captain himself has gone a long way down that path of transformation. I did not realise how far. He always seeks the arts of the lost races, such as those that lived in Shung Nang.'

'Would I be correct in assuming,' said Aru wryly, 'that you have a vast source of these substances, Jubaia? That you barter with it?'

'Not vast,' said Jubaia sheepishly. 'Enough to hold a degree of power over the elementals. Stormweave can be controlled, you see. He needs the drug, more than I knew, so in the end he will put aside other fancies in pursuit of it. You, good lady, and the gliderboat, would serve him only as a means to purchase more of what he really desires.'

'You have promised him all that you have,' said Ussemitus. 'Will it be enough?'

'Well, I have a further inducement for him. Not something I wanted to resort to, but if I must, so be it.'

'What do you mean?' said Aru suspiciously.

'There is an island near to the coast we seek. It is a small, uncharted place, one bare rock among many, hidden from ships and sky alike, ignored and forgotten. But over the centuries, certain creatures have secreted quantities of the elements we spoke of there. If I were to let Stormweave have the key to this island, he would grant us any wish. How could he resist such a thing? It would make him as a god.'

'How did you learn of this island?' said Fomond.

'From the lips of a tavern wench, I'll wager,' snorted Armestor.

'No, no. The winged men of Shung Nang know of the island. I merely stole the secret of how to find it. It is something I learned when I slipped into the dreams of the Aviatrix – '

'Hardly a tavern wench,' murmured Aru. 'But you were right about it being a woman, Armestor.'

Jubaia looked briefly indignant, but said nothing.

'Then you'd better call Stormweave,' said Ussemitus. 'We must bargain for our lives.'

Jubaia shrugged. 'I had hoped to preserve the secret. But under the circumstances – '

They were about to seek out the captain, but they found him standing close to the gliderboat, wrapped in his strange shroud, his figure as misty as the surf that curled in the waves behind him.

'The storm will burst soon,' he told them. 'It will require all my attention. So we had better come to a final agreement.'

Jubaia stepped forward. 'I'll not waste words,' he said. 'We are both creatures who enjoy deception, argument, the winning of prizes. My simple desire is to get across to Umtal with my companions – all of them. I will not expose the reasons for this, and I am honest when I tell you that it would benefit you nothing to know them.'

'Keep your secrets,' nodded Stormweave. 'Though they intrigue me. Especially with that dark messenger following you.'

'The price, the true value of the voyage – '

'Which I will judge.'

'Quite.'

'Your offer?'

Jubaia seemed to hesitate, though Aru guessed that it was for dramatic effect. 'I am sure you must have heard of the island of Scurrakhan?'

There was a sudden silence, a lull in the racing of the wind, as though Stormweave had pulled an invisible canopy over his ship. All of the crew had gathered, their faces fixed on the little thief. No sailor on this Ocean had not heard of the legendary island.

'I know its exact location,' said Jubaia. 'The secret is yours. You know what is buried beneath it.' He waited quietly, watching to see how the captain would react to this unprecedented news.

Stormweave, however, hardly moved, his face, though shadowed, hinting at amusement.

Jubaia felt a sudden stab of warning from the gliderboat. Words rang out in his mind as it spoke to him.

Jubaia! You underestimate the ship. *It has been listening to your every word. It reads your unguarded thoughts. It knows the island is a myth, and that you, yourself, have no real belief in it!*

The ship? Jubaia felt confusion reaching for him. The *ship* had heard his thoughts? But if Stormweave found this out –

Fool! hissed the mind of the gliderboat. *The ship, Stormweave, they are the* same. *The captain is not real. He is an illusion, sent by the ship. The ship is the entity!*

Jubaia's mouth sagged.

Beyond him, the image of the captain shifted in the air, and it was as though the spray passed through it. 'Scurrakhan? A worthy prize, Jubaia. But it is no more substantial than I am.' He laughed, and as he did so, his body drifted apart like clouds.

Corvash and his fellows had slipped their weapons from their belts, their faces ugly with fresh greed. 'Never mind, little thief!' laughed the fat pirate. 'There are other things our master desires. The woman and that craft of yours will fetch a pretty enough price, and maybe there'll be compensation enough for the island that isn't!'

14

CYCLONE

Ussemitus put himself between Aru and the first of the attackers, but she pushed him aside, eager to defend herself. Armestor and Fomond unslung their bows, but there was little room on the deck to put them to good use and they had to resort to their swords. The crewmen moved in, pinning their passengers back, forcing them away from the gliderboat: two of the pirates fell, run through by Aru, who was far more skilful with the sword than they had expected, and by Fomond, who narrowly escaped a serious wound as he made his kill.

Stormweave reshaped himself, his figure hovering at the edge of the skirmish, barking commands. His men drew back cautiously, spreading their circle. Stormweave stood beside the gliderboat, looking down into it. He touched it with a hand that was almost transparent, but Jubaia felt a response in the craft, as if it had been stung by an insect.

'Don't harm her!' he cried instinctively and there was a meaningful smile on the face of the apparition.

'If she means anything to you,' his voice rasped above the wind as it raced furiously about the ship, 'you'll surrender yourselves to me.'

'What do you intend?' said Ussemitus.

'This storm gathers power to it. We must go back to Kelpoora. I've no desire to continue our voyage. And you've broken the charter. Drop your weapons and be sensible.'

Jubaia stepped forward. 'Listen to me, Stormweave. It's true that I deceived you about the gliderboat. But you dare not go back to Kelpoora.'

'I've no fear of the League.'

'No. But you have no knowledge of the thing that follows us. It will be making for Kelpoora, following our trail.'

Stormweave scowled. He recalled the shadow he had sensed in the east. 'Why should I fear this thing?'

'It is indiscriminate in what it kills.'

The motionless figure studied Jubaia, the waves thrashing at the side of the ship, the membranous sails stretched back in a tight curve as the craft arched up and over another huge surge of water. Stormweave pointed to the bow. 'Go there. Open your mind and let me see your thoughts. Show me this thing that comes. Quickly, or I'll turn about very soon.'

Jubaia put down his weapon on the deck and carefully walked up towards the prow, the shape of Stormweave gliding behind him. The water that showered over the little man was icy, but he gripped ropes attached to the sides of the ship and held on grimly. Jubaia knew that the living ship would read his thoughts, so he pictured to himself the shadow he had glimpsed in the east, Zellorian's creature that followed them. He was careful to shield other thoughts, projecting only the image of the dark gliderboat.

The shadow figure of Stormweave called something above the raging seas. Lightning seemed to answer him, spearing down ahead of them.

'What is this thing?' he called to Jubaia.

'An engine of death.'

'There is danger to Kelpoora?'

'Only if we return there. But it will not attempt to cross the Ocean of Hurricanes.'

Jubaia could sense the ship as it pondered over the terrible vision he had shared with it. Stormweave's eyes flashed, reflecting another tongue of lightning. 'Then it will be the storm for us. Do you know what that means? We are elementals. Water is our power. Understand that your companions will suffer if we sail on into this storm. Be sure that the ocean is less dangerous to them than what follows, though. And when we are through, if you survive, you'll pay me well.' He looked back meaningfully.

'The girl is her own mistress. We serve her,' said Jubaia, steadying himself as the ship plunged down into a deep trough and then swung up violently to ride another wave.

'Then I'll have that craft. Or your lives. You decide. Now get back to your companions while I steer us into the heart of the storm. I sense anger within her. Something in the Mother is moved by your coming here.'

Jubaia could not argue further, almost toppling as the ship juddered to the impact of another wave. Rain had begun to lash down, mixed with the flying spray; the wind tore white sheets of spume from the tops of the waves. They towered over the craft as it dropped down into the heaving valleys.

Ussemitus and the others held on to each other for support, though the crew were unmoved by the storm, standing up to it, watching and waiting for a fresh command from the prow. The two dead members lay where they had fallen, unattended. But the figure of Stormweave shouted back, mouth forming words that should have been lost. His men must have heard him: they broke ranks, each looking to the ship, helping to take her on through the increasing violence of the storm.

'Into the gliderboat,' Jubaia told his companions and they responded at once. Aru sensed that the craft had closed its mind to what was happening, which was a relief to her.

'Can we possibly survive this?' she gasped, drenched to the skin, her hair plastered to her face.

'*This* ship will not founder,' said Jubaia. 'It was born in such a storm.'

'They've put away their weapons,' said Ussemitus. 'So what does our captain intend?'

'He knows of the thing that follows us and is very wary of it. Though he may rail at the dangers of this storm, he'll sail through it. He fears the pursuit more.' He explained how he had let the mind of the ship read his own terrors. 'I did not have to exaggerate. Stormweave is the ship. The being we see is merely a vessel, a means of communication. I spoke directly to its mind.'

As he spoke, huddled down in the body of the gliderboat, the ship plunged on through mounting seas, struck from all sides, slowing but mastering the storm. Corvash had gone to the prow, eyes scanning every wave, reading its curve, its strength, his own mind attuned to that of the ship as he helped it.

Beside him the shape of his master hovered like mist, attention fixed on the water, ignoring the swirling of the skies, the gathering of winds into a cyclone.

Corvash could sense the unease of the ship. 'What is it that pursues us, master?'

'I do not fear that so much,' came the voice beside him. 'But something in the Mother. In her darkness. It stirs in its old slumber.' Suddenly the shadow-shape turned to Corvash, pale eyes gleaming. 'We must rid ourselves of this cargo! They are cursed. If we do not destroy them, we may all be lost.'

'But we are children of the storm,' protested Corvash. 'The Mother will not swallow us –'

'There is a darkness in her that rises. We must prepare.'

Corvash slipped back to tell the crew, and again they took up arms in preparation for whatever it might be that Stormweave feared. Corvash felt it in the vibrations of the ship, and in the colliding waves. As he studied them, he saw the first of the manifestations.

Water that should have collapsed on itself formed instead into a flowing shape, a long body, a head, with a face carved from the foam. Its white eyes studied him before it broke apart and the wave had moved on as if it had never been. Another formed, collapsing as the first had, but then there were more, the shapes becoming less amorphous, more substantial. Cold laughter hissed in the sound of the breakers.

Stormweave's figure shuddered as it saw something rush down towards the prow of the ship from the skies, an aerial horror formed from cloud and light, claws held out like those of a great bird of prey. For a moment Stormweave thought it must be the shadow that Jubaia feared, but then the thing had dissipated, pulled apart by the winds. It was as though Innasmorn fought herself: nightmare things were forming from sea, from cloud and from the wind: the same elements were conflicting with them, breaking them up.

Stormweave's figure drifted back to the deck, where his men confirmed the terrible conflict in the air and sea around the ship.

The wind howled with renewed fury, all other voices lost in the din, and the seas flung the ship this way and that mercilessly. The crew were flung to the deck.

Ussemitus watched in amazement. He saw a score of the elemental shapes in the seas rise up, huge and destructive, then drive down on the ship before they could be broken. They tore at it with watery talons. The ship swung round under the impact, and the vision of Stormweave shimmered and disappeared.

'Servants of the darkness!' Ussemitus said, and Jubaia nodded.

'Something has woken them,' he said.

'The pursuing craft?' said Aru.

Jubaia shook his head. 'I cannot believe it has that power, even if it bears Zellorian himself, though I think not. But we are the targets.'

'Why?' said Ussemitus. 'The Windmasters?'

'They must have links with other powers. Even Stormweave fears these horrors.'

They knew Jubaia was right, for Stormweave's men were at the sides of the ship, watching every wave, desperately trying to keep the ship out of difficulty. Winds circled like massed eagles; one of the masts was gripped and uprooted like a sapling, flung back across the deck, disappearing in another explosion of foam. They heard an agonised cry beneath them, as if the very ship cried out in excruciating pain, a limb torn from it.

Something half-seen dropped on to the deck and gripped a crewman, dragging his head back, snapping the neck and spine and flinging the man high into the air. The wind punched him over the side of the ship; he was eagerly swallowed by the massing elemental shapes. Wave after wave of them rose up on all sides, mouths wide and silent, eyes filled with hatred that was blind and relentless. There was an unbridled, raw desire to kill in those ranks, and no ordinary weapon could oppose it.

Another of Stormweave's crew was torn apart and flung out into the eager seas.

The image of Stormweave appeared beside the gliderboat, though its shape faded. Its eyes were haggard, alive with distress. 'Who has brought them? Who has brought this terrible death to me?'

In answer the winds roared the louder, swinging the ship around effortlessly, and as it began to wallow, Stormweave cried out, arching in pain.

'He'll die,' said Jubaia softly, but Aru heard him.

'The ship?'

Jubaia nodded. 'Innasmorn has no control over this madness. See how the waters prepare to engulf us!'

Aru felt the stirring of the gliderboat, and as she did so, Jubaia straightened. He was conversing with it in a way that she had never been able to.

'What is it?' she asked him, gripping his tiny arm.

He was shaking his head, arguing it seemed.

'What is it?' Aru repeated. Ussemitus and the others could feel the urgency in her voice, even though the wind tried to crush all sound.

'She wants to take to the sky!' gasped Jubaia. 'But it is far too dangerous.'

Armestor cried out, pointing. A dozen watery shapes had flopped over the side of the ship. They rose up, full of grim purpose, their limbs shaped from the sea, their faces contorted. As one they slithered forward, intent on reaching the gliderboat and its occupants. Two of Stormweave's men slipped to the deck before these creatures, and as they moved forward, the wave-beings pulped the men beneath them, blood running ahead of them in a tiny, scarlet tide.

The gliderboat throbbed with life. Jubaia leapt to its prow. The others held on, though their eyes were fixed on the impossible shapes that still came towards them across the bloody deck. Behind them a fresh wave of the monsters formed. Stormweave's fading image hovered on the very edge of his craft, shouting something that was lost, and the lightning crashed about him as though he had called it into play. It burst, ripping a line of giant waves apart like the fall of a mountain, but still the writhing shapes in air and sea formed themselves.

Jubaia guided the gliderboat into the air, hovering uncertainly.

Stormweave will die, she told him. *I have no choice but to rise from his deck*.

'The skies are even more dangerous than the waters!' Jubaia protested, his eyes filled with tears.

As the first of the water beings reached the side of the gliderboat, Ussemitus swung at it with his sword. It tore through the water as if it were wood, and it took several such wild blows to undo the creature, which suddenly burst like a ripped bladder, emptying its contents over the deck. The gliderboat rose in time to avoid the clutching arms of the other water beings, but it hovered unsteadily as the winds tore at it.

Ussemitus toppled back into the craft. Aru held on to him, with both Fomond and Armestor knocked flat to the deck, unable to do anything other than look up into the raging cyclone above them.

'Use your power!' Jubaia was screaming, his voice almost hoarse. The wind elementals seemed to shriek with laughter at his efforts, trying to pull him off the prow, but he had locked himself there, his mind fused with that of his beloved gliderboat.

'Power?' repeated Ussemitus.

'Act as you have before,' Aru told him. 'If not, the dark will take us.'

Ussemitus crawled across the narrow space, getting behind Jubaia, the wind snarling at him. Slowly the gliderboat rose.

'Help us!' cried Jubaia. 'Beat back these fiends. Use your power.'

Ussemitus closed his eyes and concentrated on the sources he had discovered within himself in the Dhumvald, knowing that something must be drawn up to hold back this storm.

Below him the ship that was Stormweave was being ripped apart by the seas, both masts gone, the stern torn away, trailing blood and organs. Corvash alone seemed to have survived the onslaught, the others sucked down into the depths. But Corvash began to scream, racing about on a deck slippery with the blood of his fellows. He swung his weapon uselessly, and beyond him the hunched shadow of the captain watched as the waves reformed yet again, hands reaching out and pulling at Corvash, tossing him up, swallowing him, disgorging him again and again until he became a bloody rag.

The shadow image collapsed. Under it the ship was dying, reduced to an agonised carcass. Slowly the shadows seeped into the water, all power spent.

Aru looked down and saw a face in the waters about the wreck, larger than life, with a glaring white eye. Beneath it, like a hole in the sea, a bloody mouth opened. Kill them! it seemed to gasp. Kill them for bringing this nightmare to birth!

Then the waves rushed over the huge face, covering it in a blanket of surf. Aru shrank back into the craft, exhausted. The ship below was no more.

Something burst, light dazzling the company, as Ussemitus probed at the wind creatures around them. Jubaia was bent over the prow of the gliderboat, lifting the craft in a gentle spiral, away from the horrors of the sea. Ussemitus could feel the sheer weight of malice of the storm, its evil jubilation at having its prey rise up to meet it. He fought it from within, shaping what power he could, though there was no help from beyond, no gathering of Windmasters to focus his energy.

Jubaia raced the gliderboat, dropping fast and skimming along over the crests of the waves, which reached up hungrily, only to grip nothing, foiled by the speed of the craft. The air creatures whirled down, also foiled by the sudden swerving of the alien craft, the superhuman speed.

Aru gaped as she saw Jubaia's face. It was pulled back in a mask of acute joy, as though something within the little man had snapped, something that laughed to scorn the writhing madness that was trying to pull them from the skies. Aru knew that whatever control she had had over the gliderboat was truly lost to her now, for there was a symbiosis between it and Jubaia that went far beyond her own relationship with the craft. Their minds linked, and it seemed that Jubaia's own powers had found something far down in the lost depths of the gliderboat's mind, even its soul, and the process was reversed. Jubaia grew in stature when he was in harmony with the craft – for it was his craft now. Something of his past, perhaps, of the days when he had wings and flew through the skies of Innasmorn. Aru understood then what it must have meant to him to have been stripped of the power of flight, the devastating blow it must have been. But here, watching his fierce exultation, his staggering control of the gliderboat, she felt herself buoyed, her own resistance to the evils about her strengthened.

Fomond and Armestor also understood something of this, amazed by the speed of the gliderboat, its evasive actions in slipping through the cyclonic fury.

Below them the ocean gave up its lunatic shaping, though the waves yet rose and fell like mountains. It was the sky that focused the full fury of Innasmorn's rage. Ussemitus felt something within him pulling at things beyond the storm, as if he, like Jubaia, had established a link with another power. It was nameless, this power, but there was pity in it, and a will to counter the darkness.

Jubaia turned back to his companions. 'We must find land soon. She tires.' He said no more, and the others tried to see through the darkness. There was no visible break in the wild seas.

The gliderboat began to drop closer to the sea again, having soared high above it for some time, and the company realised that it was exhausted, having used up almost all the energy that it had stored. Jubaia, too, seemed tired, but he would not relax his concentration for a moment.

'There!' called Armestor, pointing down at a dark stain on the sea. They studied it, the gliderboat winging in towards what turned out to be the first of a chain of small islands. The craft flew between them, bare outcrops of rock, exposed and wind-raked. Aru wondered if one of them could have been Jubaia's mythical Scurrakhan, but smiled and said nothing.

At last the little thief was satisfied that there was a stretch of terrain they could land on, and he took the gliderboat down, plunging between two steep-sided escarpments. The worst of the storm raced on overhead. Jubaia found an area that was composed mostly of soft rock, broken down by erosion, and the tall crags closed about the craft protectively.

Ussemitus stood up in the stern of the gliderboat, using his power to create a web that held the winds in check. Like angry dogs they darted in, snapping but unable to fasten on their prey. Gradually their attack weakened, the sounds dying down, the hunt over.

Fomond and Armestor were with Jubaia, who had slumped over the prow.

'Jubaia!' called Fomond, trying to lift the little man. He was as light as a child.

Aru could feel the sheer exhaustion of the craft, but she could not reach it. It was as though it had slipped into a deep slumber.

'I can't rouse him,' Fomond said, turning to Aru with a look of alarm on his face.

'He's used up his own energy to fly the craft,' Aru nodded anxiously. 'Jubaia!' she said, shaking him. 'You must wake. Fomond, try to wake him. Sleep may be dangerous.'

'How can I?' protested Fomond. He tried to wake the little man, but to no avail.

Aru turned to Ussemitus, but he was occupied with his defence of the craft and did not break his concentration on the skies.

'What has happened?' said Armestor.

Aru grimaced. 'The gliderboat ran out of power. I didn't know it. But Jubaia put himself into it, using his own energy to bring it these last miles to the island. But at what cost to himself!'

Fomond put the frail body down in the prow of the gliderboat, appalled to think that Jubaia had brought himself so close to death for their sakes.

'You must help me,' said Aru suddenly.

Both Fomond and Armestor looked at her, puzzled, but they nodded.

'I *must* reach him, or he may slip away. I don't know how I am to do it, but I must try. And you must try with me.'

'But we have no powers,' said Armestor.

'We'll see,' said Aru, her mouth set. She bent over Jubaia's inert form, closed her eyes, and concentrated. She emptied her mind of everything, as she had been trained to do when learning to control the gliderboats. And into the black well she sent her probe.

Fomond and Armestor shut out the last despairing blasts of wind above them and thought of the little man, calling upon the Mother to help them.

As they worked at their power, Ussemitus fought back another assault from the air. But it was far weaker. He knew they had thwarted the storm. Something in the Mother had responded to the madness of that cyclone, the unchained dark, and had come to his aid, both directly, through a counter-storm, and indirectly through him. Now the cyclone had moved away, collapsing in on itself, and the remnants of its manic army were in disarray, retreating over the seas, absorbed by them.

Ussemitus sank down for a moment, knowing the danger was past. The powers he had tapped again frightened him. He could not understand them and still felt afraid of them. He had had no teaching in such matters. Only that to reach for such things was heresy, the prerogative of the Windmasters and other chosen shamen. But what choice had he had? And the Mother had not rebuked him. Perhaps that would come.

When he turned, it was with a cold jolt of realisation. The others were arranged as if they were dead, stricken by the storm. Quickly he went to them, fighting off nausea and exhaustion.

Fomond opened his eyes. 'It's Jubaia,' he said softly.

Ussemitus nodded. He could see what had happened. He stood up, straddling Jubaia and the girl who tried to revive him. With his right hand he reached upwards, calling out once as loudly as he could. Something cracked in the sky overhead, the sound of a boulder being broken in half.

Fomond thought he saw a stab of light, then shrank back, too tired to do any more. Armestor had already succumbed to sleep.

Aru felt something reach into her, a hot flow, power. She shaped it as if it were molten, making it into a spear that she jabbed down into the darkness she wanted to penetrate. Then she felt her fingers loosen on the haft and in spite of the intensity of her efforts, she fell backwards.

Ussemitus caught her and let her down, putting her beside Fomond, who was also unconscious. He touched the brow of the little man, and it was warm.

'Sleep, Jubaia,' he whispered.

Another presence alerted him and he looked up, but there was no one here. A breeze, no more than that, stirred the dirt.

He lives, a voice called to Ussemitus, as if from across a vast gulf.

Ussemitus nodded. He had so little energy left to project his thoughts. He knew that this may be the only time the gliderboat ever chose to contact his mind, for its link with Jubaia had become a sacred thing. But in those two words he felt such a depth of emotion, such a yearning, that it made him draw in his breath. And he knew that Jubaia would survive, sustained by a special power, a unique thing.

Ussemitus turned his attention away from the little man to the girl. He reached out a hand and lightly touched her alien face. He knew its every line, the shape of its brow, the curve of her mouth. His fingers lingered for the briefest of moments, then touched his own cheek, his lips. A stolen kiss? He smiled at that. Would she object to such a theft? But he had read something in her eyes. The thought of love made him shy. Foolish! he told himself. How could we love, caught in this confusion? It would weaken us. Or would it give us strength?

He turned away, suddenly afraid. The Mother had given something of herself to him. What other demands would she make on him? And what would the price be? His freedom? His devotion?

He closed his eyes, but sleep evaded him for a long time, and the waves on the distant rocks seemed to mock him, echoing his thoughts.

15

PURSUIT

The black gliderboat moved in absolute silence above the dunes, dipping down, moulding its flight to their shapes effortlessly as if riding an aerial current. Beyond it was the sea, the waves racing in to the beach, churning the sand, grey-backed, propelled by the storm over the waters. Vymark dared not attempt flight over this sea: the voices within him warned him against it. Some other force ruled the skies there, unwilling to permit intrusion. While the storm raged, there would be no safety, only chaos and brutal retribution.

Vymark listened constantly to the sounds that came to him, a dark chorus, a whispering that had begun at the back of his mind but which now had become a fugue of sound, not always clear, but fierce, compelling. Zellorian was not a part of that sound, though he could be reached if Vymark wanted to speak to him. This power came from elsewhere, from somewhere deep down within Innasmorn's lost past. And as the power grew, so it fed Vymark, drinking the fury in his own blood, using it to strengthen itself.

His enemies were at sea! They were somewhere across that heaving expanse of water, but he dare not seek them out, not directly. The darkness told him there were other ways of hunting and attacking them, powers in the sea. But if he flew towards the storm, it would gather him to it and pull him apart.

He came to the low dunes that reached towards the town of Kelpoora, pausing to study the curious outline of its structures. He could sense the life there, smell it, the gathering of Innasmornians, huddled together against the storm. Had the Casruel bitch been there? She must have. It was where she would have taken the ship.

Like a huge bat, the gliderboat soared across the last

expanse of sand, veering from the walls and swooping around the town, searching for movement. Rain lashed down as the edge of the storm caught the buildings, the wind slanting it across the misshapen roofs, blurring their lines. In this grim weather, Vymark could detect no one out on the walls or in the watches. Perhaps the townspeople felt secure from attack.

He found an expanse of relatively level roof and lowered himself gently, melting into the shadow. The falling rain meant nothing to him; he closed out the roar of the wind, the battering of the waves against the quay below. Folding his wings over himself, he settled to listen to the town, picking up the vibrations of movement below, the remote murmur of voices.

Hours passed, day and night fused by the raging of the storm, though it meant nothing to him. Time was shapeless to him in his present form. He could rest but never sleep, his existence no more than a degree of awareness that varied according to his own self-control. He thought of Zellorian, but there was no need to reach out for him. Not until he had found his enemies. Inside him, the darkness curdled, the dark whispers pulsing gently, echoing the far waves, soothing.

At last he heard a name whispered below in one of the many alleyways. *Jubaia.* One of the party of fugitives. Stormweave. The ship that had sailed out into the fury.

Vymark focused on the conversation, trying to locate its exact source. He lifted himself from his hiding place and drifted across more roofs, unable to get lower, as the streets and alleys were like pinched veins in this squalid town. But the object of his interest emerged on one of the quaysides. The storm had moved further out to sea, raging away on the northern horizon. All that remained in Kelpoora was the blanketing drizzle. The wind had fallen away.

On the quay, two figures talked guardedly, but Vymark could pick out words as though they were sparks. He dropped over the lip of the buildings, swung round in an arc, extending his talons. It took him seconds to find the creature he wanted, and like a striking hawk, he had him, fastening on him with dreadful accuracy. His companion screamed and flung himself for cover. But Vymark rose, his struggling captive shrieking.

Away out over the dunes Vymark flew, knowing that nothing in that village could follow him as quickly as he could fly. He tightened his grip, feeling bone and muscle in his claws crushing, the blood running thickly. He could smell it, intoxicated by it. It heated him, brought his hatred for his enemies boiling up anew.

The creature he held screamed for a long time, until its voice fell to a moan of pain, but Vymark cut through this, reading the thoughts of a mind that had become a whirl of confusion, clarity obscured by agony. But Vymark read what he wanted: this creature had seen the Casruel bitch, had talked with her companions, the Innasmornians from the east, and the dwarfish Jubaia. They had gone with the sea elementals to the north. Bound for where? Vymark probed with the question as if with a scalpel, and although the tormented creature below him screamed anew as his mind was subjected to the same merciless damage that was being done to his body, an answer was torn from somewhere within it.

Shung Nang. Jubaia claimed to seek Umtal, but his true destination was the sacred city of Shung Nang. The city of winged ones, the windriders.

Vymark dropped his prize into the sands below, ignoring its last cries, its pathetic flapping. He swung away, paralleling the coast. The darkness within him warned him once more about the Ocean of Hurricanes. To attempt to cross it would invite the Mother's retribution. But there was a way around the waters, and to fly swiftly would not delay the pursuit too much.

Protected by the dark, Vymark beat at the air, his new course set.

Zellorian opened his eyes and glared at the mural on the ceiling above him. Its colours confused him and he swung away to avoid them, as if they had taken concrete shape and were about to unleash something dangerous. He shook himself, wiping the perspiration from his face. Dream confused with reality. He was in his private chambers. The ceiling was no more than a decoration. But his dreams had merged with the reality of Vymark's flight.

What was happening to the gliderboat? He had tried to find it and had been rewarded with a chaotic vision. Vymark was now able to shut his Controller out at will, something that Zellorian had never expected. But Zellorian had seen something. It had not all been a dream. Vymark had killed, as a bird of prey takes its prey. But it had not been for food: Vymark had no need of food. It had been for knowledge. He had drained the creature, just as though he had eaten it. How had he developed this power?

Yet it disturbed Zellorian, as did other matters. He had equipped Vymark with the purpose of locating the power in the west. But Vymark now had a purpose of his own, more and more so. The Casruel girl had become an obsession with him. There was a danger that he would focus all his attention on her and her companions.

Something further in Zellorian's half-dream alerted him. Other voices within the image of Vymark's mind. The sea of darkness beyond it, power that Zellorian himself had drawn upon and fed into Vymark. To be used. And yet, *it grew*. Its rebellion was clear. It gave power to Vymark, permitting him flight through alien skies and in regions where others dare not go, and yet, what price would it demand? Did it have a purpose of its own?

Cursing, Zellorian tried again to contact the black gliderboat, but darkness frustrated him. As he probed at it, he felt the stirring of something vast, a deeper darkness that threatened to overwhelm with its mere contemplation. He pulled his robes about him and stared again at the ceiling. There were faces in the design, and for a moment he imagined he could see Gannatyne grimacing at him. And with him was Pyramors, the Consul who, he knew, schemed his fall.

A great silence closed in on the Prime Consul, but with it there was no sleep.

Korborus led the Csendook party onwards, moving down through more hills to a wide expanse of land beyond. His eyes were darkly ringed, filled with dread, his head flicking from side to side constantly. He muttered to himself, though whether in prayer to his gods, or whether in anger at having to lead the company further west, Vorenzar could not say.

The Csendook had, in a way, admired the spirit of the old man as he took the Zemoks away from his village and people. He knew of this western power, but he had sacrificed himself in order to divert the Csendook away from his people, who no doubt had fled these lands. Vorenzar understood all that, but it was not fear of the Csendook that had so changed Korborus. He looked down at him with a growing contempt.

'Superstition rules these primitives,' he told Ondrazem. 'I've seen this on other worlds. They read magic in every breeze, every twist of grass.'

Ondrazem nodded. 'Quite so, Zaru. The events of the storm were confused. Innasmorn is an unusual world – '

'It is easy to be confused, to have one's eyes tricked in such a storm. Whatever came to life was flesh and blood. Powerful, perhaps, but of the earth. I'd match Csendook steel against these aerial spirits.'

Ondrazem grinned, glancing at the skies, which were overcast. There did not seem to be any danger of a storm, but rain had threatened the party since dawn. 'The Innasmornians are not a strong people, Zaru. Such races have to resort to false powers, having little of their own. They use their shamen to good effect.'

'If they attempt their trickery again, I'll have an example made of them. Windmasters? We'll see how their people react to their heads on poles! Resistance might dwindle, I suspect.'

As they laughed, one of the outriding Zemoks came riding swiftly through the low trees on their right. The warrior raised his war helm, his brutish face creased in a mixture of anger and confusion.

'What is it?' snapped Vorenzar.

'Zaru, we are followed.'

Vorenzar swore. His xillatraal bared its fangs, needing tight control, but the Zaru spoke sharply to it, quelling it.

'Who follows us?' demanded Ondrazem.

'I did not see them clearly.' The Zemok seemed reluctant to say more.

'Hostile?' said Ondrazem, annoyed that the Zemok should be so disturbed. He would have to be disciplined, though this was not the time for it.

'I think we should prepare for another attack, Zaru.'

Vorenzar nodded, immediately searching the land about him, looking for a place where they could defend themselves. He pointed to a rise, strewn with outcrops of rock. The company made quickly for it, the scout galloping away in search of the other scouts, calling them in.

'The Zemoks are uneasy,' said Ondrazem. 'I'll ride them hard for this – '

'When they've seen a little action,' said Vorenzar, 'they'll settle. I sense they will not disappoint us, Ondrazem. You've trained them well.'

If Ondrazem was mollified, he did not show it, but he bowed and began the deployment of the warriors at once, calling out his orders harshly.

Vorenzar took cover behind a flat-topped rock, his eyes watching the trail along which they had come. Beside him Korborus squatted like a dog, his body shivering. He closed his eyes and intensified his prayers, but Vorenzar shut the old man from his mind.

Presently the first of the shapes emerged from the trees across the dip in the land, about a hundred yards away. Even Vorenzar felt a stab of uncertainty when he saw it. It was an urmurel.

Shaped from dark loam, its features vague, unfinished, it moved out from the trees, tall as the Csendook, arms hanging limply at its sides, the blob of a head rigid, as if somewhere within its shadows there were eyes that watched them. Behind it there were scores of other shapes slipping from the trees, all formed from the same dark loam as the urmurel, all sculpted into unfinished figures that varied in thickness and height, though none were as tall as the

210

urmurel, which seemed to lead them. They had no faces, no mouths, and they made no sound, except for the soft shifting of their earthen feet.

Korborus gasped, ducking lower.

Vorenzar looked at him, a glance of absolute fury that he should fear such pathetic things. 'Get up!' he snarled. 'Show yourself!'

Korborus stiffened, but he rose with an effort. The other Csendook were in their defensive positions, swords drawn, visors down.

Vorenzar dragged Korborus to him and shook him. 'Well? These are the creatures that seemed to help us in the night. Do they now betray us?'

But he saw at once that Korborus's mind could not cope with the coming of the earth creatures. He babbled, his eyes wide with terror. Vorenzar flung him backwards brutally.

'We shall see,' he hissed.

The urmurel moved forward, lurching down to the centre of the natural arena formed by the clearing below the rocks. The things that followed it had stopped moving, as still as the trees behind it, an unnatural copse. The urmurel moved on, as if in search of something.

'Zaru, let me test this monstrous thing,' said Ondrazem.

Vorenzar turned to him. 'In what way?'

'Allow me to make an example of it. The other creatures, whatever they may be, are its servants. Without it, their strength is diminished. We should not allow ourselves to be mocked.'

Vorenzar nodded. 'Yes. Very well.'

Ondrazem climbed over the rocks easily and dropped down to the grass beyond. The Csendook watched as he walked towards the urmurel. It was motionless, like a rock poking up from its bed, as if it had been in this valley for numberless years.

As Ondrazem approached it, he could smell its pungency: packed earth, rotting leaves, the decay of undergrowth. But still he could make out no face, no hint of features. Could this thing really be a living creature? How

211

else could it move? Yet it no longer moved. It appeared to be waiting, but for what?

Ondrazem circled it, but still there was no movement. He glanced up once at the skies, but apart from the greyness of the clouds, there seemed to be no danger there, as there had been in the night. He turned for a final look at Vorenzar, who had now climbed up on to the rocks and stood like a huge sentinel. The Zaru raised his sword in a clear gesture, then brought it down.

Ondrazem stood back from the urmurel, gripping his weapon in both hands. He swung it sideways in a blow that would have cut through a young tree. The blade bit into the waist of the urmurel and met with no resistance, nothing that suggested bone. Instead it cut through the earth as if it were soft wood, the incredible strength of the Csendook taking the blade clean through. The urmurel's trunk parted, earth spilling out like a gush of vital organs. Ondrazem lifted his sword quickly and chopped down at the shoulder. Again there was no resistance and the weapon carved its way into the soft body of earth as easily as if it had been flesh. The urmurel began to collapse like a mound that had been dug up and scattered.

Vorenzar and his Zemoks watched, puzzled. Why had there been no opposition? The creatures beyond the clearing made no move to defend the urmurel. If they were waiting for a command or signal, it did not come. Ondrazem paced about his destruction, prodding at the earth, the stinking remains, but still there was no sign of movement. He wondered if he had killed anything at all.

Perplexed, he began the walk back to his companions, but a shout alerted him and he whirled, sword ready to defend himself from any attack. At last the urmurel moved. Parts of it slid across the grass like mud slicks. Into the central core of the thing, the only part of it to remain upright, these streams of earth began to flow. It was as though an invisible potter worked with a huge mound of clay.

Ondrazem's eyes narrowed as he watched his work being repaired. Somehow the urmurel was reconstructing itself, re-forming. Slowly but unquestionably it was becoming again what it had been. Ondrazem took a step towards it, thinking to hack into it once more, but he hesitated. He waited until the thing had made itself whole.

Again it stood before him, an exact replica of what he had first seen. It no longer moved.

Vorenzar had dropped down from the rocks and strode forward as if this time he would administer the execution. But he studied the urmurel without threatening it.

'How was this done?' said Ondrazem softly. 'What power could do this?'

Vorenzar grunted impatiently. 'There's no magic in it. It is merely a life form we do not understand. We are not scientists, Ondrazem. I see no reason to fear this thing, merely because we don't understand it.' He turned to face the Zemoks in the rocks. 'Bring the Innasmornian here!' he shouted.

One of the Zemoks hauled Korborus over the rocks, but the latter cried out with terror. He had to be dragged forcibly over the grass to where Vorenzar waited. He flung himself at the feet of the huge Csendook.

'Master! Master!' he howled. 'Let me flee! You have no need of me! Let me leave this land of evil!'

Ondrazem lifted the old man to his feet, but Korborus would not look at the urmurel, cringing from it as if it would sear his flesh.

Vorenzar raised his visor and looked at him angrily. 'Why are these creatures following us? Who do they serve?'

'Evil, evil!' cried the old man, trying to wriggle free of Ondrazem's huge hands.

'Tell me why they follow us,' said Vorenzar coldly. 'Or I will give you to them.'

Korborus wailed like a child, and Ondrazem pushed him a little closer to the urmurel. It had still not moved since it had reformed.

Neither Vorenzar nor any of the Zemoks felt a shred of compassion for Korborus. They would let nothing interfere with their purpose here on Innasmorn. If Korborus withheld information from them, they would pull it from him without mercy.

'Wait! Wait!' he screamed. Ondrazem held him still. 'Mother protect me,' Korborus gasped, eyes fixed at last on the dark earth of the urmurel, seeing only horror there.

'Answer my questions,' said Vorenzar. 'Now!'

'To serve you, master. They have been sent to you to protect you.'

Vorenzar scowled. 'By whom?'

Korborus shook his head wretchedly. 'The darkness. The ancient powers. The forbidden things of long ago. Somehow by coming here you have awoken them. The Mother will try again to bring you down and destroy you. But the darkness will protect you.' Korborus was speaking quickly now, the words flooding from him. 'Always the old darkness is striving for release. It seeks allies, power, ways of breaking its chains. In you it senses this strength. It will cling to you, and to your scorn for the Mother, for the gods that have chained it. Here is proof! The urmurel and its minions will kill for you. And there will be more. Things more terrible than any you can know.'

'What is this darkness you speak of?' said Vorenzar coldly.

'Evil – '

'*What* evil? Another race? Creatures who once ruled your world who have been deposed?'

'You do not understand the powers of Innasmorn. The gods – '

'Superstition! You see a storm, lightning, and you imbue it with your own characteristics! You are like children.'

Korborus shook his head. He was less afraid of Vorenzar than he was of the urmurel. 'There are gods of light and gods of the deep night. Once they warred and the evil powers were subdued. They had sought to bend all life to them, but the Mother drove them down into the gulfs of the inner dark and shackled them.'

Vorenzar snorted. 'Gods! Creatures of the mind.'

'Something has awoken them,' insisted Korborus.

'And they dwell in the west? In the World Splinter?'

Korborus shook his head. 'No, no. They do not dwell in any physical region of Innasmorn. Yet they strive to do so. It is how they have shaped the urmurel and the things that crawl after it.'

'Then what dwells in the World Splinter?'

'Other powers. Outside powers. From beyond Innasmorn. Neither of the Mother, nor of the dark.'

Vorenzar gave another grunt of exasperation. 'Confusion. A world of chaos. Of dreamers. No wonder Zellorian chose it.'

'If this darkness protects us,' said Ondrazem, 'what will it gain from us?'

'It will make you its own,' breathed Korborus. 'You will become as easy to control as the urmurel. Slaves to the dark. When there are enough of you, and when the dark is strong enough, there will be power to shape itself into something as powerful as any god.' He hung his head. 'Mother of Storms, forgive me for bringing you to this place!'

Vorenzar gripped his chin fiercely and snapped his head up. 'What is as powerful as any god? *What?*'

The tears rolled down Korborus's cheeks. 'I speak of a Malefic.'

The Csendook stared at one another, but shook their heads. This was jibberish to them.

'Once the dark is able to spawn a Malefic,' said Korborus, 'it will begin the unleashing of the old darkness. Innasmorn will be torn asunder. Everything will change.'

Vorenzar released Korborus and Ondrazem let him fall, exhausted.

The Csendook looked about them, watching the motionless shapes in the wood. 'More supernatural powers,' said Vorenzar scornfully. 'And they want to enlist the aid of the Csendook nation!'

Ondrazem laughed coldly. 'To *enslave* us? Even if these things exist, they have no concept of what waits at the portal of their world. Should our Swarms fear armies comprised of mud and air? Of storms?'

Vorenzar snorted derisively. 'I'll waste no more time

215

hearing these children's tales. We ride on to the west. If these things wish to guard our flanks, let them. You cut this one down easily enough.' He turned abruptly and climbed back up to the ridge.

As he approached it, another of the Zemoks came to him, apparently in fresh concern.

'More willing slaves?' said Vorenzar cynically.

The Zemok shook his head. 'Zaru, it is the strange being that brought us through the portal. The ghost guide. It has appeared once more.'

Vorenzar swore, looking about for the spirit creature. The Zemok took him to a place beyond the ridge, and among the rocks there the guide hovered, no less ethereal than it had been before. It lifted an arm and pointed at Vorenzar.

'The way has been prepared for you,' it said, its voice a whisper in Vorenzar's mind.

'By whom?' Vorenzar replied instinctively, speaking aloud so that his Zemoks realised at once that the spectral figure must have spoken to him somehow, though no other had heard.

'The powers in the west await you,' said the voice.

'What of Zellorian? The others who crossed from Eannor? Where are they?'

'The west calls to them.'

'The World Splinter?' said Vorenzar.

'You must go there.'

'Why? What power lies there?'

But the ghost guide was drifting back, merging with the rocks. As it did so, a shadow rose up behind it, twice its height; it folded itself around the pale shape, arms like thick branches, a fusion of earth and wood that could have been a further type of urmurel. As it covered the ethereal figure, there was a peal of sound and an abrupt crash. Earth blasted outwards, rocks hailing down, sending the Csendook for cover. The ground shook for long moments as if a minor quake was in progress, but it became still again, settling.

Where the ghost shape had been there was now only a

216

deep pit, the rocks about it charred, the earth smoking. Earth and glistening mud spread around the pit, the result of the explosion.

'That earth creature tried to attack the guide,' said one of the Zemoks. 'Both have been destroyed.'

But Ondrazem had come up to the rocks and was pointing to the trees near the brow of the hill. Beyond it, a pale light could be seen. 'Is that not the guide? Waiting for us.'

Vorenzar nodded. 'It seems to be the enemy of the urmurels and their masters. We seem to be favoured by both parties. Gods of the light and gods of the night!' He laughed harshly. His warriors echoed him.

'Perhaps both fear us,' suggested Ondrazem.

'Well, we'll trust neither. Where's Korborus?'

They could not find him at first, but when they did, he was huddled up behind yet another boulder. His face was white and when they lifted him, his chest was smeared in thick mud from the explosion. He was like a broken doll, but he was alive.

'Can you hear me?' Vorenzar asked, shaking him.

Korborus opened his eyes, but they were like the eyes of a man who had lost his reason. His mouth worked, but no words came out. He stood stiffly, unmoving, and nothing the Csendook said or did made him any more communicative.

'His gods have come for him,' sneered Ondrazem.

'Leave him,' said Vorenzar. 'He's no longer of use to us. And I'm sick of his ludicrous fantasies.'

The Csendook mounted their xillatraal and started the winding climb up into the hills where the ghost guide awaited them. Behind them in the valley the urmurel began to move, and with it the other creatures that had been formed from the earth. As they passed the place where Korborus stood, he moved, falling into step with them. The mud that splattered his chest had spread, coating his arms and lower body. By evening he would be indistinguishable from the mass of elemental beings around him.

BOOK FOUR

THE AVIATRIX

16

SHUNG NANG

It was night when Jubaia recovered. They had placed him inside the gliderboat, and one by one they had fallen asleep, unable to keep guard, though the storm had abated, and even Ussemitus had succumbed to his need for rest. Propped against the rocks, utterly spent, the company slept like children.

When Jubaia sat up, he found himself in darkness. The only sound was that of the sea below, whispering against the rocks, but in a soft, soothing way, as though approving of the company's rest. Jubaia moved slowly, scenting the air, understanding they were far to the north of the waters where the cyclone had attacked the ship.

Rest until dawn, said the voice of the gliderboat.

Jubaia grinned to himself, stretching his arms. For a moment he felt a familiar stab of sorrow, as if his wings would be there, an emotion that often caught him unawares. He rallied his acceptance of the loss, turning his mind instead to the gliderboat.

You have other wings now, she told him.

'And fly as I have never flown before,' he laughed gently, his hands running over part of the gliderboat as tenderly as they would have run over the skin of a lover.

Rest, she told him again, knowing how tired he was, having felt the exhaustion in him as if it had been in her own form.

'We're in the west,' he murmured, gazing into the night. 'I can taste the air. I know these islands.'

Are you afraid?

He leaned back, resting against the smooth surface of the craft. He could not remember when he had last been so contented. 'If I am caught, it will mean death. There will be no mercy from the Aviatrix. No pity.'

221

Think of that tomorrow, if you must. For the moment, rest. You must.

Jubaia smiled, knowing that the gliderboat would feel his reaction. It was as if she could read his mind and heart easily, even though he could set up the barriers to prevent such a thing.

Why do you smile? she said, confirming his thoughts.

'At your tenderness.'

Should I not protect you? You have taken me from the dark place. I was like one dead.

'But surely Aru spoke with you?'

Not as you do. She is a Controller, but those who made me designed me to obey certain commands, not to think, nor to make decisions for myself. Yet you taught me that such things are still within me. They could not destroy them.

Jubaia's face clouded in momentary anger. 'Who did this thing?'

Created me? I cannot remember. But I was once like Aru –

Jubaia gasped, staring at the lines of the gliderboat.

Yes, did you not realise? I was human. But I have been changed. I cannot remember why, but I think it was to do with the wars. Some of us were badly injured, spared from death by our conversion.

Jubaia shook his head, horrified by the thought of this monstrous act.

You are appalled. But I am no worse than you, Jubaia. You had your glory taken from you. You were punished, I was spared from death.

'But they shut part of your mind! Closed off your feelings – '

Until you found them. Do I seem monstrous to you now?

He gasped. 'No! Never that. It was their act that shocked me. But never think you appal me. I would not – '

Change me? To the woman I once was?

He looked away. 'No.'

In some ways you have already done that. And have I not given back to you something of what you once were? Again she spoke with such tenderness that he felt an ache within him.

'What were you called?' he whispered.

222

It was erased, as was all my identity. But you have enabled me to recall my name. Will you tell no one?

'If you wish.'

It will be our secret. Along with many others.

He pressed himself close to the warmth of the craft, as though he would hear beneath the steel the beating of her heart.

I am Circu.

He repeated the name softly to himself, over and over, until at last, soothed by her, he fell again into sleep.

Aru found him curled up like a little boy the following morning. She was about to touch him when his eyes opened and he smiled. He sat up at once, startling her, his face beaming.

'I hope Armestor has been abroad with that bow of his,' he laughed. 'Or was it lost in the storm?'

Ussemitus appeared at Aru's elbow. 'He would more easily have lost his arm. No, all the weapons were saved. And what about you, little thief?'

'Me? Once I've some food inside me, I'll be well enough. A little sore, but ready to continue.'

'We thought – ' began Aru, but Jubaia waved away her concern, standing up and stretching.

'And the gliderboat?' said Ussemitus.

'Well rested,' nodded Jubaia.

Aru did not check. She felt as though to do so now would be to intrude, as though even the smallest probing of the mind of the craft would be a personal intrusion upon not only its privacy, but also on Jubaia's.

Armestor and Fomond had been hunting, and soon they came back, both of them having caught large hares, which they skinned expertly and cooked over a fire they had already prepared. The company ate them avidly, though they all watched the skies, the speeding clouds. But the cyclone had gone, and with it the evil that had shaped it.

Aru noticed Jubaia searching the sea's horizon as he ate. 'Is there something wrong?' she asked him.

For a moment he looked startled, as if he had been caught in some compromising act, but he passed it off with a grin. 'No. I was trying to reach out for a hint of that other shape. The gliderboat that was following us. But there is no sign of it. I think it has avoided the storm and the sea. For now, at least.'

'Are you both well enough to travel on?' said Ussemitus. 'Or would you prefer a day of rest?'

Jubaia shook his head emphatically. 'No more rest! Shung Nang lies in the west. Three days' flight away. The gliderboat is ready.'

Aru nodded. 'She's yours now, Jubaia. I understand that.'

Ussemitus looked surprised. He knew that Jubaia had established a strange link with the craft, but Aru was apparently giving up her responsibility. It was as though she felt she had no right to control the craft. But she saw his expression and smiled reassuringly at him.

Jubaia looked mildly embarrassed, but nodded. 'Very well. Let's board.'

Aru spoke softly to Ussemitus. 'I feel guilty about controlling the craft. To do so no longer seems natural. It is more alive than ever before. Jubaia has linked his mind with it – '

'I wouldn't want to intrude,' said Ussemitus. 'Any more than I would want to intrude into your – ' He stopped himself, looking away.

She laughed gently. 'My mind? And what do you think you'd find there?' she teased him, enjoying his discomfort.

'Your thoughts are private things,' he said. 'I have no right to them.'

'Nor I yours. But there would be times when I would hope to share them.' Again she laughed.

He looked puzzled.

'We'd find it hard to resolve our difficulties if we never shared our thoughts, don't you think?' she said.

'Oh yes, I see what you mean,' he said, hiding his embarrassment. 'Yes, of course.' He hastily climbed aboard the gliderboat.

Aru followed him, noticing that both Armestor and Fomond were grinning at her as if she had said something immensely funny. She was tempted to snap something at them, and only an effort of will prevented her. But she could not help mirroring their grins before boarding.

As the craft lifted easily into the air, the company felt the last of the night's depression and fear breaking up, left behind them, though they understood well enough that there would be fresh terrors awaiting them in the west.

Beyond the islands, the Ocean of Hurricanes stretched on dizzily for another day, though the gliderboat flew swiftly over it. On the second day they reached the western continent. The land beneath them was very different to that of the eastern shores. Rivers had carved steep gorges through it, the sides of which were filled with steep slopes of scree, and forests had found a hold in the rich soil, angling down towards the raging waters far below. The trees were of a peculiarly dark hue, unlike those of the east, which were lighter, less densely packed; the rocks themselves were dark, or vivid where the sunlight struck them, glistening with bands of crystalline strata. Heat rose up in waves, and the gliderboat constantly had to check its course in the face of the thermals that rocked it, though there was nothing obviously malicious in them. They seemed mindless, uncontrolled, though Jubaia told the company that they could be used if certain powers so desired.

'Everything in or on Innasmorn can be shaped to a purpose. The cyclone was a focusing of raw energy, no different to the shaping of clay by a potter.' He was reluctant to say too much about this, as though it would dampen the spirits of the party, which had now been lifted out of all former depression.

Jubaia was extremely careful to follow the natural lines of the land, the faults and scarps, keeping the gliderboat very low as it penetrated the huge land mass of the west. He used every shadow, every bend in the deep canyons to shield the craft from the open skies. After two days he insisted that they should only travel by night.

'The windriders of Shung Nang will find us otherwise. The Deathless City is never heavily guarded by them, as it is impossible to reach it other than from the air and there are other forces at watch. We must be more than invisible. We must be silent, and we must take care not to disturb the air.'

They hid by day down in the forests, trying to sleep, though the closed canopy overhead walled them in as though they were in an arboreal cavern. There were piercing calls out in the darkness as though wild beasts hunted there. Jubaia insisted that none of these creatures would attack them, and though he was proved correct, the sound of their cries did nothing to calm the company.

As twilight fell, Jubaia readied them. 'There's enough light to see by, and enough darkness to confuse any watch.'

The gliderboat slipped out from the trees, curling around yet more towering canyon walls, while huge mesas rose up on all sides in the twilight like disapproving gods. There was a chill in the air, but a stillness as if the land held its breath.

Ussemitus and his companions studied the skies above the forests, searching for any sign of movement, and though they picked out the individual flights of a few bats, they saw none of the winged shapes that Jubaia had told them would signify the coming of the windriders. Overhead, daubed in brilliant scarlets and oranges, the last of the clouds moved sluggishly towards the darkness that spread from the sea in the wake of the setting sun.

Jubaia guided the gliderboat in utter silence to a mesa that poked up at the sky, a huge knuckled fist of rock, its features obscured by the coming night. As the craft approached it, the watchers realised how vast it was, almost a continent in itself. The craft moved between two of the great outcrops, swallowed by the thick shadows within, but Jubaia guided it unerringly, with no suggestion of fear. The walls closed in like the sides of a gigantic beast, and even Aru shrank back from them. But the craft emerged near the flat top of the mesa and Jubaia brought it to a level place where there were pools and a copse of low trees. Again he found a place to conceal the gliderboat, speaking softly to it, reassuring it of its safety.

'Come with me,' he told his companions, and he set off at once across the broken stones of the mesa's top. The terrain was fragmented, a mixture of huge, cracked slabs and jagged rocks and pockets of soil where trees and shrubs grew in wild profusion, tangling with each other as if vying for soil in which to sink their roots.

Jubaia ducked down, blending uncannily with the dark, and the others had to keep very close to him for fear of losing sight of him altogether, for he seemed completely at ease with the awkward land. He was watching the skies, and twice ducked down lower when the hiss of something far above caught his attention. The others wondered if it could be one of the promised windriders, but they could discern no details. These things were like clouds, shadowed and elusive.

Jubaia led the way down through a sharp cleft in the edge of the mesa, stopping at a ledge. The company climbed out on to it infinitely carefully, thankful for the screen of bushes which prevented them from seeing directly below them into a darkness that must have dropped away for thousands of feet.

Beyond them, limned by moonlight, was the legendary city of Shung Nang.

Across that vast chasm, there was another mesa, even more immense than the one on which they now stood. Carved from its upper ramparts was the Deathless City, its walls falling away like black glass in the moonlight. Jubaia had not been exaggerating when he had said the city was only reachable from the air: Ussemitus could not imagine anyone being able to climb up those immense walls of polished stone. The city itself was extraordinary, for even in the poor light it seemed extremely intricate, its buildings carved and fashioned with infinite patience, piled one on top of another, fused into each other, the work of centuries. Tiny walls and parapets were picked out by the moonlight, even at this distance, a thousand windows gleaming with pin-pricks of light as though a constellation had been set there, jewels in a masterpiece of engineering. The higher levels of the city had been fashioned into towers and domes, each one in its own shape, some carved modestly into simple forms, while others were extravagant, even precarious. Tiny threads of stone ran between some of the towers and Jubaia explained that these were a kind of walkway, favoured by some of the inhabitants, although everyone in the city was winged and could fly.

Ussemitus and his companions feasted their eyes on the stunning city for a long time, amazed by its complexity, its size. Aru was staggered by what she saw. How her people would have gaped in wonder at this! The city must have a vast population. She wondered what level of civilisation these people had attained, though she said nothing to Jubaia for fear of insulting him. Certainly Shung Nang had gone far beyond Amerandabad in its development.

They heard the hum of wings overhead and immediately pressed themselves to the rock wall. Aru was able to look up, and she had her first proper glimpse of a winged man of Shung Nang. The windrider was drifting on the air, seemingly as light as a feather, his wide wings spread out to steady him, though they seemed so frail it was a miracle to Aru they could support the man. She could see starlight through them. The windrider was no bigger than Aru, dressed in thin clothing that revealed a body that was even less substantial than that of the woodsmen. His wings, those transparent membranes, linked his arms to his sides, reaching down to his wrists like a huge cloak. As he moved, moonlight shone through the wings, twinkling as if playing on water.

It was the windrider's face that captured Aru's attention the most. It was youthful, imbued with a strange kind of beauty, an arrogance that was somehow tinged with humanity, pride. And there was a serenity there, a peace that tugged at the emotions. Aru saw Jubaia's face, watching the winged man, and she caught her breath, for she could see the stark contrast. It was only now, on this remote ledge, that she could understand the true depth of Jubaia's loss, of what he must once have been. What crime could he have committed to make them rob him of such perfection?

The windrider listened attentively to the air about him,

as if it spoke to him with a hundred voices, all of them clear. But his attention was not drawn to the watchers on the ledge. Aru wondered if Jubaia's intense gaze had anything to do with that, whether he was using power to block out any possibility of discovery. The windrider swung away, catching a sudden eddy of wind, and he was gone as suddenly as he had come.

Jubaia waited before turning back to his fellows. 'The skies here are constantly patrolled. There are not that many of the watchers, for only the mad would attempt to get into Shung Nang. Don't you think so?' he whispered, his face lighting up with familiar mischief.

'How do you expect *us* to get across to the city?' said Fomond. 'By using the gliderboat?'

'There's no need for any of you to come with me,' replied Jubaia.

Ussemitus scowled. 'You can't go alone – '

'Far safer if I do. You would be killed on sight. You would not even be questioned, and given no opportunity to explain yourself. You are not of Shung Nang. Only the winged ones are permitted to *see* Shung Nang, let alone enter it. I have committed a grave crime against Shung Nang by allowing you even this glimpse.' But his smile widened. 'But my catalogue of sins would fill a dozen volumes, so I am beyond concerning myself!'

Aru gripped his arm. 'Jubaia, we cannot allow you to go on alone. The last time you attempted this theft – '

'I won't be alone, lady. I have the gliderboat. And there are ways in which you can all help me.'

'How?' said Ussemitus.

'I brought you to this ledge because it is easy to defend from the air. Let Fomond and Armestor position themselves with their bows. If any of the windriders do find you, then keep them at bay.'

Ussemitus shook his head. 'While you take the gliderboat and attempt to land in the city? No, that would be foolish.'

'Foolish!' Jubaia hissed, struggling to keep his voice low. He looked upwards for a moment, then, satisfied that he had not been heard, turned back to Ussemitus. 'You *cannot* enter Shung Nang –'

'We cannot possibly defend you from here, Jubaia. If you get into difficulty, you will be utterly powerless.'

Aru nodded. 'Of course. You must take us all in the gliderboat. Trust me to fly it for you while you're in the city. Surely you can do that?'

Jubaia looked down at his feet. 'Lady, it is your craft –'

'Nobody owns the gliderboat,' said Aru.

'No, she is not a machine,' murmured Jubaia.

'I understand that better,' Aru told him. 'The craft is one of us, is it not? Isn't that how you see it? Then let me fly it while you are in the city.'

'If anything happens to you,' Ussemitus told Jubaia, 'and we are without the craft, we would be lost. We could never find our way back, or onward to the west. The gliderboat is our only hope.'

Jubaia nodded slowly. 'I grow selfish.'

'No,' said Ussemitus. 'You think of our safety. But don't make plans for us without consulting us! You should know better than that by now!'

Jubaia flinched under the stern gaze of the woodsman. 'Yes. I think perhaps you are right.'

'How dangerous will it be for the gliderboat to fly over Shung Nang?' Aru asked him.

'Extremely. The skies are watched, sensed, closely. Think of the web of a huge spider, invisible but linking all the windriders who take the night patrol. Their sightings are pulled together in this web. When the gliderboat enters the skies immediately above the city, the web will tremble. It will take concentration to prevent the web from clinging to us, drawing the attention of the windriders. If you permitted me to go alone –'

'No,' said Ussemitus with finality.

Jubaia shrugged again. 'Then you must be corpse-still. I could use the gliderboat to avoid the windriders, fast as they are. But if I am to go into Shung Nang, no one must know. Discovery is death.'

They spent a little more time debating in whispers, but

Jubaia was forced to agree to the demands of Ussemitus and Aru. They returned to the gliderboat, checked that the skies were safe, and boarded it in silence. As the craft rose into the night, the company dropped flat to her deck, even Jubaia bending low over the prow, watching for any sign of movement ahead.

Gradually the craft slipped over the mesa top, feet above the trees, until it went out over the yawning abyss that was the canyon between the mesa and that of the city. Darkness shrouded the craft, which moved as silently as the air, dropping further into shadows, gliding like a huge bat. The thousand eyes of Shung Nang seemed to watch the craft as it moved over the gulf, expectant and tense, but as yet no movement in the air hinted at discovery. The gliderboat dropped as low as it dared into the darkness, where Jubaia said the net would be thinnest.

As they neared the walls of the city, well below the first of the buildings, deep in the gorge, Jubaia's face creased in a frown. 'They have used the elements to strengthen the watchweb,' he explained. 'The air feels us and probes at us. It will relay messages back to those who watch. Ussemitus, you must help me if I am to breach the city walls without being discovered.'

'How?'

'Use your powers. As before.'

Ussemitus scowled in the darkness, almost invisible. 'In what way?'

'Shield us. Bring currents into the air. Cause – '

'A storm?' Ussemitus looked appalled.

'Nothing so fierce, but there must be a disruption if we are to slip through this web. But a natural one. You must shield us,' Jubaia insisted.

'The city has a mind,' said Aru. 'I can feel it.'

'Shield us,' Jubaia told Ussemitus again.

Ussemitus gazed up at the walls ahead of them, then closed his eyes. He let his thoughts drift ahead into the darkness, recalling the powers he had unlocked in the east, powers that had sustained the company unexpectedly, powers that he feared. As he did so, Jubaia took the craft upwards in a wide arc, approaching the walls of the lower city but gliding up beyond them.

The air trembled about them, the wind suddenly rising up as if from the bottomless gorge below, its voice a gusting roar. There were movements along the walls of Shung Nang, but as yet the gliderboat had not been discovered, as if it blended in with the air. Its occupants saw a flight of windriders far above, searching the skies as though they knew something was in them.

'Higher,' called Jubaia to the craft, and it swung even more steeply upwards, the city very close now, a towering construction of buildings cut into the naked stone, a slumbering giant.

Jubaia's face was a sheen of perspiration, the wind gathering momentum like a tide as it got under the craft and pushed it upwards. More of the windriders appeared, their eager faces scouring the skies, their long spears waving beside them as if they prepared for a kill. But they seemed confused, still unable to locate the gliderboat in the swirling air.

'Are we invisible?' gasped Armestor, an arrow nocked in preparation for attack. Scores of the winged ones flew above and below them, though none had yet come within fifty yards.

No one answered him, but it seemed amazing that they had not been identified. Jubaia steered the craft even closer to the city, searching for a particular place. At last he found what he wanted and turned to Aru.

'I must disembark before I am seen.'

'How will we find you?'

'Tomorrow night. I will make my way to the highest reaches of the city, facing the west. Circle the skies there after moonrise. I will call the gliderboat. She will hear me.'

Aru would have said more, but the gliderboat gave a lurch and swooped very close to the carved masonry of the city, dipping between two tall columns. When it came up out of the sudden darkness, gathering speed, Aru saw that Jubaia was no longer clinging to the prow.

'He's gone!' she whispered, and within her she felt the

232

echo of her words as the gliderboat answered. And she shared the craft's stab of pain at the parting.

Aru would have attempted to guide the craft then, but she realised at once that there was no need. It set its own course, given to it by Jubaia, and it veered about, again dropping through the upper reaches of a towered avenue before going out over the canyon and down. It moved so quickly that the air tore past it, stinging the face.

Ussemitus was locked into whatever working he had used to bring the winds about the city, and Armestor and Fomond held on to the gliderboat in fear at its sudden abrupt speed. Aru could see a dozen windriders falling from the sky in a possible pursuit, though they seemed to be having difficulty maintaining speed as the troubled winds hit them.

The gliderboat fell deep into the darkness before breaking its fall and gliding across to the base of the mesa they had first left. Slowly it spiralled upward, making for the upper crags of the mesa, searching for a place where it could hide itself and wait.

If the windriders were in pursuit, they were unable to find the craft in the restless darkness. Ussemitus listened to the night winds, but none of them spoke of discovery. He sank back into the gliderboat.

'Is he in the city?' he asked, his voice no more than a breath.

Safe for the moment, was the reply.

Though he knew it was the craft that had answered him, he wondered how loyal it had become to the little thief. Would it abandon him if he could not escape, if he were trapped? But there was no answer in his mind, the gliderboat was silent as the night, its mind as dark as the blanket that shrouded them all.

17

RYUNG-HSU

He dropped without a sound on to the smooth stone of the tiny street, slipping quickly into an alley between two high walls. Listening with his ears and his mind, Jubaia reassured himself he had not been seen. But he moved away as quickly as he could, knowing that the city would feel him, its countless nerves alert for any intrusion, its winged guardians attuned to every variation in the winds. He deliberately blocked off his mind, severing contact with the gliderboat, closing in on himself. It was a disturbing darkness, but there was no other way to pursue his quest.

Ahead of him the alley narrowed so that he had to squeeze along through it. He was in a part of the city that he did not know well, though he knew that he had to move upwards to stand a chance of reaching his goal. When it became evident that the alley closed up, he started the precarious climb of the wall, which seemed to stretch up like the face of a large cliff. Even so, he decided it would be better to take such a difficult route as the likelihood of his discovery would be reduced. The smaller side streets, narrow as they were, would be too open a place to walk in this city.

As he climbed the wall, a spider in the thick darkness, the gliderboat that had dropped him in Shung Nang also took refuge in darkness, hidden once more in the upper clefts of the mesa beyond the city. Around it the winds had blown themselves out, now no more than a gentle breeze. Overhead the windriders flew in greater numbers, minds confused by the brief storm, as though they knew something had breached the security of the city skies, and yet unable to find it.

Ussemitus could hear the faint voices of the hunt, for the winged ones were bent on uncovering this mystery. The

234

gliderboat was very still, seemingly as dead as the rock. Like Jubaia, it had closed itself off completely.

'Can you understand them?' whispered Aru, her lips inches from Ussemitus's ear.

He shook his head. 'They have their own language. But I sense their concern. They know we are here. It's as if we broke an invisible webbing that covers the city. These guardians know it.'

Fomond leaned close, face obscured by shadows. 'Perhaps we should create a diversion for Jubaia. They may be looking for someone in the city.'

Ussemitus shook his head again. 'We dare not wake the gliderboat. The windriders would hear it at once. You know Jubaia's skills: these winged ones have them. Every thought would be a shout to them.'

'I never considered myself a poor Controller,' breathed Aru, 'but compared to Jubaia, I'd be clumsy. I'd be afraid to take the craft up now.'

'I'm sure silence is our best tactic for the time being,' said Ussemitus.

Fomond nodded and shrank back into the darkness with Armestor. Aru joined them and together they listened to the beating of wings in the still night air, the occasional calling voice.

Ussemitus sat in the prow of the craft, his back to his companions so that they could see no more than the vague shape of him. The calling of the storm had disturbed him as the use of his powers always did. They tugged at him persistently now, like a lover wooing him, teasing him away from other things. It would be easy to give in to them, to let himself go, to test them to the full, and yet the thought of that was rich in fear. Fomond had joked that he was a Windmaster and did not know it, but such thoughts made him go cold. He would do what had to be done, but no more. He would not allow power to dictate to him. Surely that must have been what happened to Quareem and others like him, who had let the dark into themselves without understanding what it would do.

His dilemma grew. Though he had told the others that

they should be utterly still, body and mind, he was uneasy at the plight of Jubaia. The windriders would concentrate a search on the city for certain, knowing that whatever had come here must have come in search of a way into the city. And for all his skill, Jubaia would be pitting himself against vast odds.

Ussemitus closed his eyes, focusing his mind. He pulled a mental cloak about himself and allowed his mind to rise, as though in a dream. He could feel part of himself soaring upwards into the night, just as the gliderboat had risen in flight. Over the mesa he sent this projected shadow of himself, and the city of Shung Nang rose up to meet him.

At once he was conscious of its extraordinary power, as though countless threads reached out from it like the filaments of a huge creature, sensitive to light and movement. Linked to these probes were the shapes of the windriders, the guardians who flew in increasing numbers about the mesa, like wasps about a nest. Their own minds linked with the city, probing the darkness like the beams from a hundred torches, and in their rays Ussemitus could see a complex pattern of light, like minute droplets of dew gleaming on the web of an unimaginable spider.

He twisted his projection like a fish, darting this way and that, evading the minds of the many beings that sought to net him as well as the intricate strands of the city's mind. At first his speed evaded them so successfully that they were not aware of him among them. But their minds glanced from his passing presence and the alert was passed through a cloud of them; they wheeled uniformly and began the hunt in earnest. He had one aim: to pull as much of their attention from the city as he could, leaving Jubaia with an easier path.

Rising up, Ussemitus could feel the concentration of thought behind and below him. The web of the city pulsed, and he felt its awesome conglomeration of minds. For a moment he wavered, knowing that he was drawing on powers of his own that were untested, as if he were crossing a new land, unsure of his footing.

The windriders closed in, and as they did so, he let

himself fall into the well of power that had lured him for
so long.

As Jubaia reached the top of the wall, muttering softly to
himself at its inordinate height, he could feel the abnormal
activity above him in the skies. Shung Nang was awake to
the intrusion, though he had known it would be. No one
came close to the city without alerting it. But it would not
be impossible to find safety. Provided the gliderboat and
its crew kept silent, they would be safe. Shung Nang would
not expect a single intruder, and certainly not one of its
exiles, to be lunatic enough to try to get through the delicate
net of its defence.

He scuttled across a flat rooftop, peering up at the dark,
a thick blanket, obscuring the upper city. The moon had
disappeared; banks of cloud remained after the storm, as
though like celestial hounds they debated whether to
unleash themselves on the carcass of the city.

Windriders flitted past occasionally, but they did not
discover the little thief. He grinned to himself. No, they
would not bother themselves with rats in the alleys, nor
the tiny bats that swooped about their towers. And one
more moth meant nothing. Even so, he was cautious,
moving extremely carefully over the walls, across gardens,
sometimes clinging to the sides of buildings like a fly. How
many times had he done this as a child? Yes, and been
caught and punished, he mused, though the children of
Shung Nang were secretly expected to learn their skills in
such a way. He clung to these inner thoughts, using them
and his past as a blanket, knowing it would protect him
from the intensity of the search that still went on around
him.

It was his past that focused his mind on the present,
however, for he searched for a particular house. The
memory of the one who lived there warmed him, though
at the same time it sent a shiver of apprehension through
him. Ryung-Hsu, who had once been as near a thing as he
had ever had to a companion, might be hostile to him now

in the city. Jubaia had been popular among his fellows as a thief, but when he had fallen from grace, none of them had been able to help him. If they had done so, they would have been clipped as he had been, and cast out with him. But he would not have expected that of any of them, even Ryung-Hsu.

The thought of his friend, the times they had spent together as young men, their shared madness around these very buildings, saddened Jubaia. And there were far sadder memories. No sooner had he touched on them, shut away for so long, than they pushed forward, eager for recognition. They would not be stilled now, as though the very city sensed his weakness and sought to build upon it. He felt himself trapped, wanting to call out with his mind to the gliderboat for strength, but it was the last thing he dared do. She must not be endangered. But she prompted a far older memory.

For a moment he saw Imlukan. She stood before him as if she had physically stepped from his past, a solid entity, touchable, her superb lips opening in a smile that called him to her. Jubaia almost fell into the dark trap of the city, though it was his own mind that had formed this memory. As quickly as it came, he shut it out, his former lover dissolving.

He climbed, clenching himself against the self-pity that threatened him. Looking about him, he saw he was in a narrow street that he recognised. The house of Ryung-Hsu was not far. Ducking down, Jubaia ran, his mind again dark. But the ghosts had been woken: they pursued him and he could hear the whisper of their feet behind him. Ryung-Hsu, Imlukan, and other friends from long, long ago.

Turning up the incline of another narrow street, he fought to close his mind to their coming. If they over-whelmed him, his reaction would be like a siren and the city would fall on him, a score of windriders dropping down like a cloud.

Then he saw the house, cut back into another wall that reared up like a cliff. It had not changed, not by one stone.

He hunched into the shadows of a doorway opposite it, the ghosts temporarily pushed back by the hard reality of his surroundings.

If he were to succeed on this quest, he would need shelter. He dare not climb to the upper city tonight, not with the Deathless City alerted. And he could not hope to hide in the streets for long, not without discovery. He had not told Ussemitus this, knowing that he would have prevented his coming here and taking the risk he was about to take.

But Ryung-Hsu had been more than his friend. Their bond defied time, they had promised each other that. And even though Jubaia's sin had been, in the eyes of Shung Nang, a cardinal one, in Ryung-Hsu's heart there had been only sympathy, pity. He could not help Jubaia, nor save him from his fate, but he would not have turned away from him.

Jubaia clung to this belief, using it to help him across the road and to the side of the building. He knew the way in, the short climb over the wall beside it. As a youth he had walked along the top of the wall many times, climbing to the room where Ryung-Hsu feigned sleep. Then the two of them would be off over the rooftops in search of entertainment.

Ryung-Hsu would be master here now. His parents would no longer be alive, and Jubaia thought of them fleetingly as he moved up over the steep roof. It was easy to drop in through an open window. He was on a wooden landing, a faint light burning below him, though he could not be sure if anyone in the house would be awake.

Even though the city was on alert, not all of its citizens would be awake to the hunt. Jubaia had no idea what position Ryung-Hsu filled, but it would be a sorry coincidence if he were on night patrol. Jubaia grinned, favouring the odds against it.

He moved down the narrow stairs, himself like a ghost. Light leaked from a doorway below him. He reached the opening, looking in with care. The furnishings were rich, the room filled with carvings and statues of breath-taking beauty, the walls hung with tapestries of incalculable value.

Ryung-Hsu was a typical citizen of Shung Nang, a collector of things of wealth and rare beauty. Jubaia almost laughed at the surfeit of glories.

The room was a long one, the light positioned at its far end. A lone figure sat there, gazing down at something spread before it on the tabletop.

Jubaia knew at once that he had found his companion of so long ago. And yet Ryung-Hsu did not seem to have aged by a single year. His face was as youthful as it had been the last time Jubaia had seen it. His exquisitely handsome features were drawn in a vague frown, his delicate fingers interlaced before him, his chin dipping to rest on them as he looked up.

'Come in, little friend,' he said softly, and in his voice was the echo of all those lost years.

Jubaia heard him as if he had been struck. He steadied himself against his emotions, crossing the priceless carpet slowly.

Ryung-Hsu's eyes dropped once more to his work. But there was no doubt he knew who approached him. He raised his eyes, seeing the shadows thicken. Then, very slowly, he stood up, his magnificent wings folded down along the line of his back on either side, his features as regal as those of an eagle, a monarch. Jubaia could almost hear the power of the wind stirring in those wings, as if they had been woven from the very air. Ryung-Hsu lifted the wooden candlestick, an intricate, priceless ornament, and held it aloft so that the soft light from the candle spilled over his visitor.

'Jung-Bara,' he said softly.

The little man bowed. 'How long have you known I was here?'

'I heard you climb my wall, though I did not know it was you until you were inside my house. You hide your thoughts well.'

'Had I not done so, I would not have reached you.'

Ryung-Hsu nodded, studying the face of his former friend. He could not hide his surprise. Jubaia marked it, but had anticipated it. He had once been as handsome,

240

as terribly proud as this magnificent winged being. How impoverished he must seem to Ryung-Hsu! A beggar before an emperor.

'Are you well?' said Ryung-Hsu, setting down the candle.

Jubaia chuckled softly. His own voice seemed harsh to him. 'I get by. I have lost few of my old skills.'

Ryung-Hsu did not smile. He seemed tense, uneasy, but it was no more than Jubaia expected. Being here threatened his friend's safety.

'How did you get into Shung Nang?'

Jubaia grinned, looking around him. Ryung-Hsu really had done remarkably well for himself, although why not? He had always been talented, a reason why Jubaia had enjoyed his company so much, their constant testing of each other a key to their developments. 'I was always difficult to catch.'

'Forgive me, but you have placed yourself in grave danger –'

Jubaia's grin abruptly melted. 'No, old friend, you must forgive me. I have acted unpardonably. By coming here –'

'You have taken me unawares, that is all,' said Ryung-Hsu, suddenly embarrassed, an emotion that sat uncomfortably with him. 'I did not mean to protest about my own safety. But you, Jung-Bara, why are you here? The city will pull you limb from limb –'

'I had to come back. I promised myself, when they cut my wings from me and flung me into the world, that I would come back –'

'Not for revenge –'

Jubaia shook his head, smiling. 'I've not lost my senses entirely! No. I have wandered Innasmorn for many, many years. You can see that in my face, no doubt.'

Ryung-Hsu looked away, his eyes troubled.

'Spare me your pity. I've no need of it. I am not of Shung Nang, not any more. I have another world to enjoy. But I wanted to see the Deathless City for a last time. Can you understand that, Ryung-Hsu?'

The latter nodded, though he still could not meet the little man's gaze.

'Aye a last visit. One night, moving through the streets of my childhood. Feeling the air here, listening to the breath of the stones. Tomorrow I'll be gone again, forgotten. I'll not be back to haunt you.'

'Haunt me!' gasped Ryung-Hsu. 'Why should you do that?'

'I make you uneasy. You should kill me –'

'As a citizen, yes. Without a word. But we were friends –'

'Are we no longer? In spite of what I have done?'

Ryung-Hsu sat down, his face tired, though even now he seemed to be no more than a youth in his prime. He gazed at the chart on his table. 'You were caught. That was your crime, Jung-Bara. Neither I nor any of our other companions thought of you as anything but one of us. But we knew the law.'

Jubaia nodded. 'Indulge me this one night.'

Ryung-Hsu looked up, his eyes narrowing for a moment. 'What is it you want of me?'

'Only your protection.'

'They hunt you.'

'Like a swarm of hornets. The night skies are filled with your winged brothers. But in this house, they will not find me. Nor ever suspect you of harbouring me. They cannot know it is Jung-Bara who has returned.'

Ryung-Hsu hesitated for a few moments. Then he looked directly at Jubaia. 'It is difficult to refuse you.'

'But you owe me nothing –'

'Jung-Bara, I would that this had not happened to you. To see you as you are –'

'I told you I will have none of your pity!' Jubaia suddenly snapped, turning away. 'Your friendship, or what remains of it, I would cherish. It is the most treasured of my memories, and worth more to me than the contents of this treasury you call home. Though perhaps there is one other memory I cherish more –'

'You should not torment yourself,' said Ryung-Hsu, again rising. 'If you have come back to Shung Nang to see her –'

Jubaia swung round, tears glistening in his eyes like frost. 'No! I would not inflict upon her the embarrassment I have clearly inflicted on you. Do you think I would have her witness my humiliation? If she remembers me, let it be as I was, as you are, Ryung-Hsu.'

They looked at each other across time for a moment. Then Jubaia moved away, breaking the tension. 'But tell me, is she well?'

'She is.'

'No doubt she has found a position, married into one of the great Flights of the city – '

'Jung-Bara, you should not talk of such things. You say you did not come back here to find her, to give yourself more pain – '

Again Jubaia whirled round. 'They cut off my wings, my powers, Ryung-Hsu, but they did not cut out my heart, nor could they close up my mind. These streets were my life, my veins. Shung Nang sings yet in my blood.'

'Of course – ' Ryung-Hsu was about to say more, when he heard something beyond the room.

Jubaia heard it, too, and at once shifted into the shadows by the wall.

Someone else stood in the doorway, but Jubaia could not see who.

'Did I disturb you?' said Ryung-Hsu, going to meet the intruder. 'I must have been talking to myself. The charts I've been looking at are extremely complex.'

Jubaia heard a woman's voice, though he could not catch the words. Of course, why should Ryung-Hsu not be married! Foolish of him not to have thought of it. And selfish, perhaps. He thought only of the past. He wondered now if there were children. Ryung-Hsu a father? Suddenly he longed to ask him, longed to see them, even in sleep.

Ryung-Hsu had lowered his own voice, and Jubaia knew that he was trying to persuade his wife to go back to bed. They spoke together for a few moments. Ryung-Hsu seemed suddenly angered.

'It is nothing, I tell you! Go back to sleep.'

His wife must have pushed past him, for Jubaia was

suddenly aware of her presence just beyond the circle of light from the candle. He could not see her in the gloom, but he could feel her eyes on him.

'There is someone here,' she said softly, an edge of fear in her words.

Ryung-Hsu stood behind her, his arms about her. 'You must not trouble yourself. Go back to sleep. This is a private matter.' He spoke tenderly, and the woman responded with a brief touch of her lips to his shoulder, a gesture that revealed so much about them, their unity.

Jubaia felt a sudden rush of cold air inside him, the voice of the woman slicing into him, opening a fresh wound that bled yet more memories. He could not close his mind completely.

The woman shrank back further against her husband, her delicate hand across her mouth, as if trying to prevent the name from slipping out. 'Jung-Bara,' she gasped, her eyes widening, though she could not see him in the dark.

'Jung-Bara, yet not Jung-Bara,' he answered her softly.

The three figures were motionless for a long time. Outside the house they could hear the sudden rustle of air as a winged guardian flew by, though it did not pause. They might have been alone in the city, or ghosts.

'Let me see you,' said the woman softly.

'No. Let the darkness hide me,' said Jubaia. 'As it has done for so long. If you remember me at all, remember me as I was, Imlukan.'

When she finally spoke, it was hesitantly. 'Why are you here?'

'To see my home. That is all. For a night. I did not come to disturb you. I could not have known – '

Ryung-Hsu shook his head. 'You should not have come, old friend. Shung Nang can only mean pain for you now.'

Imlukan took a step forward, her face filled with anguish. 'But how did you get here? Do they know?'

'Never mind,' said Jubaia. 'With a little help, I'll slip away as I came. Please, forget that I was here. If I had known – '

Ryung-Hsu held his wife back, sensing that she would

attempt to see the man she had once loved. 'Go back to bed,' he told her once more.

She drew in her breath slowly, straightening herself, trying to crush whatever it was within herself that fought to break free of her. Jubaia felt himself tensing at her beauty, the long graceful line of her neck, the shape of her face, the eyes that had snared him as a youth.

'Do as he bids you,' he told her.

At last she nodded, backing away, until, near the door, she quickly turned and fled up the stairs.

Ryung-Hsu closed his eyes as though some inner crisis had passed.

'Then she did marry into a good family,' came Jubaia's voice. But there was no bitterness in it, only a long remembered warmth.

Ryung-Hsu turned away and went back to the table, his fingers pressing down on the chart. 'She loved you. You would have been wed – '

Jubaia emerged from the darkness to stand close to his friend. 'I am a ghost, Ryung-Hsu. And a foolish one. I should not have brought this fresh suffering to your house.'

Ryung-Hsu turned slowly and put his hands on Jubaia's shoulders. He was a head taller than him, though once they had been equals. 'I bear no ill-will. How could I? And the Jung-Bara I knew is honoured in this house.'

'I will quit Shung Nang at the earliest opportunity. But for me to try to leave tonight would be dangerous – '

'Yes, you cannot leave tonight.'

'Nor by daylight.'

Ryung-Hsu released him, turning away. 'No, you'd be found at once. Tomorrow night.'

'I'll not return.'

'That would be best. For us all. Do you want food?'

Jubaia felt his throat constrict. After all this time, after all they had once been to each other, Ryung-Hsu could ask him only if he wanted food. 'A little.'

Ryung-Hsu nodded stiffly. 'Wait here. I'll fetch something.'

'Will you share a little wine with me?'

Ryung-Hsu paused as he moved to the door, his back as straight as a javelin. 'Perhaps a glass.'

'And will you talk?'

But Ryung-Hsu had gone.

Jubaia sat beside the table, glancing at the charts, though he did not pay attention to their lines, their intricate detail. He was thinking of the face of Imlukan, the face that he had once caressed, the lips that once he had kissed. Her beauty was undiminished, indeed had grown. He closed his eyes. *I must shut her out. She weakens me. In Shung Nang, that will undo me.*

The moments dragged by, the candle burning low, the dark closing in, though he welcomed it. At length he heard the soft tread behind him. He turned, expecting to see Ryung-Hsu with a tray. But there were three other figures there.

They were windriders, one holding aloft a bright lantern that flooded the room with light. The others held short, hooked weapons, their faces set. There was nowhere that Jubaia could hide. He stood up, the chair clattering over behind him.

One of the winged men, his face emotionless, pointed with his weapon at the little man. 'You are known in the Deathless City. You are Jung-Bara, former citizen.'

'Today I am known as Jubaia,' said the little thief, bowing. He was trapped. There would be no escaping these three angels of death. They circled him without fuss.

'The Aviatrix has pronounced your banishment. You are aware of the penalty for returning to Shung Nang.'

'I am,' nodded Jubaia.

'You will be taken to the Interlocutor.'

Again Jubaia bowed. 'Put away your weapons. I am not dangerous.'

Where was Ryung-Hsu? He had not shown himself. How could he do this? Who else could have called the guards? Was it jealousy? Fury that his wife's former lover had returned? No, it could not be so. But another icy thought struck him. Could Imlukan have done this? He could not believe it of her. It was chance, his trail had been picked

246

up by the sensitive city. Perhaps Ryung-Hsu had also been arrested.

As he was being escorted through the corridors of the house, Jubaia saw something hanging on one of the walls. It was a magnificent cloak, the bright blue of the sky, azure. Unquestionably it was Ryung-Hsu's.

Imlukan had indeed married into a good family. Her husband was a member of the city's highest order of windriders, the elite protectors of the Aviatrix, the Azure Wing.

18

THE INTERLOCUTOR

Jubaia closed his mind and let the inner darkness take him.
It was easy for him to do now, with so much despair seeking
to destroy him. Despair was an emotion he had dealt with
once before: he had felt its full onset years past and had
veered away from potential madness then. He walked in
silence beside his captors, the tall and haughty winged
guards. They took him out into the street. There were no
other windriders here. This had not been a chance capture.
Ryung-Hsu must have summoned them. It had been his
sacred duty. However, there was no sign of him now. Jubaia
wondered if it could be shame that prevented him from
appearing.

The windriders would have flown him up to the higher
reaches of the city, but as he could not fly they took him
by a tortuous route through narrow streets and steep alleys.
Shung Nang had not been designed for pedestrians. The
guards were irritated at having to spend so much time on
the ground when a short flight would have taken them to
their destination, but they said nothing. They did not so
much as glance at Jubaia. But had he attempted to escape,
they would have cut his legs from under him. He was
surprised that he had not already been killed, though he
assumed this was Ryung-Hsu's doing. As an Azure, he had
power.

An hour after they had left Ryung-Hsu's house, they
came to the walls of the palace of the Aviatrix, and as there
was no gate, Jubaia was ignominiously tossed into a net
and flown over the moonlit stone.

Ussemitus opened his eyes, for a moment confused by the
wall of darkness. But as the shadows thinned and he saw

the moonlit landscape of the mesa beyond the gliderboat, he brought himself into focus. His mind had journeyed beyond this place, searching the night-walled city of Shung Nang.

Jubaia! He had seen him, or rather, his thoughts. He had strained to hear them as if listening to a distant voice.

What has happened?

Ussemitus turned abruptly, hand going to his sword. Aru was dozing beside Fomond and Armestor, who were also asleep.

Cautiously Ussemitus probed for the thoughts of the gliderboat.

It is dangerous to communicate, it told him. *But we must. What have you learned? I dared not go with him.*

Ussemitus whispered that he had sent out his own guarded thoughts, searching the skies above Shung Nang, probing its streets, deflecting the countless probes of the city and its winged guardians.

You found Jubaia. I heard your concern.

Ussemitus started. If his stab of anxiety had awoken the gliderboat, had it alerted the windriders?

What has happened? the gliderboat called, more urgently.

'He's been discovered. I could not catch his thoughts clearly. But there was a sudden feeling of despair, a shock. It can only mean that he has been caught.'

Then what –

'I don't know. He closed up his mind like a fist. To protect himself from them. Now I've lost him. He may be on the run.'

We cannot leave him –

'Nor can we go to him.'

We must! The thought came from the darkness like the thrust of a knife and Ussemitus winced at its intensity.

'We cannot risk all our lives. The skies of Shung Nang are teeming with these winged ones. I have been through their ranks – '

Now that they have their prize, they'll not expect other intruders.

Ussemitus sagged back. The gliderboat was probably

right. The alert would no longer be on. Perhaps it would be safe to attempt a flight over the city.

'Ussemitus?' It was Aru. She crawled over to him, her face peering up at him. 'I heard your voice.'

'I spoke to the craft. Jubaia may have been discovered. I don't know if he's been caught, but the city is quiet.'

We must try and help him, the gliderboat said again.

Aru jolted as she heard the voice in her mind, more plainly than she had ever heard it before. She could feel the pain in it, the terrible fear that Jubaia might be harmed. It was an emotion she recognised, and it stunned her.

You understand, said the gliderboat. *We must help him.*

'There will be danger to us all,' said Ussemitus. 'To our cause.'

Aru was nodding. She knew what it was to sacrifice men to a cause. She still remembered the taste of the bile of war.

Ussemitus looked torn, anguished. 'Even so,' he breathed, 'I cannot leave Jubaia to his fate.'

'If we fail here,' said Aru, 'what of the World Splinter and the powers there? What if Zellorian finds them and uses them?'

You think only of your revenge! came the savage thought of the gliderboat.

Aru lurched to her feet. 'I've seen what he does,' she retorted bitterly, holding her voice down with difficulty. 'And who knows better than you, gliderboat, what Zellorian does when he has power?'

'We all have our reasons for being here,' said Ussemitus, sensing the sudden conflict.

'The gliderboat thinks of Jubaia, not of us, nor of Innasmorn. I care about Jubaia, of course I do. But there are times when sentiment has to be tempered with practicality,' snapped Aru.

'So you'd leave him, even if he has not been caught?' said Ussemitus.

'If the servants of Shung Nang have him,' came Fomond's level voice, 'then what chance would there be for us to free him? We'd be flying to our own death.'

'He's right,' said Armestor, woken by the argument. 'I used to loathe that truth-bending little thief, but not any more. Yet how could we possibly hope to rescue him –'

We don't know that he's been taken! cried the gliderboat, so that they all heard.

'Be careful!' said Ussemitus. 'You'll bring the winged ones.'

Please Ussemitus, said the gliderboat more softly, and only to him, *find out where he is. If he's safe. Don't leave him to die until you know he is beyond saving.*

Ussemitus closed his eyes. 'Very well. I'll try and find him. But you must not attempt it yourself. Shung Nang is well protected. If they hear your thoughts, we are all dead.'

'What are you going to do?' said Aru.

'I'll search for him,' said Ussemitus, explaining. 'But if he closes his mind completely, I may not be able to find him.'

Search the minds of others, said the gliderboat. *They may be aware of him.*

'An even more dangerous game.'

You must find him, came the plea again, and Ussemitus was moved by the depth of anxiety in the words.

Jubaia had been here before, countless years ago. The great hall was no different now. Its walls rose up, glistening like crystal, curving at their peaks to form a point. Many lights blazed up on high, the light cascading downwards, gleaming in the floors, which had been polished so smooth they were like ice. Tiers rose up on all sides in a circular mass; a number of windriders sat there, though usually the hall was filled. Dawn was yet a few hours away, and most of the city slept. Few of its servants had woken this early to hear Jubaia defend himself.

The little thief was led by his guards to a huge stone set in the heart of the chamber, a scarlet object that looked like the frozen heart of a leviathan. Jubaia was chained to it, his chains of pure gold, for Shung Nang remained the centre of extravagance, proud of its ostentatious treasures.

Presently Jubaia was left alone, apart from the dozen or so officials beyond him in the tiers. They talked in soft tones, ignoring him completely. It suited him, enabling him to keep a close grip on his own thoughts, shielding them from the powers that would be trying to tap into them. The Aviatrix would be deep in star-slumber, contemplating other, greater mysteries.

Jubaia heard footfalls behind him but did not move, looking straight ahead of him at the wall of light. It seemed to sparkle like the firmament above Innasmorn, though tonight it was a cold vault, offering no solace. He turned from such thoughts of despair.

A figure appeared before him, tall and erect, the face like the face of an eagle, the eyes as merciless, the features sharp, gaunt, pitiless. Hands like talons clasped each other, rings reflecting light like beacons. The man's cloak was sewn with two curving arches that represented wings, though his own wings were folded neatly beneath the cloak. As the man moved, his slippered feet soundless on the polished floor, he was like the passing of the air, and as he turned his head to study his prisoner, he seemed for a moment like a wraith.

Jubaia knew better. This was Feng-Shai, the Interlocutor. And Jubaia had stood in chains under his gaze once before. This was death, inexorable, without compassion. Duty, the law, the way.

'Jung-Bara,' came the voice, a soft and compelling whisper, with as yet no trace of malice, nor pain.

Jubaia attempted a smile, but in this place he found it impossible to draw on the flippancy that so often sheltered him. 'Feng-Shai.'

'You have chosen a strange bedfellow this night,' said the Interlocutor, his eyes widening a little, as though mildly surprised to see his prisoner. His hair gleamed, slicked to his high skull, its scent filling the air.

Jubaia understood the riddle. 'I hesitate to seem impertinent, Feng-Shai, but I sought only my own companionship this night.'

'The more pity then, that you have found death.'

Jubaia did not answer. The words had been said with quiet finality.

Feng-Shai moved away as if no longer interested and turned his attention to the seated audience. A few of the Azure Wing had come to stand at the base of the raised seats, their cloaks folded like blue wings about them: they watched the Interlocutor with interest, as did the seated officials, but no one spoke. The hall remained strangely silent, the air motionless, as if the place was a vacuum. Fear uncoiled within it, cold and primal.

'When you were here before,' Feng-Shai said, his back still to Jubaia, though his voice was perfectly clear, 'you were able to call upon citizens of Shung Nang to speak on your behalf. A number of them did so. But at the end, not one of them saw fit to question the sentence that was imposed upon you. Even those closest to you – ' And Feng-Shai turned, his eyes flashing like those of a hunter about to dip its muzzle into the prey – 'did not question the sentence. Can you deny this?'

Jubaia shook his head.

'No. Then you would not expect me to permit anyone to come forward and speak for you now?'

'I would not, Feng-Shai. Indeed, I would wish it understood that none of the citizens of Shung Nang had any idea that I was here. It is my fear that I may have implicated some of them unwittingly. If so, I would speak in their defence.'

'No one is so implicated,' said the Interlocutor flatly. He looked up at the officials and they nodded in unison, marking the statement as a record of this hearing.

Ryung-Hsu would be safe, thought Jubaia. Though it was clearly he who had betrayed him. Duty. But there was consolation: Imlukan would not be threatened.

Feng-Shai's dispassionate voice drifted across the hall. 'You would be forgiven for wondering why it is that you were not destroyed on sight, since that is the sentence that was passed on you, was it not?'

'It was, Feng-Shai. I came here in full knowledge of the law.'

253

Feng-Shai ignored the attempted insouciance. 'There are two reasons why you were brought before me and these patient officials, although it has caused us all considerable inconvenience. Firstly, the Aviatrix desires to know how it is that you came to be in the Deathless City. You have had your wings removed. Only a winged one can enter Shung Nang. You are a riddle, Jung-Bara. And one that must be explained.'

Jubaia felt the coldness clutching at him in spite of the inner defences he had erected. They must not find out about the gliderboat, nor about his companions.

'And the second reason, Feng-Shai?'

'We shall address that once we have discussed the first.'

Jubaia knew that if Feng-Shai used all the powers at his disposal and brought certain of his elemental servants into this interrogation, they would rip the truth from Jubaia as beasts could rip the entrails from a carcass. He must somehow deceive the Interlocutor, though Feng-Shai was a shrewd man.

'No doubt you will enlighten me in due course,' Jubaia said, every second invaluable as he tried to concoct answers to the questions that were about to be put to him.

'Yes, you will achieve enlightenment,' nodded Feng-Shai, his lips curling in a smile, though one without warmth. 'Now, your story. How did you come to be here?'

'You must think me a fool to return to Shung Nang. Why, you must wonder, did I come? What could have brought me here?'

Feng-Shai's eyes narrowed. 'This would appear to be obvious. You are of Shung Nang. There could be no peace for you elsewhere on Innasmorn. I am surprised that you did not take the honourable way and cast yourself from a high place once you had been banished. The flight from which there is no return. But I understand well enough why you came back to the Deathless City, the heart of Innasmorn. Your own heart would have been empty.'

'This is so, Feng-Shai.'

'And yet it has been many, many years since your banishment.'

'Weary years, Feng-Shai. Years spent in despair, in seeking a new life. But, as you say, there is only Shung Nang, even for a creature like myself, a wingless bird – '

'Who does, it seems, manage flight perfectly well.'

The officials stirred, though not with amusement. Shung Nang's safety was paramount, and Jubaia knew that his presence in the city had come as a distressing shock to them all.

'How did I get here? On other wings.'

'Other wings,' Feng-Shai echoed, as if in indifference. 'Where are they now?'

'The breath of the Mother is all about us, Feng-Shai. There is power immeasurable in her skies. On my travels, and I have been far, far across Innasmorn, I learned many new things. Secrets that have been lost to even the savants of Deathless Shung Nang.'

'You must share these wonders with us.'

'Certainly I must. I remain the slave of the Aviatrix, in spite of my many sins.'

'So you fly without the aid of wings,' said Feng-Shai, his voice thickening with scepticism.

'It took me many months to cross the lands that lead to Shung Nang,' Jubaia went on. 'I have become adept at concealing myself on the ground, as I have had to do so to survive. But in so doing, I have learned to grow closer to the bosom of Innasmorn. I have heard whispered secrets that are not always carried on the wind.'

Feng-Shai's eyes fixed Jubaia, again the eagle with the prey, though he said nothing. He stepped closer.

'You see how changed I am,' Jubaia continued, spreading his arms so that the links of his chains tinkled like bells in the stillness of the hall. 'One of you could lift me easily. I weigh nothing. And I am agile, as a spider is agile. I have learned so many new skills.

'But I confess I yearned to see Shung Nang once more. Once I had mastered certain things, which I will speak of, I decided to return. To drink in the splendours of my home one last time.

'I came alone, of course. No man of Innasmorn could

255

travel as I travelled, and I would not desecrate the Deathless City by bringing outsiders here. For obvious practical reasons, travelling alone made it easier to travel in secret.

'At last I reached the great mesa across the canyon, and by my new arts I climbed it, for is it not the sheer wall that supports Shung Nang. It took me many days and I sensed a restlessness in the air, as if the city knew something was strange. Ah, but Shung Nang is wise. The Aviatrix must have sensed me, I am sure.'

Feng-Shai nodded slowly. 'You climbed the mesa?'

'In time. And having breasted it, I stood before the Deathless City. I called upon Innasmorn to pity me, to give me the strength I needed to end my foolish quest. And she answered me this night. You heard the wind rise, the storm that blew.'

Feng-Shai's brows rose. 'You are asking us to believe that *you* summoned that storm?' From his expression it was clear that he considered this to be preposterous.

'In a way. But I could not control it, of course I could not.'

'And then?'

'I let the storm carry me across the abyss. Like a leaf I was borne by the winds, through the swirling windriders, who were confused by the sudden storm. I thought I must surely be dashed on the rocks, falling well below the height of the city. But it was not so. By the will of the Mother, I came to be here. A little bruised, certainly shaken. But alive. And blessed.'

Feng-Shai gazed at him for a long time. Jubaia wondered if the Interlocutor would laugh, or direct some curt abuse at him for the outlandish explanation. But Feng-Shai merely nodded, turning away to the officials with a deep breath.

'This is extremely interesting. I have heard tales of certain creatures in the eastern lands who are said to be able to control the storms. They call themselves Windmasters. Perhaps, Jung-Bara, you are one of them?' His back was to Jubaia, and it seemed that he did not expect an answer, speaking merely with contempt.

'I know of them,' said Jubaia. 'But it was the Mother

who taught me my skills. I have had little to do with the people of the outer world. Such barbarians.'

'Your skills intrigue us,' said Feng-Shai, turning back to him. 'They seem miraculous. A wingless man who yet flies.'

'Hardly flight, Feng-Shai. And had the storm not been of sufficient power – '

'Quite so. Such a simple explanation. The Mother has a strange way of blessing her servants. But your story is doubly interesting. It will have greater significance than you realise.'

'Oh?'

'The other reason that you were not struck down on the instant of your discovery, as law prescribed, was that a particular example needed to be made of you.' Feng-Shai smiled as he had before, again as a predator, his hunger apparent.

'This surprises me, Feng-Shai. I am hardly worthy – '

'You are far too modest. By your own admission, Innasmorn has blessed you, and in a way which the Aviatrix would find difficult to fathom. It would have been tragic had you been executed. You may not, after all, deserve death.'

Jubaia clamped down on his surprise. This must be a trick. Feng-Shai had once enjoyed tormenting his victims, so it was rumoured.

'If you are so close to the Mother, to her very breath as it were, then you will welcome the course of action that I have planned for you. It may, after all you have said, prove your salvation. An opportunity to cleanse yourself of your past, perhaps.'

Jubaia said nothing. Oh yes, this was indeed a trap. He was not to be freed. Feng-Shai wanted him dead, there could be no doubt of that. It seemed most unlikely that he would have believed the colourful story, though for some perverse reason he seemed to want to play along with it.

'You are to be taken to the upper regions, beyond the plateau of the Aviatrix. There you will be placed in the keeping of the Septenary, the divine voices of the wind gods. Your destiny lies with them, Jung-Bara.'

Jubaia could not suppress a shudder. The Septenary! Elemental beings who roamed the uppermost crags beyond the city. Those given to them were offered in sacrifice, for the Septenary brought the killing winds that stripped the flesh from a man and cleansed his bones.

'Well?' said Feng-Shai, standing in front of Jubaia, arms folded in front of him. 'Do you not welcome such a judgement?'

Jubaia swallowed hard, struggling for a moment to speak. 'But of course, Feng-Shai. I am stunned that you should spare me a swift death – '

'Tell your story of wonders to the Septenary. They will do better than listen to you, for they will hear the words of the Mother, her response. You'll be cleansed. If what you say is true, you'll be protected from the wind that levels.'

'And afterwards?'

Feng-Shai did not respond at first. But then he seemed to gather himself. 'You'll be brought back here. The Aviatrix will have a new position for you. You must teach us more about these earth secrets. And of your kinship with the wind.'

'This is more than I could ever have hoped for,' said Jubaia, trying to sound moved by gratitude. Fear crawled in his bowels, however, and he felt the onset of the night, the winds that tore a man apart. Let it be swift, he thought. And don't let them tear from my mind the truth. Let the gliderboat escape.

But he dared not shout out for her to flee.

Ussemitus had again sent his mind out over the city. This time it was easier to avoid discovery, for the winged guards were no longer out in force. He sensed a few of them, silent as bats in the night. But the great volume of them had gone back down into Shung Nang. Jubaia's potential capture must have spared further search. Yet the city itself remained watchful, the air thick with spells, with elemental forces too discreet to perceive clearly. Shung Nang's link with these elements was startling, as though the city had tapped into the very skies, invisible cables securing a nerve network.

The gliderboat was with his thoughts. He knew it and could not prevent it. In spite of his insistence, its own mind had fastened on to his and would not let go, determined to help him find Jubaia. Ussemitus had cautioned mental silence. Otherwise the network would close in and up from the city would come an army of winged defenders.

Ussemitus's mind roamed high over the moonlit towers when he felt the jolt of energy, almost as though a bolt had struck him in a storm. It was Jubaia, trying to smother the various emotions that were tugging at him, threatening to undo him. The gliderboat felt the sudden lapse of Jubaia's defence too, and Ussemitus could feel its response. But Jubaia closed up again.

'Wait,' cautioned Ussemitus, his mind reeling from the abrupt anxiety of the gliderboat. Its feelings for Jubaia were very powerful, almost irrational. Ussemitus felt himself grappling with them, trying to prevent an outcry, a mental shriek that would alert the city.

Darkness swirled about him for a moment as if he had been plunged into a raging torrent. He felt himself lock with the will of the gliderboat, trying to stifle it; then he was awake, lying on his back, gazing up at the anxious faces of Fomond, Armestor and Aru.

'What's wrong?' she asked.

'The gliderboat!' said Ussemitus. He sat up, calling softly to the craft.

I hear you. He's alive. In terrible danger –

'You almost woke the city!' Ussemitus hissed. 'Your recklessness will cost us all our lives.'

We must go to him!

'What is it saying?' asked Fomond, exasperated. 'What is happening?'

'We cannot wait until tomorrow night,' said Ussemitus. 'If we are to see Jubaia alive again, we have to go tonight. Now.'

'Has he found a way to the Aviatrix?' said Aru.

'I don't know.'

Armestor gazed up in fear at the night sky. 'Go now? Back into the ranks of the windriders?'

'They're gone. Only a few remain. If we overfly the city, we may be able to conceal our flight. With care.' Ussemitus directed this last remark at the gliderboat.

Yes, yes. But hurry.

'If we find him,' said Aru, 'we make one attempt for him. Otherwise —'

'I know,' nodded Ussemitus. He held her eyes for a moment, but it was he who looked away. She was correct. This was a matter that went beyond emotion. She drew on her experiences, the darkness of the wars she had known. Otherwise how could she even consider leaving Jubaia? But she was correct. Ussemitus steeled himself. Yes, she was correct. Painful though her hardness had suddenly become, he had to adopt it.

The gliderboat trembled, lifting itself without waiting for instructions. Moments later they were swooping down over the lip of the mesa, bound once again for the walls of the Deathless City.

19

THE SEPTENARY

The black gliderboat sped onwards over the barren terrain. It had not broken its flight once since its journey from Kelpoora, skirting the Ocean of Hurricanes, avoiding the storms out at sea and the worst of the squalls that buffeted the land as a consequence. Vymark heard the whispering voices, the intimations of power, but he fixed his own purpose rigidly, closing out the confusion. He knew his enemies moved across the sea, and having circumnavigated it, had arrived at the western continent. His enemies! How his fury at their escape goaded him on, giving fresh strength to his purpose. He had heard the distant commands of Zellorian, but other voices had washed over them. There would be time enough to move to the west in search of whatever power lay there, but not until Ussemitus was found. Vymark bore the name like a torch before him now, hearing its echoes in the winds that were gathering about him, strengthening as he moved up from the southern reaches of the continent.

Below him, in a deep gorge that had been slashed into the rocks by an almost cosmic blow of the elements, he sensed a presence, a possible source of one of the voices that were trying to control him. At first he tried to ignore it, focusing his attention elsewhere, but it pulled at him until he dropped lower in the skies. He hovered above the gorge, a deep trench, shadow-filled, where nothing grew, as if a fire had at some time scorched everything from these remote lands.

There was movement in the darkness, but the image was no clearer than something glimpsed in a muddy pool. Vymark prepared to veer swiftly away, but the winds that eddied in that deep trough shaped their words insistently. 'What is it you seek?' their voices asked him.

261

'Power!' they laughed back in answer to their own question.

Vymark circled, fascinated by the sounds that emanated from the well of darkness.

'It lies in the west. Enough to fill you beyond imagining.'

'Seek the World Splinter!'

'In the *west* you will find it. And drink deep its secrets, gliderboat. Far greater than Zellorian shall you be. You need fear no darkness if you drink the powers of the World Splinter.'

Vymark's fevered mind thought again of the things Zellorian had told him. Of these powers in the west. Powers that Zellorian coveted. But these creatures below him, whatever they were, promised him power for himself. Power above Zellorian!

'*Yes!*' chorused the wild voices, howling like wind in the trench. 'What need do you have of a master? You will be a master of the skies. Innasmorn favours you, great gliderboat.'

'In the west.'

'The World Splinter.'

'In the west. Forget Ussemitus. He is nothing, nor are his friends of consequence. Ignore them. Seek true power. In the west.'

Vymark's mind soared, filled with images of light, and silhouetted against it was a vast shape, a leaning mass of rock.

He rose up from the trench, swerving on to a fresh course. Zellorian's words, which he had last heard so long ago, came back to him. The World Splinter: this must be the place that Zellorian had meant him to find.

As he flew onward, Vymark sent his thoughts far across the world, and he could feel Zellorian's mind trying to seek him out, groping for him. But there was no strength in that quest, where once there had been control. Vymark was free of that! And if he could find this place of power, use it, then nothing would control him again.

He had been so seduced by the voices in the trench that he had not been aware of the gathering clouds north of him, which now swept in like the advance waves of an aerial tide. They pulsed with energy, lightning licking downwards at the land like tongues.

Again he heard a voice, though this time it was whispered by a richer darkness, a cold stab in the heart of the storm that approached. Thunder rumbled across the hills below, and in its depths there were other voices, pulled together by the storm, shaped strangely in pain.

Vymark felt himself dragged towards the storm, lured by it. What he had just learned from the soft voices of the trench seemed insignificant compared to the fury in this new command. The dark spoke to him, like a voice beyond the world.

Innasmorn protected Ussemitus and his rabble. The Mother knew that Vymark hunted them and would destroy them, and so had tried to lure him away with the promise of power in the west. But that power was a trap. Why leave a path that would soon bring Vymark to his prey? He was so close now, north of this barren land, an easy victim. Kill him, and his pathetic minions, and the dark would show Vymark the real nature of power in this world.

Vymark saw himself as he had been, a warrior destined for greatness, a man who would stand beside Zellorian as he rebuilt the Empire that was. Innasmornian treachery had cut him down. The same Innasmornian treachery now lured him to the west, to his doom.

Storm clouds swirled around the gliderboat, embracing it like lovers, darkness thicker than night shrouding it. In that darkness the clouds heaved, lightning dancing as the thunder ranted. Vymark drank in this power, feeling something fresh ignite within him. His fury grew anew, his hatred seething like the clouds about him.

He swung northwards again, seeking out the city where he knew Ussemitus would be. The Deathless City.

Far across Innasmorn, in the Sculpted City, Zellorian felt a sudden silence in a part of his mind, as though certain memories had been erased. He turned his face away from

263

the colleagues he had been listening to, the fresh reports of subtle rebellion. He pretended to contemplate their words, though inwardly he felt a stab of fear. Where the link with Vymark had been there was now an utter darkness, as though the gliderboat had been destroyed. But something else had risen up from its remains, risen up and been swallowed.

Jubaia's hands were manacled. How Ussemitus and the woodsmen would have been appalled by the use of metal! But metal was common enough in Shung Nang, thieved from whatever sources the windriders could find. It did not bring disease or madness, as the other races of Innasmorn seemed to think.

Jubaia tried to close his mind to thoughts of his friends. It was too dangerous to think of them here, where the very air was sensitive to thought, a vast sponge drinking all in. The Aviatrix herself fed on that sponge, though she would not be a direct witness to the ceremony that was about to be performed.

Members of the Azure Wing led Jubaia up the steep stone stairs between the walls of the upper city, though Jubaia was relieved that Ryung-Hsu was not one of them. He had played his part, had shown his unswerving loyalty to the Aviatrix. Jubaia could expect no less from his friend. The security of Shung Nang was paramount.

The climb was an arduous one, skirting the very walls of the immense palace of the Aviatrix, until, high above its upper spires, the cleft opened out on to a wide area, a plateau that looked down on the entire city like the eyrie of a gigantic eagle. The surface of the plateau was cracked and pitted, but its far end, facing the north, was polished, dotted with pillars and columns, though they supported nothing, standing like neglected monoliths. Many of them were broken, others so badly weathered that they seemed on the point of toppling.

A group of figures had gathered before the largest of the pillars. The top of this pillar blossomed in a carving that resembled a face, though the eyes were closed, the features strange, unlike those of the windriders, or of any Innasmornian Jubaia had met. He had never set foot in this hallowed place before, but he knew the pillars were dedicated to the wind gods, the gods of the storms.

The figures moved like phantoms, shrouded in robes that fluttered about them, ribbons of light, as thin as the webbing of spiders. The faces of these beings were always hidden, sheathed in a veil of light as though there was no flesh beneath. These were the Septenary, so Jubaia assumed. He had heard of them, of their awesome powers, their communication with the gods of the sky. It was believed that no one else on Innasmorn could match their powers.

One of the figures drifted across the plateau, its movement beautiful to watch, an intimation of the glory of true oneness with the elements. It hovered near to the place where the Azure Wing had brought Jubaia. It waited, silent and motionless, like the promise of death and of a joy beyond it.

Footfalls behind him made Jubaia turn. Feng-Shai appeared, his eyes offering no warmth, his mind unreadable. He bowed to the almost translucent figure, but it did not move. The air had become very still, unnaturally so, but Jubaia knew that the Septenary controlled it.

The Interlocutor faced Jubaia. 'You understand why you are here, Jung-Bara?'

Jubaia inclined his head. 'I am to be judged by the Mother.'

'There will be a slight delay.'

'Feng-Shai?'

'One other is to be presented to the wind gods before you.'

Jubaia felt the chill of the words. Surely none of his companions had been taken. But perhaps it was just Feng-Shai's way of making things more uncomfortable for him: let him witness the ordeal of some other recalcitrant.

Feng-Shai turned and whispered to the figure. It drifted away again, joining its fraternity. Other winged guards materialised from the pillars near the Septenary, and Jubaia could see the downcast figure of another prisoner. He was relieved to see that it was one of the windriders, a stranger who had been divested of his clothes to reveal his thin body, his wings tightly bound together behind him to prevent him from taking to the skies. His hands were also manacled and now the Azure Wingman beside him undid these shackles. The prisoner, who was as motionless as a man who had been drugged might be, was taken to two pillars and chained between them, both at the wrist and ankle, so that he was stretched in a cross, silhouetted against the light beyond the edge of the plateau.

The Interlocutor stood beside Jubaia. 'This is Ang-Chu. Perhaps you knew him once?'

Jubaia watched the ceremonial chaining, the thoroughness of the act. The prisoner was completely exposed, unable to twist more than minimally. 'I think not, Feng-Shai.'

'A fine flier. Ambitious. Though ambition is not a crime in itself. The food of survival, to some extent.'

Jubaia ignored what he took to be a taunt.

'Ang-Chu could well have become a member of the Azure Wing, but he lacked patience. It was not enough that he coveted position. He also coveted the wife of one of the Azure Wingmen.'

'Indiscreet,' said Jubaia. 'And foolish, of course.'

Feng-Shai nodded slowly, his eyes fixed on Jubaia, looking to see the effectiveness of his testing. 'Quite so. The Aviatrix is not best pleased when the stability of the city is threatened. The order of things exists for a purpose. And the Azure Wing are the essence of Shung Nang, are they not?'

'I once aspired to them myself,' Jubaia agreed.

'I remember.'

'And Ang-Chu?'

'His lust got the better of him. He took the life of the Azure Wingman and attempted to abduct his wife. But the Aviatrix hears so much. The disturbance to her sleep was

266

considerable, as you can imagine. The death of an Azure Wingman is not something that can be kept silent.'

'Then Ang-Chu is to be executed?'

Feng-Shai shook his head. 'Judged. By the Mother. The Septenary have availed themselves of the facts. They in turn have spoken to the winds. Now it is for Ang-Chu to explain himself, through prayer. The Mother will decide his fate.'

'Is it necessary for me to be here, Feng-Shai? I feel as though I'm intruding – '

'Not at all. It is singularly appropriate that you should have the opportunity to see the processes of justice at work, particularly as you are to be subjected to them yourself.'

Jubaia grunted, but the Interlocutor had moved away in his seemingly indifferent manner. He joined the Azure Wingmen who had chained Ang-Chu to the pillars, and they grouped beside another pillar, well back from the prisoner. The Septenary gathered behind Ang-Chu in a semi-circle and faced north.

Beyond the lip of the plateau a great emptiness opened up, dark and star-speckled. The land beyond was far below and thus hidden by the edge of rock. At first the night sky was clear, cloudless. But as the Septenary began their work, their communion, the stars were blotted out as though celestial hands closed around the plateau, smothering it.

Jubaia felt the coming of the winds, heard the susurrations of their voices. Beyond him, as rigid as an animal before the stare of its killer, Ang-Chu had become taut, head thrown back as he tried to see into the heavens. Around him the air moved, the dust whipped up as the stillness became a breeze, the breeze a wind. It swirled, filling the top of the plateau and the walls of stone like water sluicing into a basin, a sudden roar of sound engulfing the world.

At first it did not seem that Ang-Chu said anything, his body rigid, but Jubaia noticed as his head turned from side to side, twisting gruesomely, that he was shouting, though the sound did not carry. The wind itself had become powerfully strong, tearing through the pillars, raising the dust

267

in a frenzy of movement, a dozen miniature tornadoes. Somehow the worst of the wind did not funnel back to where the Interlocutor and the Azure Wing stood. They were like statues, eyes fixed on Ang-Chu.

Jubaia lifted an arm to protect his eyes from the dust, but they were not affected. The stinging sand brought in from the desert passed him by, curling back up to the sky to begin a new downward swirl as if every particle were being directed by the ferocious winds.

Ang-Chu's wings lifted, their thin bonds snapping so that they came free, but so great was the burst of air that they snapped and tore free of him. Jubaia gasped as he saw them crumpled, tossed like twigs to the ground, rolling quickly backward before being sucked up heavenward, vanishing in yet another hysterical gust. Ang-Chu's body was lifted from the ground, suspended by the wind, caught like a fly in the chain webbing. The chains held, but the dust that seared Ang-Chu worked on his flesh like a rasp, stripping it from his body.

Again Jubaia ducked, expecting the grisly particles to gust over him, but the air broke them up into a fine spray of dust and carried them aloft, an offering to the wind gods. Jubaia watched, utterly bewildered, as Ang-Chu's body began the disintegration, the wind stripping it down, grinding every muscle, every bone, into nothing. A stream of light was all that signified this rapid transformation as limbs, organs and skeleton were ripped apart and translated into particles so tiny they could not be seen.

The Septenary turned their heads upward, their own shapes almost invisible in the cloak of dust that whirled about them, while over the plateau the storm cloud lowered, dragging up to it the last vestige of the victim as if eager to devour him. Only when the chains fell, empty, to swing from the pillars, did the wind begin to decrease. Nothing remained of Ang-Chu.

Slowly the Interlocutor walked back to where Jubaia was crouched. He gestured to the swinging chains. 'Whatever his fate, Innasmorn has taken him to be one with the elements.'

Jubaia merely nodded. He had no illusions about Ang-Chu's death. Nor had he any about his own fate. He would be similarly torn apart and scattered to the ends of the world.

'It is time,' said Feng-Shai.

The Azure Wing moved in silently, but with the surety of a wolf pack. Jubaia did not resist.

Feng-Shai led him to the Septenary and two of them made some adjustments to the manacles before drifting back. Jubaia tried to see through the dancing cloaks they wore, wondering if they were material beings, or part of the air, somehow translated by a power that was older than Shung Nang itself. But he could see nothing and in a moment the Azure Wingmen were locking his manacles to the same chains that had bound Ang-Chu. Of him, nothing remained, not even a whisper to suggest that he had even been here.

'Since Innasmorn has graced you with her gifts,' said Feng-Shai from somewhere behind the little thief, 'let her hear you now. She may spare you, Jung-Bara, or she may take you to her bosom. Blessed is the Mother.'

'And blessed her children,' said Jubaia automatically, his mind for a moment slipping back to the days when he stood as tall as the Azure Wing, his wings as proud.

Then he was alone, utterly alone, the wind lifting its voice, the clouds bearing down on him, ravening, eager for vengeance.

Ussemitus leaned far out over the prow of the racing gliderboat. They were high above the spires of Shung Nang, the night closing in around them as the sudden clouds rolled in from the north, blotting everything.

'I can see nothing!' cried Fomond. 'The light is worsening.'

Ussemitus signalled for him to be silent. 'Patrols,' he hissed. 'All around us. They may have taken Jubaia, but the city is still alerted.'

They've heard us, the gliderboat told him, dropping down.

Beyond them they could see the vague shapes of the upper mesa. Flitting through the towers of the city were tiny figures that must be the windriders.

'Can you locate Jubaia?' whispered Aru, pressed close beside Ussemitus.

'I'm trying to, but I have to be careful. It is like shouting. This air is thick with spells, traps, everything to snare the unwary. It's as if the stones have a mind that seeks us.'

Thunder rumbled in from the distance.

'Storm?' said Armestor nervously. 'Who brings this?'

'The high priests of the city, I think,' said Ussemitus. 'To protect it. They sense danger.'

And they'll use the storm on Jubaia, came the voice of the craft. *Tell them, or I will!*

'Be silent!' Ussemitus hissed.

'What is it?' said Aru. 'Is it the gliderboat? I can't hear it. It's deliberately blocking me out – '

'Conversation of any kind is dangerous,' Ussemitus told her again.

The craft swung round and brought a view of the flat top of the mesa into focus, the last few pinnacles of rock hemming it in like battlements. On the mesa could be seen broken pillars, figures.

He's down there, said the gliderboat, eager to swoop.

But Ussemitus forced the craft to obey him, keeping its nose up, making it circle. 'Wait!'

Let me go down. Let me go to him!

Ussemitus gasped and almost fell back into the craft, steadying himself on Aru. 'It's struggling for control,' he told her. 'We dare not go down yet. Help me, Aru!'

'We're discovered!' called Fomond, raising his bow. Beside him Armestor had done the same, and seconds later a flight of the windriders came out of the darkness, passing over the gliderboat, the faces of the Azure Wing very clear. At last they had seen the intruders. Angry voices buzzed in the air from all sides. The trap was closing.

'The gliderboat has given us away,' said Ussemitus. 'The whole city will be awake in a moment.'

'Look at the plateau!' cried Aru. 'Is that Jubaia?' she added, pointing to the figure that was chained to the pillars.

The gliderboat was forced to swerve aside as a host of the Azure Wing flew directly at it. Arrows whipped through the air, and both Fomond and Armestor let fly, though in the dwindling light it was impossible to be sure of hitting anything.

Ussemitus was flung back into the craft, and Aru only just managed to cling to the prow before she, too, was thrown inward. Before she fell, however, she saw something that sucked the breath from her lungs. The winds were focusing on the top of the plateau, knifing downwards with deliberate purpose, and she had seen the chained figure jerk like a fly in a web, then begin to *break* apart. Like sand, its flesh streamed from it.

The gliderboat pulled itself free of Ussemitus's control and dropped like a stone, straight into the teeth of the gale that had come tearing in from the north. The craft shuddered, rocking and bucking as though travelling through rapids in a mountain torrent.

Ussemitus crawled forward, trying to see ahead of them, but the wind beat at him. Thunder crashed directly over-head, scattering the last of the windriders who had been trying to follow the craft. Their pursuit broke up as they flew down into Shung Nang and shelter from the flaying wind.

'Call Innasmorn!' shouted Fomond, fingers digging into Ussemitus. 'Call her as you have never called her before, Ussemitus.'

'Her servants are here already,' he said, his words snatched away. 'This is not the darkness, not the horrors of the deathstorm. These are the winds that serve the Mother.'

'She is to destroy Jubaia?' said Fomond, amazed.

Ussemitus looked away, again trying to see over the prow of the craft. It had dropped down to a level with the mesa, circling, but now plummeting like a hunting bird of prey.

He's alive! came the triumphant shout of the gliderboat, almost knocking Ussemitus to the deck once more.

This time Aru heard the voice as well, shielding her eyes

from the wind and blasting sand. They were now caught in a cloud of it as it whipped up from the top of the plateau. There were figures down there, statuesque and, incredibly, unmoved by the raging wind as if they had been turned to stone by its power.

And held in the web of chains was Jubaia. The one Aru had seen had been someone else, though Jubaia was about to suffer the same fate, to be wind-blasted, stripped to nothing, scattered across Innasmorn.

The gliderboat tore over the top of the plateau, goaded to near-madness. Ussemitus could feel its mind veering from the horror about to be enacted below.

Jubaia cried aloud as he saw the dark smear of the gliderboat coming towards him. 'Get out of the path of the wind!'

The craft shot overhead. Behind him, Jubaia could feel the consternation of the sheltering Azure Wing and the Interlocutor. The wind's voice rose in pitch to a crescendo of sound, a howl of outrage, and Jubaia could sense it gathering itself, preparing for the blast that would begin the disintegration of his body.

Ussemitus had closed his mind to the chaos about him, concentrating on the skies directly overhead as they boiled. This was not the dark, he knew. This was the Mother, her black retribution, claiming her own. He used his power to speak to her, to spear his thoughts to the heart of that descending fury. In moments it would tear across the plateau like fire, gutting Jubaia as it swept by.

Feng-Shai and the Azure Wing broke formation and took to the cover of the rocks, their bows aimed at the bizarre shape that had swung round, hovering no more than a few feet from the ground. Like a giant bat it waited, wind streaming over it, somehow not battering it to pulp.

Cut him free! came the gliderboat's voice, a mental shriek, but Ussemitus took no notice.

Aru heard, however. She turned to Armestor and Fomond, who aimed their bows at the shadows behind the craft. She could see the Septenary, none of which had taken cover, their own attention turned to the skies in a unified study of ecstasy.

'Armestor! The cloaked ones. Fire at them,' Aru called.

Armestor swivelled round and released an arrow at once. It flew across the intervening space, but he watched in despair as it went straight through the first of the Septenary as if it were made of mist. Another arrow followed and another, but with no effect.

Fomond leapt down from the gliderboat, pulling out his sword. He ran across the plateau towards the chained Jubaia. Beyond him he could see the cloud gather for its thrust, but he shut out the madness, the terror of imminent death. He reached Jubaia, but could not make himself heard, instead working on the manacles. But they were of metal, and resisted all efforts to open them.

A fist of wind knocked Fomond from his feet, punching him into a pillar. He sprawled, pain shooting through his shoulder and arm, choking for breath.

Ussemitus felt his concentration snap. He opened his eyes to see Fomond on his knees at the base of the pillars. Armestor was about to leap from the craft, but Aru tried to drag him back. The Septenary closed in, arms like wings raised as if directing the wind downwards towards the company.

They were about to share to wrath of Innasmorn.

20

SECRETS

Vymark raced on through the night, tireless. Everything was blotted from his mind as he drank the wine of power given to him by the dark, everything save the vision of his enemies. Ussemitus. Aru the Casruel bitch! He understood how deeply the darkness hated the woodsman and his allies, how determined it was to destroy them all. It filled him, controlled him. And he knew his own part, his step to greater power. Beneath him he stretched his steel talons in readiness, aching for blood.

In the darkness, the mesas rose up like fortresses. On one of them, Vymark knew, a city housed his enemies, for the dark had discovered them there and led Vymark there now, giving greater speed to him, pushing him onwards at a rate that would have astounded Zellorian. But the Prime Consul was forgotten. Vymark's mind had room only for his immediate purpose, sharpened into a weapon, all other reasoning blotted.

The wind screamed beside him, taking hold of him and thrusting him onward to the city. He could feel the turbulence in the night skies as another storm rose up ahead of him, another piling of thick clouds, where thunder rolled, shaking the rock bastions. Lights below plucked at his attention, and he was aware of the city, carved out of a huge mesa. He felt its mind digging at his, but the darkness protected him from it as he swung down towards it. More light flickered at its very peak, where figures had gathered on a plateau. Figures that included his enemies. Like animals giving themselves up for sacrifice, they had come out on to this exposed slab, almost as if in readiness to meet their end.

Vymark ignored everything and aimed himself for the

plateau, a plummeting hawk, claws outspread. Ussemitus would be the first to enjoy their grasp.

Vymark's intended victim had felt the power of the winds above him. He knew he could not turn to them. They were set on their course, focused and fed by the Septenary, whose own powers far outstripped those of the Windmasters. And as the searing wind began the final rush towards the pillars, Ussemitus knew that not only would Jubaia be taken by it, but so would he and his companions, together with the gliderboat. Even the craft could not withstand this blasting air.

He steeled himself.

Overhead there was another clap of thunder, a dazzling flicker of light. Something tore across Ussemitus's line of vision. Aru and the others all gasped as they caught a glimpse of a shape in the skies, a black, winged creature, flying in the face of the wind.

Ussemitus had braced himself for the wind that would rip him apart, but something in the oncoming storm turned, twisting like a predator under the sea at the last moment. The current of killing air swerved upwards, following the flight of the dark shape. The roar of the wind died for a brief period, leaving the plateau in an abrupt calm. But it was a calm that brought with it the threat of a greater blast.

Again Ussemitus tried to fathom the aerial powers, seeking a way to reach the elements of Innasmorn. This time he found a way through the churning confusion. Something had emerged out of the dark side of the Mother, a gathering of ancient evils, honed into some physical killing force. It, too, had come here, intent on striking at Ussemitus, singling him out in its ferocity. But in its coming it had alerted the Mother.

'The dark gliderboat,' whispered Aru in the still air.

Ussemitus turned, shocked by her words.

'I saw it,' she said, pointing.

The Septenary had raised their arms as one, also turned from the gliderboat. They were directing their own power away from their original victims, finding the monstrous

275

black craft that suddenly appeared overhead, swooping down as if for a kill. The wind followed it, though not a a part of it. It was alien, an abomination.

Ussemitus and Aru flung themselves down into thei craft with Armestor. The black gliderboat tore through th air mere feet above them. The air crackled as it passed.

Innasmorn pursued it, the wind screaming afresh, roar ing after the black craft like an army of demons. Fomono clung to the base of the pillar where he had fallen, expecting the skin to be stripped from him as the wind passed, bu it did not. Jubaia's chains snapped in a burst of sparks and the little thief was flung backwards, spinning over and over coming to rest at the base of another pillar.

Vymark, his mind filled with roaring fire as Innasmorn turned on him, did not see the wall of stone rise up ahead of him. He flew straight into its edge, his right wing smashed away by an outstretched knuckle of rock, spinning him round in a lunatic circle that spared him from complete destruction against the cliff face. Catapulted outwards ove the lip of the plateau, the black gliderboat bounced of another outcrop, showered in sparks, and tumbled over the mesa into darkness, down towards the waiting fangs o stone far below.

The wind rushed over the mesa like the sea, but there was no fire in it, and no death.

Ussemitus got to his feet, peering over the top of the gliderboat. He tried to speak to it, but it was silent, as though it had shut itself away from the storm, hidden in utter darkness beyond his reach, though it was a darkness of peace. The Septenary had lowered their arms and stood like statues, as remote from all this now as the gliderboa seemed to be. Beyond them, the Azure Wing were stirring, emerging from the rocks that had protected them. Up in the skies, the storm raged, racing to the east at fantastic speed, demons chasing demons.

Feng-Shai pushed his way through the windriders, staring at the grounded gliderboat. *This* was the means by which Jubaia had entered Shung Nang. But was it an enemy, or a servant of the Mother? The Mother had judged Jubaia, and these intruders, but they lived.

Aru and Armestor rose together, amazed that the wind had died so quickly and utterly. Dawn was at last reaching out beyond the peaks, and the last of the storm clouds were thinning. They looked at each other, eyes filled with questions, but neither of them spoke.

Ussemitus climbed out of the craft. He had seen Fomond, who looked to be injured, and ran over him, still wary of the Septenary, silent ghosts on either side of him.

'Fomond!' he called, his voice hardly above a whisper.

Fomond groaned, shuffling to his feet, managing a wave. 'I'm all right.'

Ussemitus helped him up. 'Your arm –'

'Broken, I think. But the storm – '

'Something turned it. The craft that was following us. It fed on the dark for its power. Innasmorn read that, and in the knowing, saw that we were its intended victims. She tasted its vile hunger, as I did –'

'So spared us?'

'Yes. But where is Jubaia?'

Fomond looked surprised. 'He fell, but was spared.' He glanced around him. 'Jubaia!' he called. 'He must be here. Perhaps hurt – '

Ussemitus began a search of the pillars, conscious of the fact that the windriders were watching, though they were motionless.

Jubaia was not to be found.

'I can't understand it,' said Fomond, appalled. 'Surely the Mother did not take him – '

Ussemitus ushered him back to the gliderboat, one eye on the Septenary, though they remained as stone, as if they no longer took an interest in what occurred here.

Armestor helped Fomond aboard the craft.

'Where's Jubaia?' said Aru. 'We've got to hurry, before we're attacked.'

Ussemitus looked grim, his jaw set against anger, or pain, Aru was not sure which. He was studying the windriders beyond, the tall figure of the Interlocutor. The latter began to walk towards them, face like a mask. If he came in peace, it did not show.

We must leave now, said a faint voice in Ussemitus's mind. He had to exercise strict control of himself to cover his surprise.

'Jubaia?' he breathed.

Tell them he's dead, replied the voice emotionlessly, then slid back into its unreachable silence.

Feng-Shai, guards on either side of him, approached the gliderboat. He spoke, but it was in a language Ussemitus did not understand.

Ussemitus kept his eyes on the Interlocutor, his voice very low. 'Aru, get to the prow. Armestor, you and Fomond prepare. We must leave at once.'

Aru glanced sharply at him. The question did not have to be asked.

'He's dead. The boat told me we must leave.'

Aru sucked in her breath, but she went to the prow in readiness.

Feng-Shai studied the lines of the gliderboat.

'I do not speak the language of Shung Nang,' said Ussemitus, holding back the waves of loss, the bitter anger.

Feng-Shai stiffened. He recognised the language of the east, of the Vaza. 'I hear you,' he said in the same tongue. 'Why are you here?'

'We came for Jubaia. The one you chained.'

Feng-Shai looked surprised. 'Jung-Bara? What is he to you?'

'He serves Innasmorn, just as we do,' said Ussemitus coldly, gesturing to the others.

'He had no right to return to the Deathless City. Nor to bring you here. He understood the consequences.'

Ussemitus bowed. 'I accept that. As has Jubaia, whom you call Jung-Bara. But he has paid his debt.'

Feng-Shai's eyes narrowed. 'You think so? You think the Aviatrix will be satisfied to permit this appalling sacrilege?'

'We serve the Mother,' said Ussemitus. 'You have no claim on our lives, nor does the Aviatrix. We regret the intrusion. As we regret the loss of our brother, Jung-Bara.'

'The loss?'

Ussemitus waved at the plateau. 'He has been dissipated. Innasmorn has taken him. He has made the flight from which there is no return.'

Feng-Shai nodded his head slowly.

'Has honour not been satisfied?' said Ussemitus. 'We believe it was a mistake for Jung-Bara to be subjected to the judgement of the Mother in this place. We intervened for our own reasons. If we have offended the Aviatrix, we are sorry for that. But we have other work.'

'You wish to leave?'

'At once.'

Feng-Shai again studied the gliderboat. He walked closer to it, his guards uneasily following him in case of treachery. Ussemitus knew that they would not be satisfied until they had assured themselves that Jubaia was not here. He waited while they looked, though they did not come too close. Ussemitus could feel the tension in Armestor, whose hand was on his bow as if he too expected deceit. But the Azure Wing made no hostile moves.

Feng-Shai covered his surprise. He could have sworn that Jung-Bara had been spared his doom by these intruders. But he was not here. And if he were, surely his companions would not leave without him. To attack them might bring down the wrath of the Mother, who did seem to favour them. This craft! Such a creature, if living beast it was.

'We have work elsewhere,' said Ussemitus.

Feng-Shai bowed. He had discarded all possibility of killing these people and taking their craft. The men were Vaza, though they clearly had extraordinary powers, but the woman was like none other Feng-Shai had seen, almost as though she did not belong on Innasmorn.

The Azure Wing stood back as Feng-Shai spoke softly to them. They watched in amazement as the craft rose from the ground, hovering briefly before gently drifting away over the plateau, beyond the pillars and up to meet the dawn. The Septenary had not moved, nor did they now, as if in submission to the passing of the strange visitors.

None of the windriders spoke, waiting for a command from Feng-Shai, but the Interlocutor said nothing. After a long time he turned on his heel and walked stiffly back to the stone path that led down into the Deathless City.

Dazed, Jubaia sat with his back to the pillar. It felt icy, as though there was a cold power within it that sought the warmth in his veins. He shook himself, trying to comprehend what had happened. The searing wind that had come for him had not dissipated him as it had Ang-Chu, unless the flesh that still clung to him was an illusion. And if he had been turned to dust and scattered, why did he ache so! Whatever had happened, he was free of the chains. Dust clouds whirled around him, and glancing to his left, he saw a deep crack in the surface of the rock.

Alive, though Feng-Shai would never believe it, he thought to himself. If Ussemitus has done this, Innasmorn alone knows how!

As he massaged his arms and legs, trying to squeeze strength back into them, a thought began to grow in his mind, a faint idea at first, but then more sharply focused, a plan. If Feng-Shai thought him sacrificed, given to the winds —

He rolled over, out of sight of Fomond, who he could just discern through the dust, and dropped down into the crevice, which was barely wide enough to take him. Its darkness welcomed him like a maw receiving food. He waited, but above him there was only silence. The skies were calm. He could indeed have been dead.

Then he called her name, as softly as he could, using only the faintest whisper in his mind, shaping it like an eddy of wind, a private language. *Circu.*

There was no answering voice, but he knew she had heard him. And she dared not answer, not in this sacred place, where the stones had ears to catch the faintest hint of speech and thought.

Tell them to say I am dead. Then leave.

Again silence answered him, but he knew the gliderboat

280

had heard him. She must not disobey, not if his task was to bear fruit.

After a long wait, he crawled down the long fissure, which mercifully widened as he crawled away from the place of the pillars. He thought he heard voices above him, beyond the crack, Ussemitus and Fomond. Part of him longed to assure them he was safe, but he dared not speak aloud. The Septenary would be very close by. A whisper would be a shout to them.

The fault in the rock led Jubaia down towards the walls of the upper citadel, and he knew that beyond them would be the palace of the Aviatrix. He grinned to himself as he slipped beyond another curve, now some twenty feet down and well out of sight of the Azure Wing. As he moved on, he found himself going parallel to the rock wall. He could not climb it here for fear of again going up into view, but as the slope got steeper, he knew that a ledge would run around and downwards beyond the plateau, like the bed of a stream. He was correct in his assumption: he was being taken away from the mesa crest.

The climb down became easy for one as skilled in this sort of venture as he was. But he knew he must go upwards again, now that he had rounded the crags beyond the plateau. Slowly he moved up, crawling out of the crack entirely. Dawn rose on the other side of the mesa, so darkness served him yet. He had to swing quickly to one side as he almost climbed to a window ledge where light suddenly spilled out. But there were no watchers within. He climbed around it, and higher there were other, grilled windows, but no one to see him.

Before long he was above the level of the plateau of pillars. The air here was fresh, but he took strength from it, warming to his task. If they truly thought him dispersed –

High, high up he went, ant-like and confident, ignoring the protest of his muscles. Another window opened before him in the rock, a narrow, angled one that was evidently not meant for viewing the world outside, but which was to allow light and air into the upper palace. Jubaia squeezed into its pointed arch. Ah, this is where their ingenuity failed them, he mused. One of the Azure Wing, or indeed any winged man of Shung Nang, would never get through such a window. But one such as I, small as I am –

It was not easy, and he scraped himself, cursing softly, but he got through the gap and perched on the inner ledge like an owl. Light came up to him faintly from a number of lamps far below. Spars of rock crossed before him. He slipped on to one of them, feet kicking up tiny dust clouds as he went. He was in the very apex of the palace, in an area where no guard would ever think to come, unless it was to effect repairs.

He swung down, closing his mind in on itself for fear of tripping any alarm that might have been set here like a spell to guard the way. Below him, some fifty feet down, he could see corridors, though no guards. The inner reaches of the Aviatrix's palace were nearby.

Over the complex network of stone spars he went, cutting through a mass of webs where the numerous spiders had linked their own network of curtains. Under him now was a dome, completely enclosed by the vast structure he had entered. It was smooth and dusty, offering no immediate means of ingress. He dropped lightly on to it, and although it was as solid as a huge skull, he felt a tremor run through it as though it was alive.

He froze, not daring to move, and waited. But there was no repetition of the movement. Slowly he inched across the dome, near its rounded top, looking for something that would help him. The Aviatrix would be below. If she slept, her dreams were protected by the fabric of this dome, for it was constructed from unknown materials, possibly grown, fused by powers that only the Mother could understand.

Jubaia grinned. He had not come this far on his last visit. Indeed, he had not breached the inner walls of this sanctum to find this dome. Entry from above then had seemed an impossible method of approach.

The layers of dust beneath him betrayed him, and he found himself sliding down the wide curve, his fingers trying for a purchase, but getting none. He was saved from a long fall by a ledge at the edge of the dome, his toes dropping to it. The walls fell away below him, sheer, but he slithered around the ledge with a fresh purpose.

As he moved around the rim of the dome, he began to realise that he was in danger of going in circles, for there seemed to be no hint of a way in which he could breach the dome, which he must do if he were to succeed in his purpose. Time stood still: he had no idea whether he had been all around the dome. He kept moving, searching for the merest hint of a way of ingress, but still he found none. Finally, tired, his arms aching, he rested, face and body flat to the dome, as if resting against the belly of a huge parent. He could hear faint stirrings within the dome, blood perhaps, moving through veins and arteries, the pumping of a remote organ.

When the movement came, it was so abrupt that he was completely unprepared for it. Underneath him the fabric of the dome parted, and he slithered into it, the sides of the opening as slick as a fruit. The heat bathed him, his arms and legs convulsing with surprise, but down he went. He felt something solid slithering by and grabbed at it. It took several attempts to grip it and cling, wrapping his legs around it. Like a great mouth, the substance of the skull slipped over him, releasing him as if pushing out a pip.

He was clinging to some kind of beam, possibly of bone, hanging over another drop. The bone was polished, free of dust and spiders and the air in here was pure. There was very little light, but he was inside the dome, that much he knew. He tried to gauge how far away the floor was, but could not tell. Light suffused from the inner walls, which seemed to be moving in the faintest of ripples. Stone? he wondered, but they seemed more pliant. He dared not risk releasing the spar and falling. He could end up with a broken back: the depths were obscured in darkness.

These curious walls had a number of odd features, not least of which were the growths that jutted from them like thick bristles. Jubaia preferred not to dwell on the possibilities of what they were. Instead he swung along the beam to the wall that had disgorged him and swung down to the uppermost of the growths. It was dry and solid enough for his purpose. Like a fly, he used the growths, which felt disturbingly like hair, to help him descend.

As he went down, he passed places in the wall where the light gleamed, but it, too, was bizarre, its nature veiled behind skeins of tissue as thin as the membranes of a windrider's wing. Below him the pool of darkness revealed no more of its secrets, but he knew instinctively that he must fathom them.

However, on his descent, he came across an opening in the wall, a dark rectangle that offered a passage into the citadel beyond. Swinging down from the bristles, he dropped into the mouth of the opening. It was barely large enough to admit him, and as he pushed through it, he was sure he felt the soft walls about him shudder, reshaping themselves as he passed.

Beyond the vent there was a larger passage, and crawling out he was able to stand. Bathed in darkness he moved on slowly, something blocking the way, like a curtain of fine roots. He moved these aside and had come to another corridor. To his surprise it was lit by a single lamp, a metallic object, burning tallow. The corridor was clean, the floor of polished stone or a perfect illusion of it, with no hint of dust.

He moved along this gleaming corridor, but had taken no more than a few steps when he realised it was a mistake. The floor had become spongy, his feet sinking into it as if it were mud. He looked down, but the lower half of his body was invisible. Cursing softly, he tried to pull himself free, but could not. He found that he could move forward, slowly, but it was impossible to move to either side or backwards. Controlling his fear, he moved on.

The passage curved around the inside of the dome so that he could see no more than a few feet ahead of him. The floor's illusion remained fixed, polished stone, inlaid with bright patterns at various points, though he still felt himself sinking into the substance of which it was in reality made. Light danced about him, the walls seeming to expand and contract very gently, like the walls of an organ. With extreme care he sent his mind out for the first search.

And recoiled at once.

The Aviatrix was all around him. He was within her dreaming mind and had entered it without knowing. Now, instead of moving on into a physical construction, he was caught in some other dream realm, perhaps deliberately fabricated by the Aviatrix as part of her protection. This curving path, he guessed, would go on endlessly, with him plodding around and around until exhaustion claimed him. He must break its hold on him.

But which way must he go? Inward? To the heart of the dome? That would be the most likely way. But also the most obvious. Any thief would take that course.

He studied the outer wall. It, like the floor, was featureless. He angled his forward movement, barely able to veer towards the wall, but when his hand touched it, it felt warm. The grip on his feet weakened a little. He was able to flatten himself against the wall and move along it more quickly, as if he were again on a cliff face.

Above him, the ceiling sloped, low and cut apparently from stone. He decided to test this, to see if it, too, were an illusion. There were enough minute holds in the wall to permit him to climb upward for the few feet necessary. When he reached the ceiling, it was not there, merely a shadow. He pushed upward, finding a ledge. He hauled himself on to it and rolled over. Light washed over him, though it was of a strange hue, greenish and scarlet in alternating waves. The air was hot. Looking back, he found that the way he had entered had gone.

He was now in some other chamber. It was of no particular shape, its walls curved and angled alternately, its ceiling a confusion of glittering gems, some of which were disconcertingly like eyes.

Jubaia rose, and as he did so, a score of figures rose with him. He dropped at once into a defensive crouch, waiting for an attack that he thought must surely come. But then he realised what had happened. The figures were also crouching, copying him. Though some of them were his height, other were far taller, yet others were squat and broad.

The walls were carved from enormous gemstones, each facet a mirror, though one that contorted the truth in some way. A score of twisted Jubaias watched him as he stood up again.

Then they were gone, vanishing as if they had never been. Other images began to form in the gem surfaces. Each figure garbed itself in darkness, face hidden, but this time Jubaia could see that they were not images of himself, no matter how deformed.

'Jung-Bara,' a voice called softly. He whirled round to confront one of the mirrors and the beautiful winged girl who stood there. The mirror had dissolved like melted ice, and the girl stepped into the frame, no longer an image. It was Imlukan.

She looked around her apprehensively, reaching out for him. 'I knew you would attempt something like this. I guessed it was why you came back to Shung Nang. But it is far too dangerous. You must come with me.'

He almost reached out and took her slender fingers. They were inches from him. But he stopped himself. This was not the Imlukan he had seen earlier this night. It was Imlukan as he remembered her, all those years ago. Though time had aged her so very little in the intervening years, this image of her had not aged a day since he had left Shung Nang.

A trick. He drew back.

'Jung-Bara!' she cried, an echo of the cry she had emitted so long ago. She would have stepped forward into the chamber, but she remained held by the mirror frame.

'If you would help me,' he said softly, his throat aching, 'step forward beside me.'

Again she looked about her. 'There's no time –'

He reached inside his tunic and brought out a small fragment of metal, one of the last trinkets he had left about him, and tossed it through the mirror. It was consumed in bright fire at once, sizzling as it hit the ground. The image of Imlukan instantly disappeared.

Jubaia had no time to dwell on his bitter remorse. A sharp laugh behind him made him spin about once more.

286

This time he found himself confronting Feng-Shai. The Interlocutor nodded, lips drawn back in a cruel smile.

'So you lied after all, Jung-Bara. You did not come back to Shung Nang merely to see the city of your birth. Though it will be your last time. You came here to finish the thievery you began so long ago.'

Jubaia stepped back. He looked about him for an avenue of escape, but the mirrors all dissolved. In each of them stood an Azure Wingman, with an arrow aimed at his heart. Where Imlukan had stood, there was nothing, only smoke drifting up from the charred metal he had thrown.

His mind whirled, trying to untangle this knot of deceit. There was one possibility.

He locked gazes with Feng-Shai, but the eyes that studied him were like ice, unmoved by any emotion, even anger. Jubaia took a step towards him. Still Feng-Shai did not react. Another step. Another. Jubaia was now only a few feet from the Interlocutor.

'This time there will be no judgement, Jung-Bara,' said Feng-Shai, sliding a long dirk from his belt. Its point gleamed in the chamber.

Jubaia edged forward until he was a step away. 'Then plunge it into me. Let justice take its course.'

In the silence, Feng-Shai drew back his arm.

Jubaia stood still, eyes closed. The point of the dirk shot to his chest, driven up under his ribs. It was a strike that would have killed him. But he felt nothing.

He opened his eyes. The Interlocutor was gone. The mirror had dissolved to leave only an opening. Jubaia stepped through it. Mercifully his guess had been correct: the mirror that offered the least palatable alternative had been the one to choose.

The next chamber was filled with light so bright that nothing was visible. The air whispered, many voices mingling to add confusion to the ears. Jubaia tried to concentrate, but it was not easy. He moved across the chamber, the light intensifying and the whispers growing. Still he fixed his mind on a single point, until he was able to find one voice and follow it, as if following the erratic flight of a butterfly.

The dreams! his mind cried. These are the dreams of the Aviatrix! I am among them.

The realisation almost made him lose control over the one he had found. But it was an unimportant one, fading away to be replaced by another. He was swept up by them, as though he could fly as he had done so many years before. But he began to understand that he could remain here forever, trapped by these endless mysteries, led nowhere by them, his own mind lost.

He focused his attention on what he desired. The key to the west. He closed his mind to everything else and began to create a dark concept of the lands beyond Shung Nang. Gradually the dreams about him faded, thinning down. From the sleeping mind of the Aviatrix he began to build on his own dream.

At first he was not aware of it, but darkness replaced the bright light, and beyond him, looming up out of the glow, a vast shape towered, a chunk of masonry that leaned over as if it were a world about to topple, falling into another world. The scale of the thing was unbelievable, impossible.

The World Splinter, his mind cried out in a mixture of fear and triumph. A piece of another world, lodged deep in the flesh of Innasmorn, remnant of a realm that had blown apart in some unimaginable disaster. The power that had come to the west.

'How do I reach it?' he whispered to the air.

And the voices answered, sibilant and alluring.

'You choose your path so hurriedly,' they said. 'Look around you, little thief. You desire to steal a dream. You have the pick of them now.'

'I desire the key to the west.'

'A small thing. There are greater rewards available to you. See.'

Jubaia turned to look down what appeared to be an avenue that stretched across a stretch of sand. The sea lapped at this golden shore, and through the haze above the waters, he could make out an island.

288

'Walk across the sand,' said the voices, eager as lovers to please him.

'What island is that?' he said, his mouth dry.

'It is Scurrakhan. Walk across the sand and we will show you how to skip across the rocks to it.'

'I have no need of the secrets of Scurrakhan,' he insisted.

'No? But the treasures are greater than you imagine. They transform.'

'I am a windrider, even though my body is changed. Even if I had their form, I would not take the drugs, not become one with the winds – '

'Even if you had their form? You could have it again, Jubaia. Jung-Bara. Walk across the sand, through the waves to Scurrakhan. Take its treasure. You will be as you were. Innasmorn will bless you. And Shung Nang will welcome you. Nothing in the Deathless City will be denied to you. Nothing.'

And it is no illusion, he thought. I could accept this. Reject the spoils I came for. Scurrakhan. Everything I lost, restored. I have only to ask.

'No.' He turned, searching the darkness for the image of the World Splinter. 'Give me the key to the west.'

Darkness closed in at once. He thought he felt a stir of air, as though a ghost had kissed his cheek. And the voices told him what he wanted to know, speaking to him in a language he had never heard but instantly understood. It was the key, the incantation that would unlock the spells, the terrible barriers. The Mother had blessed his choice.

A deep darkness fell. The image of the huge rock was gone.

Jubaia turned, as though to catch a last glimpse of the painful memories, but they were hidden from him. He had set a new course, courted a new destiny.

BOOK FIVE

THE WORLD SPLINTER

A DARK LANDSCAPE

'There's a pass, but narrow. Otherwise the cliffs are sheer, Zaru,' the Zemok scout reported.

Vorenzar grunted, stretching up on his xillatraal to study what he could of the rising land. The spectral guide had brought the Csendook through a broken stretch of land, barren and wind-blasted, where the soil was parched, the sparse trees wasted and dying. Water had been found when it was needed, the guide showing the company where to dig in the blackened earth, or which rocks to pull apart. The rivers were no more than trickles among crumbling boulders, petering out up on the slopes that rose to the west. There was little hint that life had been here, and Vorenzar thought increasingly of a war zone, wondering if Innasmorn had at some time experienced the fury of clashing armies, the unleashing of terrible powers.

The company had been riding slowly upwards, the land sloping gradually and then more steeply towards a range of low mountains in the west; these waited like teeth for their arrival. They stretched across the horizon, blocking the way, though the ghost guide led the company directly towards them. It had not addressed them for days, stopping only when the Csendook camped, hovering nearby but never approaching.

Vorenzar looked back. Behind him the land sloped away to a remote distance. He had not realised how much of a climb this had been. The world seemed to drop away below, a featureless slope, a drab and effective barrier to anyone thinking of crossing it. Anyone without Csendook determination.

As he looked back, the Csendook commander noticed movements among the scattered boulders and gullies; movements he had come to expect during the weeks of the journey, the shambling of the followers, scores of them. Ill-shapen figures, they came on, somehow never falling far behind the Csendook party. The Zemoks took little notice of them any more, but were always aware of them in case for some reason they turned their dogged pursuit into an act of aggression.

Vorenzar stared in surprise: there were hundreds of figures below his party, as if the cracked terrain spawned an army of them. Somewhere among them was Korborus, indistinguishable, now useless.

Ondrazem leaned over to his Zaru and spoke quietly. 'Forgive me, Zaru, but they seem to be herding us. This pass that has been found – '

Vorenzar lowered his visor. 'If it is the only way through those mountains, we'll take it.'

'It could be a trap.'

'The rabble that follows us has not brought us this far across their world to attack us.'

They rode on, slowly, cresting the slope, the low mountains abruptly before them, closer than they had expected. The scouts waited, weapons drawn as if they had already been involved in a skirmish.

'An ideal place for treachery,' Ondrazem said to one of his companions, who nodded silently.

'The place stinks of danger,' he replied.

Ondrazem did not question his Zaru, but he wondered if Vorenzar was allowing his thirst for knowledge to cloud his judgement. The earth-things might want the Csendook here so that their ruler could examine them, see what manner of creatures the Csendook were. It would have been logical generalship.

Vorenzar studied the cliffs, which were exactly as the scout had told him: far too difficult to scale, and besides, they would never get the xillatraal over them. But he saw how treacherous the pass might be. Surely the ghost guide had not brought them here to sacrifice them. He could not be sure. There could be some particularly powerful element hidden within the pass, unique to this realm, that could be the undoing of the Csendook.

As if in answer to his doubts, the ghost guide appeared beside the mouth of the pass, a tall gash into the rock wall, silent and airless. The xillatraal growled at it as if at an enemy.

'The way to power lies through here,' said the ghost guide. 'But it is protected by the World Splinter. You cannot pass through without help. I will – '

Before it could say more, the ground before it erupted. From the split earth a shape arose, shaking itself free of dry dust and rock, bent over, mannish but little larger than a child. It was far smaller than an urmurel, but seemed to have been moulded in the same way. A tortured face appeared in its blob of a head. The mouth opened, toothless and black, and when it spoke, the Csendook drew back in alarm. From that twisted orifice came the voice of Korborus.

'Ignore the spectre!' it hissed, its words clear. 'It will deliver you to your doom. You have better servants. Let them prepare the way for you.'

Swinging round, the earth-thing grew, bloating, then abruptly loping over the ground. It leapt towards the rocks on which the ghost guide stood, and as it did so there was a crash, as if of thunder. Earth and dust showered the Csendook, the xillatraal almost bolting, snapping at the air. But Vorenzar held his ground.

When the dust had cleared, both ghost guide and earth shape had gone. In the sudden stillness that followed the blast, he was aware of movements behind him, among the ranks of the earth beings. They were moving forward in orderly ranks, though without menace. The Csendook steadied their beasts and drew aside, still prepared for a battle if need be. But the earth army ignored them and began to file into the pass, five abreast. For a long time they came pouring across the plain, innumerable, while Vorenzar and his amazed company watched them, stunned by the press of bodies now moving up the pass and into its shadows. There was little semblance of humanity about the creatures, some of which were better formed than others, so that the effect was like that of an earth slide, a long slick of mud sliding into the pass, choking it.

When the last of the creatures had finally gone into the pass, Vorenzar turned to Ondrazem. 'They are to be our shield, or so it seems.'

'Dare we trust them, Zaru?'

Vorenzar shrugged. 'They aided us when the skies unleashed the storm.'

Ondrazem drew himself up. He began to understand what it was the Zaru expected of him. Vorenzar was the commander of this party, and their duty was to the Supreme Sanguinary. To find the last of the Men. Ondrazem was a Csendook. Only the most able served the Supreme Sanguinary. His duty was clear.

'We no longer have an Opener,' said Vorenzar. 'Otherwise Ipsellin would have led us into this pass.'

'I claim the honour,' said Ondrazem, without bitterness. 'I will enter the pass first.'

Vorenzar bowed in acknowledgement.

Ondrazem turned away, committed. Slowly he moved his beast forward, though it was uneasy at the prospect of following the packed mass of earth beings that had gone before it. The shadows that wreathed the jagged pass folded round it.

Vorenzar waited motionlessly, without remorse. If sacrifices had to be made, he must be the last. It was his duty as leader to ensure that.

At last he saw the mask of Ondrazem in the darkness. The Zemok waved him forward, apparently unhurt. Vorenzar nodded to his Zemoks and they nudged the restless xillatraal towards the pass.

Ondrazem turned and disappeared down the muddy throat of the gorge. The place reeked of deep earth, of rotting vegetation, of decay. But the Zemoks had been through fields deep in blood: this place was nothing to them. Of the ghost guide there was no sign, as though it had given up its unbidden support, abandoning the Csendook to the power of the urmurels and their grotesque hordes.

296

Vorenzar was not concerned. How he reached the World Splinter was immaterial.

The walls of the pass were blurred, the stone slick with wet mud, which dripped downwards to make a morass through which the xillatraal struggled, their ankles gripped, sucked down. But they moved on, eyes glaring ahead, fangs barred, prepared to snap at the merest hint of danger. The air was thick and heavy, the light above almost blotted out. As the company moved deeper into the pass, festoons of earth hung downwards, trailing roots and rotted branches as if the Csendook rode through the decomposing carcass of a giant. The air crackled overhead, threatening but never harming. If power had guarded this place, the earth beings had ruptured it, so Vorenzar imagined.

Ondrazem was up ahead, visible only as a blur, his armoured figure and his xillatraal no more than a moving shadow, shapeless and mechanical.

Vorenzar heard sounds within the earth walls, deep groans and murmurs, meaningless, like the voices of the damned. A struggle went on in that darkness, a heaving contest that never broke through to the surface. But the Zaru closed his mind to it, thinking of the power beyond the gorge.

Finally there was light. Ondrazem was limned by it, a noble statue. For a moment it seemed as though he and his beast had become as an urmurel, a thing of earth and clay, a shapeless monster, claimed by the dark powers of this world. But as the Zemoks came through into daylight, Ondrazem turned and saluted them, though he did not raise his visor.

When he spoke, his voice was controlled, level, but there was a coldness in it. 'The World Splinter lies beyond us, Zaru.'

Vorenzar rode up to the dark figure, studying it closely, but he did not order Ondrazem to lift his visor. It had been an ordeal for him, to be first through the pass. Earth and muck clung to him, as it did to them all. If a little fear had also accumulated, what of it? Vorenzar searched the visor for the eyes, but they were in shadow.

The Zaru nodded, recognition of Ondrazem's courage. Then he turned, motioning his Zemoks forward. Relieved to be out of the earth prison, they spurred forward. Ondrazem watched silently.

The land before them rose sharply, ending in a ridge that stretched from the left to the right of their line of vision, with only the empty sky beyond. It was grey, though light, as though sunlight sought to tear through a thin fabric of gauze.

Behind the Zemoks the army of earth creatures was sliding from the gorge, a viscous tide of earth and rock. From this the contorted shapes began to reform, staggering upright, or crawling away like broken animals. There were noticeably fewer of them, the power of the gorge having absorbed many of them.

Vorenzar looked at them briefly. Then he spurred his xillatraal forward, up the slope. His Zemoks needed no second bidding to follow and were soon behind him, climbing the steep ridge. Ondrazem brought up the rear, but in a moment his own xillatraal was racing with the others.

In the rocks above the gorge, beyond the sight of the earth creatures, something shimmered. The ghost guide watched the skyline, where it saw the Csendook, already a thin line of silhouettes against it. It studied them, then melted away, as if dissolving with the light, silent and unnoticed.

On the ridge, Vorenzar looked out into the heart of the western lands. Clouds of dense mist obscured everything, pale and milky, and for a moment it was as if he stood on the brink of an enormous precipice, as though Innasmorn ended here, the edge of the world dropping away as a fathomless emptiness.

The Csendook all studied the clouds rolling out below them, until at last one of them pointed into the high distance. Through the swirl, the company saw the upper bastions of the World Splinter, tipped with white. The clouds parted as if pulled away by the obliging masters of these alien skies, and Vorenzar could see the far-off ridges and strata of the vast rock he had been seeking. Nothing could have prepared him for the sheer immensity of the thing.

As the clouds sank down into the depths of the lowlands, the dimensions of the World Splinter were seen to be staggering. Like a huge chunk of galactic debris, the rock, if rock it was, had embedded itself at a steep angle in the body of Innasmorn, leaning out and up, incalculable miles long. It was no wonder, Vorenzar mused, that the people of this world alluded to it as the World Splinter, for it appeared to be just that, the splinter of a world, a fallen moon, hurled through space, plunged into the bed of another world like an arrowhead.

'The *size* of it,' murmured a Zemok beside him. He had lifted his visor, his usually stern face moved by the view of this towering rock. Vorenzar noticed something else there, too. A longing, an almost palpable desire to reach out for the rock, to be a part of it. It was a desire he felt welling in himself, and its fierceness surprised him.

'No mountain range I have ever seen compares with this,' said another of the Zemoks.

'How far away is it?' said another.

Vorenzar glanced beyond the lip of the ridge. The base of the World Splinter was hidden in folds of rucked mountain. Wide plains led to them, but the lands were dark and stained as if scoured by fires, full of hostile intimation. Vorenzar snorted at his reaction to the dark images of this world.

'Is there a way down?' he heard another of the Zemoks ask.

He looked back. The wave of earth beings moved forward, eager to serve, purposeful. He needed them now, just as he needed to reach that rock. But for the first time he began to wonder what the price would be.

'Well?'

Ussemitus started. He had been concentrating on the rocks below, the broken teeth that rose up from the mesa as if to deter the gliderboat from ever returning to it. Aru had whispered, but the question touched on a nerve. They still searched for Jubaia, but it was hopeless. They had been carefully circling for over an hour, hoping that somehow they were wrong, that he had survived. The gliderboat was silent, locked into a private misery that seemed to Ussemitus to confirm the death of the little thief. He knew that Aru was also saddened, but she hid her sorrow in her impatience to be away. Later, he was sure, she would allow her true remorse to show.

Dawn spread across the heavens, seeping down into the clefts and canyons of the great plateau. The shapes that flitted lower down, near the upper city of Shung Nang, suggested that the Azure Wing were still wary of intruders.

Ussemitus shook his head. They must abandon the quest for Jubaia. He looked at Fomond, at his bruised arm.

'A fracture,' said Aru. 'It'll mend soon enough. But he won't use a bow for a while, nor a sword.'

Ussemitus nodded, about to speak, when he felt the first stirring of the mind of the craft below him, as if it woke from a sleep. Without waiting for his instructions, or those of Aru, it dived. The air rushed by as it made its first pass of the upper crags of the mesa.

'I can't control it!' Aru gasped.

'What is it doing?' cried Ussemitus. 'Is it trying to destroy itself?'

They were some distance above the plateau where the storm had been unleashed. The place was deserted now, the pillars stark in the morning sunlight.

'No!' shouted Armestor, then he laughed. 'Look! I see him!' He leaned out over the rail, forgetting his terror of the air.

Aru and Ussemitus followed the line of his pointing arm. There among the upper pinnacles, they saw a tiny figure clinging to one of the rocks, waving at them. It ducked out of sight as a sudden flight of windriders flew past it. Fortunately they had not seen Jubaia, but they were obviously patrolling the plateau.

Still the gliderboat made no attempt to communicate with its passengers, all attention focused on the figure in the rocks. Dropping down dangerously quickly, it hovered beside the sharp spires.

Ussemitus felt Aru's grip on his arm tighten. Her face had relief written over it, and something else, guilt perhaps. Ussemitus put an arm about her and hugged her to him with a laugh. 'We should have known!' he told her. 'Jubaia has learned a new trick. He thieves lives as well as everything else!'

She shook her head in amazement, her own arm going around Ussemitus. They would have held each other longer, but there was work to be done in this place yet. Jubaia moved below them, nimble as a spider, seemingly as comfortable among the precarious peaks. He leapt outwards, his hands catching at the prow of the gliderboat, and within moments he was swinging up over the side. Ussemitus gripped him as easily as he would have hauled a pet puppy aboard. Jubaia flopped down into the bottom of the craft, which now streaked away at a staggering speed. It was hard to speak above the rush of the wind.

Armestor was watching the city behind. He was certain that he had seen members of the Azure Wing circling the peaks they had just left, though it was not easy to be sure, the gliderboat travelled so fast.

Jubaia grinned up at his companions, though he was covered in dirt, his face smeared, his clothes torn.

'So you're alive,' said Aru, her hands on her hips, trying to look annoyed. But the effort was too much for her and she laughed.

Jubaia sat up, puffing out his cheeks and nodding vigorously. 'The Mother must still have a place in her heart for me.'

'We'll not risk that in these skies,' nodded Ussemitus.

Jubaia frowned for a moment, as if something had occurred to him, but then he chuckled. His laughter was echoed by that of the gliderboat, and Ussemitus started as he heard the sound in his mind. It was a sound he had not heard from the curious craft before, and he was amazed by the warmth of the sound.

'She laughs with me,' said Jubaia.

301

Aru nodded. The gliderboat had been more deeply pained by the thought of his loss than any of them.

'Well,' Jubaia went on, hopping to his feet. 'I have no need to return to Shung Nang. I have what I sought.' He tapped his head. 'The key to the west. The World Splinter.'

Both Ussemitus and Aru gasped, and behind them, Fomond struggled to sit up.

'You found the Aviatrix?' said Ussemitus.

'I did. And I understand how we are to enter the western lands. How we are to foil the spells and storms that guard them, and how we are to bind the skies of the World Splinter. The skies of Shung Nang are nothing to those above and around the place of power. Without the key – ' He smacked his hands together as if squashing a fly.

As the gliderboat soared on over the rocky lands below, Jubaia explained how he had won through to his goal, although he omitted from his tale all references to Imlukan and Ryung-Hsu. As he talked, answering the eager questions of his companions, he felt the impatience of the craft, her own desire for knowledge. By the time he had told his tale, Fomond was beginning to tire, his eyes drooping, and Armestor was again settled at the rear of the gliderboat, constantly watching for signs of pursuit, his arrows ready at his feet.

Aru and Ussemitus sat beside each other, resting, and Jubaia went to the prow, guiding the craft on a precise course, using the knowledge he had taken from the dreams of the Aviatrix to hasten the flight. When he was sure that the others were all resting, he spoke to the craft.

'You were superb,' he told her.

You were confident of success.

'Not really. Very afraid – '

I knew that. It was difficult to leave you.

'No one was aware that I had reached within. By the time I was at the heart of things, the Aviatrix had left it too late to protect herself. And yet, she could have destroyed me.'

Then why not?

'She serves the Mother and the secrets she keeps are

302

sacred. What she has allowed me to bring away is dangerous knowledge. But she approves, of me, of us all. The
Mother works through us. I was tested, Circu. And will be
again. We will all be tested.'

Did she hurt you?

Jubaia winced at the question, shutting out other memories. 'She used what weaknesses she could find in me. My
fear – '

Your sadness.

'Sadness? No longer. Not with such spoils – '

*I read your sadness, Jubaia. Your friends do not. You conceal it
well. But not from me.*

He did not answer, his eyes fixed on the distance ahead
of them.

Did she hurt you?

'If you read my sadness,' he said a little roughly, 'you
will also read that.'

I do. I understand what love is, Jubaia.

'Let us speak of other things. Of the west.'

If we must.

He felt himself tensing, as though the craft could see
him, reach into him. But he switched his thoughts to the
images he had received of the World Splinter, closing himself off from the gliderboat, building a cold wall.

She withdrew, and they moved on in silence.

Aru leaned close to Ussemitus. 'I wonder what it is he
hasn't told us,' she breathed, watching the back of the little
thief.

Ussemitus frowned. 'I sensed it, too. He made light of
the task. But Shung Nang was once his home. And you
have seen how they look, the windriders. If he was once
like them, it is a great loss to him.'

Aru nodded, but she sensed something deeper in Jubaia,
a truth hidden behind his eyes as he had told his story of
the theft. His exultation at success was marred. Where once
there would have been only glory, bravado, now there was
a fragment of darkness, perhaps of despair. She had felt
the edge of it in herself, just as she had felt – what, jealousy?
– at the relationship Jubaia was forming with the

gliderboat. She had never had such a unity, though for Jubaia it was different, as the craft was, to him, a woman. It made her think of Ussemitus. She looked at him as he studied the skies, wanting to hold him as she had done over Shung Nang, to kiss his face. Yes, she was jealous of the gliderboat and what it had.

Ussemitus leaned forward, calling out to Armestor, unaware of Aru's thoughts. 'If they follow us, they'll not travel as we do. They'll need the wings of a storm.'

'I see none,' replied Armestor.

'Will they know what we have?' said Fomond sleepily.

Jubaia heard the exchange and leaned back. 'The Aviatrix will wake them to the theft. She would not be able to prevent Feng-Shai knowing.'

'But will they follow us?' said Aru. 'Surely they have no reason – '

'Feng-Shai has a reason,' said Jubaia, seemingly drained of his earlier humour. 'In his eyes, I have violated the Aviatrix. For that he will instruct windriders from the Azure Wing to search to the ends of Innasmorn to find me. And take me back.'

'But does the Aviatrix not favour us in our quest?' said Armestor.

'Feng-Shai controls the windriders.'

'Then the gliderboat will outdistance them,' said Ussemitus. 'And in the west, how could they hope to find us?'

'They will try. Perhaps it is their own test,' said Jubaia.

'How many?' said Aru.

Jubaia shrugged, still without humour. 'There may be as many as a hundred. But once we are in the west, there will be no need for concern.'

You're being morbid, a voice told him. *Stop it. Concentrate on the work ahead. These are your friends, Jubaia. They aren't going to desert you, any more than I am going to fly off and leave you to your fate.*

In spite of his anxiety, Jubaia did smile. 'With the power we shall find, I shall hurl them back,' he told Ussemitus.

'Will it come to blood?'

'It may be that nothing else will assuage them.'

* * *

304

The two windriders met above the broken rocks where dawn splashed bands of crimson and orange below.

'Under the shadow of that big rock,' said one. 'Did you see it?'

The other lifted his long lance, the point wavering as he hovered. 'Yes. What is it?'

'From above. Something fell here. See the tracks in the dust?'

'Dragged. Is it broken?'

'It cannot be the little thief. Too large.'

'We'll see.'

They flew down towards the large overhang, peering into the recesses where the sun could not reach. Softly they dropped on to the sand at the mouth of the cave, their long weapons probing the shadows. Cautiously they moved in, ducking down. Something made a coughing sound in the blackness ahead of them, as if spitting out gouts of blood. It was what they expected, a victim of the storm and the events on the plateau.

They used their minds to probe as they did with their lances, but there was only a darkness there, the darkness of terror.

Something reached out and gripped one of the winged warriors. He was pulled from his feet with a cry, hauled forward. His companion rushed to his aid at once, but he felt his own waist clamped and squeezed. His scream was cut off as his bones turned to splinters within him, his trunk pulped in that merciless embrace.

The two warriors died quickly. Something probed at their mangled corpses, tasting the blood, draining it easily, thoroughly.

An hour later, as the sunlight reached tentatively into the cave, the thing moved. It was less painful for it to move now, and it used its strong metal wing as a long claw, pulling itself to the daylight, the power of the sun. Its other wing had been snapped off, exposing wires and coils of leaking artery. But something fresh grew among the severed strands.

Outside, the wind rose, bringing clouds with it. They

scudded in low like diving hawks, clustering around the rocks and pillars of the mesa's foot, obscuring the thing in the cave as it lurched out from its hiding place.

Vymark, or what was left of his mind, felt the darkness pouring down from above, a liquid stream, its cold race enveloping him. His shattered wing stump pulsed as if it were still a part of him, and the shadows festered about his wound like tangible beasts. He felt the caress as they worked, the steady throb of a new vigour.

When at last he rose from the ground, veering awkwardly, he knew he could fly. His talons released the last shreds of flesh they had been gripping, and a new creature was born, fuelled by the dark, veined with hatred and a purpose that stabbed at it, goading it like a naked blade.

It began to weave its broken flight towards the west.

22

THE AZURE WING

I have to rest, Jubaia.

He blinked, realising that he had been on the point of falling asleep. Evening had darkened the world and it had been a long day. They were all tired, but Circu most of all. *It was unfeeling of me not to realise,* he told himself.

'Of course,' he told her gently.

Something in this western air drains me. I don't know what it is, but if I could set down for a while –

'For the night.'

Perhaps. But it may not be safe to remain anywhere on the ground for long. I sense many things here, shifting powers that I can put no name to.

Jubaia did not answer. He, too, had sensed a strangeness about these lands, as though the earth was permeated with the ghosts of another time, a time of blood and death. Throughout the afternoon they had flown over them, looking down sombrely on a dark landscape where nothing seemed to move and where banks of mist slid lazily along like thick, engorged serpents.

The gliderboat dropped earthwards, coming to rest on a bare expanse of stone from which the turf had been scorched away.

Jubaia explained quietly that the gliderboat needed to rest. He did not embellish his words, though something about the exhaustion of the craft surprised him. The air writhed silently, filled with imagined horrors.

Ussemitus, however, was acutely aware of the atmosphere, its numbing gloom. 'This must be the beginning of the lands around the World Splinter,' he said, peering through the murk beyond the edge of the charred rocks. A black stretch of wasteland was humped up against the last of the smooth rock outcrop like a morass. He turned away, unwilling to let his mind wander into its misery.

'It would be easy to go mad in a place like this,' said Aru. 'We'd better not stay here long.'

'Does anything live here?' said Armestor. He was watching the edge of the rocks as if he expected something to crawl up out of the black soil, hungry for flesh.

Fomond laughed at his unmasked fear. 'Best not to ask.'

They ate a little food that they had brought, and when they spoke it was in low tones. Aru tried to probe the gliderboat, but since the escape from Shung Nang she knew that an even greater barrier had developed between her and the craft. Probably it had been angered by her insistence that they abandon Jubaia when they had thought him dead. Whatever its thoughts, only Jubaia was a party to them now.

She looked at the little thief, who sat quietly watching the mists. He had achieved so much, and yet in his moment of glory seemed subdued, possibly more affected by the dreary lands about them than all the others. As she looked, she saw his neck arch, as if he were trying to look over an obstacle. He stood up, muttering under his breath.

'Do you hear?' he suddenly called.

The others rose, straining to catch the slightest sound out in the wall of silence. Ussemitus was the first to nod. 'What is it?'

'The beat of wings,' replied Jubaia.

'How far?' said Armestor, unslinging his bow.

Ussemitus concentrated for a long moment, then turned to Jubaia. 'Half a day?'

Jubaia nodded. 'They fly fast. They won't rest overnight.'

'The Azure Wing?' said Aru, amazed that they could be sensed at this distance.

'Then let's leave,' said Armestor.

Jubaia shook his head. 'She cannot. Not yet. Not until a new day. We will have to rely on the dark to hide us.'

Armestor turned to Ussemitus, face pale. 'Wait *here?* Surely it is far more dangerous.'

'You heard Jubaia. The gliderboat needs rest.'

'But it's a machine!' protested Armestor.

Jubaia looked at him coldly, and there was nothing of the old Jubaia in that expression, nothing of the buffoon they had met in the east.

Armestor was taken aback. Ussemitus put a hand lightly on his arm. 'This is not the time to argue among ourselves. Jubaia counsels rest.'

'The Mother protects us,' said Fomond, massaging his arm as if it gave him sudden pain.

'And the windriders?' said Armestor. 'Are they not the servants of the Mother?'

'They seek only me,' said Jubaia.

They looked at him, saying nothing.

As night thickened, Ussemitus kept a watch on the skies, though he relied on the soft voice of the wind to bring him news of the Azure Wing and their inexorable approach. Armestor, Fomond and Aru tried to sleep, though none of them was able to do more than doze for periods. Jubaia had become like a statue, eyes closed, mind focused elsewhere.

Something holds me here, the voice told him.

He remained as still as the stones, but felt himself shudder. 'What is it, Circu? Not the Azure Wing? The Aviatrix cannot have given them such powers. I was tested. She could have withheld the key from me but did not. And she would not send the Azure Wing to take revenge. That is Feng-Shai's doing, I am certain.'

No, not them. Though the Mother lends them a swift wind to hurry them.

'What then?'

Not these lands either. The powers that were once here are crippled, horribly damaged. Other forces are at work, preventing our progress. The World Splinter is well guarded.

'I have given you the key, all the mysteries that went with it.'

Yes. But something else holds me here. Your goddess.

'The Mother? How? And why?'

Perhaps she doesn't want us to go on. Perhaps she's angry with the Aviatrix for letting you steal the key.

'I can't believe that.'

Well, you cannot find the World Splinter without me, and I am trapped.

'What must we do?'

Tell Ussemitus he must speak to the Mother.

'You understand his gifts?'

Yes! No one of my own race ever had such power, and I doubt that the windriders of Shung Nang could ever attain such levels either.

Jubaia was able to smile. 'This is no time to tease me, Circu.'

There was gentle laughter, itself a powerful gift to him. *No. But he is certainly blessed by your strange goddess. She may listen to him. She'll have to if I'm to carry us to our goal.*

Jubaia nodded solemnly. 'I will ask him. But I will have to wait.'

Wait? Why? Time is precious, Jubaia. Your enemies are coming. You know what they will do.

He grunted, standing up and stretching, going over to where Ussemitus sat. He did not turn, but nodded to acknowledge that he knew Jubaia was there.

'They quicken their flight,' said Ussemitus.

'The Mother gives them a gale. It is an old saying in Shung Nang.'

Ussemitus turned to him. 'Jubaia, why are you doing this?'

Jubaia frowned. 'I don't understand.'

'I think you do. You seek a meeting with these warriors. Do you intend to give yourself into their hands?'

Jubaia shook his head. 'No. But it concerns me that you will be drawn into any conflict. The gliderboat cannot lift us away.'

'Does it concern you that windriders will die if there is conflict?'

Jubaia winced. It was a perceptive question. He nodded. 'We had to have the key to the west. But the windriders are naturally outraged. It is their sacred duty to the Mother to protect such things. We will not be able to reason with them. They will seek me, and if I do not give myself up to

310

them, they will attack us, and if necessary, kill us all. The gliderboat is pinned here, I think by the Mother.'

Ussemitus gasped. 'But *why*? Why now? If the Mother disapproved – '

'Speak to her. Use your gifts, Ussemitus. We need an answer.'

'If I do, and the Mother answers me as she has done in the past, the windriders may die. I cannot control what is unleashed. It may be that the Mother is prepared to destroy the Azure Wing. To teach Shung Nang that Feng-Shai has overstepped his position.'

'I don't want them to die.'

Ussemitus leaned close to him, whispering softly. 'And we'll not give you up. And we'll not permit you to give yourself up. It's no use arguing.'

'Ussemitus, I have set the key in the gliderboat. You have no need of me now. If the Azure Wing claim me, you can go on to the west. They'll not know you have the key. They'll assume it is I who carries it. To them, the gliderboat is just a machine, without a mind.'

'And do you think the gliderboat would approve of your sacrifice?'

'What do you mean?'

'I cannot probe its mind as you do, but I know enough to understand that the craft is as human as Aru. As sensitive and as emotional as you or me. And as capable of love – '

Jubaia looked uncomfortable. 'Your imagination over-exerts itself – '

'Then if I explain to the craft that you intend to sacrifice yourself – '

'No! Say nothing – '

Ussemitus grinned. 'We wait for the Azure Wing together.'

Jubaia breathed deeply, looking away.

It was deep in the night when they came. The world was clamped in silence. But the beat of wings broke that silence, and the Azure Wing were all around the place of scorched rocks, hovering but unseen. They had known precisely where to find the runaways, as though guided by a beacon.

Armestor and Aru held their bows at the ready, while Fomond gripped a sword. Ussemitus stood high on the prow of the gliderboat, Jubaia behind him.

'Who hunts in the dark?' Ussemitus called. It was an old woodsman's cry, a relic of days past, he thought, though it was not so long ago that he had lived in the forests of the Vaza. They were as remote now as his childhood.

'You know who we are,' came a reply, no more than a few yards away in the night air. Something ignited, spreading like a candle-glow above, and in that halo of light the windriders could be seen. They hovered easily, effortlessly held aloft on their wings, which seemed huge in the night.

'There is no need for the shedding of blood,' came another voice, behind Ussemitus. The circle of lights spread, showing countless forms. Jubaia had guessed that a hundred would follow. His guess had not been wrong.

'Jubaia is under my protection,' said Ussemitus.

One of the Azure Wing dropped lightly to the stone beyond the gliderboat. He wore a thin mesh of armour across his chest, and his face was masked. But he lifted the mask.

'Ryung-Hsu,' breathed Jubaia. 'As I knew it would be.'

'We will discuss Jung-Bara's fate later,' said the windrider in perfect Vaza speech, though without a trace of emotion. 'Will you permit me to speak to him? I am unarmed.'

Armestor had his arrow trained on the windrider, nor did he drop his arm.

'Step forward,' said Ussemitus. Beside him, Jubaia waited in silence, his heart beating so that Ussemitus could feel it.

Ryung-Hsu held out his arms to show how defenceless he was. 'I have something for Jubaia.' Slowly he reached behind him and pulled a small bag from his belt. He let it slip softly to the stone. Then he called out to his warriors.

At once their wings beat at the air noisily and they rose up in a vast flock, taking the light with them as they went.

'Capture him,' hissed Armestor. 'Before he can take to the sky.'

Ussemitus ignored him. 'What have you brought?'

Ryung-Hsu stepped back from the bag. 'The last time I spoke to Jung-Bara, it was in the room of my house in Shung Nang. You remember it, Jung-Bara?'

Jubaia nodded. 'Of course. You left me and sent your windriders to deliver me to Feng-Shai.'

'Fetch the bag,' said Ryung-Hsu.

There was a long pause. Silence crowded in as though the Azure Wing had flown far away. But Jubaia did not move.

Before anyone could prevent it, Fomond had slipped over the side of the gliderboat. He ducked down and retrieved the bag, making sure he did not get in Armestor's line of fire. He withdrew, dropping the bag into the arms of the startled Jubaia.

'Open it,' called Ryung-Hsu, who had not flinched. 'There is no serpent within. Nothing that will harm you, Jung-Bara.'

'Careful,' said Ussemitus, but Jubaia had loosened the leather thongs that bound the bag. He put his hand within and pulled out some round objects. After them there was a bottle that glinted in the faint glow.

Aru looked puzzled. 'What is it?'

To her amazement she saw tears in Jubaia's eyes.

Ryung-Hsu had seated himself, his legs crossed. He waited, vulnerable.

'I must go to him,' said Jubaia. 'He will not harm me.'

Ussemitus allowed him to gather up the small loaves and the bottle and climb down on to the rock.

Jubaia walked over it and sat down opposite Ryung-Hsu, and whatever the two said to each other, no one else heard their words.

'You asked me,' said Ryung-Hsu, 'if I would drink wine with you.' He indicated the bottle. 'I have brought the wine. It is the best I have.'

313

'And a little food, as you promised.'

'That, too.'

Jubaia gripped the cork of the bottle in strong fingers and levered it out easily. From the bag he took two glasses. They were priceless, as were all the things in the house of Ryung-Hsu. Setting them down, he poured the wine.

Together they drank, chewing the bread, which was excellent.

'I betrayed you,' said Ryung-Hsu. 'I gave you to the guards. But even so, Feng-Shai knew that we were once friends. For that he chose me to lead these Windriders to find you. As a test.'

'It is your duty. In Shung Nang, duty comes before friendship.'

'I have denied you everything.'

'But you brought me the food, and the wine. It is excellent, Ryung-Hsu.'

'There is no better wine in Shung Nang. It is incomparable.'

'You honour me.'

Ryung-Hsu stiffened, his proud face outlined by the light from the gliderboat, where a torch flickered. Tears gleamed in the eyes of the windrider. 'You once attempted the impossible, Jung-Bara. The theft of the dreams of the Aviatrix.'

'And paid for my audacity.'

Ryung-Hsu nodded slowly. 'Such a price, my friend. Yet you have returned. And this time – '

'This time I have succeeded. But this time, unlike the first, it was not pride that prompted me. This time I was not seeking to impress a beautiful young girl of Shung Nang, not seeking to capture her heart by showing her that no other warrior could match my skill at theft. This time I was not seeking to place myself above all other suitors in her eyes, though she loved me already.'

'Yes, she loved you dearly.'

'But I came back for what you might call noble reasons, old friend. Reasons you would understand. Duty, Ryung-

314

Hsu. Duty that transcends friendship, and love. Duty to the Mother.'

Ryung-Hsu was motionless, his face set. 'I know of duty,' he said at last.

Jubaia sipped his wine. 'Duty. We needed a key.'

Ryung-Hsu lifted his hand. 'Say nothing. Your quest is your private affair. You are not answerable to me.'

Jubaia finished his wine. 'You would rather I addressed the Interlocutor.'

Ryung-Hsu shook his head.

'The Azure Wing have not followed me to drink wine with me.'

Again Ryung-Hsu shook his head. 'But I command this Flight. They obey me.'

'It is their duty.'

'Just so.'

'My duty is to the Mother. It is why I came back to Shung Nang, and why I stole the key. My companions will defend it to the death. And they will not release me to the Azure Wing.'

Ryung-Hsu nodded slowly. 'No.'

Jubaia put down his glass, finished the bread. 'The meal is ended.'

'Where will you go?'

'To the western lands. To the World Splinter. To do the bidding of the Mother, in all things.'

Ryung-Hsu reached out slowly and put his fingers against the heart of the little thief. 'One's first duty is to one's friends,' he said.

After a moment he rose, very gently, spreading his wings.

Ussemitus felt a qualm, thinking perhaps the warrior was about to betray the trust put in him, but Ryung-Hsu showed no hostility.

'We leave you and your companions in peace, Jung-Bara.'

Jubaia had also risen to his feet, seemingly dwarfed. 'They will kill you – '

Ryung-Hsu shook his head. 'We are the Mother's, Jung-

315

Bara. She protects me as she protects you.' Smiling, he rose up into the darkness.

Jubaia watched in silence, not moving until at last he felt the soft fingers of Aru on his arm.

'Is it safe?' she whispered.

He nodded. 'Though I fear for my friend.'

They went back to the gliderboat. Overhead there was a stirring of the air, not the beating of wings, but the sudden rush of the wind, as if Innasmorn had woken in the night.

'Is it a storm?' said Fomond.

Ussemitus tried to read the darkness, the low moan of the wind, but shook his head. 'The winds are restless across these lands.'

Above him, invisible, Ryung-Hsu was lifted by the wind and carried swiftly to where his Azure Wing waited. The air streamed about them, whipping at the lights so that their faces squinted at him as if he were partly invisible.

'What have you found?' called Sung-Ru, his second-in-command.

'Is there any sign?' called another.

Ryung-Hsu frowned, not sure what they meant. 'Sign?'

'Our prey, commander,' said Sung-Ru, forced to shout. 'We thought there must be a sign of them.'

Ryung-Hsu heard the moan of the wind, the voice of the Mother. But – these warriors had *seen* Jung-Bara. They had discussed the little thief, agreed to Ryung-Hsu seeing him alone.

'Illusions,' said Ryung-Hsu, his voice carrying to the hovering windriders. 'The lands below us are dangerous. We are too near the west.'

'Jung-Bara will surely perish if he goes further,' said Sung-Ru.

'It is perilous to go beyond here,' said another, openly questioning the value of continuing the search.

Ryung-Hsu remained perplexed. He looked back and down, but the land under him was as black as pitch, without a trace of light. He drew in a deep breath, readying himself for the anger of his warriors if it must come, the consequences of his decision. 'I saw no one. Jung-Bara has escaped us. If he is alive.'

Sung-Ru looked down, shielding his eyes against the fierce wind that gathered strength with every moment. 'What are we to tell Feng-Shai?'

'We'll rest for the night. Tomorrow we'll move southwards and see if there are signs. But these winds are from the west. They speak to me of death. The Mother will protect us. But those who have sinned against her will not be safe.'

Sung-Ru nodded. 'I am sure you are right, commander.'

Ryung-Hsu motioned them away, and the Azure Wing soared above the worst of the gusts, looking for somewhere to shelter from the stinging winds that had, it seemed, stripped away certain parts of their memory, for which Ryung-Hsu gave thanks.

'Where are they?' said Ussemitus.

Jubaia frowned. The dark was impenetrable, and the whine of the wind made it impossible to detect any other sound.

'Have they gone?' said Armestor.

Jubaia nodded. 'I think so. They were led by Ryung-Hsu, who was once a friend of mine. That is, he remains a friend of mine,' he grinned. 'How could he forget the times we had together as children, eh? You saw how we shared wine?' He was laughing, struggling to control other emotions that threatened to convulse him.

Jubaia! called the gliderboat, and it was enough to prevent the tears from falling afresh. At once he rushed to the prow of the craft.

Whatever held me here has released its grip. I'm free to fly.

'Are you rested?'

Yes. And this wind is strange. Full of power. I can use it, Jubaia! It will lift me, arrow me to our goal.

'Innasmorn,' he breathed. 'She has done this.'

Aru watched him, baffled. 'Ussemitus, what has happened? Why have the windriders not attacked us?'

Ussemitus shrugged. 'Perhaps they have honoured Jubaia for what he achieved. They place great importance on theft in their society. I can only think that the winged men came to praise him. It had the look of a ritual.' He said no more, watching the darkness, though it did not weaken.

Armestor sat with Fomond, his own face creased in a frown. 'You hear that, Fomond? You think the windriders came to praise Jubaia?'

Fomond grunted thoughtfully. 'Who can say? He was certain they wanted his blood. Perhaps they do.'

'What do you mean? They'll follow us?'

Fomond shrugged. 'Nothing Jubaia does is simple. And he never tells us the entire tale! I'm just wondering what we'll find in the west.'

'Better pray to the Mother to heal your arm. You'll need it.'

Fomond's humour dissolved as he unconsciously moved his fractured arm. He lifted it, bending it, then grunted again. Carefully he unwound the tight bandage that Aru had wrapped around it.

'You ought to leave it,' said Armestor. 'It's too soon – '

'It's mended.'

'Don't be foolish, Fomond, put – '

'It's mended, I tell you.' Fomond demonstrated by waving the arm, flexing it, gripping with it. 'Believe me. As good as new.'

'A strange sight,' came the voice of Ussemitus as he suddenly appeared above them, making them jump.

'You did this?' began Fomond, but Ussemitus shook his head.

'Strange winds. They've blown away our enemies and given us strength.'

'You summoned them?' said Armestor.

'Not wittingly. But I'm sure we are willed to the western lands. Jubaia included.' He glanced again at Fomond's arm. 'I should keep it wrapped awhile. We're going aloft once more.'

Jubaia sat in the prow of the gliderboat and as it lifted

into the wind, he felt its rush of elation. It took him too, as if Innasmorn spoke to him of a new beginning.

The gliderboat rose up and soared westward, while far behind in the darkness the Azure Wing beat steadily southwards, away from their prey.

It seemed to Jubaia as though the craft flew with greater strength than ever before, as if her mind had been cleansed of something that had restrained her. The threat of Shung Nang, perhaps.

'Fly with caution,' he whispered. 'Impetuous Circu.'

She laughed in his mind, the sound like music. *Jubaia! Share this with me. Taste the wind for me. Let it caress you. Drink its power!*

He gasped as the craft accelerated into the night, the wind howling in glee, tearing at his hair, his face.

Were there ever wings like mine, Jubaia?

He laughed with her. 'Never.'

Not even in Shung Nang?

'Not in all Innasmorn,' he shouted, so that the others stared at him. 'Not in all Innasmorn.'

23

MAN ONE

The gliderboat flew on through the night, no longer hampered, its energy unbounded, and although the winds swirled about the craft, nothing threatened it. As dawn streaked the heavens, the landscape below revealed itself to be empty and seared, the only features the cracked knuckles of rock that poked up through the endless black waste of sand. The company said little to each other, each pondering on what might be at the end of the journey, and whether the deserts below them would give way to something more heartening.

Just after mid-morning Jubaia gave a sudden cry, pointing ahead. The land rose up, then abruptly fell away as though the world ended. Approaching carefully, the gliderboat circled, and the company could see the clouds that filled the world beyond the huge drop.

'We've reached our destination,' said Jubaia, though he looked uneasy.

Ussemitus nodded, and they flew on, the craft gliding out over the drop, into the land of cloud. Ussemitus felt something out in the void, a vague probe, though unlike the probes that the city of Shung Nang had projected across its skies. But there seemed to be no hostility in the probe, as though it searched for him eagerly, urgently.

Presently Jubaia called out to him, drawing him to the prow of the craft. Again the little man pointed, and Ussemitus saw a streak of blue light in the clouds, drawing nearer. Something swooped under the craft, the air faintly crackling. The gliderboat dipped, and the light swirled, forming itself into a hovering shape, though this was no windrider.

'What is it?' said Aru, her eyes wide.

'A wind elemental,' said Fomond. He studied the

320

creature as if it would attack them, though it remained placid, hovering just beyond the nose of the craft.

Ussemitus felt it call to his mind, though he knew that the others could also hear it.

'The land of the World Splinter welcomes you, Ussemitus. And your companions. Who bears the key?' The aerial creature, which appeared to be formed more of cloud than flesh, looked at Jubaia as it asked this, as if it had already read his thoughts.

'Are you the guardian of these lands?' Jubaia replied.

'I am one of the spectrals. We serve the World Splinter.'

'You'll lead us there?' said Ussemitus, wondering how it had known his name. And about the key. Why should they be expected?

'Have you the key?'

Jubaia straightened. 'It is in my keeping.' He closed his mind over the truth, that the details were with the gliderboat, but the spectral seemed indifferent to the mild deceit.

'You will need it if you are to cross these skies. Do not attempt to go down to the land. There are guardians there that would contest your passing. Even the key would be of no use to you against them. Follow me.' The spectral swirled away, the gliderboat following.

'You hear it?' Jubaia whispered to the craft.

It tried to penetrate my mind, too. But being alien, I am less easily read. But it knew the key was not lodged with you.

'Caution then.'

They followed, and as they did so, the mists swirled apart, the clouds pulling back, though the land far below them was not revealed. Ussemitus considered this a blessing, as there was a darkness there, an intangible something that shrieked out silently in torment and outrage, as though whatever lands were there had been stretched and twisted far beyond the ravages of the lands they had already crossed. Watching the spectral, he had his first glimpses of the towering buttresses of the World Splinter, the immense rock that thrust up from the body of Innasmorn, rising up before the craft like a vast sliver of another world. All of the crew gasped at it as it was revealed, high over them,

321

and they studied its unique shape in silence, amazed by the sheer scale of the thing.

'The chaos of the lands around us is explained,' whispered Jubaia. 'When this monstrous rock fell, it must have sent out such waves of power!'

'Is it evil?' Armestor asked Fomond.

Fomond shook his head slowly. 'I feel nothing. It is cold, dead. Alien.'

Aru seemed less bewildered by the rock, though she looked at it in no less fascination than her companions. 'It has a strange morphology. Strong in metals. But other worlds share the rock types commonly.'

'There's power there,' said Ussemitus. 'Locked away, deep within it. If the legends are true, it is immeasurable.'

They fell silent, each of them pondering the rock. It took two hours to fly close to it. As they drew on, its size amazed them further, for it spread across the horizon in front of them, endless miles thick, and equally as high. Its peaks were lost in the upper skies, beyond the highest reaches of the clouds, seemingly a bridge with the regions of darkness beyond them.

Jubaia could sense a growing fear within the gliderboat.

I am drawn, Jubaia, it told him. *Something in this mass has found me and locked on to me. If I wanted to turn away, I could not.*

'Is there danger?'

I have no idea. But it has been waiting. There is a hunger in this power. Other emotions I cannot fathom. But something craves release.

Jubaia turned to Ussemitus, but the woodsman had closed his eyes, his concentration deep and unbroken as if he were communicating with his god, the cord not to be broken.

They drew nearer to the rock, the face of which now blotted out everything before them, above and below, and to the sides. Still the gliderboat sped on, its speed increasing. The spectral was a blur ahead of it, coalescing into an arrow of blue light, and it seemed intent on dashing itself like a wave on to the bare face of the rocks. Armestor

322

and Fomond sagged back into the vessel, overcome by the immensity of this mountainous object, which weighed down on them oppressively, a vengeful god.

Aru searched for an answer to their accelerating flight, seeing destruction at the end of it, but Ussemitus was locked into something else, another realm, perhaps. Jubaia glanced at Aru, though there was uncertainty in his own eyes.

'Innasmorn?' said Aru.

'I fear we left her keeping when we crossed the lip of the crater,' he answered, a thin smile crossing his features. He turned back to face the oncoming rock, and as he did so, his eyes bulged.

Aru had seen it, too. A wide crack in the surface of stone, a black gash. As they sped nearer to it, it widened, no longer a small fissure, but something far bigger, a huge slash, cavernous, that prepared to engulf them. The glider-boat hurled towards it, unable to free itself from whatever pulled it. The power of the rock had read the key within the craft and used it to draw it forward.

Ussemitus was immobile, and nothing would break his trance, just as nothing could deflect the flight of the glider-boat. Jubaia called out to it, but to no avail. His mind met darkness and silence. The spectral evaporated, its task done.

The cavern yawned as they neared it, its dimensions huge, and within it, night beckoned. There was no glimmer of light, no intimation of anything but utter darkness, as if the emptiness between worlds beckoned.

'Can't you turn us!' yelled Armestor, suddenly leaping to his feet.

Jubaia shook his head. The onward swoop continued until the lips of the huge cave passed high above and below them. They were inside.

Movement ceased.

They were hovering. Armestor whirled about him. He could see the brightness of Innasmorn beyond him, outside the cavern. But only the clouds massed there, obscuring the distant land. He leaned over the craft and looked down, but only into further depths of night.

Jubaia! came the sudden voice of the gliderboat. *What has happened?*

'We are inside the World Splinter.'

I felt it gripping the key. It was like a dream –

'You feel danger?'

Only silence. And a kind of peace. I cannot see. Nor move. It is as if I am floating. Powerless.

'Ussemitus,' Jubaia breathed, touching his friend.

Ussemitus stirred, opening his eyes. He blinked, turning to squint at the light behind them. 'We are close,' he said at last.

'Close to what?' said Aru, trying not to be impatient. There was still no way of knowing whether or not the powers in this place were hostile.

'We'll soon know,' said Ussemitus, though he seemed a little dazed.

The gliderboat began to drift forward and down, though not of its own volition, and Jubaia could understand nothing of what powered this new flight. The movements were slow, but something bumped gently up under the keel of the craft, as if they had touched the sandy bottom of a cove. Glancing over the side of the gliderboat, they could still see only darkness.

Ussemitus looked up, and before the prow of the craft the spectral had materialised once more. It said something in a faint whisper that only Ussemitus heard. He nodded and spoke to the gliderboat.

Jubaia watched, puzzled, as the woodsman climbed down from the prow, standing on something invisible.

He turned, almost as an afterthought. 'Remain here,' he said. 'I am in no danger.'

Aru was about to protest, but Jubaia pulled her back. Ussemitus had walked forward with the spectral into the crowding shadows and was gone. It had happened so quickly, they could not prevent it.

'We must protect him,' Aru said.

'He says he is safe,' said Jubaia. 'We must trust him.'

He has the key, said the gliderboat.

Jubaia gasped. 'The key? How? It was within you – '

He read it easily. I could do nothing to stop him. He has learned it all. But it does not matter –

'He entered your mind? As I do?'

It was not an intrusion. It is as it should be, Jubaia. We must not question Ussemitus. The rock was waiting for him.

Aru's face was creased in concern. 'What are you saying? What is the gliderboat telling you?'

Jubaia explained.

Aru shook her head, perplexed. 'How can we be sure he's safe? That he isn't being used?'

'For what?' said Fomond.

Aru shrugged. 'Nothing is clear. We no longer have control over what is happening. Does Ussemitus?'

'What do you counsel?' said Jubaia. 'He warned us not to follow.'

'Perhaps we should.'

'I will not leave the gliderboat,' said Jubaia, and Aru could see that nothing would persuade him to change that decision. She turned to Armestor and Fomond.

Fomond shook his head. 'Ussemitus has gifts that are rare among our people. This power has sought them out. He told us to wait. Armestor and I will do so. I think you should. Do you fear for him?'

Aru grimaced. 'There is something here, something vast, unthinkable. I am not convinced of its motives. Ussemitus cannot know what he is going forward to meet.'

'It may be,' said Fomond, 'that only one with his gifts can go forward. If you follow, Aru, it may be you who are in danger. And you may jeopardise his safety.'

She drew in a deep breath, thinking that perhaps Fomond was right. As she looked back at him, she saw beyond him the light at the mouth of the cave. It filtered inwards, and for once there were features visible within the vast area. Rocks, or smudges that could have been rocks, a pale grey floor, as if of fine sand. The others saw her expression and turned, all seeing the faint details for the first time. The scale of the cavern was confirmed: it was

325

vast, its sides lost in distance and darkness, and apart from the floor visible between the gliderboat and the entrance, nothing beyond the craft could be seen.

They climbed down on to the sand, sifting it. It was cold to the touch, twinkling in the light. Aru frowned: some of the sand was abrasive, like rust. They moved slowly about, not going far from the craft. Jutting from the floor there were jagged rocks, though Aru wondered if they could be metal spars, in view of their odd shape.

Jubaia preferred to sit on the prow, legs dangling over it as he watched. 'Don't stray too far,' he warned.

Fomond grunted. 'There's nothing here. Empty. Like a huge shell.'

Armestor tugged at his sleeve, pointing to the entrance, fifty yards away. 'I think I saw movement,' he hissed.

'You exaggerate,' Fomond grinned, but ducked down at once.

A silhouette shaped itself against the sunlight, and then another. There were creatures out there and they were entering the cavern.

Armestor and Fomond quickly slipped back to the cover of the gliderboat. Aru was standing out in the sand, rooted. Fomond hissed at her, but she paid no attention.

'Get her aboard!' snapped Jubaia. 'Quickly!'

Fomond leapt down to the sand and rushed to Aru. She was in some sort of trance, her eyes wide, her arms shaking.

'Aru! Come, to the craft. What is wrong?'

She shook her head, but her legs moved mechanically in response to Fomond's urgency. 'It can't be,' she murmured. 'Can this place conjure illusions?'

Fomond had to help her to the craft, and Armestor pulled her aboard. She seemed weak, as if suddenly drained of energy. Once aboard, she whirled, looking back at the mouth of the cavern.

'What did you see?' said Jubaia, kneeling beside her. Fomond and Armestor lifted their bows, ready to let fly at anything hostile that showed itself, but the silhouettes had fused with the darkness.

'They have a certain smell about them,' said Aru softly. 'It is not something you forget.'

'Who?' said Jubaia.

She looked at him, still shaken. 'You must get the craft into the air.'

He shook his head. 'She cannot move. Perhaps when Ussemitus returns. I have tried.'

She gripped his arm tightly. 'Get us into the air, Jubaia. Or we are dead, I promise you.'

'Why? What have you seen?'

Aru gazed out at the shadows, dreading their movement. 'I pray the light is playing tricks. They cannot be here.'

Ussemitus walked slowly into the darkness, his limbs responding to some subtle command that seemed built into the very air. There was no resisting this power, but it brought no pain, no fear. He had no need of vision, not yet, for he seemed to be responding to something primitive, atavistic, a memory from beyond time, long before his birth. The spectral was no brighter than the flicker of a candle, equally as silent. Its light dimmed, a beckoning point. Downward he drifted, into a vault of emptiness and silence, the well of a world.

He ceased his descent. His mind was empty, adrift from his body, though he could feel the rush of blood through his veins, the pulsing of his heart, the rise and fall of his lungs. It was as though the darkness thrilled to the awareness of flesh.

Light winked out, but grew again, changed, a golden glow. There was other power in this light, though it was cold. Whether evil or beneficent, he had no control over it, no resistance to it.

A figure stood before him. It was taller than he was, naked save for a thin garment wrapped tightly about its loins. By the growing light he could see that it was a man, though proportioned and muscled strangely. In many ways it was like the Men of Aru's race, but its skin was grey in hue, its contours too symmetrical. The face was perfectly

327

sculpted, the eyes wide, staring, and it was hairless, its skull like a smoothly polished stone. In fact, Ussemitus saw that its entire body was hairless, and he thought of stone, or of wood. The being bowed his head as if in respect.

Ussemitus felt something snap within him, and he came alert as if he had been on the fringes of dreaming. But this was real to him now. The darkness pressed in, only the tall figure visible, and the latter's expression was fixed, as though the being looked through him, studying his organs, perhaps, and the structure of his mind, the intricate network of his thoughts, the pattern of the key. Ussemitus was certain this being had greater power than the Aviatrix of Shung Nang. Was he an elemental?

'Ussemitus of the Vaza,' came the deep, musical voice, speaking as if the being had known Ussemitus for many years.

Ussemitus nodded but did not answer.

'Servant of the Mother.'

Ussemitus nodded.

'It reads in your heart. It is part of the key that has admitted you. But if you are to penetrate the Mystery of the World Splinter, you will need more than your faith, your devotion to the Mother.'

'Is this place dedicated to the Mother?'

'Yes, it is now, though it has not always been so. The World Splinter is not of Innasmorn, as her people know. But it serves the Mother. And it is ready to give up all of its remaining power to her.'

'The legends of my people speak of this power.'

The being nodded. 'If you wish to go on with your quest, to seek the heart of the Mystery, you will need the key. I see that you have it.'

'Taken from the Aviatrix.'

'It was given into her keeping. Locked into her dreams. It is dangerous knowledge, power that can destroy the weak.'

'Am I to impart it to you?'

'No!' The being raised a hand as if in warning, like a man backing away from a terrible spell. 'Not to me. I am

328

a servant. I am Man One. I was the first to wake, the first to look upon Innasmorn. And I am the last. The children have all gone out into your world. Come with me.'

Ussemitus watched the figure turn away, thinking it might dissipate, but it did not. It appeared to be substantial, unlike the spectral, and it moved in a natural way, its limbs rippling as it walked.

Ussemitus followed, going downward into more darkness, and after an eternity he felt the growing of light below him, and the murmur of winds. Powers beyond imagining were stirring, raising their eyes to seek this intruder, this bearer of the key, and Ussemitus felt the weight of the ages bearing down upon him and heard the thunder of Innasmorn's heart, a rhythm that filled him with fear.

The skies swirled thickly like the dark and turbulent waters of an ocean, streaked with flashes of light, oppressive, lowering. Day had quickly changed into a false night, obscuring the monstrous shape of the World Splinter, and up from the depths of the precipice further clouds roiled, as though intent on linking their own turgid powers with those of the skies.

Vorenzar growled in approval, enjoying the play of powers on this bizarre world, this so-called Mother of Storms. Dark or otherwise, it did not matter to him if they chose to give aid to his own cause.

Ondrazem called out above the roar of the winds. 'Zaru, we have found what we seek. The precipice is not impassable. There is a way.' The Zemok spoke almost impassively, as though still partially numbed by his passage through the earth tunnel, but Vorenzar's mind was interested only in the World Splinter, its potential power, and the finding of Zellorian.

He rode beside Ondrazem along the dipping edge, and below them, where the scouts had gathered, they could see a huge crack in the edge, and what looked like a landslide of mud and rock, disappearing into it as if a mountain had slipped. The skies echoed to another rumble of thunder and the earth shook, as if the heavens sought to dislodge more of the cliff face, sanctioning the way downwards.

Rain fell heavily, but the Csendook ignored it, their xillatraal eager to ride forward, descending from the ridge. Vorenzar looked about him. Along the rim of the rift the strange army yet watched, statuesque, immune to the sudden deluge, like dead beings waiting to be reanimated.

Ondrazem went to the head of the Zemoks, silent again, as if his thoughts strayed back to the tunnel, but Vorenzar ignored him. There was power somewhere below, along the route to this World Splinter, and with it the possibilities of – what? A place beside the Supreme Sanguinary? Or maybe something better, the very office itself?

Lifting his weapon, Vorenzar gave a shout to ride forward, and his Zemoks saluted him with a loud roar, goading their xillatraal on over the edge and down the long earthfall into the writhing darkness.

Vorenzar and Ondrazem rode at the head of the column, knowing that behind them the earth creatures followed. These were in no danger from the storm, black though it was, for they, like the Csendook, were protected by it, its children. Vorenzar would have spoken to Ondrazem about this, but deliberately avoided the conversation, knowing that it was unheard of for a Csendook to speak of sorcery. It was a jest, something to mock. And yet the voices licked at his mind, their alluring promises firing him. He felt his blood stir at the thought of power, supernatural or not, it did not matter. Here in this outlandish region, he would fasten on to it if it was to be offered.

Pelted by the rain, they rode downwards, the xillatraal sinking deep into the earth that turned quickly to a mire, sliding like cold lava down to where the mists swirled. Mile after mile the company rode downwards, seeking the floor of the titanic crater, while overhead the skies raged, lightning scything over Innasmorn, darkness closing in to ward off any creatures intent on barring the passage of these armoured invaders.

When the company reached the bottom of the earth ramp, they found themselves riding through an even more uneasy terrain, the land full of pits and bogs, treeless and shattered. The earth creatures spread out around Vorenzar and his Zemoks, protecting them from anything that might attack, as these lands were evidently guarded. And the attacks did come, out on the edge of vision, though the Csendook saw nothing clearly on their dismal ride.

Huge shapes flung upwards from the depths of the crater, twisted and ugly, trying to dash themselves forward like a tide across the path of the intruders, but the earth creatures amassed and tore into them, forming and reforming, a slick wave that shielded both eyes and mind from the torments beyond.

The Csendook tried to shut out what they thought they saw, the screams and roars of huge powers, mutated beasts, as if they were trapped in the past, in memories of the bloody wars they had fought. But the thought of the rock, the World Splinter, called to them like a god, though they knew none. As they drew closer to it, they felt themselves responding to a lust, a fierce desire to reach it.

Vorenzar's own desire was a firebrand. The voices that called to him grew more daring in their intimations, and he found himself laughing aloud at their blasphemies, enjoying them. If this was power, he would bathe in it, feast upon it.

Worse things than death and madness crawled about these swamps, trying to rip out the minds of the Zemoks, but they fought them off, urging the terrified xillatraal forward. The storm roared on, but the Csendook would not be cowed by it as javelins of light tore earthwards, bursting in the marshes beyond the lines of the earth army. Vorenzar howled. How could anyone doubt such power! If he could harness *this*!

Days later, utterly exhausted, the Zemoks called out to Ondrazem and Vorenzar to bring a halt to the ride.

Vorenzar swung his xillatraal round and confronted Ondrazem. 'Stop? What do they mean? We cannot stop now.' He flung up his visor, eyes blazing.

Ondrazem, one of the fittest, most able warriors he had

ever known, looked worn out. Behind him the Zemoks had fallen back, leaning wearily on their beasts.

Vorenzar rode to them, cursing them, shaking his weapon at them, and though there was fire in their expressions, the hunger for the rock, they were yet drained. In another blaze of lightning, Vorenzar saw the change that had come over them. Coated in mud and slime, they seemed half-Csendook, half earth creature.

Then let the power claim us! his mind laughed. Let it feed us!

Snarling, he rode back to the head of the company, ignoring Ondrazem, whose eyes were dull. His body was thick with mud, his helm clogged with it.

'How far?' Vorenzar screamed above the wind.

Ondrazem lifted his arm, a muddied stump, pointing upwards. Through the sheets of rain, Vorenzar saw the chunks of naked rock gleaming, the mangled spars of some vast edifice or artefact, long gutted. The base of the World Splinter rose up from the debris.

Vorenzar felt a brief stab of reason. What should he do now? Ride around the base of the rock, which must be endless? Or attempt to find a way up?

Ondrazem got off his xillatraal mechanically, like a hound being given instructions. He walked raggedly towards the stones, disappearing into the mists.

Vorenzar turned. His Zemoks had all dismounted. They all intended to follow Ondrazem. Beyond them the last of the earth creatures sank down into the mire as if they were a part of it, the entire company dissolving, slithering like reptiles into the substance they had been moulded from.

Something gleamed in the shadows at the base of the rock, among the tangle of metal and stone. At first Vorenzar thought it must be Ondrazem, but as he looked, he saw the curtain of rain part. The ghost guide waited. It had come to guide him upwards.

He craned his thick neck, but the clouds rolled in once more, filled with energy and a new kind of greed, and he could taste it, savouring it as a wolf savours fresh blood.

Vorenzar laughed, fresh strength filling his veins, and he

ran forward, eager to begin the climb, eager to grasp at his destiny.

24

ORACLE

Ussemitus was drifting rather than walking down into the heart of the World Splinter, bathed in brilliant light, unable to see anything within its radiance other than the vague form of Man One. They had gone downwards, entering a chamber, although in some ways it was as though they had left Innasmorn through a portal and come beyond it to another realm. Ussemitus expected the light to weaken so that he would see an alien terrain stretched out for miles before him. The light did lessen in intensity, but he could still see nothing ahead of him. Man One stopped and turned to him, his own eyes unaffected by the glare.

'The Mysteries,' he said. 'The Abyss of History. Only those with the key can pull aside the curtains of light.' He waited.

Ussemitus closed his eyes. On the journey to this place, he had spoken to the innermost part of the gliderboat's consciousness, to the place where the secrets of the Aviatrix had been hidden away at Jubaia's express command. But there had been no contest, no debate. Ussemitus had gently lifted away what he had needed, almost without the gliderboat knowing. There had been a soft cry, to Jubaia, and Ussemitus had felt a stab of guilt as he understood how deeply the craft felt for the little thief, but he closed his mind to the knowledge.

He drew out what he had learned from his mind now, speaking ancient words, lost incantations that he did not understand, words locked in their own meanings, words that could only be of value to one being, one power. And that power resided here, in this fragment of another world.

Man One withdrew as he heard Ussemitus whisper the words of the key. They meant nothing to him, but he understood well enough the reaction they had on the air around him. Out into the Abyss of History they went, arrows of thought, silent almost, but as effective as shouts.

Light faded around the two figures, and up from below a shaft of it concentrated into a huge beam, the source far down, too brilliant to look into. In this light, shapes drifted easily to and fro, amorphous and ill-defined, twisting and pulsating like swimmers in a pool. Ussemitus opened his eyes to gaze at them, fascinated, but each time he tried to focus on one, it faded to be replaced by others.

'What is this place?' he said.

Man One reached out his hand, as though about to pluck fruit from an invisible tree. 'You have unlocked knowledge, Ussemitus. The powers of the World Splinter will speak to you, through me.'

'What are you?'

'The keeper, if you like.'

'What is this World Splinter?'

'It is just that. A piece of a world, the last of it, a surviving fragment, hurled from its own cycle of worlds, centuries ago. It would have been destroyed, blown apart by the destructive forces acting upon it when its world exploded. But the Mother guided it here.'

Ussemitus looked started. 'Innasmorn *guided* the World Splinter here?'

'And lodged it in her own body, nurturing it.'

'But for what purpose?'

'You must hear the greater history before you understand the Mother's reasons for shaping the future.

'Beyond the cycle of worlds to which Innasmorn belongs, there are other such cycles, though these cycles are not linked to each other, nor to Innasmorn's cycle. Events in each cycle do not affect those in another, and indeed, each cycle is considered by those indigenous to it to be unique, alone.

'Long ago on Innasmorn, there was conflict, a grim struggle for power between forces that shook this world with their war. You know the stories of this conflict, of the legends and myths that have come down through the ages.'

Ussemitus nodded. 'Of the darkness that was subdued.'

335

'Subdued, yes. But not destroyed. Innasmorn was weakened by the war, and although the races of the world transformed, becoming one with the elements, taking fresh strength from that, the Mother has always felt vulnerable, divided. It would take her countless millennia to grow strong again.

'So there was war on ancient Innasmorn. But in other world cycles there were also wars. In one particular cycle of worlds, where Man dwelt, there was a war of such vast proportions that the destruction spread in an unprecedented way. Man had an empire that stretched across most of the worlds of his cycle of worlds, and he moved easily between them, using the gates.

'But Man stumbled on a race of beings that were more than his equal, and which in time proved to be his better. The Csendook. Whether Man found them by chance or design, history obscures the truth. But once provoked, the Csendook grew in power until they rose up and brought ruin to the worlds of Man. Many of the worlds of Man and of the Csendook were destroyed utterly in their wars. One such world was the one from which the World Splinter derives. The Csendook wars caused its disintegration, and there would have been no survivors if the Mother had not intervened.'

'How was it possible?' said Ussemitus. 'If Innasmorn was part of another cycle of worlds?'

'The destruction and havoc caused by the Csendook wars knew no barriers. Whatever forces worked on this world to destroy it, they ruptured the very frontiers of Innasmorn's world cycle. Innasmorn brought the World Splinter here, to herself, rather than let it drift through limbo to a final doom. And with the World Splinter came life, life alien to the Mother.'

'Survivors?'

'Man had survived the crossing. Though his worlds fought on in his own world cycle, locked for centuries in combat with the merciless Csendook, a few of his kind reached Innasmorn.'

'And brought artefacts with them!' cried Ussemitus. 'Weapons of steel, machines – '

'Alien objects. And the races of Innasmorn abjured them, and saw the coming of the World Splinter as an intrusion, the birth of a plague. A Curse. It is said that the gods of Innasmorn argued over the World Splinter, even those who had fought together to subdue the ancient darkness. But there was a great purpose behind this, one that only the Mother understood and would not reveal. She had seen the Csendook war, the potential for disaster. For in Man's cycle of worlds, the Csendook would triumph, sweeping everything before them in a tide of death. And once Man perished, removed from his world cycle like a plague, what then? Where would the Csendook turn their attentions? For they are avaricious, greedy for conquest, as terrible an enemy as the darkness of old, just as if they had been spawned by it.'

'You think they would come here, to our world cycle?'

'Innasmorn knew that if they found us, they would do so. And begin again their slaughter, their world harvest. It would take them time, for Man fights even now in his world cycle. Man is not exterminated there. But during that time of war, Innasmorn began to work on her own plans for war. The Mother knew that Man must not perish, and that somehow he must be made strong again, strong enough to rise up against his ancient enemies and drive them back. The Csendook had to be eliminated, from all worlds. That or they would destroy Innasmorn and all the worlds of her cycle.

'When the World Splinter lodged here, the transformation of the people of Innasmorn had already begun, and there were few races left who were not one with the elements. Innasmorn began the workings that would transform the survivors, the Men who came. There was an exodus down from the World Splinter, out into the world. Over the centuries, these people became the people of Innasmorn, and they themselves abjured artefacts, which to them represented their past, their dark history. They forgot, or had the past washed out of them.'

Ussemitus gaped into the light, the writhing shapes, his own thoughts as restless, confused. 'Then the races of Innasmorn, the Vaza, all the others, are descended from *Man*?'

'There has been a fusing of the original races. Those who came to Innasmorn have evolved into something very different, as you know. You have met the girl, who comes from the world cycle of Man that exists today. You understand the differences between you. Innasmorn changed the nature of Man, developing skills normal Men do not have. Does Man speak to the wind? Or control storms? Does Man use his mind as you, or the Windmasters can? Man may be physically stronger, but what good has that done him against the Csendook, who are even more powerful physically?'

'I am a child of Man,' Ussemitus murmured.

'You are a child of Innasmorn. You are closer to the original races than to Man. The Mother has shaped you and your people, Ussemitus. But you must not think of divisions. It is not why you have been permitted entry to this sanctum.'

'Why am I here?'

'In a while, you will know. There are other things you must understand first. About the defence of Innasmorn.

'The Mother guided the World Splinter to her and began the preparation of its people, the shaping of their destiny. But it did not end there. The Mother has drawn others to her.'

Ussemitus felt a flush of apprehension, his mind trying to wriggle free of the things Man One was about to tell him, as if they would assault his reason, eat into the fabric on which his world had been built. 'Others?'

'As Man's empire collapsed around him, the Csendook sought his rulers, who were united under his Imperator Elect, the rallying point of all Man's hopes. And his men of power, his scientists.'

'Zellorian,' breathed Ussemitus, recalling everything that Aru had ever told him.

'Yes, Zellorian in particular. Somehow he had sensed

338

that there were other world cycles, though the Csendook did not know this. They have no belief in sorcery, as they call it. Zellorian knew that if he could escape the world cycle of his empire, Man would be safe. So he searched, using every dark art he could. The pain he inflicted on others, the cruel rituals he perfected, were felt beyond his realm. The Mother housed no love for him, but even so, used him. She gave him the key, though Zellorian has never known it. She gave him the last shard of power that enabled him to bring the Imperator Elect and his chosen few through to our world cycle, to Innasmorn.'

Ussemitus felt himself weakening. He could not fathom the logic of this. It went against all reason. To *bring* Zellorian here! The cruellest of them all, a monster –

'But it is true,' avowed Man One. 'And the crossings do not end there. Zellorian and the Imperator Elect were brought here as bait.'

Ussemitus shook his head. Bait? For a trap? But that could mean only one thing.

'Oh yes,' nodded Man One, reading his thoughts as if they had been cried aloud. 'The Csendook. And they are already here.'

'I cannot believe this,' murmured Ussemitus. 'The Mother would never do such a thing – '

'Man must be strong again, Ussemitus. Man must rally himself and all the allies he can find. He must defeat the Csendook, and throughout his cycle of worlds his survivors must understand that the Csendook can be defeated. It will begin here, on Innasmorn. The Mother has been preparing the way for centuries.'

Ussemitus shook himself, trying to piece this fantastic puzzle together. 'You say the Csendook are here already?'

'A few of them. Just as the Mother sent help to Zellorian without his realising it, so she aided this war party. It is little more than a scouting party, a handful of warriors, searching for clues to the whereabouts of the Imperator Elect.'

'And if they find him?'

Man One shrugged. 'That may never happen. Like you, they are to be subjected to certain tests.'

'*Tests?* You speak as though this were a game. Of risk, of chance – '

'No. But decisions have to be made. Choices, Ussemitus. Innasmorn has merely drawn the forces together. How they unleash themselves, how they resolve the future, is a different matter.'

Before Ussemitus could answer, Man One pointed outwards to the light, and the shapes changed, flowing into a landscape as swiftly as a gushing mountain torrent passes, and Ussemitus found himself gazing down as though from a high peak on the wooded lands of the Vaza.

'In disparity lies defeat,' said Man One. 'Innasmorn learned that millennia ago when she was forced to take her own children closer to her bosom in order to hold back the darkness that would have riven her, dragged her down to chaos. Now she has brought an even greater range of children together. Your own company, Ussemitus, epitomise it. Aru, from the race of Men. Jubaia, a true descendant of Innasmorn, and yourself, Fomond and Armestor, the new breed. And there is the gliderboat, also a living entity.'

'Then it is no accident that we are all here?'

'Innasmorn did not contrive at your union. That was part of the testing. You all have qualities that have enabled you to find this place. But there have been many before you. Many have come here, seeking truth, power, the key to the Mysteries. They were not ready. Though they serve the Mother in other ways.'

Ussemitus glanced across at the false skies, where earlier the shapes had turned like fish below a lake's surface. 'They are there?'

'Yes. Blessed by the Mother.'

'And is this to be *our* fate?' Ussemitus said tersely.

Man One lifted his hands. 'Possibly. But there may be a greater destiny awaiting you. If you wish to go on. We shall see.'

'Why am I here?'

'Someone must lead. They must take the mantle of

power, of knowledge, from me. I have served my purpose. You and your companions have priceless gifts. A unity rarely found in any cycle of worlds. The time approaches when you must put that power to the test. If it serves you as it should, if it can be the weapon that the Mother seeks, then you must carry the responsibility, Ussemitus. You understand that. It is why you came. It is why you chose to seek this place. It is what brought you here.'

Ussemitus wanted to protest, but the words would not come. In his heart he knew it was true. He had been lured by the power in the legends. And he had sought it for the very reasons that Man One had given him: to prevent the war with the Men who had come to Innasmorn, Aru's people. 'What must I do?'

'You must face the true enemy.'

'The Csendook?'

'Like you, they have been lured to the World Splinter. They seek power, though they scorn sorcery, powers of the mind. But they are strong, Ussemitus. One blow from their arms would split you from brain to crotch. You will have to use other weapons.'

'Sorcery – '

'A word. Since the Csendook use it, let them. It obscures the truth, and they must not taste that. Only as they die.'

'I must face these intruders?'

'You will be given power, if you are ready for it. I will take you to a place within. The gifts you already have will be enlarged upon. But there are other things you need to understand.'

Ussemitus frowned. Nothing without a price. He could not expect to be granted power as though it was something trivial to be given away.

'You will be the Mother's. Completely. Of the Mother and for the Mother. You can never be as others are, not if you take the powers. In many ways, you will be alone. Some will curse you, being jealous of you. Others will love you. Some will never trust you. But you will be apart. And you will be the last of your line. Do you understand that, and what it means?'

341

Ussemitus's frown deepened. He had not given a thought to children. They did not seem important to him, not yet. But to be apart, unable to share the love of a woman: was that what Man One meant? He thought at once of Aru, the possibility that they might become lovers. It was what he wanted, he knew that. But he quickly blotted the thought from his mind, as if Man One eavesdropped on his thoughts, or worse, they were fully exposed to this sanctum. Such things were private.

'I have no wish to read your thoughts,' said Man One dispassionately. 'Yet I can see that you understand me. To wield power, you must be able to forge your mind into a weapon, Ussemitus. It will take great concentration, focusing of will. Love is for others, itself a mighty force, and a vital one to the survival of Innasmorn and all other worlds. But love can only weaken your resolve, if you receive power. Just as other emotions will weaken you. Hatred, anger, jealousy. Your enemies will bring out the vilest of your emotions, and if you let them run unchecked, you are lost. The darkness will feed on them and turn you, in the end destroying you.'

Ussemitus studied Man One. He was like a machine, a being without emotion. But without it, how could he understand the emotions of others?

'Others have been here before you, over the years, Ussemitus. They tasted power. But not success. Not enough to enable the Mother to release them so that they could begin the work, the cleansing.'

Ussemitus looked beyond to the shapes in the well of light. He thought of the times he had summoned the storms, struggled with the evils that beset his world. How could he turn away from them now? But love: had it not given Jubaia strength when he needed it most?

'The Mother is a demanding goddess. If you give yourself to her completely, you will receive as fully.'

Ussemitus nodded slowly. 'I will go on.'

Man One said nothing. He began a fresh descent. Stairs of light dropped endlessly beyond them into the shaft that seemed to pierce the very heart of the world, whether that of Innasmorn or that of some other realm, Ussemitus could only guess. The strange, alien power of the Splinter seemed to have been long since absorbed into Innasmorn, as though she herself had taken a lover, and from that union had sprung an even greater knowledge of the world cycles.

When they came to a halt, they were standing on a circular outcrop of stone, surrounded by light, nothing visible beyond the perimeter of rock. Man One raised his arms.

'It is fitting that you are shown something of the things that I have told you. Here, in the Abyss of History, you will know the truth. Unless you desire to go back. If you do, your mind will be cleansed of all that I have told you.'

Ussemitus shook his head. 'Show me.'

At once he was alone. The light writhed, darkening, and from it flickered distant lightning, the far walls of the enormous shaft rumbling to the coming of a storm. He felt the first blast of that storm, winds that swirled around him, winds of such power that they could strip flesh from bone, the very breath of the Mother. And beyond him, in the sudden tumult, he saw vast plains, stretching as far as the eye could see, and mountain ranges that plummeted, pulverised by the striking light from the skies. Storms beyond imagining, world-storms that shook the very core of the earth. And in them there were shadows stalking, colossal things that mocked reason, monstrous deities and subdeities that clashed and smote against each other, unleashing catastrophe, maelstrom and holocaust.

The Mother beat back these evils, but among them something central spawned itself, a howling child from the deep, feeding on the darkness, on pain, torment, destruction. Shaping itself into something that threatened to grip reason and crush it. Ussemitus felt his own reason wavering before the realisation of this horror, but the Mother drove it down, pouring energy into its subjugation.

Around it the clouds tore through the night, tangible nightmares, screaming in agony as the Mother seared them, attempting to obliterate them all.

'Malefics,' came the soft voice of Man One, and in that

one word was all the darkness and pain of the conflict 'Terrible servants of the dark. Once there were many, lik the swarming of bees. Physical manifestations.'

Mercifully light burst around them as the battle fumed and gradually they were absorbed into the body of th central darkness and driven down into it, the plain opening receiving its sacrifice. Seas boiled in over it and the jaw of the rift closed, the darkness and all its evils thrust deep into some other region, some limbo outside the physica reality of Innasmorn. This had been the subjugation.

A final rumble of thunder boomed out far below, an Ussemitus stood before soft light, the storm quickly reced ing back into its womb of the past.

'You once heard the coming of the storm-of-the-dark came Man One's voice. 'When you were in the Dhumvald.

Ussemitus turned. 'Is that what you have shown me?'

Man One shook his head. 'What you saw in the Dhum vald was only the beginning of the storm-of-the-dark. Ha it been unleashed, a force would have taken the lives o everything that moved in those mountains. Used it to shap something far more terrible. A Malefic. But you served th Mother well in preventing the storm.

'The darkness never sleeps. It searches for evil in us all for a means to drag itself back from its prison abyss. Thu it used Quareem, as it uses other Windmasters, other crea tures of power on Innasmorn. You begin to see, Ussemitus how many fronts there are to this war.'

Ussemitus nodded. He understood the nature of the rea enemy. 'It is not the Csendook the Mother fears most.'

'They are an immediate danger,' said Man One. 'Bu think of them as weapons, unwitting tools.'

'Then why bring them here, where they will be mos dangerous! If they are exposed to these horrors –'

'Yes, the dark will find them. Wherever they are, what ever dark place spawns them. And it will use them to focu itself. They are perfect hosts for the evil the dark coul become. Unwatched, on some remote world, they coul grow into a force so powerful that the Mother could no subdue them. So she has brought them here, to begin their undoing.'

'Before the dark claims them.'

Man One did not need to answer.

'You say they are here already?'

'A few of them. Seeking this very place. The Mother has sent out a spectral, a guide to bring them, to lure them.' Man One indicated the void, and fresh visions appeared here.

Ussemitus saw another plain, another world. Smoke wreathed it, figures running through it. Men, warriors, clothed in thin metal armour and bearing steel swords. A group of them turned, and out of the smoke other shapes appeared, tall, black-clad beings, faces masked by their war helms. They, too, carried steel swords, and in a moment there was a clash of metal, sparks sizzling as the two companies attacked one another. The larger Csendook were outnumbered, but they moved with incredible speed, easily deflecting the blows of the Men. They cut into them with grim strength, ripping through them clinically, hacking them apart effortlessly as if cutting down beef. The victors lifted their war helms and studied the corpses. Ussemitus saw a Csendook face for the first time, and though they were not unlike those of the Men they had slaughtered, there was a bestiality about them, a cruel hardness that enjoyed havoc. And strength, staggering strength.

The dark would find them, Man One had promised. And now well they would house it, Ussemitus thought.

'No Man could stand alone and defeat a Csendook,' said Man One. 'Not without additional power. The Csendook are fast, you have now seen how fast. And you have seen their physical strength. Before it, Man is weak. It is why he has almost been eliminated.

'But Csendook power is limited. Speed and strength of arm is not everything. They cannot converse with the elements. They scorn any thought of what they call sorcery. They have no understanding of true power. Thus they are vulnerable in two ways. Firstly, they are vulnerable to the dark. You see how easily it could fill them.'

345

'Yet to have brought them *here*,' Ussemitus persisted, thinking of the possible consequences of these warrior taking greater powers on themselves.

'They are also vulnerable to power wielded by true servants of the Mother,' went on Man One, ignoring Ussemitus's outcry.

'How vulnerable?'

Man One shrugged. 'A Windmaster could better a Csendook, or so it is thought. This truth needs to be tested. there is to be conflict, war, then an army will have to meet these Csendook, and it will have to be better armed than Man ever was.

'If you choose power, Ussemitus, you will have to test it against these alien warriors. Here, in the World Splinter.'

Ussemitus considered this. 'And what of Zellorian?'

'Innasmorn has sensed his anger, his loathing of the Csendook. It is like a madness in him. Such an emotion weakens him. He is ruthless, destroying all in his path There is no reasoning with him.'

'If Man is to rise against the Csendook, Zellorian is an obstacle. There is irony in that,' Ussemitus snorted.

'So it would seem. His fate will be one of the decision that will have to be made, Ussemitus. Subdue him, conver him, or destroy him.'

Ussemitus shuddered. 'You are asking me to decide the destinies of nations, *worlds*.'

'You will be the voice of Innasmorn. Her vessel.'

'*The hand of a god*,' he breathed.

Man One looked at him for a long moment. 'I have carried out my duties as keeper for long enough, Ussemitus. I am unable to take on the role that is before you. I was not designed for such a task. You are young, strong, and your reasoning is good. No child of Innasmorn is pure or selfless or uncorruptible. But you and your companions have qualities that give the Mother hope.

'Will you put them to the test?'

Ussemitus looked again into the wall of light. It waited in silence, the mind of a world, not prompting him, but waiting, as it must have waited for millennia.

He stretched out his fingers to the light.
'I am ready.'

25

CONVERGENCE

Vorenzar attempted to see into the cavern that loomed ove
him, vast as a moon. But it was impossible. Nevertheless
for all its oppressive darkness, he knew instinctively tha
this was the place he had been seeking, the open arter
that must lead to the heart of this World Splinter, thi
colossal rock from another realm. He and his Zemoks ha
spent three weeks climbing it, and it had taken its toll o
their strength. Two of the Zemoks had slipped and falle
to their deaths, but Vorenzar never faltered in his determi
nation to get here, goaded on by a deep yearning, a
irresistible drive. Standing on the lip of the great cavern
he felt himself lifted, fresh purpose filling him. If this plac
fulfilled its promise, a new age would dawn for th
Csendook.

Impatiently he gestured for his Zemoks to follow him
and stepped over the threshold into the darkness. Once ou
of the direct light, he could make out vague shapes or
the floor around him. This was smooth, sandy, with a
occasional jutting object. As with the debris at the far bas
of the rock, these seemed to be as much of metal as of rock
like the broken ribs of machines that had been scattere
and forgotten. The floor looked to stretch for an infinit
distance, while overhead the ceiling was out of view. Vine
and trailing plants hung down from the high upper lip o
the cavern, obscuring the rock surface, though sunligh
gleamed on elements within it.

Ondrazem grunted something beside him and he turne
to speak. What he saw made him growl with surprise
Whether it was a trick of the light, the play of shadows or
illusion of another kind, Ondrazem seemed to have altered
his shape changed, thickened out, blurred. Like an urmurel
Vorenzar glanced at the other Zemoks, but they, too, were

348

ttle more than amorphous shapes in this poor light. He
looked down at himself, but he was as he should be, the
complete Csendook warrior.

He gestured with his drawn sword and moved inwards.
As he did so, he was aware that something had stirred
ahead. Peering, he discerned other shapes. Waiting. There
was some kind of craft there: to his amazement it looked
like something that might have been built by Man. And
here were figures inside it. Three small ones and one
larger.

'Bring light,' he told his Zemoks and at once two of them
ignited torches they had prepared. As they flared, casting
beams into the cavern, Vorenzar realised that the figures
ahead of him intended to challenge his passage. Two of
them were Innasmornians, the third was even stranger,
though doubtless native to this world. But the fourth! It
was a *woman*. One of Man's breed.

Vorenzar lifted his visor as he stepped forward, conscious
that the two Innasmornians had arrows aimed at him. He
had absolutely no fear of them: arrows would snap on his
armour.

'Who are you, and what are you doing on Innasmorn?'
he called across to the woman, using a common tongue.
Even in the vastness of the cavern, his voice was clear,
powerful.

But the woman did not answer him.

Aru bit down on the fear that threatened to crush her,
born anew at the sight of these, the terrible enemies she
had thought never to see again. Behind her, Armestor and
Jomond were staggered, as was the incredulous Jubaia.
Nothing Aru had told them about these aliens had prepared
them for this, for they had known instinctively that these
metal-clad monsters were Csendook. They dwarfed Aru,
being some seven feet tall, but their girth, their incredible
broadness of shoulder, took away the breath of the Innasmornians. This was power incarnate, sheer strength, and
in it the promise of annihilation, no mercy. The leader of
the beings, who had lifted the face plate of his black war
helm, showed his face: it resembled that of a Man, but only

superficially. The eyes were narrow, blazing, the jaw wide
the teeth almost vulpine. Bred as war machines, engines
destruction, these Csendook looked remorseles
invulnerable.

'You serve the Imperator Elect,' called Vorenzar. 'I hav
a message for him.'

Aru gripped her puny sword more tightly and stoo
defensively. She had told her companions they would di
if they attempted to stand in the way of the Csendook. Bu
Jubaia would not leave the gliderboat. Aru knew that h
would rather die than do so. There was no point in arguing
And she could not let him defend the craft alone. Th
Csendook would unquestionably try to destroy it.

'We must not let these creatures pass,' said Fomonc
though he was still numbed on seeing the size and girth c
the enemy. 'They will endanger Ussemitus. He will b
defenseless, whatever it is he does.'

Armestor nodded, gritting his teeth on his terror.

Vorenzar waited for an answer, but had none. Did th
woman understand him? He tried several human language
that he knew, but still received no answer from her. Instea
he turned to Ondrazem.

'I want the woman alive. But kill the others.'

At once the Zemoks moved forward. They stalked easily
slumping down, their shapes even more strange, but thei
purpose clear. Ondrazem led them, sword raised.

Armestor and Fomond unleashed their arrows, and t
their horror saw them sink home into the necks of thei
intended victims, but they had no more effect than if the
had buried themselves in wood. Or earth. What kind c
bizarre armour were they wearing?

Aru looked desperately at Jubaia. 'Are you certain th
gliderboat will not rise?'

'I've told you, she cannot!' he cried, his frustration clear
Jubaia! the shout was fierce in his mind: he almost reeled
'What is it?'

*These creatures are not true Csendook. Except for their leader
who spoke. The others are replicas, shaped from earth and stone an
from metal from the base of the World Splinter.*

350

'Can you see into their minds?'

I tried! But they are a fog. And in them something vile is stirring. A power that frightens me, Jubaia.

'Dhumhagga,' Jubaia breathed. 'Though these are far worse than what we have seen. We dare not attempt to fight them.'

Not with your weapons. But if we lock minds?

Jubaia watched the enemy approaching stealthily, though with a fearful assurance. 'Very well. Choose one of them.'

They agreed on the Csendook to the left edge of the advance and between them concentrated their mental efforts on halting it. Aru and the others could see what they were doing, watching in silence.

The Csendook creature stumbled, but still came forward. Jubaia suddenly fell back with a cry.

'What is it?' said Aru, helping him to his feet. He looked aghast, his arms shaking.

'We dare not attempt to probe its mind! What in Innasnorn has found its way into these monsters?' He turned to whisper something to the gliderboat, but it had gone silent.

'Jubaia, we'll have to flee if we are to live,' Aru told him. *They want me, more than anything. I know where the Imperator Elect is, and that's what their leader is after. Somehow they've followed us from Eannor.*

Jubaia rose unsteadily. The Zemoks closed in, preparing for the last dash that would enjoin the battle. 'I'll not leave the craft,' he breathed.

'Then you're a fool,' snapped Aru.

She was about to shout to Armestor and Fomond, warning them to flee, when a sudden gust of air from the far end of the cavern almost toppled her into the gliderboat. The air lifted itself, like the very breath of the mountain, for it came from within, not from without. It gathered in force quickly, a strong breeze, then a wind, and both Aru and Jubaia had to duck down into the craft to avoid being blown out of it. Armestor and Fomond also crouched, hanging on to their weapons.

They all watched as the wind whipped about the

351

Csendook shapes. These still trudged forward, as though immune to such gales, but as they did so, they began to disintegrate. One of them abruptly flew backwards like a tossed boulder, arms flailing until they snapped off like rotted boughs. The creature tumbled over the floor of the cavern, churning up sand and dust, clouds in the wind. Over and over it bounced, shedding clumps of its unnatural skin like clods of earth, until its head burst, though in a welter of mud and soil. Other Csendook shapes also toppled, rolled and punched by the wind, and they, too, broke apart, spilling mud where blood should have gushed. One by one the warriors were picked up like toys by the wind from inside the World Splinter and hurled across the cavern floor, rupturing and falling apart.

Only one of the figures had survived. It stood, upright and defiant, in the midst of the smashed warriors that had served it, its helmeted head down into the wind, its twin swords gripped, thrusting itself forward as though it could divert the very air as it battered it. And, like a boulder in a river, it turned the current to either side. Beyond it, framed by the black fangs of the cavern mouth, the Innasmornian sky had darkened, like a canvas cracked by flickering tongues of light. Another storm proclaimed itself, an echo of the powers surging outwards from the great rock.

Vorenzar straightened as the inner winds abruptly died down. He gazed about him at the destruction. But there was no flesh, no bones poking from the ruined heaps that had been sham warriors. No blood. Only earth and clay, ripped sacks. The darkness had taken his Zemoks. Somewhere below, on the bleak crossing of the crater, the night had closed in. Ondrazem and the others were no more, already victims of this most alien of worlds.

Yet he had survived. And the hunger burned in him, the fierce elation, the joy of having reached this wild place.

He glanced at the craft before him. Inside it he could see the bobbing heads of his enemies. They, too, had survived the scorching wind. Had they controlled it? But he could not believe such a thing. He must not! To go down that path was to give in to madness.

And yet power had seduced him here. Power of a kind that he and his race had never known.

Behind him there was a distant growl of thunder, the snarl of a hungry beast moving forwards toward a kill. A sound he had heard before in the black skies of Innasmorn.

His purpose was clear before him. He must enter the heart of this cavern and discover where that wind had come from. The source. Something had protected him from it. Again the thunder boomed, closer outside, an echoing voice of affirmation. So hungry, like himself. So eager.

'Then give me your power!' he hissed at the closing dark, stepping forward.

Aru had seen him, stunned by the way he had ignored the destruction, had been spared by the wind of death. And now, *behind* him, the skies contorted themselves.

Fomond looked staggered. 'Is it the storm-of-the-dark?' he gasped. 'Surely *he* does not bring it upon us?'

'It cannot enter the World Splinter,' said a voice behind him, and he swung round, as did the others.

It was Ussemitus who had spoken. He stood, bathed in a glow that emanated behind him, deep in the rocks of the cavern, a counterpoint to the horrific darkness that swirled outside the cavern. In his arms he carried the limp form of Man One, though it had shrunk to the size of a child.

'Who is this?' said Aru.

'He was the keeper of certain knowledge,' said Ussemitus. Gently he put the body down inside the gliderboat. There was a soft sound of metal on metal as he did so.

'What has become of you?' Jubaia asked softly, seeing the strangeness of Ussemitus's expression, but the latter merely shook his head.

'Quickly!' called Armestor. 'The warrior.'

Ussemitus watched the lone Csendook approach. Though he had been shown the Csendook in his visions, Ussemitus was not prepared for the shock of seeing one of the monsters in the flesh. It was huge, twice his height, armoured in black scales that looked as though a dozen swords would have shattered on it like glass. The helm was up, brazenly, the face within it cold, eyes wide with lust

for the kill, the nostrils flared like a beast's. What resem
blance there was to a Man was superficial. Here was powe
incarnate. The fury of a storm embodied in one creature.

Its swords hissed through the air, one in each hand, i
what Ussemitus took to be a ritual gesture, a preparatio
for slaughter. The Csendook had not come here searchin
for him, but it would kill him and the others for the mer
pleasure of it. But something warned him that it was no
that simple. He caught sight of the foaming darknes
beyond the cavern's mouth. The dark gathered there. An
it had sent this warrior here, *as its ambassador*. Did it posses
him?

Ussemitus turned to Aru and Jubaia. 'I have been to th
place of power. I must test that power. But none of you
safe. You must not attempt to interfere – '

Aru gripped his arm. 'But what will you do?'

He could see the concern in her eyes, and could fe
something else, the love that he had known had been grow
ing. But he had to turn from it, just as he had been warne
'I must prevent the Csendook from entering the place
power.' He lifted his sword from the deck. It seemed
pathetic thing compared to the twin weapons of th
Csendook.

Vorenzar had seen this other creature, another Inna
mornian, preparing to do battle with him. What were thes
people protecting? They were insane if they thought the
could stand in his way. He'd spare the woman, who woul
be useful later, but the others he'd gut. Starting with th
impudent newcomer.

Ussemitus dropped from the gliderboat, landing softly i
the sand, and he moved away from the craft. The Csendoo
watched him silently, its visor still raised.

Vorenzar could see that the Innasmornian was trying
lead him away from his companions. He grinned at tha
It did not matter. But he moved away, choosing a place i
the sand where his feet would not be impeded by rock,
by the damp mounds that had once been his mock warrior
He felt no pity at their passing. In time, he would repla
them with untold thousands.

354

Ussemitus faced the Csendook, aware that the eyes of his companions were on him.

Power, Man One had told him. The speed and strength of the Csendook against a new kind of power. They would call it sorcery.

Ussemitus had tasted it. He had been plunged into the pool of fire, the heart of the Mysteries. The light of worlds had bathed him, the furnace of their energy. Crystallised.

He had seen the nature of the Csendook, the darkness at the core of them. He saw it now, its stark outline.

Vorenzar dropped his visor. He took one step forward, a lightning move, one of his swords driving downward as quickly as a serpent's tongue. It would have ripped through the vitals of any Man. But it struck something and slipped by Ussemitus as if turned by a shield. Sparks fizzed in the air. Vorenzar recovered instantly, as though he had not moved. He felt mildly surprised; the creature was deceptive.

Ussemitus had still not tried to probe the mind of the Csendook. Would he find surprise there? Fear? No, not that. Not in this beast. Fear was utterly alien to this warrior. Just as pity would be. And love.

Vorenzar waited. Would this impudent warrior attack him? With that toy? Yet the Innasmornian had used something to turn his blade aside. He admired his quickness.

Again Vorenzar shot out an arm, this time aiming a blow that would have easily sliced through Ussemitus's left knee. But the little figure hopped over the stroke, a blur of movement. Vorenzar grinned within his helm. Extraordinary agility.

Fomond and Armestor watched in appalled silence, their bows lowered. Ussemitus had evaded the blades of the huge warrior, but this could be no match. And their own weapons were useless.

Jubaia studied the face of Man One. But he was like a machine without power, no spark of life or energy in his glazed eyes.

Aru knelt down, lowering her voice. 'How can we help Ussemitus? Can he not call upon Innasmorn? Can you?'

Her eyes were desperate, her fear for Ussemitus, her love for him, like fire now.

Jubaia shook his head solemnly. 'The Mother will not let us interfere.'

'Interfere!'

'Softly, Aru. Innasmorn has brought us here, I am sure of it. Just as she has brought that creature. It is as if she designed this battle. I don't know why. I think it is a test. And we, too, are tested.'

Aru grimaced. 'But that's a *Csendook*! A full Zaru, a military commander! You've no idea how powerful he is! He'll laugh at your powers. You saw how he broke the winds that struck at him.'

Jubaia stood, nodding slowly. He watched as Ussemitus somehow deflected another chopping blow.

Vorenzar grunted to himself. So far he had merely been testing this youth, finding out his speed, his preferred movements. They were not easily predicted. But the youth was moving gradually towards the mouth of the cavern, away from his companions. Ah yes, that was to be expected. Their safety concerned him. He was as emotional as a Man, though he seemed to be faster. This was something to do with the remarkable elemental nature of the beings of this world. Perhaps the youth was using this fight as no more than a ploy to draw him away so that his companions could flee. In the craft? But why had they not all done so when they had had the opportunity? Was it damaged? That must be it. They had made no attempt to use it.

The Csendook changed his attack, abruptly stepping into the line of his opponent and raining several blows at him, weaving twin networks of steel about him that defied the eye. It was a tactic that could have maimed three or four Men in minutes, but still Ussemitus avoided being hurt, though he was forced backwards. Death hovered over him, but again he swung aside.

Vorenzar lifted his blades in a fresh challenge. As he did so, a crackle of lightning overhead lit up the mouth of the cavern, bathing the Csendook in garish light. Ussemitus gasped as he saw the warrior stab down at the sand floor. There were scattered mounds of earth and rock, the remains of the warrior shapes. Light licked out from the Csendook blade, aimed at the debris.

Vorenzar had felt something lance down from the skies, a livid javelin of energy. He was reminded again of the conflict between the winds and the urmurel. He shook his head, uncertain of what was happening. He must remain in control, and not allow these forces to seep into him. Something groaned on the floor, a sliding movement. Rock grating on rock, the protest of metal scraped on metal. Fusion.

Earth coalesced like shadows. Something rose, darkness feeding it until its face was revealed, not quite complete, dripping.

'Ondrazem!'

Ussemitus heard the Csendook warrior speak to the thing that had staggered up from the ruined earth. And he felt its power, the throb of darkness, the gift of the churning skies beyond the rim.

The Ondrazem-thing bowed, then lumbered forward, arms lifting, preparing to take hold of Ussemitus and hurl him from the cavern mouth into the precipice. Light burst within Ussemitus's skull. Other powers danced, almost blinding him. He looked and saw before him only a silhouette, reeking with evil, with the slaughter of a world, a lust older than Innasmorn.

He shaped the light he had been given and flung it, a spear of thought.

Vorenzar watched as the Ondrazem-thing reached out for its prey, about to grip and pulp it, but before the hands closed, it shuddered, lifting from the ground. It was flung backwards, crashing into a spar of metal that jutted skywards, bursting like an overripe fruit, earth showering outwards.

Ussemitus gaped at what he had done, at the power he had released. It had blown the earth creature into nothing, the explosion detonated by the contact with the darkness within it. But that darkness had not been destroyed.

Ussemitus knew that instinctively. Instead it had lodged itself in the warrior, the Csendook ambassador.

Vorenzar felt the grip of ice, the sudden chill as power from the skies flooded him. His own hungers, lusts, desire for power fountained up, blotting all reason, filling him with a fresh craving, a wild, uncontrollable need. It jolted him into movement.

He attacked Ussemitus with sweeping blows, his weapons alive as they met whatever force it was that protected the youth, whatever powers the World Splinter had invested in him.

Ussemitus lurched back. The blades did not strike him, nor bite into his flesh, but he could feel them hammering into the forces that shielded him, buckling them as if they were real armour. There was nothing he could do to contain the overwhelming onslaught. He tumbled back, closer and closer to the brink of the precipice. A blow that should have sheared off his head battered into the power of the light; he felt his senses reeling, as if he had been punched. He was down, head ringing. He tried to focus his powers, but they swam away like elusive fish. The Csendook blades scythed down into his field of light again and again, the power of the alien warrior enhanced by the flow of darkness from beyond.

Aru saw Ussemitus topple and screamed. 'We must help him! He'll be cut to pieces!' She leapt from the craft, holding her own slim blade, shouting at the top of her voice, though the cavern swallowed the sound.

Vorenzar neither heard nor saw her. The roar of the dark fires was all about him, and he looked down at the slaughtered mounds of his enemies at his feet, the screaming of worlds. The glory that was coming, the drive onward. Over him the skies shrieked out their approval.

'Circu!' cried Jubaia. 'Death closes in on us all. Lift yourself! Break the bonds!'

The gliderboat responded with an unintelligible sound, but Jubaia felt her shudder.

Fomond leapt over the side of the craft, sprinting after Aru. She ran for the Csendook, and Fomond could see that she would fly into him but be smashed like an insect by his fury.

Armestor tumbled from the craft, landing awkwardly. He was about to give chase, utterly confused, but the glider-boat at last hummed into life and rose from the ground, sweeping over him so that he had to flatten himself to avoid being knocked senseless.

Vorenzar now stood astride Ussemitus, who was stretched out over the rock's edge, his head thrust out into the air. Vorenzar raised both blades, about to drive his opponent out into the emptiness, where the dark waited with its thunder.

Aru was almost upon the Csendook, but before she could launch herself, she felt something wrap itself around her calves and she was sent thumping into the sand, winded by the fall. She tried to speak, to scream protest, but the air had been punched from her body. It was Fomond who had stopped her.

Vorenzar turned to see what was happening. There were two forms sprawled in the sand, a few yards away. He laughed, preparing to kill Ussemitus. As he did so, he saw a shape coming out of the blackness of the cavern. It was like a huge bird, great wings outspread, and at its neck sat a tiny figure, a single lock of hair trailing behind it like a pennant as the machine gathered speed.

Roaring his defiance, Vorenzar twisted to meet this thing, swords flashing as he readied to carve it from the sky.

The gliderboat took him in the chest, ripping the top half of his body from the bottom. It tore out into the howling of the storm, the crescendo of madness.

Ussemitus felt something strike his legs, then slide away, out into the abyss. The Csendook was gone.

Shaking himself, Ussemitus rose, head ringing. The power had left him. Beyond him he could feel a new element of rage in the killer storm.

Armestor came running up to him, helping him to his feet. Fomond was holding Aru upright, though she was gasping for air, unable to get her words out. They all tried to see what was above them, but the darkness had closed in like a talon. The gliderboat had been absorbed by it.

'Get back into the cavern!' Ussemitus warned them. 'Quickly!'

They obeyed him as lightning licked out for them, blasting at the rock around the cavern opening, ripping chunks of it away.

Fomond studied the darkness. 'Have we – lost them?'

Ussemitus closed his eyes. He sent his mind out into that turmoil, the darkness writhing about it, the voices of nightmare howling at him, the claws of terror trying to prise his mind from its moorings. He veered this way and that, searching for the fear, the panic that he knew would be at the core of the craft, of the little thief. And found them. Tossed and tumbled, the craft was losing height, spiralling downwards on a disaster course that would have sent it into the floor of the crater. He dragged at it, wresting control, lifting it, turning it.

Up through madness it came, like a fish rising through burning oil, trawled against its will.

Into the mouth of the cavern, and through it, beyond the reach of the dark, the maw of the storm. It flopped down, raising a cloud of dust like a shroud about it.

'Jubaia?' gasped Aru, recovering her breath.

They all gathered around the craft as it dropped. Jubaia's head poked up over the rail. 'I'm alive, I think,' he muttered.

'The Csendook?' said Aru.

Jubaia nodded. 'Gone.'

Armestor scowled at the nose of the gliderboat. There was blood smeared over it, and score marks as though metal had ripped into it. But it was all that was left of the alien.

Ussemitus looked down into the craft. 'And Man One, the keeper?'

Jubaia looked puzzled, surprised to see that the tiny body was no longer there. 'But – '

'There is a power even in death,' said Ussemitus.

Beyond him the storm rumbled, but it could not pass

the mouth of the cavern, as though the World Splinter was forbidden to it.

Ussemitus put an arm about the shoulders of the little thief. 'You and your beloved gliderboat have saved us all, Jubaia. I could not do it. The Mother works through you both.'

'Through us all, I think,' replied the little man.

They were silent for a while, reflecting on the implications of what they had been through, the clash of wills.

Ussemitus broke into their thoughts. 'I fear there is a darkness awake to us now. Man One explained many things to me before he died.'

Aru watched him sadly, controlling her needs, her fierce desire to go to him and hold him. 'It's not over then?' But she knew that he had taken onto himself the greatest burden of them all, the sharing of powers from within the rock, the bequest of the Mother, his goddess.

Ussemitus shook his head, avoiding her gaze as if he understood that their paths would divide here, when they could have joined, become one. 'Innasmorn is on the threshold of war. We have witnessed the inner turmoil that still tears at her, how it still seeks to find a way to break free of her control. How it tried to use the Csendook. And it will go on trying.'

Aru looked suddenly drained. 'The Csendook. But how did they get here? *How?*'

'We may never know,' said Ussemitus. 'But they can only have been the spearhead.'

'Then they'll find us?' said Fomond.

Ussemitus nodded. 'Yes. It is for us to prepare the shield that will take their next thrust.'

While they rested, Ussemitus began to tell them some of the things that had been revealed to him in the Abyss of History. As he spoke, the dark storm withdrew, though somehow it seemed to hover at the edge of the day, a constant promise of pain to come.

EPILOGUE

EPILOGUE

The black gliderboat was almost dead, flopping on broken wings into the mire, clinging with the determination of its madness to a rock. Its journey through endless night and agony had taken its toll, and its destination was still beyond it. Above it the storm raged, and the final night began to close in.

In the murk, shadows surged forward, a dozen shapes, converging on the wrecked craft. If there was anything left of Vymark's consciousness, it did not register the armoured warriors who stood around what he had become, coated in the filth of this desolate region. Themselves animated by strange fires, the warrior shapes looked up at the storm, where lightning chased through clouds that were black and swollen.

The warriors obeyed the darkness. They listened to its whispers and lifted the broken craft, staggering with it through the knee-deep bogs. For mile after mile they trudged, though they showed no sign of tiredness, and never uttered a word. Like dead men, they ignored the pelting rain and the sucking mud, the things that crawled and slithered through it. They were like machines, locked into their grisly task.

In the foothills below the World Splinter they finally stopped and set down their burden. Fluid leaked out of it on to the flat rock where they rested it like an offering. They gathered around it like acolytes at a ritual, heads bent. Lightning crackled, gleaming from their armour. They waited with the patience of stone.

High above, where the World Splinter soared to the heavens, the storm raged on. Something fell from the clouds.

Two of the armoured shapes slipped away from the

circle, searching the terrain. For a long time they searched, until one of them returned, dragging something behind it with the same unrelenting determination that had brought the crippled gliderboat here.

The other warrior also returned, also pulling something. It was the lower half of a corpse, enclosed in buckled armour, a black shell that had partially protected it when it had fallen from above.

On the flat stone the warriors layed out the bloody remains of Vorenzar, their Zaru. His blood mingled with that of the gliderboat, trickling from the rock down into the mire.

One by one the Csendook removed their war helms, letting them sink in the mud. Ondrazem was the first to tilt back his head, exposing his thick neck. He drove the point of one of his swords hard up into the flesh, dropping to his knees, spilling his blood into the pool before him.

The others followed his example, around the circle, until every one of them had sacrificed himself.

Darkness closed in on the circle, a hand that hid these deeds from the Innasmornian skies, a hand that dipped down to stir the blood of the fallen. To draw strength from it, and life.

Something surged through the storm, as though a vast beast shuddered. Power bred power.

The storm winds of the night laughed. They had felt the Csendook warrior as he beat aside the powers of the youth, Ussemitus. An ill match.

The circle of warriors converged in death upon the stone. Light faded, banished from this final act. Darkness began the shaping of its servant, tugging at the evils of a world, trawling them in, binding them, moulding them.

And before the storm broke, the night creature rose from the scattered remains, called by the storm as it retreated. It howled in jubilation at its birth, and was swept upwards, wrapped in dark clouds, hidden from the cleansing light.

Only the darkness saw it, felt the malevolence of its thoughts. Heard it savour its name.

Malefic.

RETURN TO AMBER...
THE ONE *REAL* WORLD, OF WHICH ALL OTHERS, INCLUDING EARTH, ARE BUT SHADOWS

ROGER ZELAZNY

The Triumphant conclusion of the Amber novels

PRINCE OF CHAOS   75502-5/$4.99 US/$5.99 Can

The Classic Amber Series

NINE PRINCES IN AMBER   01430-0/$4.50 US/$5.50 Can
THE GUNS OF AVALON   00083-0/$3.95 US/$4.95 Can
SIGN OF THE UNICORN   00031-9/$3.95 US/$4.95 Can
THE HAND OF OBERON   01664-8/$4.50 US/$5.50 Can
THE COURTS OF CHAOS   47175-2/$4.50 US/$5.50 Can
BLOOD OF AMBER   89636-2/$3.95 US/$4.95 Can
TRUMPS OF DOOM   89635-4/$3.95 US/$4.95 Can
SIGN OF CHAOS   89637-0/$3.95 US/$4.95 Can
KNIGHT OF SHADOWS   75501-7/$3.95 US/$4.95 Can

The Epic Adventure

THE OMARAN SAGA
by
ADRIAN COLE

"A remarkably fine fantasy...
Adrian Cole has a magic touch."
Roger Zelazny

BOOK ONE:
A PLACE AMONG THE FALLEN
70556-7/$3.95 US/$4.95 Can

BOOK TWO: THRONE OF FOOLS
75840-7/$3.95 US/$4.95 Can

BOOK THREE:
THE KING OF LIGHT AND SHADOWS
75841-5/$4.50 US/$5.50 Can

BOOK FOUR: THE GODS IN ANGER
75842-3/$4.50 US/$5.50 Can

Three Wondrous Stories
of Adventure and Courage by
B R I A N
J A C Q U E S

MOSSFLOWER
70828-0/$4.50 US

The epic adventure of one brave mouse's quest to free a
enslaved forest kingdom from the claws of tyranny.

REDWALL
70827-2/$4.50 US

A bumbling young apprentice monk named Matthias
mousekind's most unlikly hero, goes on a wondrous quest to
recover a legendary lost weapon.

MATTIMEO
71530-9/$4.99 US

The cunning fox, Slagar the Cruel, and his evil henchmen hav
kidnapped the Woodland children, and Matthias and his band o
brave followers must rescue their stolen little ones.

Coming Soon
MARIEL OF REDWALL